PRAISE FOR CAITLIN ROTHER

Praise for *Hooked*, the first in the Katrina & Goode thriller series

"Rother delivers a gripping expertly woven crime thriller from the first page. *Hooked* is a tense, multifaceted plot filled with murder, secrets, and a brilliantly plotted cover-up that keeps the pages flying."

—Audrey J. Cole, *USA Today* bestselling author of *Missing in Flight*

"Smart, gritty, and intricately plotted, this addictive police procedural features unforgettable characters and a plot that cuts as deep as it twists. The chemistry between investigative reporter Katrina Chopin and homicide detective Ken Goode is electric . . . and the plot multilayered, delving into corruption and the many masks it hides behind. I was hooked from the start!"

—Christina McDonald, *USA Today* bestselling author

"Caitlin Rother sets the hook early and reels you in chapter by chapter in this fascinating murder mystery. Rother's attention to detail and crime scene knowledge, which has made her the best true crime writer of our time, gives the novel a gritty sense of verisimilitude. Goode and Katrina are layered and complex characters who come together to make a formidable investigative team. I can't wait to read about their next case!"

—Matt Coyle, author of the bestselling Rick Cahill crime novels

"*Hooked* had me hooked from the first chapter. Rother's true crime fans will devour her new thriller. Sharp dialogue and fast-paced, *Hooked* is an excellent start to a new series. Can't wait for the next one!"

—Alana Albertson, #3 Amazon bestselling author of *Badass*

Praise for *Naked Addiction*, the prequel to *Hooked*

"With a journalist's eye for the telling details of life, Caitlin Rother is a keen architect of the most important part of storytelling: character. The people in her prose grip you tightly with their truth."

—Michael Connelly, *New York Times* bestselling crime novelist

"*Naked Addiction* is a strong debut from a perceptive and unflinching writer. Detailed and tightly focused, the story unfolds on the sun-drenched but dangerous streets of San Diego."

—T. Jefferson Parker, *New York Times* bestselling crime novelist

"Caitlin Rother walked the walk as an award-winning journalist, and now she talks the talk in her debut novel, *Naked Addiction*. Rother's honed reportorial eye gives us the five *W*'s of murder set out on turf she knows so well. With a deft hand, Rother puts a bloody fingerprint on the picture-postcard setting of San Diego. The sun and surf are a gorgeous backdrop, but in Rother's *Naked Addiction*, trouble in paradise abounds."

—Alan Russell, author of *Political Suicide*

"*Naked Addiction* . . . is one of the most well-constructed murder mysteries that I have ever read in forty years of reading that genre. Rother's years as an investigative reporter put her on the front line of crime, and she has used that experience to construct real and authentic characters and scenarios that are so factual that you feel you could be reading a newspaper account of a crime. The plot . . . is so complex and elaborate that you never suspect who the murderer is until Rother decides to let you know—at the end of the book. Rother's debut into the fiction genre is impressive and has a long life ahead of it."

—Book Hunters

Praise for *Down to the Bone*

"Rother presents the riveting story of a botched investigation, multiple suspects, and a web of lies. Was justice ever served? The question will remain with you long after you finish reading."

—Diane Fanning, author of *Written in Blood*

"If you love true crime books where the author goes far beyond what is already known, and raises questions that need to be asked, this is a book for you."

—Justin Brooks, founding director, California Innocence Project

Praise for *Death on Ocean Boulevard*

"The Rebecca Zahau case is one of the great crime mysteries of modern times. It took an author of Caitlin Rother's caliber to bring it into sharp focus. A riveting read."

—Gregg Olsen, #1 *New York Times* bestselling author

"Gripping. Propulsive. A tour de force of true crime storytelling. Rother is a rare talent, and *Death on Ocean Boulevard* an instant classic of the genre."

—Kevin Deutsch, author and host of *A Dark Turn* podcast

"Caitlin Rother skillfully chronicles one of the most fascinating and controversial cases of the past decade. Big money, sex, and a questionable death makes for an addictive read."

—Kathryn Casey, author of *In Plain Sight*

Praise for *Poisoned Love*

"A true-crime thriller that will keep you on the edge of your seat. This first-time author has done a brilliant job of captivating the inner workings of a female killer . . . someone who uses her cunning ways to commit murder."

—Aphrodite Jones, author of *Cruel Sacrifice*

"Caitlin Rother, a seasoned reporter with integrity, class, and skill, weaves this complex story seamlessly, offering it up in the page-turning fashion of a suspenseful novel . . . An exciting debut from a tirelessly hardworking reporter."

—M. William Phelps, author of *Obsessed*

Praise for *Twisted Triangle*

"A harrowing tale of one woman's struggle to maintain a balance between being a mother, an FBI agent, and dealing with a corrupt husband, also an FBI agent. A must read."

—Joseph D. Pistone, a.k.a. Donnie Brasco, author of *The Way of the Wiseguy*

"Hitchcock wishes he'd dreamed it up. Capote wishes he'd written it. Rother's mesmerizing narrative chronicles a wife's heroic struggle against great odds to survive her psychopath husband's elaborate scheme to make her murder the perfect crime. This spellbinding tale offers an added treat—it's true."

—Marcus Stern, Pulitzer Prize–winning journalist and coauthor of *The Wrong Stuff* chilly. To get there I needed to travel by propeller plane with a pilot younger than pilots should be. The entire harrowing journey overwhelmed me and when I finally landed back in Boston, I made my way to the oldest and most refined hotel I knew. I took off all my travel-worn clothes and sunk into an enormous tub of hot water.

This is what I am thinking, the pause in a journey, the blessed rest at the end of a tiring flight. I go back inside the cottage to grab a sweater and passing the bedroom mirror, I take a quick glance, routine for me, always trying to tame my hair into something sensible. My face is flushed from the lake breeze, my eyes still large in the wonder of swans. But something else stops me. Is it the color of my eyes? The shade of gray not my own? Or the depth beyond my depth, the wisdom beyond my wisdom, the traveler come to a journey's blessed end?

Like the swans, this is not anything I expect, but a figment, solitary and decided. I hold my breath and when I exhale, I say what I know is true but cannot be true. I look to my own image, my own presence and I say what I see:

Franny.

Absorbed into the timbers of this cottage, pulled through the smoke chamber of the old chimney, a sure part of my story with all the others as we spin at one thousand miles per hour on our earthly axis, returning each day to where we were the day before. Everyone coming back, as it were.

In some manner, always coming back.

news, until the man and his lame horse did not have to go to war, which was good news, and so on, good stumbling into bad and back to good again. Tell any story you choose, fill it with tragedy, strip off garments, destroy, march over mountains if you like, eventually it will come to some end, a last breath or scream or sigh. But is that the end?

Franny and my long-gone family speak otherwise. One way or another, the story goes on, rowing out into the middle of the lake, watching the ice layer begin to form along the shore then extend until all is frozen and the landscape gone from green to gold to white, the sky a different blue, cooler and higher, and still the story goes on—elusive, contradictory, disconcerting—but not undone.

This morning, surveying the lake from shore, I notice birds too large to be anything I expect, as though I am seeing what cannot be true, another figment of my mind. But then there is the neck of one, of two, eventually all those white tumbles raise long, thin necks of trumpeter swans. I am too far away to trouble them but not so far away I can't observe their fishing and fluffing and gliding about. Unlike the blue heron, swans are not beyond themselves in any way. They swim almost one with the water. Believe your eyes, I tell myself. Migrations happen and here is proof, the rare swan, indeed a small bevy of swans just across the bay.

I do not take the sight of rare swans as a sign exactly, but they signal a change, another season and the start of whatever will happen here in this season. I watch them until they pull themselves onto the shore over there and seem to settle in for a rest. They've come far, from Canada, I guess, and are not at their winter destination just yet. I imagine their relief, pausing to take a swim, find food, tuck into the wetland grasses where they are just now.

I once did a project in a small town on the southern coast of Nova Scotia where the only hotel gave me no peace, drunkards fighting at night and worrisome types all around. The work was challenging, the light in the office dim, the air damp and seaside

Praise for *Body Parts*

"This kind of frightening and fascinating glimpse into a killer's mind is rare, and an extremely intuitive Rother makes the most of it."

—Ron Franscell, *New York Times* bestselling author

"Caitlin Rother is the model for serious crime journalism today. She's bold, meticulous, and exhaustive, returning to cases with loose ends to update us on the latest innovations and developments."

—Katherine Ramsland, author of *The Serial Killer's Apprentice*

"The updated material in this new edition of *Body Parts* not only brings the story full circle by giving a name, face, and tragic backstory to the mystery that set the nightmare in motion, it adds another layer of depth. Caitlin Rother never lets the horrific nature of the crimes overshadow the humanity of the victims."

—Simon Read, author of *Scotland Yard*

Praise for *Dead Reckoning*

"Well researched and a quick, engrossing read, this should be popular with true crime readers, especially the Ann Rule crowd."

—Starred review in *Library Journal*

"We've finally found the next Ann Rule! Caitlin Rother writes with heart and suspense. *Dead Reckoning* is a chilling read by a writer at the top of her game."

—Gregg Olsen

"*Dead Reckoning* by Caitlin Rother is one of the best true crime books I have read in years. First, it's one of those 'too wild and crazy to have made up' stories about the horrific murder of Tom and Jackie Hawks on their yacht *Well Deserved* off Catalina Island by Skylar Deleon, a con man, killer, and hermaphrodite, along with his wife Jennifer and three other accomplices. However, it took Rother's investigative journalist's tenacity and eye for detail and her knack for telling a good detective story that reads like a novel to set this book above most in the genre."

—Steve Jackson, *New York Times* bestselling author

Praise for *Lost Girls*

"*Lost Girls,* by veteran journalist and true-crime writer Caitlin Rother, is a deeply reported, dispassionately written attempt to determine what created that monster and predator. It is a cautionary tale and a horror story, done superbly by a writer who knows how to burrow into a complex case without becoming captive to her sources."

—*Los Angeles Times*

"[Caitlin Rother] is one of the best storytellers going in the true crime genre today. Written with the verve, pacing, and characterizations of a detective novel, combined with her reporter's eye for detail, *Lost Girls* should be on every true crime fan's bookshelf."

—Steve Jackson

Praise for *I'll Take Care of You*

"Rother has written another 'ripped from the headlines' page-turner. Journalistic and thorough, this title is sure to be popular. Purchase for public libraries with large true-crime collections."

—Library Journal

"Riveting . . . a story that will haunt you . . . Rother presents a fascinating study of one woman's evil and greed—that ultimately leads to the murder of a kind-hearted millionaire. The compassion the author shows for the victim and [his] . . . family makes this book an emotional, gripping tale."

—Aphrodite Jones, *New York Times* bestselling author

Praise for *Then No One Can Have Her*

"I honestly could not stop reading Caitlin Rother's *Then No One Can Have Her*. It's riveting, revealing, and insightful . . . Her closing chapters, written in first person, made my eyes water. What a fabulous, fabulous book!"

—Suzy Spencer, *New York Times* bestselling author

"Prepare to be hooked by Rother's absorbing narrative of greed, desperation, and twisty relationships . . . Between lies, financial shenanigans, shady legal maneuverings, and divided families, this tale sounds like fiction, but it's all true. And very dark."

—Katherine Ramsland

HOOKED

ALSO BY CAITLIN ROTHER

Poisoned Love (updated)

Twisted Triangle (by Caitlin Rother with John Hess)

Where Hope Begins/Deadly Devotion (by Alysia Sofios with Caitlin Rother)

My Life, Deleted (by Scott and Joan Bolzan and Caitlin Rother)

Lost Girls

I'll Take Care of You

Then No One Can Have Her

Hunting Charles Manson (by Lis Wiehl with Caitlin Rother)

Naked Addiction

Love Gone Wrong

Secrets, Lies, and Shoelaces

Dead Reckoning (updated)

Death on Ocean Boulevard

Body Parts (updated)

Down to the Bone

HOOKED

A THRILLER

CAITLIN ROTHER

This is a work of fiction. Names, characters, organizations, places, events, and incidents are either products of the author's imagination or are used fictitiously. Otherwise, any resemblance to actual persons, living or dead, is purely coincidental.

Published by Thomas & Mercer, Seattle
www.apub.com

EU product safety contact:
Amazon Media EU S. à r.l.
38, avenue John F. Kennedy, L-1855 Luxembourg
amazonpublishing-gpsr@amazon.com

ISBN-13: 9781662532351 (paperback)
ISBN-13: 9781662532344 (digital)

Cover design by Shasti O'Leary Soudant
Cover image: © Philip Thurston, © Tom Grubbe, © lingqi xie / Getty

Printed in the United States of America

Hooked is set in 2015, as newspapers were starting to transition from print to online editions, but long before newsrooms were decimated by the resulting industry implosion and many were closed entirely due to COVID shutdowns. This was before "fake news" evolved into the misinformation and disinformation campaigns of today, when communities relied on the media to print the truth and to keep politicians honest, and on the police to keep us safe. When journalists were held to higher ethical standards and when people still believed in science and technology.

Dopamine, *noun*: An organic chemical compound present in the body as a pleasure-seeking neurotransmitter that serves as a precursor to adrenaline. It can also cause feelings of infatuation, attraction, or sexual chemistry between two people in the initial stages of a relationship. Even the anticipation of rewarding activities, such as sex, can trigger its release. Ingesting stimulants, such as cocaine, triggers a dopamine rush, though subsequent doses must be larger to achieve the same high. THC, the psychoactive component in marijuana, generates a smaller amount of dopamine, as does the use of social media. It's this addictive response that keeps people repeatedly engaging with the stimuli, even as the rewards decrease. While a dopamine deficiency can cause symptoms related to Parkinson's disease, such as shaking, stiffness, and loss of balance, an overload may result in hallucinations, delusions, paranoia, or mania.

PROLOGUE
VICTORIA

Halloween Friday

Victoria Fontaine struggled to break through the brain fog, her body aching from a no-sleep hangover. Her head pounded, and her limbs felt like lead weights. Even her eyelids were too heavy to lift. But the struggle was worth it. She felt satiated. Content, even.

She rolled over and reached out blindly, expecting to grab a handful of warm flesh next to her. Instead, her fingertips found only the folds of wrinkled sheets, where Alex Battrelle had kept her up most of the night with his hot, whispery breath. Rolling her over and around until she screamed as he brought her to climax. Not that she was complaining.

As she pried her eyes open, the orange numbers on the clock read eight fifteen. She heard Alex's motorcycle engine gun up the driveway to the locked gate, idling long enough for it to open. She imagined him smiling at the memory of rubbing her belly one last time before he left.

She reached for the phone, which pinged on the bedside table with a sweet text from him. There had been an emotional connection between them ever since they'd met in rehab a lifetime ago, but Alex had always denied it. She'd waited so long to hear those words. It felt safe to be happy, for once.

Best ever, babe. It only took 18 years. I'll let u get some sleep. Love u. Feels good to say that. See u tonight???

But then there it was. That bile rising up again, like a bullet train, same time every morning for the past week. Throwing off the covers, she then ran into her bathroom, where, in one fluid motion, she lifted the toilet seat, knelt on the mat, pulled her hair back, and threw up into the bowl. After flushing it down, she pushed herself to her feet and lowered her face over the sink to rinse with mouthwash.

"God," she said, "how long is this going to last?"

She crawled back into bed and she closed her eyes again, reliving the feeling of Alex's soft, wet lips on hers, his scratchy chin rubbing against the crook of her neck, and his hard, muscular ass in her hands, tight from all the mountain-bike riding he'd been doing in Ramona the past six months.

He's right. That was our best night ever. Everything is different now.

Victoria wanted to see him again, but she couldn't commit to another night of no sleep. At least not right now. Hopefully her stomach would settle later in the day.

Tummy still not good, but it was worth losing some sleep to see u. Luv u too.

She didn't feel well enough to drag herself out of bed and into the office, not with the shitstorm going on right now. It was Friday *and* Halloween, so she might as well take a sick day, because that's what she was. Sick. All she wanted to do was lie there and sleep. Watch some TV. Drink ginger ale.

It had been a rough week, wondering if it was stress or an ulcer that constantly made her feel like retching. She'd finally faced reality and bought a pregnancy test. As the little purple cross emerged, it was like an apparition showing itself to her.

Simple math told her it could be Alex's, but she couldn't be sure, because she'd been seeing his younger brother, Michael, for the past five months. Still, after the last abortion debacle, she called Alex right away this time. He was at her house within an hour, happier than she'd ever seen him. Clean and sober too. Her ultimatum had worked.

It's all coming together. I know I need to tell Michael we're over, but he'll be devastated. So, I'm not going to tell him about the baby. Or Alex. Yet.

She'd been trying to deal with the "morning" sickness without anyone knowing at work, especially Michael. But that was tricky, because she felt nauseated off and on throughout the afternoon, when round two often hit without much warning. Luckily, she had a private bathroom in her office. She didn't want to seem weak, with the human vultures watching her every move. Not now, with so much at stake.

She didn't take extortion sitting down, so she'd issued another ultimatum, this one very different from the one she'd given Alex a year earlier. If the vultures didn't comply with her demands, she would follow through on her threat to notify the full board.

If any of this becomes public, we're all going down, and Daddy's life's work at Vitaleron will be ruined.

Four hours later, Victoria Fontaine was dead.

CHAPTER 1
GOODE

Halloween Friday

Ken Goode spent the whole flight home from Maui craving a dry martini with extra olives, followed by his usual bowl of steamed mussels and ciabatta toast to dip into the broth.

But after landing in San Diego, he had to make one stop before heading to Piatti, his favorite Italian restaurant in La Jolla. Cutting through Pacific Beach and Bird Rock, he cursed the traffic lined up at the stop signs, wishing he'd taken the freeway instead. He needed to get to Windansea before Sunset, the neighborhood's daily ritual he'd attended habitually since he was a kid. Every evening, he stood with the locals along the block with their dogs, watching the sun slip lower in the sky, while the surf rats gathered in clusters, vaping and drinking beer from red cups to skirt the no-alcohol laws. As soon as he headed down Nautilus, he breathed easier, taking in the full panoramic view of the reddish-orange horizon that stretched across the ocean as far as the eye could see. Even better once he eased his vintage sky-blue Volkswagen van into the last open slot in the parking lot, closest to the shack.

Originally built with simple eucalyptus poles and palm fronds to provide shade for the surfers on the rocks below, the iconic shack had been smashed to bits by huge waves numerous times since 1946. But the surfers always reconstructed the structure, where they gathered at dawn for a paddle-out ceremony every time another brother died too young.

Windansea was Goode's go-to place for calming his brain, a respite from the blood, fractured skulls, and darkness that made up his life as a homicide detective. Even fifteen minutes could be restorative as he meditated to the hypnotic rhythm of the waves crashing on the shore, breathing in and around the rocks and smoothing them into shapes like the curves of a woman. The rippling patterns and soothing reflection of light on the water was enough to lull him into a Zen state.

Although he'd just spent ten days riding some gnarly twenty-five-footers at Jaws, an epic surf break on Maui, he still needed to come back to this, his emotional docking station for the past thirty-seven years. Like a homing pigeon returning to the roost before setting off again.

Meandering down the dirt path to the sand, he kicked off his flip-flops and approached the water's edge. He let the foam lap over his toes before backing up a few steps to lean against the ledge and watch the whitecaps crest and tumble.

The Maui trip had been energizing and Zen in its own way, because it had pulled him out of his head for a long stretch of time. That was unusual for him, because he was constantly stuck in there, thinking about thinking. Knowing he still had another couple of days of vacation before obsessing over his next case, he was determined to spend it lollygagging.

Finished with his Albert Camus deconstruction phase, he was ready to read some inspirational Paulo Coelho, and get together with his sister, Maureen, whom he hadn't seen in many moons. She was all he had these days, orphans that they were. Other than their aunt Katherine, that is, who raised them after their parents passed, one tragic death at a time. Goode had just had dinner with Katherine and her husband on Maui, where she'd moved after Maureen graduated high school.

Maureen was smart, but in his view, she was a career underachiever. He'd tried to persuade her to follow him into police work, because, like him, she'd always been good at solving puzzles. But she preferred the freedom of waiting tables at a high-end restaurant, which left her plenty of time to surf and seemed to subsidize her low-end lifestyle. She was also a little crazy, like him, often driving two and a half hours north to Malibu after the dinner shift to surf solo by moonlight.

That's why he wanted to talk to her about his trip. She might be the only person who would really *get* his Jaws revelations. What it was like to be pushed down and tossed around in a giant whitewash machine and still go back for more, not really sure what he was trying to achieve other than the thrill of riding a glassy aquamarine tunnel that closed around him. The high took him to a new plane of existence. But she was elusive. Always busy, and hard to pin down.

For now, he was grateful to be home for Sunset, to watch the yellow orb dip lower still, narrow into an orange strip, and disappear with a flash behind the flat line of the ocean.

Feeling recalibrated, Goode climbed the path to his van and drove through town to La Jolla Shores, where the wealthy lived among the palm trees. Although they stood tall, like soldiers guarding the beachfront, the trees were no match for high winds, to which they bent in surrender.

As a public servant, he could only afford a one-bedroom rental cottage near the high school, where his parents taught when he and his sister were very young. Goode's rental was right down the street from their old house, just a few blocks from Windansea, only it was smaller and more cramped, crammed with remnants of a lifetime. Divorce could do that to you.

But then so could trying to love again. He'd had no serious romantic entanglements since his ex-wife Miranda had left him at the altar. It was some years ago now, but he still felt humiliated by his misguided attempt to give her yet another chance. It was simpler to stay celibate.

After a brief, covert, and unwise interlude with Alison—an attractive witness from the Tania Marcus murder case, his first big case, which greased the way for his official transfer to Homicide a year ago—he'd crawled back into his cave of celibacy. Technically, he'd never left that cave, because he knew in his heart that Alison was another wrong choice, so they'd never actually slept together. Clearly, he needed more time alone. It wasn't as often lately, but he still heard that voice in his head, saying *Never again.*

Women weren't an addiction per se, but he was honey to the Queen Bees of Damage, which made him fall prey to manipulative love addicts like Miranda, who'd bailed on their second wedding for a Caribbean escape with her boss. These women were drawn to him, and he, unable to resist the urge to rescue them, went down trying. It was a vicious cycle. He had a hard time repressing the savior in him, because it was, in part, what made him a good detective. But it could also compel him to take risks that he shouldn't, which sometimes worked to his disadvantage.

After bumper-bumping into a tight parking spot, he changed into a dress shirt and shoes in the personal greenroom of his van before heading into Piatti. He preferred flip-flops, but as a man of law enforcement, rules were rules. Piatti was a white-napkin-and-tablecloth kind of place, with an unwritten dress code communicated only by raised eyebrows.

There was one seat left at the bar, next to a stunning thirtysomething brunette who was staring off into the distance as she cradled a glass of amber liquid. Scotch, most likely. Goode didn't even have to order. Matt, the bartender, started making his usual martini as soon as they made eye contact.

As he came closer to the woman, he sensed that she, too, wanted to be alone with her thoughts, so he felt safe sitting next to her. In hindsight later, he realized that it was silly to think he could have resisted her.

"Are you waiting for someone?" he asked.

"No, not really," she replied, sighing, though not in an off-putting way.

"You're not sure?"

"Well, I was wondering if my dad might show up."

"Okay, how 'bout I sit here, and I'll move if he comes?"

The woman smiled and shook her head. "I wouldn't worry. I meant his spirit might visit, because our family used to come here together. But I thought it would sound weird to say that out loud. Like I'm a crazy person. Which it did, right?"

Actually, it didn't. Goode knew exactly what she meant.

"Thanks, Matt," he said as the bartender placed the martini in front of him. "No, not at all," he said, turning back toward the woman. "I've always talked to my mom on the Coronado Bridge, where she died when I was six."

"Bad accident?" she asked, hastily adding, "Unless you don't want to talk about it."

"No, it's okay. She jumped."

"Oh," she said, pausing. "Wow."

"Yeah. It was brutal. She pulled our car over to the side and left me sitting in the front seat. I looked in the rearview mirror and saw her throw one leg over the railing, then drop out of sight. So, I just sat there, waiting for her to come back."

"I know," she said, nodding.

"You do?"

Another long pause. "Yeah, my brother died by suicide too. Allegedly. I'm still not sure he did it on purpose. We were fraternal twins, and I had no clue he was going to do that."

For all his good intentions, Goode's overactive brain was firing up a storm. He felt an immediate connection with this woman. Not the usual stab of the old pain, but a brief flash of bright hope. Kismet, even.

Oh, get ahold of yourself. This isn't a frickin' rom-com.

Maybe it would be her, maybe it wouldn't, but he felt a glimmer of possibility, nonetheless. Unlike Alison, the pretty witness who proved to be another one of his vulnerable savior cases, this woman didn't need saving. She seemed strong, as if she might fight any attempt to do so.

"I'm so sorry," he told her, trying not to look too long into her hyacinth-blue eyes. He felt drawn to her, beauty aside, partly because she seemed familiar, and partly because she looked at him as if she felt the same way. He took a sip of his martini.

"Yeah, me too," she said. "About your mom."

They chatted away, introducing themselves, but only by one name. She by her first, Katrina, and he by his last, because no one had called him Ken or Kenny Jr. since he was a kid. Somehow, talking about an immediate family member's suicide—one of the most intimate subjects imaginable—was easier with a stranger he might never see again.

"You're a surfer, right?" she asked.

Goode cocked his head. "How can you tell?"

"Just the vibe. The way you carry yourself, I can see your upper body strength," she said. "You remind me of my brother. I used to watch him surf at the OB pier. He was a kamikaze surfer, the kind who would fly to Maui to ride these ginormous waves. He would have died even sooner if he didn't make a habit of wearing a life jacket. These guys on Jet Skis had to ride out and tow him in through the whitewash. It's called Jaws. You heard of it?"

Goode felt the breath go out of him for a moment. "You're not going to believe this, but that's where I spent the last week," he said.

Katrina looked as surprised as he did, when, of all the times for his cell phone to ring, Stone called. Goode couldn't believe the bad timing, but he couldn't ignore the boss. Talk about a buzzkill.

Mouthing "sorry" to Katrina, he held up his index finger to indicate he'd be quick as he stepped outside to take the call.

Sergeant Rusty Stone had been there for Goode ever since he'd lost his parents. Five years older than Kenny, Rusty was a big, stocky kid who lived down the street and stepped in as an older brother by another mother. Rusty brought his young friend to the beach, where he taught Kenny to surf. Although Rusty initially called them "Tuber" and "Mini Tuber," it wasn't long before the student surpassed his teacher, and the nicknames fell away. Rusty simply didn't have the skill or coordination, nor the desire, to ride big waves, let alone in stormy conditions.

They started going by their last names when Rusty hit seventeen. Stone thought it made them sound more macho, but he also loved making puns with Goode's name. After graduation, Stone stayed in touch, because he still lived at home while he took classes at San Diego State. Later, Stone often drove up to party with his buddy once Goode started at UCLA, where he majored in psychology.

Stone was hired by the San Diego Police Department (SDPD) right out of college and immediately started trying to convince Goode to join him. But Goode chose to stay in Los Angeles with Miranda and went to work for the LAPD instead. After Goode's marriage fell apart, Stone didn't give up, lobbying him to come home rather than apply to law school.

"We need smart guys like you," Stone said. "You'll go far, fast. You can always take classes at night."

Goode took his buddy's advice, put law school on hold, and transferred to the SDPD, where he did his requisite time in Patrol before moving on to an undercover narcotics gig. From there, Stone recommended him as a relief homicide detective, and after Goode's exceptional work solving the Tania Marcus case, Stone helped facilitate his move from Vice to Homicide.

Officially, Stone was now Goode's supervisor, but they were such good friends they worked more as a team.

"You're up," Stone said. "Where are you?"

"I'm at Piatti. Flew in a couple of hours ago. Maui was awesome, by the way. Thanks for asking. What do you mean I'm up? You know my shift doesn't start for a day and a half, right?" Goode asked this rhetorically, because he already knew the drill.

"I hope you're not trashed."

"No, not at all. I was just getting started, and my mind is pretty damn clear after facing down those waves."

"You're crazy," Stone said. "But it's lucky you came out of it alive, because we've got a mondo suspicious death case. Slausson and Fletcher were supposed to be up, but they're both down with food poisoning again. I keep telling them not to eat carnitas from the street vendors in Tijuana, but they're pigheaded."

"Bada boom."

"You're in luck, though. It's in the Farms, right up the hill from you: two victims, one older male and one female, mid-thirties. The property is owned by a plastic surgeon, Simon Fontaine, so he's probably the dude. The 911 call for 'shots fired' came in at nine o'clock from an anonymous male somewhere on the 9800 block. Wouldn't give an address, so Patrol had to go door to door. The Fontaines were the only ones who didn't answer. We had to call private security to open the gate."

"Who's there now?"

"The patrol officer, his sergeant, and the security guard. They did a sweep of the house and the grounds, but no shooter. The male victim was found with a gunshot to the head on the back patio. The female was unresponsive on the bedroom floor, no gunshot. I texted you the address. Punch the intercom and they'll buzz you in. You'll be the lead on this one."

"Thanks."

"Don't thank me yet. Simon Fontaine isn't just any plastic surgeon, he's *the* go-to cosmetic guru in San Diego County. He's also head honcho at Vitaleron, a biotech company that's developing a new sex drug with Vincent Battrelle. So it's going to be a major news clusterfuck on all fronts. See you in a few."

Goode knew exactly what Stone meant: The next forty-eight hours were going to be living hell because the likely victim was not only superrich, he was in business with another superrich dude, who owned the only newspaper in town.

The brass is going to be second-guessing our every effing move.

Rejoining Katrina, Goode tapped her on the forearm. "I'm really sorry. I was supposed to be on vacation for another couple days, but that was work calling," he said. "We've got two dead bodies in the Farms. I've got to go."

"You're a homicide detective?" she asked with amusement—or surprise—he couldn't really tell.

"'Fraid so. Is that bad?" he replied, frowning curiously.

"No, not at all," she said, shaking her head and chuckling.

He gave her his card and asked her to write her number on the back of a cocktail napkin.

"The next few days will be nonstop, but I'll call. I promise."

"I know," she said.

CHAPTER 2
GOODE

Halloween Friday

It was only a five-minute jaunt up the hill to La Jolla Farms, but Goode had to backtrack to grab a triple espresso, or he wouldn't make it through the next forty-eight hours. He'd driven his personal vehicle from the airport to Piatti, so he didn't have time to drive across town to trade it out for the department-issued Ford Explorer he drove during work hours.

After purposely parking his VW van down the street from the Fontaine estate in case any TV cameras showed up, he got out and leaned against the door to switch out his leather loafers for a pair of sneakers. Death scenes could get messy, and he didn't want to get blood on his only pair of dress shoes.

Downing the last of his coffee, he watched the particles of wet fog dancing in the beam of a streetlight as he slipped out of his button-down shirt. He applied a quick wipe of deodorant before pulling on a T-shirt with the slogan **RIDE A SURFER**, topped by a thick sweatshirt. Winter nights were cold and damp along the coast.

A salty breeze of rotting seaweed rolled up from Black's Beach, a hard-to-access surfing spot that doubled as a nude beach, popular with gay men. Whenever he surfed there, he always looked up at the cliffs, wondering how many centuries had passed to create the staggeringly tall, jagged accordion of stone. It made him feel like Charlton Heston at the end of *Planet of the Apes*, when he rides his horse up the beach to find the Statue of Liberty's head and arm jutting out of the sand.

As Goode approached the Fontaines' motorized gate, he measured with his feet the distance and privacy from the closest neighbor. Because the backside of the properties on that side of the street ended with a sheer three-hundred-foot drop into a canyon that led down to Black's, the sound of gunfire would have carried far and away, blending into the sound of the waves breaking on the shore.

Those shots could have come from anywhere.

Goode wondered how long the doctor had lived in the Farms and the nature of his relationship with the young chiquita found dead in his house. It wasn't unusual for second and third wives in La Jolla to be half, or even one-third, the age of their husbands.

Pressing the white intercom button, he heard the buzz of a camera motor as it turned to watch him.

Excellent. There should be security video.

"Yes?" a young man said.

"Homicide," he replied. "Detective Goode."

Heading down the steep, sloped sandstone driveway, he passed a silver Mercedes and a red Miata parked at the bottom. The double-doored entrance pictured two stained-glass mermaids reaching out to each other. The siren's call.

An antique clock chimed at eleven thirty as he pushed one of the doors open, noting it was spring weighted to close on its own, with no signs of forced entry. Before going any further, he slipped on booties and latex gloves from his go bag, which contained everything he needed at a crime scene—flashlight, notebook, protein bars, Faraday bags, and a few bottles of water, all replenished after each call.

This place has more square footage than a Nordstrom.

"Out here!" the same voice called out as Goode entered a kitchen big enough to serve an entire restaurant. Beyond two sliding glass doors that opened onto the back patio, a security guard was chatting animatedly with a newbie patrol officer. Both were in their mid-twenties.

"Did you open these doors, or were they like that when you got here?" Goode asked the officer, who should know better than to touch anything. But he remembered being their age, brimming with young, hot enthusiasm and endless curiosity.

"They were open," the two lads said in unison.

"You guys are supposed to be waiting out front, not walking all over my crime scene. We treat all suspicious deaths like homicides. So, you didn't move anything, right?" Goode asked this facetiously because he'd already eyed a wallet on the ground next to the male victim's body, with a driver's license on top of it.

"No, sir," the officer said.

"Except for this man's driver's license and wallet," Goode said. "And what else?"

"Nothing," the officer said quietly. "We thought we should see if the victim lived here or if he was an intruder who killed the woman upstairs. His license shows this address."

"Yeah, well, that doesn't mean he didn't kill her, though, does it?" Goode asked rhetorically. "Or vice versa."

"Um, yeah, I guess not."

"Never move a victim," Goode said. "Don't even touch him unless you think he might need medical aid."

Crouching down, Goode shined his flashlight across the victim's face and head until he found the bullet wound Stone had mentioned.

There it is, a perfectly round hole in his right temple. But gunshot wounds to the head are usually big bleeders. This one didn't bleed much at all, and even that little bit is gelatinous. By the looks of the driver's license photo, this is Dr. Simon Fontaine.

A 9mm pistol—standard issue by most law enforcement agencies—lay inches from the man's right hand. The skin on his neck felt surprisingly cold, so even the newbies knew he'd been down too long to call for paramedics. Since this guy was a plastic surgeon, Goode wondered if he could have partially embalmed himself premortem with Botox, creating clots or slowing his bleeding somehow. Either way, he looked remarkably well preserved for sixty-five, with tight skin and a full head of white hair.

The body lay about ten feet from the edge of the terra-cotta-tiled patio that flowed down a flight of stairs to a lapis-colored lap pool and a pool house. Up above was a second-floor exterior balcony, where a bystander would have had a direct view over the body.

"So, I hear you guys did a sweep and there's no armed nutjob hiding in a closet somewhere?"

"Yes, sir," the officer said more brightly now, as if he'd finally done something right. "My sergeant and I searched top to bottom before he alerted Homicide."

"Did you try the pool house too?" Goode asked, prompting the newbies to look at each other, then take off down the stairs.

"Guess not," he muttered.

Fontaine's body was in an unnatural position. Not the way someone would land after shooting themselves. Goode glanced up at the balcony again, then reexamined the doctor's face, noticing some red abrasions on his forehead.

Did he fall or jump from the balcony? Or was he dumped?

The officer and security guard returned a minute later, grinning sheepishly.

"All clear, sir," the officer said. "Other than my sergeant catching a nap. He's on back-to-back shifts and figured it would be a while before the briefing."

"Okay, thanks. I'm heading upstairs," Goode said.

The Berber-carpeted stairway ascended in dogleg fashion to the second and third floors. One flight up in the bedroom closest to the stairs, a pretty, dark-haired woman lay on her back on the carpet next to a queen-sized bed. No wedding ring. Dressed in panties and an oversized T-shirt over her well-toned, tanned body.

Must be the lap pool. If she lives here, that is. So, is she a girlfriend, his daughter, or a roommate?

If Goode had a few moments alone with her before the rest of his team showed up, he might be able to figure that out. He'd work solo if he could, but homicide investigations were, by definition, a team effort.

He knelt to check her neck for a pulse. Nothing. The soft skin along her jawbone was about the same temperature as the doctor's.

Two pill vials were open on the bedside table: Xanax, a sedative for anxiety, and oxycodone, a narcotic painkiller. Both prescriptions had been filled earlier that day by Dr. Simon Fontaine for Victoria Fontaine, but the vials seemed pretty full, so it didn't look like she'd swallowed a handful of pills.

He'd heard the name Victoria Fontaine before, but he couldn't remember where or when. Only that it was long before he worked undercover in Ocean Beach, a neighborhood known as OB, where gentrification still hadn't managed to wipe out all the old hippie drug culture.

Also on the table were a clock, a cell phone, some saltine cracker wrappers, and an empty bowl with a yellow residue that smelled like chicken soup. Goode put the phone into a Faraday bag, which would prevent it from receiving a signal, thereby blocking new texts, emails, or calls from coming in until he could get the device to the Regional Computer Forensics Lab (RCFL).

Password protections could be challenging, but the protocol was to copy all the data, then search the duplicate to avoid disturbing or accidentally deleting anything on the original device. He was antsy to go through the emails, texts, and voicemails so he could start building a timeline for when she died, and if he was lucky, find some clues as to motive.

The bathroom had a double sink carved out of gray marble, a glass-walled shower with two heads facing each other, and a whirlpool tub with multiple jets. However, he saw only one set of seafoam-green towels and one electric toothbrush. The proliferation of perfume bottles, but no cologne or aftershave, also indicated it was hers alone.

Peering into the trash bin tucked between the toilet and the vanity, Goode took a pen from his bag to move a couple wads of tissue to the side, revealing a white pregnancy stick with a purple plus sign.

Bingo.

"Now, that's what we call a clue," he whispered.

Looks like she was living, or at least staying, here in this bedroom. The question is whether she took the pregnancy test before or after filling the prescriptions. Unless this isn't Victoria Fontaine.

Back in the bedroom, he searched for some form of identification and found a green crocodile bag on the floor next to the bed. He couldn't tell if it was a genuine Hermès or a knockoff like his sister carried around.

"I like to mess with people, because the real thing costs $85,000," Maureen had told him, laughing.

He found his answer in a wallet stuffed with hundred-dollar bills, a stack of credit cards, and a driver's license with a photo that resembled the victim, listing her age as thirty-five and an address on La Jolla Farms Road.

No, it's her. But this address says she lives down the street. Odd.

Seeing her age triggered his memory: Victoria Fontaine had been two years behind him at La Jolla High, so he'd already graduated when she was high on oxy and crashed her father's vintage Corvette into an oncoming car, severely injuring a seven-year-old girl. He'd heard about it through the grapevine, because Victoria came from a wealthy family. They'd never met because they ran in very different circles. Being around uber-rich people like the Fontaines made him uncomfortable.

So, does she live here or not? Seems kind of weird for a thirty-five-year-old woman to be under the same roof as her father.

Kneeling down again, he noticed three purplish spots in the inner fold of her left elbow. They looked like sloppy injection sites, but there were no syringes or paraphernalia in sight. He also saw several rows of white horizontal scars in the soft flesh of her inner thighs. Old scars. Which meant she'd been cutting herself for years. Looking closer, he found some pink, fresh marks on the inside of her upper left arm.

Wow, that's sad. Given the brand-new prescriptions and cutting marks, this one looks like it could be a suicide. Maybe the pregnancy created complications because the father is married or didn't take the news well. But why would her own father prescribe oxy and Xanax for her now, when they are contraindicated, especially when she had a problem with oxy as a teenager, and even more so when she's pregnant? Maybe she stole one of his prescription pads or had someone else call them in for her?

Following a hunch, he went back downstairs to reexamine the doctor for injection marks. As he scanned the areas of exposed flesh, Goode located a purplish area on the side of the doctor's neck.

Looks like Victoria's arm, only not as badly bruised.

He couldn't see very well with a flashlight in the dark, but if that was another injection site, he saw no syringe or empty drug vial there either. None of this added up. But maybe that was the point.

It was never fun to request a search warrant from a judge after midnight. But that wasn't his problem. That was a job for Ted Byron, his team's warrant czar.

In the meantime, Goode had the techs search the front yard and photograph along the driveway up to the gate, because, technically, they weren't supposed to mess with anything inside until the warrant came through. Nor could he go through the victims' phones. Some impatient detectives did this prematurely because they thought they knew better, only to screw up the evidence or render it inadmissible in court.

"Where's that warrant?" he yelled to no one in particular.

"It's coming, buddy," Stone said as he walked through the sliding glass doors from the kitchen and handed Goode a more powerful flashlight.

"Thanks. 'Bout time you showed up," Goode said, taking the light and returning the smaller one to his bag.

"Yeah, I got waylaid. Norman Klein called me after hearing the 911 call on the scanner in his car. He said it was past deadline, but he could call in a few details, so I gave him enough to hold him until we've officially identified the victims. Based on the money in this neighborhood, I'm betting the chief will want to do a news conference."

"Not too soon I hope, because I can't tell what this is, a double suicide, a murder-suicide, or a double murder," Goode said, filling Stone in on the doctor's gooey gunshot wound, his daughter's history with oxy, the bruising and cutting marks, and the red flag raised by her new prescriptions.

Stone looked a little overwhelmed. "Well, the good news is that the lieutenant says we've got anything we need on this one. I mean, look at this place, it's huge. Must be worth a frickin' fortune. Hopefully the warrant comes through sooner than later. Judge Brockton, that longboarder from Bird Rock, is on call tonight. But if I know you, you'll have this thing solved before it even gets here. No pressure."

"I wouldn't count on that, but thanks. We need to make sure to get one for the security video too. I saw a camera out front."

"Yeah, I already told Byron. He's on it."

"It's too late to talk to neighbors," Goode said. "Foster can do that first thing."

"Yep."

As they walked out to the driveway, Ted Byron was dutifully typing up the warrant affidavits on the hood of his car, and Bill Foster, their newest team member, was walking toward them with a roll of yellow crime-scene tape.

"I had Patrol string this up to keep the lookie-loos out," Foster said. "How was Maui, brotha? Gnarly?"

"Totally," Goode replied, but then turned away, all business. He was in no mood for small talk.

CHAPTER 3
KATRINA

Halloween Friday

Katrina Chopin was on edge that night. She had no problem sitting by herself at the bar. She could talk to just about anyone. Or no one.

But she'd come to Piatti for self-reflection, so she took the seat nearest the kitchen, which left one between her and a constipated-looking couple in their fifties. They were eating their meal in silence, barely acknowledging each other. Another reason not to get married.

"Glenlivet with one big rock if you have it, please," she told the bartender.

This one is for you, Daddy. Your favorite.

She was still feeling a bit disoriented after her reentry into San Diego a week ago. It had been a bit bumpy. Parachuting into her hometown after living five years on the East Coast, and five years in the Chicago area before that, had given her a jolt of culture shock. She'd visited only occasionally while attending undergrad, and later grad school, at Northwestern University, which was her mother's alma mater as well. Her mom majored in theater; both of Katrina's degrees were in journalism.

But it went deeper than that. Katrina normally felt like the confident investigative reporter she was, but for the past week, the demons and memories of her younger self were creeping back up: The insecure tomboy who didn't like men staring at her new breasts—high, firm, and slightly larger than one would expect for her petite frame. The teenager who was attracted to guys who weren't good to her, and vice versa. And the young woman who took risks and bad turns, telling herself she could use the experience as a writer and musician, all of which ultimately landed her in therapy.

"Sex is not love. Lust is not love," her therapist told her. "Look somewhere else. Or better yet, stop looking."

The bartender set the tumbler of scotch in front of her with a quick grin before splashing vodka into a glass, pushing the tonic button on his soda gun, and muddling mint in the bottom of another glass.

Having tended bar at a Chicago steak house for several years, Katrina grew a little nostalgic watching him create trendy infused cocktails. But that chapter was closed for her. Listening to customers' stories was entertaining when the tips were flowing, but her attempt to weave them into a novel was a major fail. Once she realized that making stuff up was a better fit with her songwriting, she joined a band for the first time since she'd played dual guitars with her brother. She performed at night, mostly on weekends, and earned her master's by day.

Her parents were set to fly out to Evanston for her commencement ceremony one Saturday in June when her mom's sister, Athena, called.

"Katrina, honey, I don't know how to tell you this, but your mom and dad won't be coming," she said, bursting into tears.

From the mutterings between the sobs, Katrina gleaned that her parents, both federal judges, had been gunned down in their driveway in Point Loma. Katrina was on a plane to San Diego two hours later.

In just six months, she'd lost her three closest family members, starting with the overdose by her brother, Francis, who was named after a distant ancestor, the composer Frédéric François Chopin, and went by the nickname Franny.

Dazed and numb but efficient, she spent the next week in crisis mode—comforting Athena and speed-sorting through her parents' affairs. After hiring movers to transfer the antique furniture and sentimental belongings into three storage units, she sold the remaining odds and ends at an estate sale on the lawn.

The house had been in her mother Aphrodite's family for many years. Being in one of San Diego's older, wealthier neighborhoods, a nicely groomed yard wasn't unusual, but Peter Chopin had taken great pride in such matters. Katrina made sure to pay their longtime gardener every month so the task wasn't left to the new rental tenants.

That done, she took off for a reporting job at a little paper in Northampton, Massachusetts. She was fine as long as she stayed active, but that meant she never really stopped to mourn. She simply pushed the emotions down, then down some more. At least that's what her therapist told her.

As Katrina swirled her Glenlivet around the giant cube, she tried to remember the last time her family had dined at Piatti together. Franny loved their veal piccata, her mom went for the risotto, and her dad had the daily special, no matter what it was. But toward the end, their family get-togethers were downright unpleasant.

Looking over her shoulder at the adjacent room, Katrina recalled Franny slamming down his fork and storming out the night Daddy called him out on his boozing. Another evening, Franny performed a dramatic wine-bottle drop on the patio, splashing Zinfandel on every diner nearby, before silently turning to leave. Each time, their mother stared straight ahead, her bottom lip shaking, until Franny's tantrum was over. Only then did she order her usual glass of Cabernet and finish her dinner in peace.

As Katrina faced forward again, the bartender was salting the rim of a glass. He shook the silver canister vigorously, pouring out two foamy margaritas with a flourish. Maybe she'd have one of those next.

She didn't like to dive too deeply into these family memories because they made her sad, and who needed that? But she'd made a deal with herself—and her therapist—to visit Piatti, pull some out, and start processing them. Or the trauma would keep bubbling up and festering, as it had on those sleepless nights while she was writing the award-winning series that had brought her back home, recruited by the *San Diego Sun-Dispatch*.

It was a tad surreal to work for the "conservative rag" her parents wouldn't have in the house when she and Franny were growing up. They preferred the *Los Angeles Times*. But other than the comics and Dear Abby, teenage Katrina had no interest in either paper. And now look at her, a member of the Watchdog reporting team, driven to succeed as much or more than her parents ever were, trying to live up to the legacy they'd left behind.

That said, she almost dreaded seeing anyone from her past life here. What would she say to them? Of course they'd ask how she was doing after Franny's overdose, followed by her parents' very public death, which the media dubbed the "Double-Judge Murders."

They always came up with catchy phrases for high-profile cases, but this one made her wince. Like her parents were a pack of gum or something. She was frustrated that neither the cops nor the FBI, which was called in to assist, had made any significant progress in the case, allowing the killer to go underground or remain hidden in plain sight. She had no idea, really, but she was determined to find out.

Feeling a presence next to her, Katrina heard a male voice to her left.

"Is this seat taken?"

She turned to see an attractive man, slightly older than her, with a mirthful smile. His opening salvo didn't sound like a pickup line. More like a polite question.

"No, not really," she said.

She'd imagined saving the seat for her father as if he were the prophet Elijah. She wasn't Jewish, but she'd been to a few Seders. The host always left an empty seat and a glass of wine for Elijah, knowing he would never show up.

The man seemed friendly enough, but he was almost too handsome, with his sun-bleached brown hair and his pecs and shoulder muscles pushing against his long-sleeved fitted shirt. Royal blue made his tanned skin glow.

As a general rule, she mistrusted men who looked this good because they were usually self-centered. Too often, they started a conversation, then picked up their phone to read messages while she was trying to tell them a story. She could read most anything upside down, and on two such occasions, the asshats were trolling for Tinder dates right in front of her. But she could tell this guy was for real as soon as their conversation went to death and suicide. He also had kind eyes.

She talked to her parents too. Sometimes aloud or in her head, sometimes in her dreams.

It's not the same paper. It's better these days. They've won a Pulitzer since you've been gone.

In just minutes, she and Goode had gone deep, yet barely touched the surface, when he stepped outside to take a call.

He apologized when he returned, touching her lightly on the forearm. "We've got two dead bodies in the Farms," he said. "I've got to go."

"You're a homicide detective," she said, laughing a little.

"'Fraid so," he said, apparently confused by her amusement. "Is that bad?"

She shook her head. She was laughing because she'd realized why she felt such a connection with him. They were both investigators, but on opposite sides of the fence. How much of a no-go was that right off the bat? He was one of *them*. A potential source, which could be a problem when he called her for a date. She knew he would. Despite his cool exterior, she could see it in his eyes.

But he was gone before she had a chance to tell him what she did for a living. Or that she was going to be a burr in his department's ass, pressuring them to pull her parents' cold case out of the freezer and bring it back to a boil.

Goode's abrupt departure took the breath out of her evening, so she paid the check and headed back to the La Jolla Sheraton, where the paper was putting her up until she could find a place to live.

CHAPTER 4
GOODE

Saturday

Once the two forensic tech teams arrived—one for each victim—Goode called everyone together for a briefing in the driveway. Thankfully, their lieutenant, Doug Wilson, had decided to wait until morning to swing by. Wilson aspired to be chief someday, and morning lighting was better for face time in front of the TV cameras.

While they waited for the warrants to come through, Goode walked up to the street to determine how an intruder might have gained access to the house when Patrol had to call private security to open the gate.

Could've scaled the wall, I guess, but I'm betting they knew the security code or got buzzed in somehow. So, if it's a murder, that says inside job by a family friend or associate.

Turning toward the ocean, he caught a whiff of night-blooming jasmine and tried to imagine the pristine ocean-bluff neighborhood before Texas oil baron William Black carved it into residential lots in 1947. It was called "La Jolla Farms" because Black and his wife bred and trained horses there, but every deed came with a covenant: Only "Caucasian[s] with European ancestry" could buy a parcel or join their Beach and Bridle Club of white supremacists.

Such local covenants, which also banned Jews from buying property, had to be changed during the 1970s, when the new University of California, San Diego, began recruiting faculty members nationwide. But that didn't eliminate the residual elitism that Goode felt from his classmates at La Jolla Elementary all the way through high school. While many of his classmates lived in mansions like the Fontaines', his family's bungalow was in the same hood, near the high school, in which the "help" for those mansions used to live.

Many homes in the Farms were built during that same era but had since been upgraded or expanded to reflect the occupants' wealth, often leaning toward the ostentatious. The Razor House, for example, which he'd passed on his way to the Fontaines': With walls of glass and cold cement, the home had water flowing over its outside edges. Designed by a famous architect in 2007, the property, originally valued at $34 million, was used as a backdrop for high-end fashion and credit card shoots. Goode couldn't even imagine living there. He felt like a trespasser just walking by.

Once the warrants came through, Goode headed back inside the Fontaine mansion, pointing the techs toward items to photograph and mark with evidence numbers, such as the pregnancy stick. He liked his numbers to progress in logical order, to tell the story he would present to the prosecutor, and he—or she—in turn, to the jury. Other areas were identified for fingerprint dusting and swabbing for DNA.

"Bag the hands of both victims, please," he said. "We'll need to check them for gunshot residue."

Although they'd turned on most of the lights, it still wasn't very bright in the house. But even as a death scene, the stark rooms of wall-to-wall glass seemed right out of *Architectural Digest*. During the day, the ocean view had to be spectacular.

Six bedrooms and five bathrooms were spread over three floors, including a master suite on the top, where Goode focused the next phase of his search. Because the enormous walk-in closet was half-empty, with men's clothes and shoes on the other side, Goode figured the doctor was recently divorced or widowed.

This was confirmed by the reading glasses perched on the spine of a book, opened and pages-down on one bedside table, but nothing except a clock on the other. Female companions usually left remnants of themselves, like earplugs or eye cream, which indicated that Simon was not in a serious relationship. Maybe a regular sex partner, but nothing more.

Down the hall was a big office, where two wide-screen computer monitors spanned most of a massive cherrywood desk, most likely for viewing X-rays and medical records simultaneously. Several framed family photos showed Simon with a younger Victoria and an even younger blond man with the same nose and chin. Probably her brother.

Simon had his arm stiffly around Victoria's shoulder. Not the affectionate type, apparently. A framed news article hung on the wall, featuring a photo taken at the ribbon-cutting for Vitaleron Corp. at their HQ in Sorrento Valley. It identified Simon as founder, chief executive officer, and board chairman, and Victoria as the company's chief financial officer.

So, they worked together. That's a start.

Another photo featured Simon fishing on a yacht with an almost identical white-haired man. His brother most likely, possibly a twin. Neither of them looked particularly happy to be together, but at least they were trying.

The rest of the wall was hung with Simon's medical licenses and degrees, and photos with local celebrities and elected officials, including the mayor and several council members and port commissioners. Always with the serious expression, Simon was captured in a posed handshake with Police Chief Tom Baxter at a civic event.

Just what we need. A victim who was a friend or associate of the chief and every politician in town. A major clusterfuck, indeed.

There was also a plaque commemorating the groundbreaking of the Fontaine Room at the McDonald Center, a rehab facility for alcohol and substance abuse. With Victoria's history, this was a strong indicator that she'd spent time there, because major donations are often gestures of thanks. Again, this pointed to suicide, or even an accidental overdose, at least for Victoria.

Checking the master bathroom, Goode found a black medical bag of first-aid items: gauze, white tape, and an unopened box of syringes.

This box hasn't been touched. Still, people don't shoot up a lethal dose, dispose of the needle, then go downstairs to make chicken soup.

It also contained a silver-dollar-sized plastic box with several blue pills and two green capsules under the snap lid. He knew the blue ones were Viagra, but he didn't recognize the green ones. That was a job for the medical examiner's toxicology lab.

But other than the dead bodies, he didn't see any signs of foul play anywhere in the house—no blood, broken glass, splintered doorjambs, or forced locks.

"Listen up, everyone," he called from the top of the stairs. "We need to search every trash receptacle on site. Keep an eye out for syringes, drug vials, paraphernalia, and any traces of blood inside the house."

Walking down one flight, he identified the room with the balcony he'd seen from the patio below, and it felt as lifeless as the bodies. The only piece of furniture was a long, U-shaped sectional green couch facing a big flat-screen TV, where a family could gather to watch movies or play video games. Yet, he saw no toys or photos of children anywhere in the house. No flowers, sentimentality, feminine touches—or liquor—either.

A set of French doors opened onto the balcony, which was enclosed by an ornate wrought iron railing. The door on the right was slightly ajar. The left side was closed.

Odd. Did someone forget to close both doors after pushing him over? If he was going to jump, he probably wouldn't have closed them first.

Still, with a gunshot wound to the head, it seemed unlikely that he would've shot himself, then fallen. The small amount of his thick blood on the patio also made a jump implausible because his noggin would have split open. In fact, the whole scene screamed oxymorons. Goode had seen some weird crime scenes, especially when they'd been staged, and this one was right up there.

We should dust these doorknobs for prints.

Heading back to Victoria's bedroom, Goode opened the white, shuttered doors of the closet, which contained designer suits and casual business attire, sexy dresses and fancy gowns in plastic bags, a must so close to the ocean. But he didn't see any computer or work area. Although she could have shared her father's office upstairs, he figured she preferred keeping her personal and professional lives separate.

Even if Victoria or Simon had a health issue, Goode still couldn't conjure up a motive for either one to commit a murder-suicide. But it seemed like more grown children killed their parents than the other way around.

Maybe I missed something in her bag.

Although he had lost his mom on the bridge shortly after his sixth birthday, she'd already taught him not to go into her purse.

"It's like going through a woman's private secrets," she told him.

But it was his job to paw through Victoria's. After removing a heap of clothes from the armchair to sit down, he was pleased to find a laptop on the seat.

Excellent. Got to get this to the RCFL to see if we can find some leads in her files or browser search history.

Victoria's bag was full of random pens, paper napkins, sticky wrapped cough drops, Stevia bags, a lipstick case, and her laminated Vitaleron security badge on a cord. But then, tucked in a side pocket, he found a surprising yet important clue: a single unspent 9mm round.

Where did this come from? Is that her gun on the patio? Was she planning a round of Russian roulette when the events took an unexpected turn?

It was an interesting find. But it only raised more questions.

Googling Vitaleron, Goode found the news stories Stone had mentioned. According to *The New York Times*, the promising experimental sex drug was billed as a dopamine enhancement vehicle, more effective and broader in scope than Viagra. Unlike the little blue pill, which was for men only, this drug came in different gender-based formulations, to address men's and women's respective hormonal and other physiological needs: Mantabulis and Femtastica.

You've got to wonder about side effects, though. Like Viagra's four-hour erection warning.

Goode had taken a brain chemistry class at UCLA, but he did a quick internet refresher on dopamine functions and its reward-seeking receptors before reading the rest of the article.

The goal of the new drug was to heighten physical pleasures during sex. But what made the drug unique and unprecedented was the psychological boost it reportedly would provide to prolong or rekindle lost attraction to a long-term partner. In essence, this pharmacological rebirth of youth and virility was billed to maintain that new-relationship feeling, the butterflies and infatuation that typically lasted only six to eighteen months before fading away. The ramifications could be sweeping.

"You know that euphoric feeling when you're first attracted to someone? What if you were able to reinvigorate that excitement later in your marriage or relationship? Or, even better, if you never lost it?" Dr. Fontaine told the *Times*. "Studies show that's often why married partners have affairs. They miss that desire, that urge. Having it with your spouse or significant other is certainly safer—and socially preferable—than trying to find it with strangers online or in dark bars."

Amen to that. Sounds like Simon was speaking from experience. I wonder if he or his wife was the one who lost the feeling?

As a regular *Times* subscriber, Goode didn't know how he could have missed this story when it came out, unless he was investigating a fresh murder or testifying at trial.

Per Food and Drug Administration (FDA) protocols, Vitaleron had already completed animal trials and the first of three phases of human trials more than a year ago. But Goode couldn't find any updates online.

He pictured the rich white men lining up in the steam room at the La Jolla Beach and Tennis Club—with their limp penises, droopy bellies, and fantasies of eternally youthful erections—lobbying Simon Fontaine and Vincent Battrelle to let them into the human trials.

If these deaths were related to Vitaleron, Simon's phone might also hold some leads. Heading back downstairs, Goode went hunting for the device, which was covered by the warrant.

Out on the patio, he waited for the criminalist to finish his measurements around the victim's body. Careful not to disturb Simon's position before the ME's investigator arrived, Goode felt around and eased the phone from the front pocket of the doctor's Bermuda shorts and dropped it into another Faraday bag.

Goode picked up the gun in his gloved hand and opened the chamber. It was empty, which left one bullet in Victoria's purse and one in her father's head.

Stone joined him outside. "Find anything else?" he asked.

"Yeah, check this out," he said, showing him the gun and the single round, which he dropped into two respective bags the tech held open for him. "This unspent cartridge came from a pocket in Victoria's purse. We'll need to check if either of them owned a gun, but if this was a murder, it could also be stolen."

"Appearances can be deceiving. Remember the Loricelli case?" Stone said, referring to the man who had staged his own suicide to look like a murder so his kids could collect on his life insurance.

"Point taken," Goode said. "But if that's what happened here, then who benefits?"

When the ME's investigator showed up around 4:00 a.m., Goode was pleased to see it was his buddy, Artie Hayes. Goode had learned a lot from him over the past few years.

"Don't you usually work days?" Goode asked.

"Yeah, but we had a five-car pileup on the 805 that took forever to process," Artie said, his voice ragged from exhaustion. "Bunch of gang members chasing and shooting each other. They're going about a hundred and twenty, and two of them lose control. Boom. Five cars totaled, two fatalities, two drivers in critical condition. Only one guy walked away."

Goode briefed Artie on his findings so far but let him examine both bodies and come to his own conclusions about the gunshot wound and bruising.

"We won't know for sure until we do the autopsy, but it seems like this guy was dead before he was dumped here, and was shot postmortem," Artie said. "If he was killed in a fall from that balcony, you'd see a lot more blood, and it would have spread further. His skull would have cracked open like a melon."

"That's what I thought."

"Even if he was shot somewhere else and the killer did a cleanup, we'll probably still see blood in his hair. We'll check for powder burns on his temple and hands, and his daughter's too. She could've shot him, then killed herself some other way."

"Right. I had them both bagged," Goode said. "We'll have the gun dusted for prints, but if the shooter was an intruder, he probably wiped it clean."

"Good move, grasshopper. Find any blood in the house?"

"No, not yet anyway."

"So, if this was a staged suicide, the question is how did Simon Fontaine actually die? Hey, wait. Is this an injection bruise here on his neck? That's interesting."

"That's what I said. Victoria has something similar on her arm."

"Really? Show me."

Artie followed Goode upstairs, where he confirmed the detective's assessment. "If she didn't shoot herself up, whoever did wasn't very good at it," he said. "People don't generally inject themselves in the neck, though. Dr. Thompson can take a closer look at both injection sites at the morgue."

Goode made sure to point out the pregnancy test and Dr. Fontaine's name on the prescriptions for his daughter. "Can we get a rush on the tox screen?" Goode asked.

"We'll need a request from your chief, but I'm sure that won't be an issue in this case," Artie said.

Once Simon's body was taken away, Goode was tempted to come back with a weighted mannequin and dump it off the balcony to see how and where it landed.

You never know. This smells like a murder for the good doctor. Victoria, I'm still not sure about.

CHAPTER 5
KATRINA

Saturday

As soon as Katrina woke up, she reached for her phone to search for news about the two dead bodies that had interrupted her evening out.

But all she saw on the *Sun-Dispatch* website was a measly brief. It didn't say whether the dead man at the mansion was the homeowner, Dr. Simon Fontaine. Nor did it explain his relationship with the young woman who was also found dead there. It didn't even mention that Homicide had been called in.

After only a week on staff, she hadn't met many of her colleagues, including those who worked in bureaus, like Norman Klein, whose name was on this shoddy little brief.

Is he an intern or an actual reporter? Where was his editor? I thought this was a real paper. What have I done, coming back here?

She'd taken the job at the *Northampton Record* in part because it had won awards, but the primary reason was that the detectives working her parents' murder case had advised her to keep a low profile or get out of town until they could catch the killer. She figured the little town in Western Massachusetts was about as far away and under the radar as she could get without leaving the country.

Under the circumstances, she suggested the cops look into any possible connection with the "suicide" of her brother, Franny, a developer who was blamed for a multimillion-dollar loss to a group of investors when his hotel resort project on Mission Bay was aborted due to "environmental issues." But if the cops had found, or even looked for, a connection, no one had shared it with her.

As advised, she secreted herself away in an apartment in Northampton. When she wasn't at work, she hid out at a dive bar where she and her colleagues drank beer or whiskey and played pool after deadline. But she wasn't very good at keeping a low profile.

Sniffing out several iffy contracts on her beat led her to the revelation that the head of a waste-hauling company with reputed ties to the Polish mafia had bribed two school board members, then killed Katrina's source—the superintendent's estranged wife, who had leaked the explosive documents to her. Threats on Katrina's life ensued, but she still came to work every day, bleary-eyed from lack of sleep, and wrote the hell out of a series of stories.

Just hours after the national investigative award for that series was announced, Metro Editor Linda Kelley called to offer her a job at the *Sun-Dispatch*. Katrina reflexively said yes and gave notice that same day.

Although Katrina was relieved to have an excuse to come home, her therapist, whom she'd started seeing after the death threats started, cautioned that she would be bringing her PTSD with her. Katrina had tried to deny it, but she had to admit that over the past week, she'd jumped whenever a Massachusetts area code, or even an unknown number, showed up on her caller ID. Not to mention the couple of voicemails she'd gotten, with heavy breathing but no talking, since her first stories had run in the *Sun-Dispatch*. She couldn't help but keep her eyes peeled for black Town Cars like the one that had parked outside her apartment at night while she was writing the mafia series.

The prosecutor on that case had called this past week, trying to persuade her to testify at the upcoming trial. So far, she'd put him off, saying her stories spoke for themselves. But he was persistent, so the possibility of a subpoena was hanging over her like an evil spirit. Nonetheless, Katrina was determined not to let her anxiety take a toll, or to tell anyone about any of this.

Katrina wasn't scheduled to work that Saturday, but she wanted to "hit the ground running," as they said in the biz, by submitting a list of story ideas to her new boss, Joanne Wagner, one of the assistant Metro editors. After that, Katrina planned to find a short-term rental before her few boxes of belongings arrived by UPS. Her longer-term plan was to move into the family house in Point Loma as soon as the tenants' lease expired.

The elevator rattled its way up to the third floor of the brick building, circa 1973, which overlooked Interstate 8, the freeway that ran east to west through Mission Valley. The elevator bell sounded with an antiquated *ding* as the doors opened onto a blue carpet with worn patches.

The newsroom was a big open area with desks configured into pods for the reporters, surrounded by glass-walled offices for the editors. Just like at her last newspaper, the cleaning staff vacuumed occasionally, but wasn't allowed to disturb reporters' desks, or their stacks of books, yellowed newspapers, and notebooks, full of scrawls no one else could read. That meant the dust blown around by the computers' internal fans coated every exposed item and layer of paper. Like the photos of reporters posing with politicians or celebrities they admired or detested, the campaign buttons with slogans like "I'm not running for Congress" or Obama's "Yes we can," and the random keepsakes like troll dolls, petrified Twinkies, and purple Peeps.

Because she'd only been there a week, her desk, which faced the editors' meeting room and the executive editor's corner office, was comparatively naked. Several minutes after Katrina sat down, a woman's voice erupted behind her.

"Hello, Katrina."

She turned to see it was Linda Kelley, the woman who had hired her.

How long has she been standing here?

"Oh, hi," Katrina said, whirling around in her swivel desk chair. "I didn't hear you come up."

"Sorry," Linda said. "Didn't mean to startle you. I thought you'd be out looking for an apartment."

"I was putting a story list together."

She'd heard from her pod-mates that Linda didn't know how to take a day off, but Katrina made no judgment because they shared that trait. Journalism was a hungry vortex. Filling the endless black hole of anticipation with stories distracted her so she didn't feel lonely. But the reward lasted only a day or two at a time. Until the next big scoop came along, and the adrenaline rush that came with it.

She hoped she wouldn't wear the long-term consequences like Linda—the purplish bags under her eyes, the thick middle section, and the untreated white roots. It was too soon to tell whether Linda's eye bags were caused by insomnia or whiskey, but Katrina wanted none of them.

Her editor, Joanne, had already warned her that Linda's crusty exterior came with an unpredictable temper, a common trait among female senior editors who lacked intimate contact with other sentient beings and weren't home enough to have pets. But it was because of women like Linda, who had fought their way up in a formerly all-male industry, that Katrina had a job at all.

"I was actually going to call you in, so it's good that you're already here," Linda said. "I'd like you to work on a story that broke last night. We'll pay you overtime for today, and you'll still have time to look for a place to live."

"Sure, no problem," Katrina said, cringing inwardly at the assignment she sensed was coming, which would cost her a date with the sexy surfing detective. As she grabbed her notebook and pen, Linda rolled closer, as if she were going to reveal a secret.

"Did you see the crime brief about the two deaths on La Jolla Farms last night?" she asked.

Dammit.

"Yes, I did," Katrina replied.

"We had to chase it in because it came in after deadline. The reporter, Norman Klein, had already left his office at the cop shop when he heard the 'shots fired' alert on his scanner, so he called Big Ed, our nightside editor. Ed used the crisscross directory and online property records to figure out who owned the house."

"Uh-huh."

"Dr. Fontaine was a newsmaker, quite influential in the La Jolla medical, biotech, and philanthropic communities, where we have a lot of readers. He was working on a groundbreaking sexual enhancement drug at a local pharmaceutical company he founded, Vitaleron, and we need you to find out if the deaths are somehow related to that. We still don't have IDs on the victims, but we figure he's probably one of them."

Katrina nodded, excitedly taking notes. Since she had no choice in the matter, she was pleased that it sounded way more intriguing than your basic cops story.

"I'd like you to get a feel for the neighborhood and introduce yourself to the lead detective," Linda said, as Katrina suppressed a smirk to hide her secret. "We need to get a handle on how these people died. For all we know, Dr. Fontaine had a heart attack during a romp with some floozy. If he was taking his own sex drug, that would be a bombshell because it's still in experimental trials. We also want to know how far along those trials are. They've been very hush-hush about that."

"Got it."

"I've created a special database access for you to run full background checks—criminal, civil, and financial—on the Fontaine family and its holdings in Vitaleron. You can sign in at the office or the hotel from your laptop."

Linda paused, as if she were deciding whether to say more.

"FYI, the paper's owner, Vincent Battrelle, and his son Michael are both on the Vitaleron board, so there is great interest in this story. John Palmer, our executive editor, suggested I give it to Jerry Kennedy, our

City Hall reporter, so he's doing the daily today. But I want you to do the bigger investigative takeouts from here on out. If you run, you can make the ten o'clock news conference. This is the perfect chance for you to show us—and the community—what you can do."

"Great," Katrina said. "Thanks for the vote of confidence."

"I don't know how they did things at your last paper, but ours is family owned, so you'll need to tread lightly on the Battrelles. Don't call or put them into the story without talking to me first. I'm guessing the police will say these deaths are suspicious or they wouldn't have called a news conference. But either way, let's talk to the Fontaines' friends, family, and business associates to see if their company was in trouble. You'll be working directly with me on this."

"I can tell you right now that Homicide was called in last night," Katrina said.

"What?" Linda asked. "How do you know that?"

"Oh, I have my sources."

The editor's mouth, which normally turned down at the edges, broke into a smile, the first one Katrina had seen since she'd arrived. "Terrific! I knew you'd be a good hire."

It's too bad, but that date with Goode is just going to have to wait.

Katrina was about to head out when her desk phone rang.

"Ms. Chopin?" a woman asked.

"Yes, speaking," Katrina said, surprised that the caller ID showed a four-digit extension inside the building.

"Please hold for Mr. Battrelle."

Vincent Battrelle? Why's he calling me, and on a Saturday? I'm not even scheduled to work today. Are there hidden cameras in the newsroom?

The cheesy hold music was barely tolerable as she waited for the newspaper owner to come on the line.

"Hello, Ms. Chopin. How are you this morning?"

Smooth as whipped butter.

"Pretty peachy, Mr. Battrelle. How are you?"

He laughed. "I'm pretty peachy too. I'll get right to the point, because I'm sure you're still getting settled in. Can you come over for a drink this evening? I'd like to talk to you about a personal matter."

Now she was really confused. She wasn't allowed to contact or mention the paper's owner in her story without Linda's permission, but he was inviting her to his house for a drink?

Personal for him or me?

This couldn't be a typical new-hire welcome, or surely Linda would have prepared her. She didn't know how old the guy was or whether he was married or divorced. Only that he had two grown sons, one of whom was a playboy who often embarrassed the family. But being new on the job, she couldn't say no, so she accepted his invitation.

"Great. I live on Whale Watch Way, overlooking La Jolla Shores," he said, rattling off the address. "I'll see you around six forty-five. Come hungry."

Hungry for what?

CHAPTER 6
GOODE

Saturday

Goode was grateful he didn't have to handle media calls, because he didn't trust reporters. He watched Stone's stress levels escalate around 6:00 a.m., when the sergeant's phone started blowing up. After listening to Stone argue with a reporter, Goode patted his buddy on the shoulder and went back to supervising the forensic techs inside the mansion.

Before he left, Artie asked Goode if he could access the contact list on Simon's phone to find a relative to formally ID the bodies. Luckily, Simon was old school and didn't have password protection, so Goode was able to find a William in his contacts. A check on Google and Facebook confirmed that he was, in fact, Simon's brother.

When Artie called William on speakerphone, Goode could hear how broken up he was. William, who had already connected the dots from the brief in the newspaper, agreed to come to the morgue within ninety minutes to ID his brother and niece. Simon's son, Cal, was last known to be surfing somewhere in Costa Rica, where William had been trying to reach him, with no success. Same with Simon's estranged wife and Victoria's mother, Nancy, who was out of the country and had been in an acrimonious divorce battle with Simon over the division of property.

William had strong feelings about what did and didn't happen at the mansion. "This was no suicide—single, double, or otherwise," he said before hanging up.

"He sounded more upset about losing Victoria than his own brother," Artie told Goode. "I guess he and his niece were close."

"Seems like it," Goode said. "I'll follow up with him myself to ask a few more questions."

Artie gave Goode an ETA for the autopsies, which he knew Goode would want to observe.

The brass tried to control the narrative by scheduling a news conference in front of the security gate at ten o'clock.

"Seems weird that Lieutenant Wilson is taking the lead," Stone said. "The chief usually likes to talk about the big cases."

"Maybe he's having a bad hair day," Goode said.

Dr. Henry Largo, the chief medical examiner, showed up too. It disturbed Goode how excited the man got talking about dead people.

Among the media gathered on the street, Goode recognized Jerry Kennedy from the *Sun-Dispatch* by his arrogant posture.

"Yo, detective, whassup?" Kennedy said as he approached Goode, who kept walking toward the podium, reminded of how much he disliked the reporter's miscalculated familiarity.

"I thought you covered City Hall," Goode said.

"Yeah, but I'm on the rotating Saturday shift, so I got saddled with the cop beat today. No offense. Your bro, Norman Klein, will be back at it Monday."

"Sergeant Stone is handling media," Goode said dismissively before turning to stand behind Wilson, who was about to speak. The lieutenant was celebrated for his ability to release as little information in as many words as possible, which kept the media at bay.

"We're here today due to the great public interest in the tragic deaths of Dr. Simon Fontaine and his daughter, Victoria, whom we are able to identify publicly now that their next of kin has been notified," Wilson said. "Reflecting our usual policy, we won't be releasing details about the scene or last night's events at this time. I can, however, tell you that we have opened a suspicious-death investigation. The case has some unusual characteristics, but as always, we're approaching it as a homicide to ensure that no evidence is overlooked. We will get to the bottom of this case, because we're committed to keeping this—and every other neighborhood in San Diego—safe. We won't be taking any questions. Thanks, everybody."

"When will the autopsies be conducted?" Jerry yelled out.

Didn't the lieutenant just say he wasn't taking questions?

Largo stepped up to the microphone to introduce himself. "I'm Dr. Largo, chief medical examiner, here at Chief Baxter's request to let you know that we had a busy night due to a car-racing pileup on the 805, so we'll be doing multiple autopsies this weekend, including these fine folks. We should know more by Monday. That's all, everybody."

After the news conference, Goode leaned into his van to grab another bottle of water before taking off for the RCFL.

"Hey, Surfer Man," a familiar female voice said behind him. "Is this your fine-looking surf-mobile?"

He turned around and was so surprised to see Katrina—holding a notebook, no less—that the bottle fell out of his hand and started rolling away. He had to run over to pick it up.

"Wait, you're a *reporter*?" he asked. "How did I not know that?"

"And to think, you call yourself a detective," she said, smiling mischievously.

Now that she was standing before him, he couldn't help but notice that her dark-brown hair had wavy curls underneath, falling past her shoulders to a pair of nearly perfect breasts. Her slender runner's body was about five-foot-six, with long shapely legs below her flowered skirt, which fell, professionally, right above the knee. Her eyes reflected the same sarcastic wit they'd shared the night before, and the emotional wall that masked whatever was behind them. It was like a dare to him.

"Who are you with?" he asked.

"The *Sun-Dispatch*."

He was confused. "Really? Because I saw Jerry here, one of my least favorite people, I have to say. This story needs two reporters?"

"Jerry's doing the daily today, but I'm writing a bigger story. Whatever that turns out to be. Because, as my editor said, they were such 'high-profile and influential people.'"

"Is that code for rich folks?"

"I'm sure that's part of it," she said. "Listen, I didn't say anything when you got the call last night, because I'm not a police reporter. I'm on the Watchdog team, and I didn't even get assigned to this story until an hour ago. I only started working at the paper last week."

"Figures. Just my luck."

"What do you mean?"

"Well . . . this . . . just . . . complicates things a bit, that's all," he said, choosing his words carefully. Those knowing eyes made him nervous. It was like she could see into his brain, and reporters could be so manipulative. He needed to proceed with caution, especially given his attraction to her, which was formed before he knew who she worked for.

"It doesn't have to," she said. "I've got a job to do, and so do you. You'll get to trust me, you'll see. I'm good at what I do."

See? She's starting the charming manipulation already.

"I'm sure you are," he said.

As much as he'd wanted to stay and chat the night before, he now felt the need to flee before he said something that got him in trouble. "Listen, I've got to run and drop some stuff at the RCFL."

"What's that?"

"The Regional Computer Forensics Lab. You know, computers, phones."

"Oh, okay. Could you possibly show me around the house first, point to where you found the bodies?"

"Sorry, no can do."

"Okay, then can you describe the death scene to me? Tell me how they died?"

"That's what we're investigating. If we release specific details, we could tip off the killer that we're on to him. Or her. If this turns out to be a homicide, that is."

"So, you think it might be a female killer?"

"Simmer down now, Ms. Investigative Reporter. I was simply attempting to avoid sounding sexist. Women kill too."

"What about the condition of the victims? Were they shot, strangled, or beaten up? In the same room, or in bed together? My editor was wondering if they were having sex, because of the drug Simon Fontaine was developing, although that was before we knew the victims were father and daughter. Do you think one of them killed the other? Or does it look like a hit of some kind?"

It was hard for Goode not to smile a little.

She's a firecracker. A much better reporter than Klein, that's for sure.

"Seriously, I can't tell you anything on the record. You'll need to talk to Sergeant Stone for that. But maybe later I can tell you a few details *off* the record," he said.

"Great. So, when can I call you?" she asked.

I'm going to have to be careful with this one. I had my guard down last night, but that changes now. I have the information, and information is power.

"How 'bout I give you a call when I have something?" he asked rhetorically.

"You gave me your card last night," she said. "With your cell phone number on it. Remember?"

"That's right, I did," he said. "But I've got a lot on my plate with this case. You know, the first forty-eight, and all that."

"Yes, I know. That's exactly why I think we should talk."

CHAPTER 7
GOODE

Saturday

Antsy to see the most recent texts and call logs on the victims' phones, Goode headed east to the RCFL office, which was housed in the FBI building in Sorrento Valley, the region's high-tech and biotech hub. Byron, his teammate, had submitted the search warrant affidavit for the security footage that morning, hoping the judge would approve it in time for Goode to serve it that afternoon.

Goode called ahead to let the RCFL know he would need a cart to transfer the Fontaines' computers and phones out of his van, which he realized needed vacuuming to suck up the small dunes of sand on the floor.

But first he needed to grab some lunch. The triple espressos made him smarter, but they also caused his blood sugar to drop. His protein bars were gone by 6:00 a.m., so it was time for something more substantial, like a ham-and-cheese sub.

Goode briefed the RCFL examiner, John London, at the kiosk in the lobby, where he copied the data from Victoria's and Simon's phones onto two thumb drives that he would review on his laptop. Goode also gave London a preliminary verbal list of keyword search terms for combing through the computer data.

"I'll be back with the security video that you can upload to the CAIR system," Goode told London, referring to the Case Agent Investigative Review system, which allowed him to log in from a private connection and access the RCFL's "data dump" of case documents or images. "In the meantime, it would be great if you could send me emails and browser-history pages from both computers so I can read them tonight."

"Sorry, we're down a couple of guys, plus it's the weekend. No way that gets done today," London said. "I'll get to it when I can."

Back in his van, Goode plugged the drive with Victoria's phone data into his laptop with great anticipation and pulled out his notebook to flag anything important to check or print out later.

Her last texts and calls were with an Alex B. and a Michael B., both of whom were in her contact list, which listed other contacts with their full first and last names. To him, this indicated the two men might not only be related, but also familiar enough to be listed in this shorthand manner.

She called Alex briefly on Thursday night, apparently to leave him a message, because he texted her back a few minutes later: On my way. Can't wait to see u.

He texted her again Friday morning at eight fifteen: Best ever, babe. It only took 18 years. I'll let u get some sleep. Love u. Feels good to say that. See u tonight???

Victoria responded right away: Tummy still not good, but it was worth losing some sleep to see u. Luv u too.

She called Michael a little later, around 9:45 a.m. That call was also a minute or less, indicating she had left a voicemail. Her only other call was to her father's surgery office, one of two work numbers she had for him in her contact list. The other one was at Vitaleron.

Was that to ask him to call in those prescriptions? If so, I still can't understand why he would agree to do that.

Michael called her back a few hours later, which was also a short call, but she didn't respond. He called her again at 3:00 p.m. and followed up with a text at 5:00 p.m.: Did u get my messages?

His text at 6:30 p.m. sounded frustrated: R u there? Was shocked and bummed by yr voicemail this morning. Can we talk? I love you. Pls call me.

It sounded like a love triangle was unfolding. Googling "Victoria Fontaine and Alex and Michael," he confirmed his hunch that Michael B. and Alex B. were, in fact, related, based on the society photos that came up.

The Battrelle brothers. Of course. That makes sense, and it also adds a layer of complication to this case. A messy love triangle could even give us a motive. The question is, which one is the baby's father? Or did she even know? I'll need to interview them both, obviously.

Goode checked a folder on the phone called "Notes," which contained a variety of journal-like entries. The top two were written in the last few days before she died.

The most recent one read: Having a latte at the Pannikin. Lots on my mind. On top of all the crap at work, my period is late, but I've lost track of how long it's been, so I just bought a pregnancy test to find out. I've been feeling like using again. But so far, I've stayed strong. Not even a glass of wine, especially if I'm pregnant. God, grant me the serenity to accept the things I cannot change, the courage to change the things I can, and the wisdom to know the difference.

Recognizing that as the serenity prayer for AA, Goode thought it was telling that was her last note.

The next one read: I'm going to write a memo to the board tonight about all the shit that's going on, because it's too long to type here while I drink my coffee. I don't know if I'll send it or not, but I need to get it out of my head and down on paper. I'll probably show it to William first to make sure it's the right way to proceed, because at this point, I don't know who to trust.

Figuring that memo would be on her laptop, Goode made a note to keep an eye out for it.

Sounds like a road map to the challenges she was facing at work, which hopefully will give us some leads on motive. Like whether she was a target, i.e., murder, or was just having a rough time, i.e., suicide.

Moving on to Simon's phone contents, he read the last outgoing text first, which was to his surgical partner, Dr. Warren Russell, just before noon on Friday: Wish I'd scheduled a back-up tee time. These women are going to kill me. See you at the golf tournament tomorrow.

Was that reference to "women" killers a joke? Hard to say given the circumstances.

A few minutes earlier, around 11:45 a.m., Simon had texted Esperanza Cepeda, another coworker, apparently: Surgery cancelled. No need to come back to the office.

Later that day, Simon received a call and several texts from a lady friend, Lucinda Robinson, asking whether they were still meeting for dinner. He never responded.

Her first text landed at 5:15 p.m.: What time r u picking me up?

The next one came forty-five minutes later: Are we going casual for sushi or did u feel like going to George's downstairs tonight? I made 7pm reservations for both. Let me know.

She texted again at 7:00 p.m.: OK, I'm getting annoyed—and hungry! Where r u?

Her last message was at 9:00 p.m.: Now I'm worried. R u OK? Did u get stuck in surgery or are u still mad about this a.m.??? Pls call me.

At that point, Stone texted Goode the approved warrant for the security footage, so Goode fired up his van, which had a recognizably loud engine as most old VWs do, and made a mental call list as he headed toward Fullerton Security in Kearny Mesa.

Besides Simon's brother, I also need to get ahold of these coworkers to see what was going on in his life.

But first, he tried Lucinda, who he hoped could fill him in on Victoria's love triangle and interpret Simon's remark about the women trying to "kill" him.

"I still can't believe it," Lucinda said, sniffling, saying she'd learned about Simon's death on the TV news that morning. "He spent the night Thursday. We had dinner plans last night, but he never answered my texts. I thought he was mad at me or was out with another woman, because we argued yesterday morning."

"Yeah, I saw your texts," Goode said, proceeding to nail down the timeline: She said they'd had a spat around 9:30 a.m. over coffee on her veranda, then he left in a huff. "What was the argument about?"

"Whether he should get involved in Victoria's mess with the Battrelle brothers," Lucinda said, blowing her nose. "I told him to give her some fatherly advice. He disagreed."

"What mess, exactly?"

"She'd been dating Michael Battrelle for five months, but she's always had this *thing* for his brother Alex, ever since they met in rehab when she was just a seventeen-year-old kid. After being AWOL for months, Alex showed up unexpectedly Thursday night, right before Simon left for my house. That's all I know. When I said, 'Alex is bad news, always has been,' Simon said, 'I can't help who my daughter is in love with, and it's none of my business anyway. Or yours.' Then he stormed out, saying he didn't like me 'meddling.' But I didn't see it that way. I was trying to offer help and support. Lord knows Nancy never did that."

"Nancy, Victoria's mother, right? Where is she now, do you know?"

"Off gallivanting to Wherever with the Prince of Whatever."

"Do you know how we can reach her? I'd like to talk to her," he said. *And see if she's a possible suspect.*

"That's all I really know. Simon said she left a week ago for a Mediterranean cruise on some Saudi prince's yacht and thankfully would be out of touch. He only mentioned it to me because they had a hearing date coming up next week on a property that's holding up the divorce settlement. You can probably get her number through Simon's attorney."

"Okay, thanks. So, Friday morning was the last time you saw or talked to Simon."

"Yes. He had a rhinoplasty scheduled for one o'clock."

"I see. So, he had narcotics, syringes, the whole deal, at his office?"

"Yes, it's an outpatient clinic. That's actually how we got together. He gave me an eye lift. Did a great job too."

"Uh-huh. What was his state of mind lately? Any depression?"

"No, none of that."

"Problems at his practice or Vitaleron? Or any serious medical conditions, like heart trouble?"

"Other than high blood pressure, he was healthy. Virile, even. He was relieved to finally be getting divorced, and he was optimistic about the drug trials."

"Any women bothering him besides Nancy?" he asked, mentioning the text.

"No, not to my knowledge. That's just his dark sense of humor."

"Any idea who might want him dead?"

"No, I mean, he wasn't the easiest person to be around, but he was well respected, and he was in charge. Maybe someone resented that or wanted what he had. I know he and Vincent Battrelle haven't always gotten along. I have to wonder about Nancy, since they were fighting over that property, but Victoria's dead too, and Nancy would never hurt her own daughter. Maybe she hired a hit man who wasn't expecting Victoria to be home?"

"Sounds like Simon wasn't supposed to be home either."

"Yes, I guess that's true."

"What else was going on in Victoria's life?"

"Oh, well, she's a whole other thing. Lots of emotional baggage. Never been able to commit to one man. I blame her mother, although Simon wasn't around much either. That's why William stepped in. That was ages ago, but who knows. You should talk to him."

"Yes, I plan to. How do you know all this history?"

"I was Nancy's best friend until she ghosted me. I still have no idea why. Simon and I didn't get together until after she stopped talking to me, and that was after she and Simon split up. I saw my chance to grab him, and I took it."

"Do you know why Victoria didn't have her own place? It seems a little odd for a thirty-five-year-old executive, who I assume is financially solvent, to be living at home with her father."

"Well, the house was so big and empty. After Nancy left a few years back, Vincent told me that he could use some help taking care of it. Victoria moved in earlier this year because her house, which is down the street, was undergoing some renovations and they found mold. Personally, I think they both liked the living situation so neither one had to commit to a romantic partner—Simon with me, and Victoria with Michael, or anyone else for that matter."

"Can you think of anyone who might want to hurt her?"

"It could have been a jealous lover, although good luck trying to figure out which one. Poor Michael. He's such a good man, and so loyal too."

"How would Simon fit into that?"

"I don't know. Wrong place, wrong time?"

"Did Simon own a gun?"

"No, he wasn't interested in guns."

"Victoria?"

"Not that I know of. They weren't that kind of family."

"Was Simon seeing other women?"

"If he was, I didn't know about it. But we also weren't officially exclusive. I'm—I was—still working on that. Simon definitely liked his personal space."

Goode ended the call as he pulled up to the Fullerton Security office, a glass box with dark-tinted windows that reminded him of a drug dealer's car. He jotted down some notes from the call, then tried to reach William Fontaine. No answer, so he left a voicemail, then tried Alex Battrelle. Goode left another message, then went inside to serve the warrant. He didn't see an immediate need to try Nancy or Cal Fontaine since they were apparently both out of the country on Friday.

Although you never know.

He pressed the intercom button because the door was locked and he couldn't see inside. When the buzzer sounded, he entered the reception area, which had two sets of back-to-back chrome-framed chairs with black vinyl seats, reminiscent of an oil-change waiting room, only cleaner.

The owner, Charlie Fullerton, came to the lobby to apologize, saying he couldn't get the footage copied until Monday.

"It's just me in the office today," he said. "Skeleton crew on the weekends."

"But isn't that when you have the most security calls?" Goode asked, bemused.

"Yes, which is why there's no one else here. They're all in the field."

CHAPTER 8
KATRINA

Saturday

On the short drive back to the Sheraton, Katrina wondered why the police would hold a presser simply to ID the victims and characterize the Fontaines' deaths as "suspicious." They could have done that with a simple news release.

That was the worst kind of dog and pony show. San Diego may have a population of 1.3 million now, but it's as small-town as ever.

A murder-suicide scenario seemed highly unlikely for a father and daughter, unless they had a horrible degenerative disease like Huntington's, which ran in Katrina's family on her dad's side, and gave her more insight into such matters. That left a double murder, or maybe a homicide mixed with an accidental overdose. She wanted to dig deeper, but she really needed to find a place to live.

After quickly arranging to see a few apartments on Sunday through a rental website, she had just enough time for a run at the Shores and a shower before heading over to Vincent Battrelle's.

Around six thirty, Katrina cruised down Whale Watch Way and parked in the cul-de-sac. It was the gloaming, that wonderful time of the evening when it's barely bright enough to read home addresses from the street, but before the streetlights have turned on.

It was hard to miss Vincent's palatial cream-colored home, which was so big it could have been designed for an Arab sheikh. She could see two stories from the street but figured it had additional hidden levels, or even a pool, that stepped down the hillside behind it. The silver Jaguar at the bottom of the steep slate driveway had a personalized license plate that read "SDPUB."

Wearing heels had been a mistake, because they kept slipping out from under her. She was relieved to reach the bottom of the driveway without falling into the spiky succulents that ran along an undulating sea of gray river rocks and coral-pink gravel.

After ringing the doorbell, she waited almost a full minute before she heard the thud of footsteps inside. In the meantime, her cell phone rang in her purse, but assuming it was Linda, she let it go to voicemail. Vincent said the visit was "personal," so therefore none of Linda's business.

To her surprise, Vincent opened the door, when she'd expected to see an assistant or a young trophy wife. She was impressed by his trim build and well-preserved face, albeit a little sunspotted.

Probably a lot of tennis, sailing, or golf. And some Botox.

"Come in. Sorry, I was down in the wine cellar, and it took me a minute to get upstairs. My wife and daughter are in Europe, spending my money on more of these overpriced trinkets," he said, leading her through a long hallway of handwoven rugs and shelves lined with hand-painted boxes, carved wooden masks, and tiny statuettes made of jade and ivory.

Vincent put his hand on the small of her back to guide her down the steps into a spacious sitting area with the magnificent ocean view she'd envisioned and motioned her toward a beige leather couch that wrapped around a cherrywood coffee table. Most of the wall was taken up by one of the largest flat-screen televisions she'd ever seen, far too close for her screening comfort. Luckily, it was turned off.

"I have Chardonnay, Pinot Grigio, or Sauvignon Blanc," he said, approaching a bar where several chilled bottles of wine were sweating. "Isn't that what you young ladies drink these days? Or am I out of touch?"

"Pinot Grigio would be perfect," she said, smiling politely.

Any wine, including a red, would have been fine, but she didn't want to seem too excited at the prospect. This was a professional visit to her employer's home, after all, not a night out with her coworkers, most of whom swam in booze without a suit. It was a high-stress job, and they needed to come down from the adrenaline somehow, which didn't make for a healthy lifestyle.

"I picked up some Thai coconut prawns that my wife won't let me eat, because of my cholesterol numbers. So, I only eat them when she's out of town."

Is he flirting with me?

"This house is gorgeous, Mr. Battrelle," she said, watching him struggle with the corkscrew, a mundane task that, apparently, others usually handled.

"Oh, please call me Vincent," he said.

"Vincent."

"Yes?" he said, turning toward her.

"You said, 'Please call me Vincent.'"

His face lit up like a child's. He would be eating out of her hand in no time.

"Funny girl," he cooed.

"This how you welcome all the new recruits?"

"No, actually, it isn't," he said, pouring her glass gauchely to the brim. "In fact, I hope you don't think less of me, but I've never asked a reporter over to the house before." He paused, adding impishly, "Is that awful?"

"Uh, well, that's not for me to say. I never met the owner of my last paper."

"Good. Then I don't feel so bad."

The wine was light and crisp. "This is delicious," she said.

Tapping his pinky ring on the bottle, Vincent replied, "There's more where that came from, so have as much as you like."

She wished he'd stop with the seduction act and get down to it. He was old enough to be her father, and he was her boss's boss several times over. Despite, and possibly because of, Linda's warning, she wanted to ask his reaction to the Fontaines' deaths and whether Vitaleron was in any trouble. But she didn't.

"You're probably wondering why I've invited you here," he said, unfolding the take-out container and holding the savory fried prawns under her nose. They smelled like a heart attack in a box, but heavenly.

"Very nice," she said, eyeing his hand on her forearm. "Yes, do tell."

Picking up her discomfort, he removed his hand. "Sorry, you'll have to excuse me," he said. "I'm a little shaken up by the news about the Fontaines. They were very close friends of mine. Anyway, I took a personal interest in your hiring."

"Really?"

Is that the "personal" matter?

"Yes, you may not know this, but I dated your mother many years ago. Shortly after we broke up, she married your father. It was all rather fast. The three of us went to law school together. Such a tragedy what happened to your family. I'm so sorry."

Wait, what? That was an unexpected information dump.

Katrina was temporarily speechless. Vincent spooned the shrimp onto two plates, and after adding a dollop of sweet-and-sour sauce, he handed her a plate with chopsticks and a cocktail napkin.

"Dig in," he said, stuffing a prawn into his mouth before settling into an armchair adjacent to her.

"Thanks," she mumbled, still tongue-tied. "I wasn't aware that you knew my mother. She never mentioned you."

"Ah, well, it was a long time ago. So, back to your hiring, we thought it was a coup to get you, and without a big-ticket price. I mention that not to upset you, but because I've got a business proposition for you concerning my son. If you're interested, that is."

Which son? The playboy or the dull, steady one?

Katrina was hesitant, but curious. Was she supposed to feel naïve and stupid that Linda had taken advantage of her, or was he merely stating the obvious, that he was in charge of her future? Either way, it made her a little nauseated.

For someone who was allegedly grieving, Vincent was acting rather playful. In fact, she felt a predatory vibe from him, as if he were a cat and she were a hummingbird, wrapped in catnip, that he wanted to toss around.

"Okay, let's hear it," she said. She hoped it wasn't something twisted, sexual, or both.

"First things first," he said, his tone changing abruptly from coy flirtation to serious business. "I need your word that you won't mention our meeting to anyone in the newsroom. I make a point of staying out of the day-to-day operations and let the staff make their own decisions about coverage. But if you agree to move forward, I'll need you to sign an NDA prohibiting you from discussing with editors or reporters what you learn working for me and also from writing about it in the newspaper."

Katrina's brain raced ahead. *What the hell?*

"If you'll sign this, we'll be good to go," he said, handing her a stapled document he'd pulled from a briefcase under the table.

"I'll have to read it more carefully and then think about it," she said. She dutifully skimmed the front page, then folded the papers and tucked them into her purse.

"I need you to do more than think," he said gravely. "I need you to say, 'Vincent, I give you my word.'"

Surely the publisher of a major metropolitan newspaper would have considered the ethics of what he was asking. Did he not anticipate that she, as an investigative reporter, would get pulled into the Fontaine story and that the Battrelles, as primary investors and board members of

Vitaleron, would top the list of logical sources? That by asking her to do this, he was creating a conflict of interest that could ethically hamper, if not prevent, her from covering the story properly?

Unless he doesn't know Linda assigned me to it. Although he reached me in the newsroom this morning, when the story was breaking.

"Which son are you talking about?" she asked noncommittally.

Vincent picked up a photo album from the coffee table and moved to sit beside her. Close enough that she could smell the sweetness of the alcohol he'd been drinking long before she arrived.

"Alex, my older son," he said, pointing to the cute tyke squeezing his mother's cheek. "He's the quintessential middle child, always acting out to win my attention. And it's worked. Michael is smart and steady, and Meredith is a good girl, but Alex has always been my favorite. I had such high hopes for him, but, unfortunately, he's been my biggest disappointment."

As Vincent turned the pages, Alex went from an apathetic adolescent at La Jolla Country Day, a private prep school, to a surly teenager at Dartmouth, where he leaned against his black Porsche 911 Carrera in a James Dean stance of invincibility, with an air of entitlement.

"He was a very bright and good-looking kid, so he never had to try that hard in school," Vincent said. "But he thought rules were for other people. In high school, he drank our liquor, refilled what he'd consumed with water, and thought we wouldn't notice. After he graduated from Dartmouth, I got him a job at an investment firm on Wall Street where my roommate at Yale was a partner. That's when the cocaine started.

"It's common for brokers to party together; it's an intoxicating business, investing other people's money. But he had no boundaries. No self-discipline. We were sending him an allowance until he could get a client list established, but he never told us that he'd been fired. Or that he was running around with a bunch of trust-fund kids in the West Village, by which time he'd moved on to heroin."

Vincent stopped to sip his wine, his eyes transfixed on the ocean.

"So, what did you do?" Katrina asked.

Alex sounds like Franny, only worse.

"An intervention, of course. We flew him home and put him in rehab, but he kept relapsing," Vincent said, pointing to Alex's puffy eyes, the skin sagging like a sad clown. "He'd get very drunk and go Jekyll and Hyde on us, say the most horrible things to his mother, punch doors, throw wineglasses at the wall. The day after, he'd offer contrite apologies and claim he couldn't remember any of it."

Katrina had lived this story with Franny too. The seesaw between the brief stints of sobriety and the hope-crushing calls at 3:00 a.m.

As Vincent talked, Katrina's mind wandered back to the Skype call with her parents the night of her and Franny's thirtieth birthday. He was seven minutes her junior, so she'd been confused when she didn't see him on the shared screen.

"Where's Franny?" she asked.

"We have some terrible news," her mother said, her eyes reflecting a blank numbness. "Franny is dead, honey. He OD'd."

Katrina felt a blow to her gut. "On what?" she asked softly.

"A little bit of everything: OxyContin, Xanax, Ambien, Adderall, and Absolut Citron vodka."

"But he doesn't even like lemons!" she blurted out.

The three of them sat in silence for a few moments while she tried to absorb the news.

"Are you sure he did it on purpose?" she asked, casting about for an alternative reality. "Maybe he couldn't sleep and took too many by accident."

Her mother speculated that Franny was unable to face another decade of causing turmoil for her and Katrina, who cherished him. Franny wasn't as close with their father, who took a more methodical approach.

"He'd been sober for a whole year," her dad said. "He really seemed to have turned a corner. Why didn't he come to us if he was in trouble?"

"Maybe he was upside down on a deal and couldn't dig his way out," her mother said.

"Or maybe someone wanted him dead and used the knowledge of his addictions to take him out," Katrina replied, wondering if someone had forced him to drink a lemon-infused cocktail spiked with drugs.

"It could also have been the Huntington's," her father said, "so I feel partly to blame. But we don't know."

Although her father had managed to escape the plight of the genetic degenerative illness, it had sent his mother to a nursing home to die in bed, unable to swallow her own food, so Katrina was plagued by the fear of coming down with it. The symptoms generally hit between ages thirty and fifty but could strike at any time. The disease gradually ate away the nervous system until a person had no control over his or her withering body and mind.

Even though she and Franny knew they could have the Huntington's ticking time bombs in their bodies, both were too scared to take the genetic test that would either confirm they had the disease or release them from that gruesome plight. But in light of this news, Katrina wondered if he'd gotten tested without telling her and learned he was positive.

"You know about my brother, Franny, right?" she asked Vincent, feeling the tears start to well up.

"Yes, Katrina, I'm sorry, I do," he said. "That's actually how I ran into your mother and father again, at the McDonald Center's family support group. Alex and Franny were there again too. We all had kids in and out of there over the years, including Simon and his daughter, Victoria."

Wow, that's a weird coincidence . . . Or is it?

"I think Franny may have been murdered," she said.

"Really?" Vincent asked, sounding surprised.

"Yes," she said.

She couldn't tell if he was playing innocent, but she quickly wiped away a tear to erase any sign of vulnerability. Even though he seemed sincere and earnest for the first time since she'd arrived, she still felt like she couldn't trust him after the NDA ploy.

But there was an invisible bond between people like them, those who had ridden the roller coaster of their loved ones' addictions. That bittersweet ache of truth and pain that lay beneath the surface that only hurt when you poked it. Like they were doing right now.

"Anyway, Alex is missing," he said. "He's disappeared before, but never for this long. It's been six months. He's been known to binge and hide out until one of us brings him back, but as far as I know no one's seen him. He could be dead for all I know."

Vincent said he'd stopped by Alex's house on West Muirlands Drive several times over the past few months but saw no sign of him or his golden retriever, Talula.

"Alex loves that dog, so someone must be taking care of her. I'm worried he's done something to harm himself. Given up," Vincent whispered. "Couldn't live with his addictions, couldn't live without them."

He turned toward her. "I want you to find him—if he's still alive. Talk to his old party buddies, ex-girlfriends, whoever. But you need to do it with discretion," he said, explaining that the *Advocate*, the alternative weekly newspaper in town, loved to expose the Battrelle family's peccadilloes. "They take some sort of sick joy in it. No sense of decency. It really upsets Ruth, my wife."

"Yeah, I've been there myself," she said. "I'm sure you read the article loosely tying my brother's suicide to my parents' murder."

The *Advocate* article connected a bunch of random dots to suggest that her parents could have been murdered as payback for one of Franny's projects tanking. But the reporting, based on conjecture and speculation, was superficial and lazy. Checking out a few of its claims, she found more holes than a sprinkler head. However, she did recall that Vincent had been one of Franny's investors.

"I'll match your weekly salary if you can spend some of your off time looking for Alex," Vincent said. "And sign the NDA."

"I'd like to help you," she said, "but, like I said, I need to think about it."

It was hard to say no after this intimate discussion, but she wasn't going to even consider signing his agreement without a careful read. She hoped that she'd broken through his psychological armor and derailed whatever game he'd been playing. In the meantime, she was determined to remain noncommittal for as long as possible.

"I'll give you some names and phone numbers to start with," Vincent said, handing her a list with Alex's home address and his favorite local haunts—George's at the Cove for drinks or dinner, Jose's Courtroom for margaritas, Harry's Coffee Shop for breakfast, the Pannikin for coffee, and Windansea or Black's Beach for surfing. Katrina was familiar with all of them because she'd dated a La Jolla boy one summer during college, though they'd spent most of it having sex in his parents' guesthouse.

"Check back with me in the next day or so, or as soon as you find a promising lead," he said.

He sounds like Linda.

"I'll let you know," she said, standing up to go. "Thanks for the wine."

Outside, she stood behind a row of tall, spindly bushes and watched him through the picture window, pouring himself another large glass. Then he folded his face into his hands and wept, his shoulders shaking.

CHAPTER 9
GOODE

Saturday

Fatigue started creeping in by Saturday afternoon. It had been more than forty hours since Goode had last slept, and he felt even more deflated after learning he couldn't get the security footage.

He'd fully intended to observe Victoria's autopsy, but he and Artie got their wires crossed. He stopped for a latte, and by the time he walked into the morgue, the deputy chief medical examiner, Dr. Clarence Thompson, was closing her back up.

"You were right," Artie said. "There are injection sites in the middle of the bruises on her arm. We also found a few oxys lodged in her throat. Looks like she fell unconscious, or died, before she could swallow them. They also could have been manually inserted after she was down."

Either way, he said, they wouldn't have been absorbed into her system to show up on the tox screen. "The injections are a more likely cause of death, and the pills an afterthought."

"The question is, what was she injected with?" Goode asked.

"Could be heroin," Artie said. "I saw that McDonald Center plaque in Simon's office."

"Yes, I saw it too," Goode said. "But with no used syringe near either body, or anywhere else in the house for that matter, the overdose scenario could be exactly what a killer would *want* us to believe."

"We'll have to leave cause and manner of death as 'pending' until the tox screen comes back," Thompson said.

"What's your gut?" Goode asked.

"If she didn't shoot herself up or take more than these three oxys, then someone else killed these folks and staged the scene as a murder-suicide or double suicide," Thompson said.

"But it looks like whoever it was went a little overboard with Dr. Fontaine," Artie said. "Did you figure out where on the property he was shot yet? Or find any possible motives?"

"Not yet, but there was apparently some shit going down at Vitaleron that Victoria was about to report to the board," Goode said, citing the note on her phone. "I don't have any details yet, but on top of that, one of the Battrelle brothers is likely the baby's father. If someone staged this scene, it had to be someone who knew her history of suicide attempts, which could be either of them."

"She was three months pregnant, by the way," Thompson said. "We took tissue samples from the fetus to get a DNA profile."

"Great," Goode said. "We'll collect samples from the Battrelle boys and see if we get a match. It's possible that someone wanted to keep her quiet. It's also possible that the baby's father had an interest in terminating the pregnancy, or a jealous lover got so angry he snapped and killed her."

Artie shook his head. "There are easier ways to end a pregnancy, let alone a relationship, than murder," he said. "I'm betting it's more likely the former."

"Yeah, me too."

Craving fresh air to clear the stench of death, Goode drove straight to Windansea, where the evening sky merged seamlessly with the ocean. He would have loved to jump in and catch a few rides, but that was frowned upon during the early days of a death investigation, where every moment counts. Besides, the waves were puny, landing gently and rolling out like lace over the shore.

He was starting to nod off and might have fallen asleep in the parking lot if his ringing phone hadn't jerked him to attention.

"What's all this vagueness and secrecy about whether it's suicide or murder?" Katrina asked. "Did you find a murder weapon?"

"Well, hello to you too, Miss Katrina. Nice to hear from you," he said, picturing those stunning, knowing hyacinth eyes.

"Sorry. Hi, how are you?"

"Just taking a break before getting back to it. Off the record, we're not being vague, we're still not sure."

"What do you mean you're not sure? And, when you say 'off the record,' do you mean 'on background,' so I can call up Stone and ask him to confirm what you're telling me? Or as in I can't use anything you're telling me, period?"

"Easy, now," he said. "I'm going to have to ask Stone if he's okay with me sharing details as long as you don't quote me. So, it's off the record, as in it might help you understand the case better. Both the cause and manner of death are still pending for a reason."

Goode wasn't going to open his investigation to a reporter he'd only just met. Besides, his emotions were jumbled after he'd googled her that afternoon. Impressed by her award-winning series about the bribes and murder in Northampton, he'd felt a gut punch when he learned that she'd not only lost her brother to suicide, but her parents to murder as well, all within six months.

He'd heard about the "Double-Judge Murder" case, but Katrina hadn't gone into enough detail at Piatti to tie it all together. She'd never even told him her last name. It had been several hours, and he still didn't know how to describe the odd mix of feelings his discovery had evoked.

Compassion? Empathy? Synchronicity? Chemistry?

Surely, her personal tragedy contributed to the connection he felt with her. It also made him want to trust her. But his physical attraction to her, not to mention the inherent conflict of their jobs, made it all very confusing—and forbidden, which, ironically, made him want her even more.

He needed to keep some distance and a clear head. As cases went, this was a big one—and everyone was watching. Big cases, big problems. It never failed. But by the same token, she had sources that he didn't, and, working for Vincent Battrelle's paper, she had access to information that could be helpful to the investigation.

"Well, okay. Did you read Jerry's story?" she asked. "It's full of holes. He's not a cops reporter, but it's like no one even read his story before it was posted online. He didn't even have the victims' ages. How old were they?"

"Simon was sixty-five and Victoria was thirty-five."

"Where was Mrs. Fontaine when this happened?"

"Out of the country somewhere. Victoria's brother too. The Fontaines are divorced, or almost."

"Do they have any other relatives in town I can call?"

"Simon's brother, William, ID'd the bodies this morning. He's a lawyer. Because every family needs a doctor and a lawyer."

"Is there a boyfriend for Victoria in the picture? Maybe love gone wrong?"

Speaking of which, he knew he should keep this to himself to protect the investigation, but he wanted to throw Katrina a bone, and this secret tidbit was so juicy he wanted to share it with her.

"Yes, but we aren't sure about that yet either. Listen, I hope you don't think it's weird, but I googled you this afternoon. I can see you're the real deal and I'm going to let you in on something we haven't released yet: Victoria was pregnant."

"You're kidding."

"Nope. I found a positive home pregnancy test in her bathroom."

"So, there *was* a boyfriend."

"*At least* one, actually. But yes, that's generally how that pregnancy thing works."

"She was unmarried, right?"

"Yes."

"What do you know about Alex Battrelle?"

Where did that come from?

"What do you mean?" he asked, his curiosity piqued since Alex hadn't returned his call.

"He's apparently been MIA for six months."

Whaat? She clearly doesn't know about the love triangle or his night of lovemaking with Victoria.

"Really? Where'd you hear that?"

"I have sources too. I had a meeting where that came up. He was in rehab with my brother sometime before he died. Victoria, too, by the way. I only just found out."

"That's a strange coincidence. A meeting with whom?"

"Can't say. It's off the record."

"Very funny. So, seriously, while I was googling you, I read the *Advocate* story linking your brother's death to your parents' murders. That was a huge case when it broke, but it was very hush-hush. I was working undercover narcotics in OB back then, so I wasn't in the loop, but I'm so sorry for everything you've been through. Like I said the other night, I understand."

Katrina didn't respond directly. Instead, she deflected, as he might in her shoes.

"Thanks," she said, pausing. "So, your mother jumped off the bridge when you were in the car? That must have been harrowing."

"Yeah, I should have known something was up when she got out, left the engine running, and dropped her high heels onto the driver's seat. She went behind the car so I couldn't see much in the rearview mirror, but she was there one minute and then she was just . . . gone. My dad couldn't stay in town, it was too painful. So, he took off for Montana and left me and my little sister, Maureen, in La Jolla with our aunt. We spent a few summers with him until he died of a heart attack, but my mom's death just broke him. I'm lucky to have Maureen, though I hardly ever see her. She's headstrong and wildly independent."

"I'm so sorry," she said softly. "It was a rough year for me, and I was thirty. I can't imagine what it must have been like for you as a six-year-old. But this week has been weird too. It's freaking me out a little that all these people with connections to my family are turning up dead or missing. Should I be worried?"

"Not that I know of. But I can see why you might be. Let's save the rest for when we can share a bottle of wine."

"10-4. Copy that."

After they hung up, Goode's mind wandered for a moment before he started up his van. Why did she ask about Alex out of the blue like that? And why would she say he'd been MIA—for six months?

Maybe he skipped town after finding Victoria's body on Friday. She answered his text that morning . . . or did he kill her and send himself texts from her phone? People usually don't disappear unless they're running from something.

A murder scenario didn't jibe with their "love you" texts that morning. It would help to know who Katrina's source was. He was confident he'd find some answers on the Fontaines' computers, specifically that memo, and the security video. He was growing impatient waiting for them.

It was just as well, though, because his brain was so fried he almost dozed off driving back to his cottage, which was just across the boulevard. But he made it home somehow, peeled off his clothes, and flopped into bed, too tired to bring his luggage from Maui inside. He was asleep within thirty seconds of his head hitting the pillow.

CHAPTER 10
KATRINA

Saturday

Katrina didn't want to tell Goode on the phone that she was close by, in case he thought she was following him. She'd needed to clear her head after meeting with Vincent and headed down to Windansea, which she and her old boyfriend frequented that one summer, although he preferred Black's.

Her heart started racing when she saw Goode's VW van in the parking lot by the shack, so she raced past him, turned left on Gravilla, and did a U-turn so she was parked overlooking Pumphouse, two blocks south of Windansea.

In La Jolla, one contiguous stretch of sand could have several different beach names, each corresponding to a landmark or street. Such as Big Rock, Little Rock, Westbourne, or Pumphouse, the latter of which was named for the little sewage building Tom Wolfe wrote about in his book, *The Pump House Gang*.

Katrina called Goode because she wanted to get her mind off the memories that had erupted talking with Vincent. But she also wanted to hear his voice again. His warm tones calmed her, and, she had to admit, also aroused her.

Even though he was two blocks away, she could feel his presence as she pictured him with that mirthful smile and the royal-blue shirt from Piatti. But then he brought up the very topic from which she'd been trying to distract herself, and she snapped back to reality.

She felt uncomfortable revealing too much too soon. It was like ripping open an infected wound. But these days they lived in the World of Google, where anyone could find her personal history with a couple of clicks. She'd only brought this on herself, confessing to him about Franny within moments of meeting him. In a way, it was a relief that he'd learned the rest on his own.

"Like I said the other night, I understand," he said.

That's really why she'd called him. But she had to face facts. At this point, he was just another unavailable man, though that drew her to him even more. She was addicted to complications. It was her chronic Shakespearian flaw.

Katrina's therapist said it was her nagging fear of developing Huntington's disease that led to these maladaptive coping behaviors, like her habit of sleeping with unavailable men.

Why get involved if I could come down with Huntington's any minute? No man wants to deal with that, so if I get too attached, I'll just get hurt. And if he gets too attached, he'll be the one who gets hurt. And forget about children. They would have to live with this nagging fear as well. What was Daddy thinking?

The obsessive behaviors started as a teenager with dieting and binge eating, progressing to boys, caffeine, wine, sex, love, and to some measure, alcohol. She'd managed to keep most of the demons at bay until the sex got out of hand. Counseling helped her become more cognizant that having "intimate" relations with unavailable men wasn't intimate at all, nor was it healthy, prompting her recent—and ongoing—hands-off phase, at least until she found someone who loved her back. No small feat.

She'd been doing better since learning to channel much of that energy into work and exercise, but she wanted to get back to her music.

She and Franny got their talent from their mom, Aphrodite, who had performed in several off-Broadway musicals before returning home for law school at the University of San Diego (USD). When Katrina and Franny were young, Aphrodite enrolled them in vocal and guitar lessons and encouraged them to perform together, which they did until Katrina left for college.

Once she got to Northampton, however, work became Katrina's primary go-to distraction. That coping mechanism failed when the mafia began stalking her and murdered her source, which sent her back into therapy. She continued the sessions until she left for the West Coast.

Now that she was home again, she was worried that her parents' killer would pick up where he had left off. She'd tried her mainstay method of walling off her emotions by diving deeper into work, but that had only led her to Goode, who was off-limits because he was a source, so she was essentially back at zero. She had no distraction. Only complication. On top of free-floating anxiety and fear. It was maddening, really.

Although Katrina was devastated by her parents' murder when it happened, she almost felt that her suspicions about Franny's death had been vindicated—that they were killed shortly after his "suicide" so they would look like the primary targets. To her, the three deaths weren't a tragic coincidence, more like a conspiracy. The *Advocate* had simply connected the wrong dots. They had to be interrelated, she just couldn't prove how. Yet.

At the time, the police were stuck on their own theory that an angry assailant, likely a past defendant in one of her parents' courtrooms, had solicited a murder contract against one of them from prison, and the spouse had gotten caught in the cross fire. That was a workable premise, but they'd never identified a single suspect, at least not to her knowledge. Still, Katrina left town on their advice because either way, someone, or a group of someones, seemed to have it in for her family.

When Vincent confessed his history with her mother today, she felt a niggling undercurrent she couldn't identify. She could only describe it as déjà vu. Did he feel guilty, somehow, so he tried to throw her some extra cash, or was it more complex than that? There were so many threads, it was hard to make sense of them in her mind:

Vincent Battrelle dated my mother, but she married my father instead. Franny was in rehab with Alex Battrelle and Victoria Fontaine. Vincent was an investor in Franny's hotel project, and then invested in Simon Fontaine's company, Vitaleron. Now, Franny, my parents, Victoria, and Simon are all dead, and Alex is missing, possibly dead. Vincent even said that, or was that to throw me off? Could he, or even Alex, have been involved in the Fontaines' deaths? Is that why he tried to get me off the Fontaine story with this side job? Whether or not these murders are related somehow, the killer must know I'm back in town because my name has already been in the paper, and any day now I'll have a byline on this story. So, if the motive truly was payback or revenge, I'll need to remain hypervigilant at all times.

Katrina wished she could talk all of this through with Goode, but there were rules about avoiding conflicts with sources. Boundaries. He was supposed to be sharing information with her, *not* the inverse.

As she replayed their exchange about Alex, she recalled hearing a slight hesitation, or even surprise, in Goode's voice when she mentioned Alex's name.

Is Alex even missing? Was Vincent telling me only part of the truth, or was he outright lying?

With all these questions hanging, she knew she couldn't just go back to her hotel or her brain would never let her fall asleep. She needed some answers. After typing Alex's address into Google Maps, she drove past Goode's van again, turned right on Nautilus, and headed up Mount Soledad to West Muirlands Drive.

Alex's street was lined with homes worth $5 million or more, yet there were few streetlights. Most of the houses were set back from the street behind walls, gates, and tall, thick hedges, and it was too dark to see the address numbers. Katrina had to cruise the block a few times, watching the little blue dot on her phone until she reached her destination.

Parking on the street, she fished the heavy-duty flashlight out of her glove compartment and got out to look around. The mailbox, posted at the bottom of a steep, winding driveway, seemed as good a place to start as any. As long as she didn't steal or open his mail, she wasn't committing a felony.

The short stack of envelopes inside was certainly not six months' worth. More like a few days.

Has someone been collecting it periodically and giving it to him at another location?

The interior of the house was completely dark, though a couple of exterior motion lights flashed on as she passed, which startled her. Katrina saw only two newspapers lying on the front step, both dated within the last couple of days.

She tried to open the side gate, but it wouldn't budge. Feeling her way over the top, she fiddled with the latch to unhook it and shined her light through the darkness to avoid tripping over cats or possums as she pushed overgrown branches out of her face.

In the rear courtyard, the moonlight revealed a four-tiered wooden deck. The top two were covered with potted plants; the lower two were lined with lounge and Adirondack chairs, with a couple of tables with umbrellas, a built-in stone barbecue, and a pizza oven. At the bottom was a rectangular pool and Jacuzzi encircled with tall eucalyptuses, firs, and peppertrees, which blocked out the view from the street or side yards.

This is a total party house. Probably even more impressive with the lights on.

Based on the vast accumulation of dead leaves, the house had been vacant for some time. Katrina put her nose to the sliding glass door to the kitchen, shining her light across the cabinets and granite countertops. She saw no signs of life until she came across a box of cereal and a half-eaten banana sitting on the island. The peel was yellow, so it hadn't been there for long.

Looks like he, or someone else, was here for a quick breakfast.

When her phone started ringing, Katrina felt a spike of adrenaline and thrust her hand into her purse to squelch the ringer. The last thing she needed was for a neighbor to report her to the police for trespassing.

She didn't know what triggered it, but an even bigger set of motion detector lights flashed on. She also heard a new buzzing sound, like a surveillance camera following her every move. Someone was watching her.

Walking as fast as she could toward the side yard, she pushed through the thicket of branches to the gate, ran back to her car, and locked herself inside. Sometimes her mind was her worst enemy, but this time, she didn't think it was all in her head.

After taking several deep breaths, her heartbeat slowed as she drove away, repeatedly checking her mirrors for anyone following her. Pushing the speed limit, she drove the twisty, narrow road down the north side of Mount Soledad and up Torrey Pines to the Sheraton. She didn't feel safe until she'd pulled the latch across the door to her room.

Katrina lay on the bed for a few minutes, trying to shake it off. Then, she changed course and set her mind on learning as much as she could about the Battrelles, and Alex in particular.

First, she searched online for connections between the Battrelles and the Fontaines—business, personal, or otherwise. Linda had mentioned that Vincent and his younger son, Michael, were on the Vitaleron board, but what about Alex?

A two-year-old news brief said Alex had stepped down and was being replaced by his brother, Michael, but gave no explanation. It also stated that the board had created a new seat for Simon Fontaine's surgical partner, Dr. Warren Russell, and the corporate title of medical adviser.

Finding nothing else, she opened the *Sun-Dispatch* archive to see if it contained items that didn't come up on Google. This was a good call, because it had an exclusive photo library, which included social events such as the Jewel Ball, a high-end charity fundraiser at the La Jolla Beach and Tennis Club. In a five-year-old shot, Alex had his arm around Victoria, but Michael did not. In one from a few months ago, Michael was holding her hand, and Alex wasn't pictured.

Katrina wondered why Vincent hadn't mentioned the relationships between Victoria and his sons or suggested she pursue any leads at Vitaleron, a curious omission given Linda's prohibition on mentioning the Battrelles in stories without permission.

Going further back, she found a story about Vincent Battrelle's sizable donation to a new meditation garden at the McDonald Center and another about a room being named after Simon Fontaine. It almost seemed like they were competing to see who could get more attention for making a better or bigger donation. But other than the philanthropic items, the newspaper's coverage of the Battrelles was nil.

The only person she could think to call about the dynamics between the families was Simon's brother, William. But it was getting late, so the call would have to wait until morning.

Switching her focus to the Fontaine family, Katrina pulled up Victoria's Facebook page. Because it was set to private, she couldn't see any photos or her friend list, but the Vitaleron website provided a decent bio: By thirty-five—the same age as Katrina—Victoria had run several start-up biotech companies before landing at Vitaleron. She held a bachelor's in economics from the University of Southern California and an MBA from Stanford.

Not too shabby.

On the board of directors' page, Katrina recognized all but one of the officers' names: Darren McMurphy, who was secretary. Simon Fontaine was board chairman and CEO, Vincent Battrelle was vice chairman, and Michael Battrelle was treasurer.

Because director seats often came as rewards for investments, she cross-checked the Securities and Exchange Commission's (SEC's) website for their stockholdings. It was no surprise that Simon

Fontaine and Vincent Battrelle were the largest stockholders by far. Their offspring followed close behind, with Victoria Fontaine leading, followed by Alex and Michael Battrelle. Warren Russell was next, then Darren McMurphy and his father, Patrick. Patrick was also on the board, and although he wasn't an officer, she figured he had broader political clout as the city's Port Commission chairman.

How am I supposed to keep the Battrelles out of my Vitaleron stories? If I can find this, so can my competitors.

She found it peculiar that previous stories were vague or silent about progress of the drug trials, but if the company wasn't bragging about it, the drug probably wasn't close to winning FDA approval.

As her brain started to spin, she decided to use an organizational tool she found helpful and drew a tree diagram of all the players. She included executives, board members, and major investors at Vitaleron, using different colored lines to designate personal or familial connections between them, placing stars next to the biggest investors, and black X's over the dead people, highlighting the power vortex that would be filled with someone else.

With the Fontaines gone, the company's management and board leadership will go through a reorganization. It seems natural for Vincent or Michael Battrelle to take over the key positions and others to move up in the hierarchy. That seems like a possible motive for murder to me.

When she was finished, she realized there were no women in the tree except Victoria. Where were Mrs. Fontaine, Mrs. Battrelle, or her daughter, Meredith, in all of this? Once Katrina got her own place, she would transfer the tree diagram to her living-room wall, like they did on the TV crime shows, so she could update it as she found new connections. She figured Goode was probably doing the same thing.

With that, Katrina closed her laptop and found some slow jazz on her phone to calm her mind. The radiation might slowly kill her, but it was the only way to shut off the static and get some sleep.

CHAPTER 11
GOODE

Sunday

Goode was awakened at 5:25 a.m. by the smell of French roast brewing in his kitchen, his favorite kind of alarm clock. His brain began compiling a to-do list almost immediately. Five hours of sleep was usually enough for him to get by, but after staying awake for two days straight, he'd needed a solid seven and a half.

With a mug of strong home brew, he wrote up his list at the table that doubled as his eating and workplace. He put the plate with his toasted bagel to one side of his laptop and his coffee and notebook to the other, where his papers, files, and books were stacked in several piles.

So much for the separation of my personal and professional space. I keep meaning to put some of these books away. Or read them. Or buy a bigger table.

His online search for background on Alex Battrelle came up empty. It was almost as if he didn't exist.

Maybe I just don't know what to look for yet.

Around 7:00 a.m., Artie texted him with the ten o'clock start time for Simon Fontaine's autopsy. Goode texted Stone and agreed to meet up at the morgue.

After showering, he headed out in the Explorer for a latte in Bird Rock, a neighborhood of La Jolla south of his cottage named for a giant rock offshore that was once shaped like a bird and also drew flocks of them. Goode always drank too much caffeine early in an investigation, which was as good an excuse as any for the worst of his addictions. But he knew not to eat anything right before an autopsy, a lesson he only had to learn once.

Sure enough, Goode was right about the bruising on Dr. Fontaine's neck. Pathologist Clarence Thompson confirmed there was a needle mark in the bruising on Simon's neck just like on Victoria's arm, on the opposite side from the bullet wound.

But Thompson didn't find the bullet because it had gone clean through Simon's brain without hitting any major arteries. Thompson also confirmed that the wound was postmortem—hours after the heart had stopped pumping blood to that area, which explained why the seepage was so scant and gelatinous.

"Do you know what kind of gun it was?" Thompson asked.

"There was a 9mm next to the body," Goode said. "We haven't found any bullets or casings yet, but I did find an unspent 9mm round in Victoria's purse. Now that we know it went through and through, I'll have them go back and look again. Problem is, we still don't know where he was when he got shot."

"See these?" Thompson asked, holding up a squeezed set of tweezers. "Rug fibers in his hair. He also had bruises on his scalp and abrasions on his face, arms, and knees. They look like rug burns."

"The house has Berber carpeting," Goode said.

"There you go."

"Can you tell how he got the bruises on his scalp?" Stone asked.

"Probably from falling, but not a long or hard fall," Thompson said. "Are there stairs inside the house?"

"Yeah, three flights, all carpeted. There's also a tile stairway that goes from the patio to the pool," Goode said. "Does he have any broken bones? What about a fall from an exterior balcony?"

"His hip is kind of splayed out, possibly due to a fall, but his skull probably would have cracked open if he fell or was pushed from a balcony. I also found no fractures in his legs or feet. You said it was a tile patio, right?"

"Yes."

"I suppose he could have injected himself with something that made him drowsy, causing him to fall down the carpeted stairs. But who injects themselves in the neck?" Thompson said.

"Devil's advocate," Artie said. "What if he saw Victoria on the floor, panicked, tripped, and fell as he was running downstairs for his phone to call 911?"

"I found his phone in his shorts pocket, remember?" Goode said.

"True. But if he was in shock he could've forgotten where he put it. I've done that."

"Yeah, but the lividity is mostly on his right side, and you found him on his back, correct?" Thompson asked.

"Correct," Goode said.

"So, what if he was pushed down the stairs, hit his head, and was knocked out cold?" Stone suggested. "Someone injects him and dumps him off the balcony, but he doesn't land on his head. That someone also shoots him, though not necessarily in that order."

"I read a book called *Kill Him Some More*. Seems fitting," Goode said.

Stone glared at him. "A little respect, please."

Goode shrugged. *Sure seems like overkill to me.*

"What if he's gearing up for some afternoon delight, tells his sex partner to inject the experimental drug into his neck so it goes to the brain faster?" Artie suggested. "But something goes wrong and he has a heart attack. His lady gets scared, calls a friend to help her move the body, and they stage the suicide scene."

"I talked with his lady friend and she said she hadn't seen him since Friday morning at *her* place," Goode said. "She mentioned she was worried he might be with another woman, but she could be lying about the last time she saw him. I still haven't seen the security footage yet, so I guess we'll find out."

"Any of these scenarios are possible, but I still say the fall from a balcony would cause different injuries," Thompson said. "We need more information, especially the tox screen, before we can definitively determine cause or manner of death for either victim. But at this point, I'm leaning toward homicide. Did you find any drugs in the house they might have injected?"

"No, that's the most suspicious part. No empty vials, no used syringes, no paraphernalia at all near either victim, which points to an outside suspect removing them," Goode said. "Based on that and the gunshot, I'd call it a murder staged as suicide for Simon. I'm still on the fence about Victoria because of her history."

"Well, she probably wouldn't have shoved three oxys down her own throat and then died, right?" Stone said.

"Unless she choked on them," Goode said.

"Good point," Stone said.

"But as a working theory, if Simon was murdered, and Victoria had no reason to kill him, then someone likely murdered her too. Is that what you're saying?" Goode asked Thompson.

"Sounds about right, yes."

Walking outside to the parking lot, Goode and Stone chatted about strategy for serving the next round of search warrants simultaneously the next morning, to catch everyone by surprise: one at Simon Fontaine's surgery office, where they would audit inventory and purchasing records to determine if any drugs were missing; the second at Vitaleron headquarters, where the R&D lab was located and experimental human trials were underway.

"They must have a private computer server. We might find internal communications that give us a clearer motive or dovetail with that memo Victoria was going to write but that don't show up on Victoria's and Simon's personal computers," Goode said. "It could be an issue with funding, FDA approval, or a disgruntled employee. Anything, really."

"I'll have Byron call RCFL to meet us there," Stone said, stopping to answer his phone. "It's the lieutenant."

As Stone briefed Wilson on the working theory and questions raised by the autopsy, Goode could hear the lieutenant yelling. Stone rolled his eyes and made the "blah blah blah" yapping motion with his hand.

"He's all fired up," Stone said after hanging up.

"No kidding."

"Yeah, he wants a news conference tomorrow afternoon to brag about what we find with the warrants. His exact words were, 'We need to show the public that we are kicking this case's ass,'" Stone said. "I guess a lot of investors are worried about their nest eggs going down the tubes."

Speaking of which, Goode said, "What do you think about me throwing a few bones to that new reporter, Katrina Chopin, at the *Sun-Dispatch*? I checked her out and she's the real deal. I think she could be helpful to us. Would also be good to keep an eye on her."

Stone, who knew him too well, gave Goode his characteristic "don't bullshit me" look. "C'mon, I saw you guys talking yesterday," Stone said. "You have a thing for her, don't you? I don't even know how that's possible, since she got to town, like, five minutes ago—"

If Goode didn't come clean, Stone would figure it out anyway. "Remember when you called me Friday night and I was at Piatti?"

"You're kidding."

"Totally random chance. I stopped by for my usual martini and mussels. There was only one open seat, so we started chatting—"

"Dude, you are everywhere, and into everything."

"I was still in vacation mode. I had no idea she was a reporter. We never even got that far. But it's not about that. She and I are both professionals. This is about the case."

"You sure about that?"

"Yes, to the best of my ability. Plus, she's the daughter in the 'Double-Judge Murder' case. She comes from good people."

"Oh, I didn't—" Stone said, falling uncommonly speechless for a moment. "All right, then. Carry on. Just be careful. I know how you are with pretty, smart, manipulative women. Your ex-wife, for example. Remember her?"

"Don't rub it in."

CHAPTER 12
KATRINA

Sunday

Katrina had been hoping to find an apartment near the beach. Ever since she'd left San Diego, she'd missed the ocean, like a long-lost lover.

Growing up, she'd always enjoyed tagging along with Franny to watch the sunsets and the sinewy surfers. Wetsuits peeled down to reveal ripped pecs and six-pack abs, dripping with salt water. Boards tucked under their arms as they jogged to their trucks.

But coastal housing prices were ridiculous, especially when she had a beautiful four-bedroom home waiting for her in Point Loma.

Out of steam by Sunday afternoon, she turned down a side street in Mission Hills to grab a Diet Coke at the market. Somehow, she missed the driveway and was about to do a U-turn in the cul-de-sac when she saw a faded **For Rent** sign at the bottom of the hill.

Thirty minutes later, she was writing a check to the chain-smoking manager of a U-shaped retro complex of apartments that were dated but spacious. They were so cheap, in fact, that she took a two-bedroom, telling herself she now had a home office or music room.

Built in the 1960s, the living room had dark wall-to-wall paneling. The tiny kitchen still had the original appliances, and the master bathroom's faux-marble countertop was stained and chipped. The apartment also came with a parking space under the carport and a convenient lap pool. But the winning feature was the panoramic view. Two side-by-side sliding glass doors opened onto a shallow balcony that looked down to a lush, green canyon. It literally felt like she was living *in* the canyon.

If she positioned a couch and chairs just so on the orange shag carpet, she could gaze all the way down to the freeway and golf course, a few blocks from the newspaper.

By 6:00 p.m., she'd checked out of the Sheraton, loaded her belongings back into her car, and moved them into her new living room: two suitcases of clothes, a sleeping bag, two pillows, her and Franny's guitars, and a few small but necessary items, such as a corkscrew. The other boxes still had yet to arrive.

Although her parents both came from old San Diego families, their wealth was nowhere near Vincent Battrelle's. Still, Katrina rejected even a marginally materialistic lifestyle. She'd maintained a nomadic mindset since college and saw no reason to change that now. If and when *The New York Times* called, she didn't want to be weighed down by armchairs, lamps, and end tables.

Walking from room to room, she pictured where she would place the few pieces of her parents' furniture from the storage units. No sense bringing much. She'd have to move it back to the house anyway.

Although she knew their antiques were valuable, they weren't really her style. She hadn't been able to face selling any of them, but she wasn't sure if she could live with them either, haunted by the memories.

Settling into her sleeping bag on the living-room floor, she leaned back on a pillow against the wall, with her laptop resting on a second pillow across her thighs. She was still doing research when Goode called around 8:15 p.m.

"What's the news today, Scoop? Figure out where Alex Battrelle is yet?"

"Have you been talking to my editor? It's Sunday, if you haven't noticed. But no. Have you?"

Either he was playing dumb, or he didn't understand that she couldn't share information with him. There was a big red line between reporters and their sources, but the sources often didn't understand this was an "us" and "them" relationship.

"Am I supposed to be looking for him?" he asked coyly.

"You know I can't share information with you, right?"

"Really?"

Definitely playing dumb.

Long pause.

"Can't blame a guy for trying," he said. "Hey, one thing. Did your source mention any bad blood between Michael and Alex Battrelle?"

"No, not at all. In fact, the opposite. Why do you ask?"

"Because one or both was seeing Victoria. But that's off the record for now as well."

"Yeah, I was wondering about that," she said.

"Oh, really, why's that?"

"I found some photos of her with each of them, holding hands and arms around each other, but not at the same time."

"Gotcha."

"By the way, you need to say 'off the record' before you tell me something—it's supposed to be an agreement between us, not a statement after the fact—or it's fair game."

"Ah, maybe that's how I've gotten myself into trouble in the past."

She couldn't tell if he was joking, but she had to lay the ground rules with him. He was one sarcastic dude.

"Sounds like it," she said. "I'll let it slide this time, because I already confirmed it elsewhere, but that's your last warning."

"Check. Autopsies are done, by the way. See you tomorrow at the news conference. Ciao."

News conference? About what? But he'd hung up before she could ask what they'd learned.

Damn him.

CHAPTER 13
GOODE

Sunday–Monday

Stone called Goode, all pumped up, right before midnight.

"Byron got the warrants for tomorrow morning," he said. "You two should team up at the surgery, and I'll meet Foster at Vitaleron. Before they open, like, 7:30 a.m. Then we'll do the switcheroo so we don't miss anything."

"Sounds like a plan," Goode said.

"The lieutenant got us a few guys as backup so no one can sneak out the side door with a computer. I have no idea why he wants to call attention to the search at a news conference. Seems unusual *and* unwise."

Goode managed to get a few hours' sleep, but he was up at five o'clock, beating his coffee brewer to the punch. By seven twenty, he was practically vibrating, fully caffeinated, in the Explorer outside Dr. Simon Fontaine's surgery on Nobel Drive, waiting for the employees to show up. His team had synchronized their watches to enter both sites at the same time in case an employee called to warn the other location.

"Let me do the talking," Goode said as he and Byron followed an older man and a younger woman inside.

"Sure, boss. No problem. I'll be the muscle," Byron said, referencing a long-standing joke about his stocky weight lifter's physique, a stark contrast to Goode's long, lean surfer body.

The older man proved to be Fontaine's partner, Dr. Warren Russell, and the woman was his daughter, Regina. Goode talked to the doctor in one of the waiting rooms while London, from the RCFL, packed up the computers.

Russell's eyes were puffy and red. He explained in a raspy voice that he hadn't slept since he'd read the *Sun-Dispatch* Saturday morning.

"Is this really necessary, Detective?" he asked, referring to the computer seizure. "We're trying to run a business here, and these contain all our patients' medical records."

"Right, we'll copy them as soon as we can," Goode said, noting that they might have to get a special master to review the medical records before they could actually read them, though he didn't know if that would even be necessary. "Don't you back up to an external drive or the cloud?"

"We've talked about it, but we aren't very tech savvy here. Regina is stretched pretty thin as our bookkeeper and part-time receptionist. Simon was always telling me—" he said, his voice breaking as his upper lip shook.

"I'm sorry for your loss, sir."

"Thank you. Sorry," Russell said, wiping away a tear. "Simon, Vincent, and I had long been scheduled to play in an annual charity golf tournament this past weekend, so it's tradition for my wife, daughter, and son-in-law to plan a getaway somewhere. Regina has been busy with her girls, so I've had to process this on my own. It was so sudden, so unexpected."

"How long have you known Simon Fontaine?"

"He's been my partner for the last twenty-five years. We met in medical school."

"Wow, that's tough," Goode said. "I need to ask, has your surgery practice been having any financial problems?"

"No, not at all," Russell said, frowning. "We've got more patients than we can handle. We had a full week lined up, in fact, but I can't do all the surgeries myself. Our only surgical assistant called in sick today, and now you're taking our records. We'll have to close up shop entirely if we can't access their files."

"Are these three your only computers?"

"Yes."

"We'll copy the hard drive of the computer with the patient records and leave it here, but we'll take the other two. Here's the warrant," he said, handing him the document. "As you can see, we're also looking for an inventory of drugs you have stored here. Who keeps track of that?"

"That would be our nurse, Esperanza," he said.

"Is she here?" Goode asked.

"No, like I said, she called in sick this morning, so we'll have to cancel today's procedures anyway."

Sick, really? That seems a little convenient. She's already on my list to interview.

"I see. You still have access to her drug files, correct?"

"Yes, I would think so. She and my daughter share a computer, the same one with the patient files. We follow all DEA protocols," he said.

"Can I get her phone number?"

"Sure, Regina has it."

Per the warrant, Russell directed Goode to the cold-storage area, then to the cabinet where they kept the drugs at room temperature.

"You keep syringes here too?"

"Yes, of course, there in the cabinet," Russell said.

"Do you keep track of those?"

"Yes, but you can buy syringes over the counter at any drug store. They aren't like controlled substances."

"Dr. Fontaine also kept some at home. Do you know why?"

"We both take B_{12} pick-me-ups sometimes. He also used a little Botox now and then. I don't go in for that stuff."

"I see. Do you own a gun, Dr. Russell?"

"No, I don't want one near me or my family. Why do you ask?" he said, frowning again.

"We can't discuss details of the investigation, but that's good to know. Detective Byron will go through your drug inventory and compare it with your daily usage logs and invoices. Can your bookkeeper help him with that?"

Russell nodded. "Regina!"

Once Goode got through that, he texted Stone that he was heading over to Vitaleron.

RCFL collected computers, copying the server now, Stone wrote back. Left Michael Battrelle for u to interview. He seems panicked re computer seizure. Let's find out why.

Heading northeast to Sorrento Valley, Goode drove toward the giant *V* of the Vitaleron logo on the futuristic, fifteen-story column of mirrored glass that reflected the pale-blue sky. He could see it from the freeway, towering above the squat cookie-cutter industrial parks surrounding it, and wondered if the architect had purposely designed it with sexual overtones.

The lot was surprisingly empty when Goode parked his SUV in a visitor's spot under the shade of a peppertree, leaving the window cracked so it was cool inside when he returned.

Vitaleron occupied the top three floors, but the directory in the lobby downstairs didn't list any additional companies. Were there no other paying tenants, or did they not want to be identified?

I wonder if they've got some black ops going on in the rest of the building.

The company's reception area was in the penthouse suite, which offered a bird's-eye view of the valley. Goode was greeted by a pretty receptionist with long blond hair who looked like a Barbie doll, only smarter. Her nameplate read **Darla Johansen**.

"Michael, the other detective is here now," she said, a sizable yellow diamond on her ring finger flashing in the sunlight as she hung up. "Down the hall, second door on your right, Detective."

That thing could sink her in the ocean. What's she doing working here as a receptionist if she's got a rich fiancé? Maybe she hooked up with one of the investors. Or a board member, perhaps.

"That's a beautiful ring," he said, seeing if she might volunteer any information.

"Thank you," she said.

As the buzzer sounded, Goode opened the hallway door and found Michael Battrelle's office, where he stood, looking a bit frazzled, behind a formidable, but bare, black desk. He was wearing gray dress slacks, a white button-down shirt, and a purple tie, though his hair was askew as if he'd been running his hands through it.

"This was Victoria's office, and your people took her computer, which has all the files I need to take over her job," Michael explained with frustration. "I'm not sure how I'm supposed to do that now."

Gesturing toward a stuffed leather armchair for Goode to sit, Michael sat down at the desk and leaned forward, resting his elbows on the surface, his fingers joined together like a church steeple.

"Should I be scared?" Michael asked, clumsily trying to make light of the situation. "The sergeant said he was leaving the questioning to you as the lead detective."

"Yes, that's right," Goode said. "But to answer your question, I don't know. Have you done anything wrong?"

"I may not have done everything right in my life, but I haven't done anything that would put me in prison, if that's what you mean," Michael said, shrugging defensively. "I work hard and do my best."

Michael tried to settle into his chair, but as it lurched back, he jerked forward, knocking his cup of soda and ice onto the floor. Opening a drawer, he quickly retrieved a stack of napkins and disappeared below to mop up the liquid.

He rose from his knees, looking embarrassed, and dumped the wet, soggy mess into the trash. "You'll have to forgive me," he said. "I've been a wreck since I got the news. It's unsettling being in Victoria's office, especially now that it's empty. I knew where she kept her napkins because we used to have lunch in here sometimes."

He seems jumpy. Anxious. And why is he overexplaining the napkins to me?

"I'm sorry for your loss," Goode said. "I understand you two had been seeing each other for the past five months?"

"Yes, although she never let me forget that we weren't exclusive."

Goode had intended to ask about Vitaleron's financial background and drug-trial status, but he took Michael's cue and headed straight to the personal details. "How did you find out?"

"About her seeing someone else or that she was dead?"

"Let's start with the first part."

Michael exhaled loudly. After taking another deep breath, his face crinkled as he fought back tears. Surviving men didn't often cry during an interview, and this was the second one that day.

"She called and broke up with me Friday morning, which came as a complete surprise. She said she really cared for me, but I wasn't 'it' for her. She'd said that before, but I really thought I'd won her over. I was nicer to her than the other men in her life, like my brother. All those years he wouldn't take his recovery seriously, and then he went wacko when he found out she'd aborted his baby. I'd hoped that she would appreciate someone more stable, who treated her with respect and didn't call her in the middle of the night, high, asking to be picked up in a dark alley after being mugged by a dealer."

"Makes sense. Did she say why?"

"Before we were dating, she always complained about her push-pull relationship with Alex, that she loved him, but they couldn't *be* together. I suspected it was him, but all she said Friday was 'There's someone else.' I didn't ask, and she didn't elaborate."

"I saw from your texts that you kept trying to reach her after that call. Did you ever make contact?"

"No, but I wish I had. Maybe I could have stopped her. I don't understand why she would do this now."

"Do what?"

"Kill herself. She had a history of suicide attempts, as you're probably aware. I'm sure Simon was devastated by the loss, since he's the one who found her."

Attempts, plural? You're the first one to definitively call this a suicide, brotha. Why are you so sure that Simon Fontaine found her? And if that's true, then why would he promptly take his own life by injection in the neck?

"You're suggesting he was devastated enough to kill himself? Why?"

"I don't know, maybe out of guilt, or because he felt like a failure after she'd stayed clean all these years only to relapse under his watch."

Is that the real reason they were living together?

"How do you think he killed himself?"

"You guys haven't released much information to the media, so I'm only speculating based on the 'shots fired' 911 call I heard about on the news."

"Why would Victoria kill herself the day she broke up with you to be with someone else? That doesn't track."

"I'm just telling you what she said. But she also sounded ragged and weird on the phone. She'd been acting so distant and irritable lately, I thought maybe she'd relapsed, and that she broke up with me so I wouldn't try to take her back to rehab. She could have accidentally overdosed, I guess. I don't know. But that's why I kept trying to reach her. Something was off."

That's what the killer wants us to think, anyway. Michael has now added himself to my suspect list.

"You said suicide attempts, plural. Tell me about that."

Michael described the fallout after the high school car crash as the first attempt. "She got really depressed about hurting that little girl, so she took a handful of her mom's oxys with a bunch of whiskey. They had to pump her stomach. She almost died. You'd think Nancy would have been more careful about leaving the pills around, but she had issues too."

"You'd think. When did the cutting start?"

"Sometime after Victoria OD'd. She went too deep and had to be hospitalized again. William finally stepped in, and she went to stay with him and his wife. They helped her get back on track."

"I see. How long ago was this?"

"This was all toward the end of high school, so about eighteen years ago."

"I saw some cutting marks that looked pretty fresh."

"I did too, but they weren't that deep. She got defensive when I asked her about them, so I didn't push. Now I wish I had."

"How did you find out she was dead?"

"I saw it on the news Saturday morning. I was totally shocked. Heartbroken, really. I'm sure Simon was too. I loved her very much and hoped to marry her someday. Our families are tied up financially, but emotionally it's always been, well, complicated."

Goode felt bad for the guy, but his double-suicide theory didn't jibe with the scene. Someone had moved Simon's body, shot him in the temple, and shoved those pills down Victoria's throat.

Was it him, angry that she broke up with him, then wouldn't answer his calls or texts? Either way, my gut says he's lying.

"Thanks for your time," Goode said, standing up to leave.

"Did you really need to take her computer, or did you do that to mess with me?" Michael asked with a half smile.

Why, are you antsy to delete incriminating evidence?

"Yes, I'm sorry. We needed its contents as evidence."

"As the new CFO, I have a lot of catching up to do. Victoria was supposed to update the board on the drug trials this coming week. But now that's my job."

Goode stopped and turned. "By the way, do you own a gun?"

"No," Michael said, his brow furrowed as he shook his head. "I don't like guns."

But he didn't seem surprised by the question. He definitely knows more than he's saying.

CHAPTER 14
GOODE

Monday

Back in the lobby, Goode waited for Darla Johansen to finish her call.

"Where can I find the lab director?" he asked, eager to learn more about the sex drug.

Darla led him down two floors to meet Dallas Fairchild, who was fortysomething and, unlike Michael, was dressed casually in shorts and a polo shirt. He had strong legs and a trim torso, which Goode attributed to the racing bike that rested on two hooks screwed into the wall.

"You ride that to work?" Goode asked.

"No, I take it out at lunch to break up the day. It's a great stress reliever," he said. "I ride my motorcycle to and from work."

As Fairchild gave him a tour, he was happy to tell Goode about the sex drug. Any topic was preferable, it seemed, to the Fontaines' deaths.

"Simon and I developed the drug here in the lab," Fairchild said, proudly gesturing toward the test tubes and other equipment on a wide countertop area that lined the room. "It's primarily a psychoactive dopamine enhancement vehicle that increases sexual desire, a little like ecstasy or THC, the primary psychoactive component in marijuana, only cleaner and safer. We've also added a couple other ingredients that were originally designed for other uses but have helpful secondary benefits, such as reupping the dopamine in your brain for a shorter recovery period. It makes for quite a powerful cocktail. It's going to help a lot of people."

At the coffee bar, Fairchild offered Goode a cup with some Danish cookies, then motioned for him to sit at a table to talk.

"How does it compare to Viagra?" Goode asked.

"Viagra works differently and is vastly inferior in scope. It's a vasodilator, which simply increases blood flow to the affected areas. It also has no psychological benefit other than, essentially, producing more confidence."

"Sounds fascinating," he said. "If it works, that is."

"Oh, it works all right," Fairchild said. "The first phase of trials went well, and we were about to launch the second phase—when all this happened."

"What about possible side effects?"

"None to speak of."

"What if you take too much?"

"That's not something we recommend."

"Humor me."

"We're still testing for the proper dosage. We will, of course, give careful instructions on how much to use, and when, to receive the optimum benefit."

"What are you not telling me?"

"Nothing. I've been slowly increasing doses and asking our subjects to track their thoughts, physical urges, and any side effects. Darla is also doing detailed interviews of our trial participants once a month."

"Darla? The receptionist?"

"No, the receptionist is on vacation this week. Darla is just filling in. She's a chemist and has several jobs around here, including administering doses to our trial participants and tracking the chemical and drug inventories."

"Aha. What kind of behavioral issues could occur if someone takes more than he should, or, say, the wrong gender formula?"

"I'd expect it would increase testosterone levels in men, and a range of behavior from an overactive libido to antisocial aggression. Mania, perhaps? The former might be fine if both partners are taking the drug, but likely not otherwise. The effects would be more unpredictable if one of them unknowingly ingests the wrong gender formula. Misuse of the drug isn't something we test for."

"So, murder is not out of the question?"

Fairchild shook his head. "I don't see why this drug, on its own, would cause anyone to commit murder. But mixed with testosterone boosters, or methamphetamine or cocaine, alcohol, or even HGH—human growth hormone, which some men use these days to try to stay virile—I guess anything is possible in someone capable of killing even without it. We didn't see any adverse effects on the rats, either, so we progressed to the first phase of human testing, with about fifty subjects. You can't effectively test a psychosexual drug on rats because it's our rational thought that separates us from our four-legged friends, at least theoretically, and rats certainly can't tell us if they're feeling more aroused than before. But we could see that they mated more often."

"Was Dr. Fontaine the type of doctor who would test this drug on himself?" Goode asked.

"I see where you're going now. I've wondered that too, but I didn't notice any behavioral changes in him. I know that he used Viagra from time to time, so it would show up on the tox screen, if they even test for it."

Goode leaned closer. "Viagra doesn't come in a form you can inject, does it?"

"No, it was actually developed as an alternative to injection therapy, although I know that some men use both after prostate surgery. Why do you ask?"

"Just wondering," Goode said. "Is your drug in pill form or is it injectable?"

"We injected it into the rats, but we give pills to the trial participants."

So, they have a supply of syringes, too, presumably.

"What about Victoria? Was she the type to test it on herself?"

"I don't think so. She was careful what she put in her body, but they say recovering addicts are always one pill or drink away from relapsing. I know she liked sex, but she didn't need any enhancement."

Goode nodded. "That sounds like personal knowledge."

"Yeah, well, V. and I dated last year. She was trying to move past her thing with Alex Battrelle—after their falling-out over the abortion, but before she started seeing Michael."

Michael Battrelle had mentioned the abortion too, but Goode hadn't wanted to interrupt his line of questioning to ask more about it. "Tell me about the abortion."

"It was Alex's baby, but Victoria thought he wasn't ready to be a father," Fairchild said. "So, she got rid of it."

Fairchild grabbed a bottle of water off the counter and took a couple of sips before he continued. "It seemed very transactional at the time. She wouldn't even talk about it, but I'm sure that's why it didn't work out between us. I really liked her. She just had too much going on. Thankfully, Victoria wasn't my supervisor—Simon was—which made the breakup a little less awkward."

"Did she seem depressed lately?"

"No. But she also didn't seem that fulfilled, either, and I'm not saying that because we had a history together. I know she was *trying* to love Michael. He's a really nice, well-meaning guy, but he's kind of, well, boring. Nothing like his brother. Alex is a real pistol."

That's a curious word to use under the circumstances.

"Was Alex ever violent with Victoria?"

"Not that I know of."

"What about Michael?"

"God, no."

"Do you own a gun?"

Fairchild's eyebrows shot up. "Yes, I do. My dad taught me how to shoot a gun when I was ten years old. Why do you ask?"

"Do you still have it?"

Goode could see the sweat beading on the chemist's forehead as he shook his head. "Um, no. I loaned it to Victoria a few weeks ago, because she said she didn't feel safe going to the underground parking garage late at night."

"Where did she keep it?"

"I don't know, exactly. Maybe in her desk drawer, or her purse? Why do you ask? Or is this another question you can't answer?"

He seems a little agitated. But if she kept it in the desk drawer, maybe Michael Battrelle took it out of there, and that's why he made the weird remark about the napkins.

"Because Dr. Fontaine was shot in the head."

Fairchild looked genuinely stunned. "Wow. Okay. That wasn't in the news. What kind of gun was it?"

"It was a 9mm. What's yours?"

"A 9mm," Fairchild said slowly, shaking his head, as if he realized how that sounded.

Goode asked Fairchild to email him the registration paperwork, showing where and when he'd bought the gun. "Here's my card."

The biochemist stared at the card as if he was holding something back.

"Is there something else you want to tell me?" Goode asked, pausing. "Like, why you chose a 9mm rather than, say, a .40?"

"My dad's a retired cop. He had a 9mm on the job, and he let me use it at the shooting range growing up, so I was familiar with it. But yeah, there is something more. I didn't really want to mention it, because the board doesn't know yet. Can we keep it confidential?"

"Well, it could come out later if someone is arrested, but I don't make a habit of reporting details of our investigation to businesses whose executives have died under suspicious circumstances. Why don't you tell me whatever it is."

"Okay, you'll find out from the emails I wrote to Victoria anyway. When I audited the doses on hand a week ago, I discovered that a bunch were missing. Of both gender formulas. I told Victoria about it right away."

"Really?" Goode said, trying to hide his excitement. "Any suspects in mind?"

"No one in particular. It could have been anyone with access to the lab. I'm here a lot, but not all the time," Fairchild replied. "It could have been Simon, I guess, wanting to tweak something, and he didn't get a chance to tell me. Or one of the board members, or even Darla, though I can't see that. I suppose it could also be one of the new investors Vincent has been parading through here to keep our funding going. I tried to tell him there was a risk-benefit ratio to allowing outsiders in, but he didn't want to listen. Said the gravy train needed to keep running."

Interesting. So, funding ***was*** *an issue.*

"What was Victoria's reaction?"

"She was pissed, so I knew it wasn't her, and that's why I thought it probably wasn't Simon either. My guess is it's a Casanova wannabe. Worst case, it's someone who wants to sell it on the black market or to a competitor. Victoria had some ideas about who it was, but she wouldn't elaborate."

Odd. Was she protecting someone? Or scared of someone? Sounds like the latter since she asked for his gun.

"What was the plan of action?"

"We were going to have cameras installed in the lab, but obviously we were too late," Fairchild said.

"Maybe not. Have any more doses gone missing?"

"I haven't had a chance to check, but it's possible. I've got jugs stored in that refrigerated tank behind you, along with new batches I've tweaked to load more efficiently into the bloodstream. Some of both were missing. The jugs are all coded separately, but a thief could unknowingly use a more potent or less stable mixture, or even the wrong gender formula."

"It would be helpful for us to know if doses are still going missing," Goode said. "Any chance you can get those cameras installed today? It would be great if we could catch the culprit in action, the sooner the better. I'd also strongly suggest that you tell no one. Everyone is a possible suspect at this point, including you."

Fairchild raised his eyebrows and his mouth fell open. "Uh, yeah, okay," he stuttered. "Victoria said she was going to use the same security company that installed cameras in Vincent's house. I'll contact them as soon as we're done here. She'd already found a guy who is going to install a password-protected lock system on the lab door. Only the two of us would know the key code, and we were going to change it weekly."

"But that didn't happen either?"

"No, she was going to oversee that this past weekend, but she called in sick Friday morning."

Goode went quiet as he mulled the sting operation. He hoped his gut was right, that he could trust Fairchild, because the thief could very well be the killer.

"I suggest you hold off on the new locks until you catch the thief on camera. How would someone know you two had discovered that doses were missing?"

"If someone had access to her emails or to the server, I guess. Or if someone was paid to gain access, like a hacker. I'm not sure why I emailed her about it in the first place," he said, his tone tinged with self-blame. "I wish I'd called her instead."

CHAPTER 15
KATRINA

Monday

Rather than use the side entrance for employees, Katrina entered the *Sun-Dispatch* building Monday morning through the lobby, where the walls were hung with portraits of Vincent Battrelle shaking hands with luminaries, virtually all male, at editorial board meetings. His smug expression revealed how much he enjoyed making powerful men pay homage to him.

Vincent wasn't a newsman; he was a businessman. A real estate developer. After buying the paper in a virtual fire sale a few years back, the *Advocate* ran a rather unflattering profile that challenged his motivations, alleging that he wanted to use the forum as a narcissistic megaphone for his personal and political projects, not to protect the public good. The sale price was reportedly based primarily on the value of the land on which the building stood. For that alone, he got a good deal. The paper was a bonus. Not surprisingly, Vincent didn't change the paper's historic tradition of perpetuating the status quo. If anything, he dug even deeper into it.

The sale came at a time when the news industry had already begun to implode as the world moved online, where readers felt entitled to free content. The *Sun-Dispatch* ultimately installed a paywall, but newspapers nationwide were losing money through a growing income gap that could not be plugged. As positions were slashed and advertisers fell away, managers echoed the mantra "do more with less" while employee morale fell further with each round of layoffs.

Given the state of the industry, Katrina initially had been surprised but flattered by Linda's recruiting call. She'd hoped that the decline of journalism was entering the "boomerang" phase, when bean counters finally realized that cutting staff and producing an inferior news product did not help keep papers afloat after all. But by now, reality had sunk back in, and skepticism had taken over. In this cost-cutting environment, how and why would a new position be created for her just three weeks before the Fontaines' suspicious deaths?

Katrina saw Linda walking briskly toward her desk at 8:30 a.m., a little frothy around the mouth.

Is she always this excitable on a Monday morning?

She wasn't planning to tell Linda that she'd done research all weekend because she didn't want that to become an ongoing expectation. But as she would soon learn, her new employer would exercise as many unreasonable demands on her as the last one.

"I thought you were going to call me on Saturday. What have you got so far?" Linda asked breathlessly.

Knowing Linda wouldn't want to hear that the juiciest tidbits were off the record because of Goode's rules or Vincent's demands, Katrina scrambled for a middle-ground response.

"There's a news conference today, probably about the autopsies over the weekend. I learned—off the record—that Victoria was pregnant and may have been involved with both of Vincent Battrelle's sons. Also, FYI, Michael and Vincent are not only on the board at Vitaleron, they're also corporate officers and major investors. It's all in the public SEC records, which anyone can access."

As the editor's expression morphed from a blank stare into a bureaucratic mask, Katrina sensed her apprehension. The more the Battrelles became involved in this story, the harder the editors would fight to keep them out of it.

"I'll let John Palmer know and get back to you," Linda said, sniffing, her voice quite pointy now, with edges. Katrina found it amusing that the executive editor was the only person in the newsroom identified by their full name, when everyone else went by their first or last names.

"Okay," Katrina said. "I'll keep poking around the SEC records to identify other investors. For all we know, these deaths could be an extreme form of a hostile takeover."

"That is a major stretch," Linda said curtly.

Feeling her abdomen cramping, Katrina tried to shrug it off. She didn't want to work for a paper that violated journalistic ethics to protect its owner from bad publicity, but she tried not to catastrophize. Linda could conceivably come back and tell her to go full steam ahead. Although she seriously doubted it.

To hell with Linda's and Vincent's instructions, I think I'm on to something.

Katrina vowed to follow her own instincts and to methodically cross-check criminal, civil, family court, and property records of all board members to see who might benefit from the Fontaines' deaths. If anyone asked, she would say she was gathering string on the victims and their company.

Right off the bat, I'd have to say that as Vitaleron's second-largest investor, Vincent Battrelle had the most to gain.

Fontaine's surgery partner was also a good candidate, because their practice most likely had a life insurance policy, with the surviving partner as the beneficiary. If there was a power struggle between either man and Simon Fontaine, Victoria could have been collateral damage.

Either one could've hired a hit man. Or had a partner in crime. Someone else on the board? I still like the hostile-takeover scenario, even more so because Linda tried to shoo me away from it.

Starting her background checks with Vincent, she found no criminal history or restraining orders. But he did have a stack of lawsuits against him, mostly related to his development projects. His dozen pages of property holdings ranged from condo complexes downtown to a structure on a big lot in the mountains near the rural town of Ramona. The undeveloped parcels, mostly zoned for large residential subdivisions, included a site in the avocado groves of the northeastern part of the county that was massive enough to build a whole new community.

Moving on to Michael Battrelle, she came up with a whole lot of nothing. He was as clean as could be. Never married, he owned a house near Vincent's in the Shores, had a JD *and* an MBA, and had worked for his father's companies his entire life. But appearances could be deceiving. Based on what she'd learned about the Polish mafia, Michael could also be the "cleaner" for his father's affairs, which required him to appear pristine.

Next was Darren McMurphy, an attorney who went to law school at USD, just like her parents, then proceeded directly to Milton Biggs & Associates. She'd heard of Biggs at the dinner table growing up, because his firm represented both of the city's professional sports teams, wealthy real estate developers, and white-collar criminals. At thirty-eight, McMurphy was a partner there, and he'd already been divorced three times, the last time quite recently.

Katrina could see why from his headshot. He was a rich, pretty boy with full feminine lips and long eyelashes. She suspected he treated women like trophies, trading them out when he grew tired of them.

Clicking through to the Biggs website, she saw Vitaleron listed among McMurphy's clients.

Isn't that an obvious conflict of interest to be on the Vitaleron board and also serve as the company's legal representative?

Since the Battrelles were presently out-of-bounds for her, she saw Darren McMurphy as her only vehicle to learn about the Fontaines. So, she searched the archives for his most recent ex-wife. Fresh bitterness would make her the most likely to talk.

Wife number three, Daisy Miller McMurphy, was president of the La Jolla High School Booster Club and sold real estate at an agency on Prospect Street.

"You can call me 'Muffin,'" she said. "Everyone does."

Daisy couldn't wait to spill the sauce on Darren, who had left her for another woman. She didn't know the woman's name, only that she was a younger version of wife number two: a sweet, soft-spoken people-pleaser. Apparently, he had a thing for Filipino women.

"I wasn't that surprised, because I was the other woman in the last round. He complained that he was bored being married to a doormat. 'I want some spice in my life,' he said. I guess I was the spice until he wanted bland and subservient again."

"Did you guys go to high school with Victoria Fontaine?"

"Yes, but not at the same time. We all went to 'Dinner Dance' Friday nights at the Beach Club, but he didn't talk to me then, because I was too young."

"Did you know Victoria?"

"Not very well. She was a year ahead of me. I actually dated her brother, Cal, before I married Darren. Cal was hot, but kind of a lost soul. I think he left the country after we broke up," she said, trailing off.

"I'm trying to find him too," Katrina said.

Daisy kept talking as if Katrina hadn't said a word. "La Jolla is a tiny fishbowl, where we all know each other's business."

She told Katrina about Victoria's crash, high on oxy. "Going to the McDonald Center in La Jolla was a condition of her probation. She was back in rehab a year later after OD'ing on oxy and whiskey."

Does everyone end up at the McDonald Center?

"She was in the thirty-day inpatient program when she and Alex first hooked up. Their families go way back. But he was five years older than her, plus he and his brother went to Country Day."

More context for her tree diagram of connections between Franny, Victoria, Alex, and their families.

"So, they dated?"

"Not exactly. Alex was a player, and Victoria was so young back then."

"Uh-huh," Katrina said, urging Daisy to continue.

"He and Victoria seemed to have a special kind of friendship, but they weren't *together*. She got around too, which made him jealous, so he'd come back for more, but never for very long."

"They were close friends, then?"

"You mean like friends with benefits? I guess so, but we didn't call it that back then. More like recovery-support buddies, there for each other on some level, but not on a day-to-day basis. Probably because Alex was never committed to his recovery. Darren said Alex's dad put him on the Vitaleron board to help him focus on his sobriety. Alex is quite brilliant."

"How long was he on the board?"

"A couple of years. But Simon forced him out, so Michael took his place."

"What about Victoria? Seems like she turned her life around."

"With her history of addiction and emotional issues, she had to prove herself first, but Simon finally asked her to help him run Vitaleron."

"Did anyone know that Victoria was pregnant?"

"Wait, what? Do you know who the father was?"

"No, I don't. Not for sure, anyway. Who might know?"

After thinking a moment, Daisy threw out a couple of names, starting with Regina Russell.

"Regina was a cheerleader with me. I know she's stayed in touch with Victoria because their fathers are so close. Simon's partner is on the board and a major investor in Vitaleron as well."

Katrina thanked her and immediately called Regina at the surgery office.

Sounding stressed, Regina seemed happy to vent.

"Funny you should ask if the police had contacted me, because they left about an hour ago after tossing the place and taking our computers."

"What were they looking for?"

"The warrant listed the obvious official stuff, but I got the feeling they didn't really know."

"Fishing for clues?"

"Yeah. Like they were hoping to stumble across one."

"A common investigative technique," Katrina said wryly.

"They wouldn't tell us anything about the investigation, but they asked a lot of questions about the drugs we keep here."

"You do actual surgeries in an outpatient clinic?"

"Yes. We follow DEA regulations for tracking our narcotic usage and keep all the drugs locked up."

"Who was in charge of that?"

"Esperanza, our surgical nurse. But she's out today. We're all still pretty upset—and scared—about the murders."

Funny she called them that, since last I heard they were still categorized as suspicious deaths. I wonder if that's changed.

"So, your dad is a Vitaleron investor?"

"Yes, like most every other wealthy La Jolla man over fifty. They're all hoping this magic drug will be the next big thing. Not just financially, but for the sake of their own virility. My dad's in the business of improving people's lives, but he gets a kick at how 'the rich man's penis' has been keeping Vitaleron afloat. Oh, there is one thing I thought was weird."

"What's that?"

"The police asked if we keep track of syringes in the office and if Dr. Fontaine might have taken some home."

"Syringes?"

"Yes. I thought that was strange, because there was nothing in the paper about syringes at the crime scene. Do you know anything about that?"

"No, the police won't tell me anything, even if it *is* a crime scene," Katrina said. "*Did* Dr. Fontaine keep syringes or drugs at home?"

"Probably. He used to joke about taking shots of B_{12} in the butt and Botox in the face. It's funny, but you and Detective Goode are asking the same questions."

"I think we're both trying to find out what happened," Katrina said. "I mean, Victoria was pregnant, dating a nice rich guy, friend of the family. She had a good job and had been off drugs for years, right?"

"Wait, Victoria was pregnant?" Regina asked. "That ought to be interesting."

"Why's that?"

"Because she and Michael weren't exclusive."

Could Michael have found out that the baby was someone else's—like his brother's—and gone into a rage?

CHAPTER 16
GOODE

Monday

Goode walked back to the Explorer with the freeway roar in his ears as he juggled various scenarios in his mind.

No wonder Victoria didn't feel safe walking to her car alone at night. Some crazy shit was going down here, and she was worried—with good reason—that she could be in danger.

"This is starting to make more sense now," Stone said when Goode called to brief him.

"What do you mean?" Goode asked.

"Why the Vitaleron honchos have hijacked our news conference this afternoon."

"Whaat?"

"Yeah, the lieutenant wanted to talk about the searches, but he was overruled by the chief—and the mayor, apparently—who said the Vitaleron execs would do most of the talking. And *not* about the searches."

"Okay, so what are we talking about, then?"

"Got me. I guess we'll find out when the reporters do. Sounds like some Tammany Hall shit to me."

"I'm going to give a heads-up to our girl, Katrina. Maybe she can get to the bottom of this," Goode said.

"Yeah, about that," Stone said.

"What?"

"I've been meaning to talk to you. I got a call while you were in Maui from the mother of Clover Ziegler, that mentally ill girl we thought was a suspect in the Tania Marcus case last year, the one who ended up jumping off the cliffs at Black's. Apparently, Clover's mother is still distraught and thinks you should have tried harder to save her daughter. She also said she heard that you had a female witness in your apartment."

"Sounds like she was stalking me," Goode said defensively, caught off guard, partly because the timeline didn't make sense. "I told you she hit on me the day I went to their house, looking for Clover. My question is why she's coming forward now."

"What witness is she talking about? And why would she be in your apartment?"

After explaining that the witness was Alison, he tried to deflect any further questions while he reviewed the chain of events in his mind. "You know nothing happened, though, right?"

He'd never told Stone much about what had happened with Alison—a friend of the victim and a key witness—because he knew he'd committed an ethical lapse that would only get him in hot water. He just couldn't figure out how Clover's mother would have known anything about it.

"Is that a Bill Clinton nondenial denial or a real denial?" Stone asked.

"Look, I let the girl stay on my couch for a couple of nights, because I heard her crying out from inside her apartment, so I broke her front door down. Remember I told you I found Tania's father straddling her on the living-room floor with his hand over her mouth? I literally had to pull him off her. I didn't tell you I let her stay with me because that would have made you complicit. But I swear I sent her home as soon as they put her door back on the hinges."

“You said she was staying with a friend,” Stone said.

“Yeah, well, sorry, chief. She seemed so traumatized I thought she needed personal protection. I wanted to make sure that dude didn’t come after her again,” Goode said. “I almost called Alison for a date after the case died down, but then I thought better of it. She’s a troubled girl, too, and she didn’t need me in her life, confusing her even more.”

“I’d agree with that. But you should have come clean. You know we have safe houses for this type of thing. That call caught me unawares, which is never good.”

“Yeah, I know. Sorry. I’m not sure what else to say.”

“Say that you won’t step over the line again, and certainly not with this reporter while we’re still investigating. And if you do, you need to tell me, pronto.”

“I won’t. Like I said, she and I both have our jobs to do. We’re professionals.”

“That’s what I’m worried about. Professional whats?”

“Very funny.”

“Okay, call her, but stay in your own lane, and don’t talk to any other reporters about this. Let’s keep this between us and your girl for now.”

“Happy to,” he said.

“It’s for your own good, Goode,” Stone said.

Goode felt relief as Stone inflicted him with the well-weathered pun, which meant the beating was over, at least for now.

CHAPTER 17
KATRINA

Monday

As soon as Katrina hung up with Regina, Goode called, but he sounded more formal and emotionally detached than usual.

Something is off.

"Just wanted to let you know the news conference will be at 4:00 p.m. at headquarters downtown," he said. "Something political is going on and I don't know what it is, so I'm counting on you to nose around, shake some trees. Your boy, Michael Battrelle, is going to be there."

Katrina was confused. "Why would he do that? I've got it covered."

"He's not coming as a representative of the newspaper. He's on the docket with the Vitaleron honchos."

"What do you mean?"

"Yeah, this came down from the mayor and chief. We're as confused as you are, so I thought you'd want to know."

"Definitely. Thanks for the heads-up. Now I have a question for you: What can you tell me about the syringes, drug audits, and the warrant you served at Dr. Fontaine's office?"

Silence.

"Okay, I can say this," he said after a long pause. "We may or may not choose to release the warrant affidavits, but if we do, they'll be the ones we want the media to have, because it might help the investigation. Why don't you ask me when the affidavits will be released by the court?"

"Huh?"

As Goode repeated his question, Katrina realized he was trying to teach her how to play his game.

He can't tell me things, but he'll confirm them if I ask the right question. That's valiant of him.

"Okay, when will the affidavits be released?"

"Now that you've asked, I'll have to say that we can't talk about the specifics of any affidavits, but those that aren't sealed would be made public ten days after they're filed with the court, and then only for a short time before they're no longer a public record. By the way, I've been cleared to talk to you, but it has to be off the record. Can we make that a standing order so you don't have to keep asking me to go on the record?"

"Um, not really," she said. "How'd you swing that?"

"I proposed it, and my sergeant said yes. We go way back."

"Are you *ever* going to tell me anything on the record?"

"Not for the moment. We'd like to give you the exclusive story once we make an arrest, but in the meantime, we'd ask that you hold off writing things that could tip off any suspects, such as the mention of syringes or drug audits. We'll do what we just did—where you ask me questions and I answer—so I'm never volunteering information or quoted directly. You can attribute the information to 'a source knowledgeable about the investigation.'"

Katrina was hesitant. She'd made deals with sources before, but not when the story was this competitive, and certainly not on her first big story at a new paper. She also wasn't going to be silenced when she had countless questions.

"I don't see how that flies. I'm not going to muzzle myself about details, like the search warrant, which I've already learned from other sources. As much as I like you, I'm a watchdog reporter. I'm not here to help you with your investigation."

Goode paused again and sighed. "Okay, I get it. You've been doing some good legwork, and you're putting two and two together. We're not used to that. Normally, the *Sun-Dispatch* reports what we tell them to—or not to."

"I'll take that as a compliment," she said.

"You should. I don't give them very often. So, ask your editor about my exclusive-story proposal."

"All in good time, Surfer Man."

"That's Detective Surfer Man to you."

She hung up smiling. It was good they could be straight with each other. She only wished she didn't like the sound of his voice so much. It made her all melty inside.

After the awkward exchange with Linda that morning, Katrina sensed she should talk to someone else about Goode's proposal. She'd been assigned to Joanne, the Watchdog team editor, her first day at the paper, but Linda had sidelined Joanne on the Fontaine story for some reason.

Katrina called Joanne's cell phone so it would sound like a personal call if anyone was around, but hung up as soon as she saw Linda waving her over to John Palmer's office.

"He wants to talk to you," Linda whispered. "Not the best circumstances for an introduction to the boss. Let him talk. Don't disagree with him. He doesn't like that, and especially from a new hire."

Katrina appreciated the advice, but she didn't like the increasing apprehension that she'd come to work at a fascist organization. "Okay, so how do I know when to say something?"

"I'll nod," Linda said. "You've got to ease into this place, but you're suddenly in the soup, as they say."

As soon as a line of suits filed out of the office, John Palmer motioned for the two women to come in, excitedly recounting the joint promotion the San Diego Padres had just proposed.

"Go, Padres!" he said.

Katrina winced inside, trying not to let the disgust show on her face.

Gawd. What are we, cheerleaders?

"Welcome," he said, extending his hand to Katrina. He shook hers firmly, then squeezed. Hard.

He's nice looking enough, but he's overcompensating because he isn't good with the ladies. Or he simply lacks subtlety in his need to exert dominance. Same difference.

"How are you enjoying it here so far?" he asked disingenuously.

"It's great to be back in my hometown, but as a reporter," she said.

Linda nodded approvingly in her direction.

"That's good to hear," he said.

Rather than seat them at the big conference table like the Padres suits, he gestured toward two squat chairs in front of his giant desk, where they were below his eye level once they were all seated.

"Linda tells me you've gotten us into a bit of a pickle," he said.

Katrina glanced over at Linda, but she was staring straight ahead at their boss.

If she wants me to follow her signals, why doesn't she look at me?

Katrina couldn't tell if he was joking, but she was prepared to defend herself.

"I was being facetious, Katrina. No need to panic."

"Okay, good," she said, laughing nervously. Linda didn't even crack a smile.

"No, but seriously, we're in a tenuous situation here," he said, cocking his head to one side, which struck her as a trick he'd learned in business school to appear compassionate.

"We want to avoid embarrassing the paper and its owner but still cover the news. Of course, we don't want to withhold important information from our readers, but at this stage, we don't need to insert the Battrelles' names—or information about their personal assets or business holdings—into any story. We can say Vincent and Michael are members of Vitaleron's board of directors, because I assume we're going to be naming the others as well, but that's it. Anything else is irrelevant."

As he waited for Katrina to answer, she looked at Linda, and this time, the editor nodded for her to go ahead.

"Okay," Katrina said, unsure of what else to say.

I guess I'll wait to see what happens at the news conference, which he doesn't seem to know about.

With that, John Palmer stood up to signal that the meeting was over. When Linda jumped to her feet, Katrina followed her lead.

"Thank you, ladies," he said. "Very nice to meet you, Katrina. I'm sure you'll do a fine job with this story. We're expecting great work from you."

"It was nice to meet you too," Katrina said, thinking the exact opposite.

"Linda, can you stay a minute?" he asked rhetorically.

"I'll come find you when we're done," Linda said to Katrina, who returned to her desk, her lower abdomen now in outright rebellion.

What's going on? Don't they understand that it's wrong to shield the publisher and his family like this, to refuse to even consider that they might be witnesses or possibly involved in these deaths somehow?

She sat with her face in her hands until she heard Linda's voice behind her.

"Katrina?"

As she turned around, Linda nodded toward her office and started walking that way. Following dutifully, Katrina felt her coworkers' eyes on her as she passed them.

"Shut the door," Linda said.

Katrina did as she was told, holding her notebook on her knee, poised to take notes.

"Let's be clear on what you're supposed to be doing," Linda said. "Just so you know, I get copied when you run database checks, and it seems you're getting into the weeds. We'd like to get you back to the Fontaines. Remember I asked you to explore their influence in the philanthropic, social, and business communities? We want our readers to know about these people, what their contributions were, and where their company is with the drug trials. Not property and affiliations between board members and how much money the Battrelles have invested in Vitaleron."

Geez. Talk about Big Brother.

"But I've been doing that," Katrina said. "In fact, I just interviewed two women who went to high school with Victoria. I'm also going to call Simon's brother, William, before I head out to the news conference at the cop shop this afternoon."

"Good. Remember, we're expecting a series of stories from you as they develop, Katrina, not one long thumb-sucker."

Series? When did it become a series?

"Okay, but it seems like there are some land mines here," Katrina said, "and I'm not sure how I'm supposed to ignore or walk around them."

"Do your best. I'm sure everything will be fine. There is no *I* in team, Katrina. There's plenty to do without wasting time going through SEC records or the Battrelles' property and lawsuits. Are we clear?"

"Yes."

CHAPTER 18
GOODE

Monday

After dropping the security footage at the RCFL, Goode reached police headquarters twenty minutes before the media event's scheduled start time. He planned to watch every Vitaleron exec arrive, checking for strange twitches, sweating, shaking, or odd behavior that could stem from unauthorized dosing of the drug.

By definition, the news conference couldn't start until the media arrived, but the rule of thumb was to wait for the network affiliates so speakers didn't have to repeat themselves. "Ready Rhona" Chen from Channel 10, who earned her nickname from the time Goode saw her wrapped around a cop at 3:00 a.m. in a Denny's parking lot, was often late because she liked to make an entrance.

Goode stood under a tree near the portable podium, a good vantage point to observe the entire courtyard. As the TV trucks pulled up, reporters spilled out with their thick makeup and hair sprayed in place, videographers trailing behind them.

Stone did the stop-and-chat on his way to help the PIO set up the speakers' podium, where the media also set up their mics, next to the fountain. "A couple national network shows called about doing a live feed this morning," he told Goode, with a mix of excitement and dread in his voice. "They've already named this 'The Sex-Drug Death Case.'"

"Great, just what we need," mumbled Goode, who wore a long-sleeved white shirt and aquamarine tie for the occasion. He hated collared shirts and ties because they were restrictive, and he felt self-conscious as he tugged at them. But he'd even stopped for a haircut on the off chance that he was asked to speak or was pointed out as the lead detective.

When Katrina arrived, she came over to say hello and compliment him on his haircut.

"Nice 'do," she said, leaning in to whisper "Is that Darren McMurphy?" as she pointed toward the men in dark suits lined up next to the podium like a soccer team guarding their jewels before a penalty kick.

"Do you mean the cocky-looking one, second from the left? We went to high school together—he was a year ahead of me. He was a dick then and I'm sure he still is. But I'll deny having said that."

As Chief Baxter approached the podium, Goode moved away from Katrina to make room for Foster and Byron under the tree, noticing that Mayor Jack Norton was AWOL.

"Thanks for coming today," Baxter said, introducing Dr. Largo, the chief medical examiner, who stood beside him, along with Stone, Goode, and their team.

"Let me also introduce some of our city's business leaders from Vitaleron. Standing beside me is Darren McMurphy, the son of our esteemed Port Commission chairman, Patrick McMurphy, who owns some of our biggest hotels on the harbor and Mission Bay," Baxter said, waving to an older man in a navy blazer standing alone by the fountain, who nodded in response.

"Darren ran the campaigns for the last two mayors," Byron whispered. Goode knew that Darren's father was an unpaid adviser to the mayor with his own office at City Hall, which in his mind was a blatant pay-to-play reward. He should have known that Darren would also be involved in politics.

It's obviously a family affair.

Ready Rhona started talking with another female TV reporter right next to Katrina, oblivious, because their mics were recording the chief's comments from the podium. Goode could see Katrina getting agitated at the women, who glared at her when she shushed them.

Baxter mostly repeated what the lieutenant said on Saturday, and he still didn't explain why the two deaths had been deemed "suspicious."

C'mon, Chief, throw them a bone.

"We can't go into too much detail right now," Baxter said. "Although we completed the autopsies over the weekend, the cause and manner of death are still under investigation. I'll let Dr. Largo take it from here."

Stepping up to the mic, Largo tried to quiet the crowd of reporters, who were buzzing about the "news" conference being a misnomer.

"Excuse me," Largo repeated several times. "Due to the suspicious and unusual nature of the death scene, the detectives are still exploring some unanswered forensic questions. We hope to know more once the toxicology tests come back. But in the meantime, we can report that Victoria Fontaine was three months pregnant. We send thoughts and prayers to her family."

"Who's the father?" one reporter yelled out.

"We don't know yet," Baxter interjected. "We're doing DNA tests to try to determine paternity, because the father will likely be a person of interest. We're also running the fetus's profile through CODIS to see if the father has a criminal record," he said, referring to the federal database known as the Combined DNA Index System.

"Who reported the murders?" another reporter called out.

"As I said, we haven't determined these were murders yet. I repeat, these are still suspicious deaths at this point. The 911 call came at 9:00 p.m. from an adult male who reported hearing 'shots fired' on La Jolla Farms Road but wouldn't give his name."

"When will the autopsy reports be ready?" the same reporter yelled.

"As you know, we always wait for the toxicology results before we complete the reports—" Largo said.

"—and because this is such a high-profile case, we may ask the court to seal them," Baxter said, interrupting. "No offense, folks, but your stories can interfere with our investigations."

The crowd erupted into a cacophony of objections. "Hey, now, everybody, calm down," the chief said. "We're not there yet. Nothing's in stone."

"What's so suspicious? Sounds like a double suicide to me," Rhona hissed at her cameraman. "I bet she OD'd and he offed himself because they ran out of funding. They haven't announced anything about the drug trials in more than a year."

"Ask the chief," he hissed back.

"Chief, why, exactly, are you calling these deaths suspicious?" Rhona yelled.

Silence fell over the crowd. "That's all we have for you," Baxter said, evoking a chorus of even louder objections. "But, before you go, the Vitaleron team wants to say a few words."

Goode, who could feel Katrina watching for his reaction, tried to maintain a blank expression. But he couldn't resist giving her a quick wink. She smiled back and glanced away before anyone saw.

Darren McMurphy started off by introducing his fellow board members, including Dr. Warren Russell, who looked as distraught as when Goode last saw him. Same with Michael Battrelle, who was still in a state of fluster.

"It's a shame that the tragic deaths of our founding partner and CFO brought us here today, but we have a few announcements," Darren said. "I'll be taking Dr. Fontaine's place as chairman of the board. Michael Battrelle, our board treasurer here to my right, will replace Victoria Fontaine as CFO. These other gentlemen, all of whom have stellar professional qualifications, will pitch in where necessary to ensure that the Vitaleron ship stays on course. We want to ensure our drug trials for this globally important marital aid move forward without delay."

So, now it's a marital aid? That's interesting marketing.

After scanning the Vitaleron execs for strange behavior, Goode saw nothing untoward in the corporate types, other than too much product in their hair.

Frankly, they all look jumpy and sweaty to me.

Michael Battrelle nodded sullenly as Darren stepped away from the mic to make way for the new CFO, who looked positively stricken, the color drained from his face.

"We want to reassure stockholders and the public that everything is fine," Michael said in a shaky voice that negated his stated intent. "We want the police to resolve this case as soon as possible so we can all get back to work and get this exciting drug out to the public as planned."

Well, he's a bundle of nerves. Did he not know about the pregnancy until now?

CHAPTER 19
KATRINA

Monday

By the end of the presser, Katrina was irritated. She no longer had the exclusive scoop about Victoria's pregnancy, which was the only real news at the event. But she did get a chance to see Darren McMurphy in the flesh. He was just as Goode described.

She made a note to ask whether the paper's attorneys could file a motion to unseal the autopsy reports if necessary, because if these deaths were in fact murders, the public had a right to know.

Although the female reporter from Channel 10 was unprofessional for talking during the chief's comments, she did ask a relevant question that he should've answered. Katrina almost never asked questions at pressers, because she didn't want to share her insights with competitors.

The police are acting extra cautious, claiming they still don't know what happened at the house, but I bet they have a better handle on the case than they're letting on. I bet they also have a suspect or two in mind.

That said, Katrina was thrilled that Michael Battrelle made a public statement, because the newspaper could no longer force her to omit his entire family from her story. She fully intended to describe Michael's pale and shaken appearance, even though Linda would probably take it out. If they didn't do their jobs, the competing media would do it for them, which would only embarrass the newspaper. The *Advocate* might even spout more of its conspiracy theories.

We could've been out in front of this, but now we'll have it at the same time as everyone else, if not later. The TV stories will probably air before mine gets posted online tonight, and way before the paper comes out tomorrow. I like to be first. Always first.

As soon as the speechifying was over, Katrina stepped away to call Vincent. They'd agreed that she should call his cell, rather than go through his secretary, to avoid unnecessary gossip. When he didn't answer, she left him a voicemail.

"We need to talk. I'd like to stop by your house after work tonight. Please give me a call."

Although she was curious about Alex's whereabouts, she had to be firm. She couldn't search for Vincent's playboy son as a side job, because she needed to do that for the newspaper. It was a clear ethical conflict.

A few minutes later, Vincent returned her call.

"Did you find Alex?" he asked.

"Sorry, no. I was at a news conference at the police station, where Michael announced that he's replacing Victoria Fontaine as Vitaleron's CFO," she said. "But you probably already knew that."

She waited for a response, but there was none.

"Why didn't you tell me that Alex and Michael were both seeing Victoria?" she asked.

"I don't even know if that's true," he retorted. "Besides, it wasn't relevant at the time, and I'm not sure it's relevant now. Our families have always been close. Simon and I had some disagreements in recent years, but I never had a problem with Victoria. She was always a good kid, and she put up with her father, which wasn't easy. He was a difficult man, but he was my business partner."

"Okay, but when we discussed talking to Alex's friends about his whereabouts, it seems like you would have mentioned that he and Victoria were so close."

"Why would I do that if you couldn't talk to her? She'd just passed away the night before."

"That's exactly why I thought you would have said something."

He also hadn't suggested that she talk to Michael, which didn't make sense either. Unless the two brothers didn't get along, as was implied by Goode's "bad blood" question. But she decided to wait to ask that until she and Vincent were face-to-face.

"I'm not sure where you got your information about her seeing Alex," he said. "They had a falling-out a year ago. She and Michael were always friends, though he told me last night that they'd been dating for the past five months until she broke up with him Friday morning. No one tells me anything."

Friday morning? The day she died?

"Is that why Michael looked so upset this afternoon, because he didn't know about the pregnancy?"

"I'm sure of it," Vincent said. "I know I am. I had to hear it live on TV just now, for Christ's sake. I was upset about Simon and Victoria, of course, but I had no idea there was a baby too. I'm not sure how this relates to Alex's disappearance."

"That's what I wanted to talk to you about. I just have to file my story first."

"I'll be home," Vincent said, "though I can't say I'll be very good company."

"That's okay. I won't stay long."

This wasn't going to be easy. Vincent was going to accuse her of abandoning him, but she had to hope that when push came to shove he would agree that the newspaper had to come first. Or she'd made a huge mistake coming here.

I left a good union job for this.

The obvious ties between the Battrelles, Fontaines, and her own family concerned her, but she wasn't ready to tell that to Vincent—or anyone at the paper. Not yet anyway.

Linda's eyes glazed over as Katrina recounted the slim news bite from the presser, but she came to attention as soon as Katrina mentioned the management changes at Vitaleron involving Michael Battrelle. Her tight lips registered surprise, then discomfort, as Katrina described the ring of TV cameras that captured his pallid face and visible distress as he spoke.

"So that's that, then, isn't it? I'll have to tell John Palmer that we have no choice but to go ahead with plan B," Linda said.

Katrina wasn't exactly sure what plan B was, but she hoped it meant she was free to do her job properly.

"Hold on, there's more," she said brightly. "The major news of the day, which other media outlets don't have, is that the police served search warrants at Vitaleron headquarters and Dr. Fontaine's surgical office this morning, where they were looking for syringes and doing drug audits. I've also got some juicy background info on Victoria Fontaine from two schoolmates."

"Oh, good. That's a relief. Start writing now so we can get it online before anyone gets wind of this. If we give our competitors something to chase, we'll stay one step ahead of them. I'll have Norman Klein feed you what he's got from the presser. He might have gotten a few tidbits that you didn't. Send me the story when you're done, and we'll run it up the pike."

"What does that mean?" Katrina asked.

"John Palmer and the lawyers will have to sign off on it," she said. "He's not going to like it, but we don't have much of a choice. For now, it's mostly about Vitaleron, so we should be okay."

Frozen in her chair, Katrina stared at the blank computer screen. It was difficult to navigate the land mines, but once she got going, the words started to flow. She had plenty of good material for a daily story.

Thankfully, the editing went pretty quickly, because she purposely pulled her punches for another day. The rest of her research needed more time to steep, anyway.

While she was waiting to be released, she ran Goode's name through the archives. She was surprised to find a year-old story by Norman Klein, describing how Goode had saved him from an armed, mentally ill woman from the cliffs of Black's Beach, right before she jumped to her death.

Wow. That is some crazy shit. Goode is a good man.

Linda let her go at 7:30 p.m., after which she headed straight to Vincent's place.

CHAPTER 20
GOODE

Monday

After the news conference, Goode headed inside police HQ to his desk, wondering why the mayor had asked the chief to hold the damn thing and then didn't show up. Maybe a politically savvy insider had warned him at the last minute that it would be ill advised to appear at a news conference with Vitaleron flunkies on city property. Because it was. Good call.

It also had been niggling him all day why the Vitaleron parking lot was so empty. Whoever owned the building could be doing more with it—unless, as he'd theorized, they were running a black ops program on the other floors that required absolute secrecy and no visible staffing.

Clicking on the county assessor's website, he learned that the building was owned by Lexicon Group LLC, registered to an address on Prospect Street in La Jolla. Lexicon appeared to be a shell company, because its corporate formation paperwork listed no other specific purpose.

Cross-checking Lexicon with the secretary of state, he found corporate formation documents filed eight years earlier, stating that Simon Fontaine was president, Peter Chopin was vice president,

Vincent Battrelle was treasurer, and Francis Chopin was the registered agent. But when its annual form was filed three years later, Fontaine and the Chopins were gone. Vincent was president, and his two sons were vice president and treasurer.

Typing "Vitaleron" into the same corporation-search page, he saw that it was formed two years before Lexicon bought the building that now housed Vitaleron's HQ, and it originally had three founding partners: Simon Fontaine, Vincent Battrelle, and Peter Chopin. But Chopin's name was dropped from the paperwork the following year, just as it was with Lexicon.

Vincent Battrelle must have bought the other partners out of the building or made some other arrangement. And this Peter Chopin character was also involved in Vitaleron as well. Was Fontaine having financial troubles even back then?

Then it hit him.

Peter and Francis Chopin? Was that Katrina's family?

Googling "Double-Judge Murders" again, he reread the stories: Peter and Aphrodite Chopin were Katrina's parents, and their son was Francis. It hadn't clicked before because he didn't focus on their names. At Piatti, Katrina never mentioned her last name or her parents', and when she did mention her brother, she always called him Franny.

Goode found it curious that the Vitaleron website made no mention of Peter Chopin as a founding partner. The man was a ghost. Vincent Battrelle wasn't credited as such either, only as the second-largest investor to the founder, Simon Fontaine.

So, Peter was either a silent partner or he dropped out entirely. Was that because he was a judge? Or something else?

Diving back into the *Advocate* story about the judge murders, he viewed the conspiracy theory with a whole new perspective, noting that Vincent Battrelle had also invested in Franny Chopin's final project, the one that tanked before he died.

Maybe it's not so crazy that the Advocate *linked all three deaths in the Chopin family to this failed hotel project. You'd think the PD would have been all over this. Did the killer have an inside guy in our agency, and if so, does this mean Katrina could be in danger? Should I even tell her about these filings? If she's already done the same research I did, you'd think she would have said something about it.*

Either way, he needed answers, because right now, Vincent and his family were looking more and more like the nexus. Growing up, Goode had learned a lesson as he watched a few of his wealthier classmates and their family members go to prison: Follow the money. That lesson had served him well in Vice, and even more so in Homicide.

With this new information and Alex MIA, he needed Vincent to explain what was going on behind the scenes at Vitaleron. He also needed a better understanding of the dynamics between the Fontaines and Battrelles, all the way back to their partnership with Peter Chopin. It was time to pay Vincent a surprise visit.

Vincent Battrelle answered Goode's knock holding a crystal tumbler of whiskey on the rocks that was almost overflowing. He was visibly surprised and disappointed to see Goode standing there.

"Detective Goode, Homicide," Goode said, pulling out his badge.

"I was expecting someone else," Vincent said, pausing, apparently, to get his bearings.

Looks like he's had a couple of those. He seems confused. And agitated.

"Can we talk inside?" Goode asked.

"Can we do this tomorrow?" Vincent countered.

"It won't take long, and we may need to follow up tomorrow at the station, because I will probably have more questions."

"Why? What's going on?"

Vincent wasn't budging, and Goode was tiring of the delay tactics. "Are you going to let me in?"

Sighing, Vincent finally stepped aside. "Yes, all right, I suppose. Let's go to the living room, right down here," he said.

Plopping into the armchair next to Goode on the couch, Vincent took a sip of his drink, then smacked it down on the table.

"Sorry," he said. "The glass is wet and slippery. So, what's so important that you needed to come to my house?"

"First, I'm sorry for the loss of your friends, the Fontaines, and second, I'm sorry for the loss of what was likely your grandchild. I assume by now you've heard that Victoria was pregnant."

"Yes, I heard it on TV. You guys could have given us a private heads-up. My son Michael didn't tell me until afterward that they'd been dating for the past five months and that it was possibly his child she was carrying."

"Yes, or his brother's," Goode said.

"Alex? No. I haven't seen him in six months."

"Well, I have texts from Victoria's phone showing that Alex was at the Fontaine house the night before they were found dead and that he left the following morning."

Vincent shook his head. "That's not possible."

"What do you mean?"

"I mean he's literally been off the radar for six months. I actually hired an investigator to find him."

"Just because you don't know where he is doesn't mean he wasn't there. I have an independent source who says Simon Fontaine saw him there Thursday night. What was your relationship like with Simon?" Goode asked.

Vincent's eyes flashed with anger. "What are you implying?"

"It's just a question. Was there some bad blood, a financial problem, or a falling-out between you?"

"No, nothing like that. The last disagreement we had was about Alex, and that was two years ago."

"Oh?"

"Simon said he wanted Alex off the board for missing too many meetings, but I just think he didn't like having my son on there, challenging his ideas. Alex is brilliant, you know. He's had his problems, but he's got a great business mind. Nonetheless, Simon seemed threatened by him, so he orchestrated a vote to remove him. When I countermanded by getting Michael appointed, Simon backed off. He seemed to like Michael well enough. He's easier to control."

"Did you know that Simon Fontaine was shot in the head?"

Like his son, Vincent was guarded, but he didn't look entirely surprised by the question.

"Yes, I think I heard that," Vincent said with a careful, if not calculated, nonchalance. Knowing they hadn't released that detail publicly, Goode threw him a baited fishing line.

"Do you think he was the kind of man who would kill himself?"

Vincent's face brightened, almost too predictably. "You know, it's curious you say that, because he didn't seem like himself lately."

"How's that?"

"He was far more irritable and irrational than usual. Like he had too much on his plate."

"Really?"

"Yes."

"You think there was more going on at home or at work than we know about?"

"I think that's a very real possibility."

Now for the zinger.

"I see that Peter Chopin partnered with you and Simon on the Vitaleron building, but then he dropped off the paperwork. And he was also one of the original founding partners of Vitaleron, yet he's not even mentioned on the website. Was he bounced before or after he was murdered?" Goode asked.

Vincent dropped his glass, which shattered on the tile floor, sending shards in every direction as the pool of whiskey crept toward the steps.

"Dammit!" Vincent said loudly, but he didn't move. Paralyzed, apparently. *I guess I hit a nerve.*

The sound of the doorbell chiming brought Vincent back, as he looked around frantically for something to wipe up the mess. Goode, who was enjoying the spectacle, didn't offer to help. He was too busy observing.

"Could you get the door, please?" Vincent muttered. "I've got to find a towel or something."

"Sure, why not," Goode muttered back, more than a little annoyed that his interrogation ploy had not only lost its spontaneous impact to the doorbell but also created a delay that gave Vincent time to conjure up a creative answer.

The detective made his way through the labyrinthian maze to the front door, where he was pleased, and a bit amused, to see Katrina. But the serendipity seemed to startle her, as she stood silently staring back at him. As if she'd been caught doing something she wasn't supposed to.

"What are *you* doing here?" she blurted out.

"I could say the same to you," he said, relishing the moment. "I'm doing a little police business. How 'bout you?"

"I came to talk to Vincent," she said. "I mean, Mr. Battrelle."

"Uh-huh."

"But I'm going to go since you guys are obviously busy," she said, turning to leave. "Can you please tell him I'll come back in a bit?"

"Sure thing."

What was that all about? I'll have to pry the details out of her later.

Back in the living room, Vincent was picking up the glass shards and placing them into the small kitchen trash bin.

"Ow, shit!" he exclaimed, dropping one of them to shatter some more.

As the blood streamed from Vincent's index finger and dripped on the floor, Goode grabbed a roll of paper towels from the coffee table.

"Here, give me your hand," he offered.

Looking panicked, Vincent extended his bloody right hand. While his finger was being bound with a folded towel, Vincent's shoulders slumped with what Goode imagined was embarrassment and humility, two emotions the man likely didn't exhibit often. As Goode squeezed tighter, Vincent grimaced and looked away.

"Am I going to need stitches?" he asked.

Opening the towel, Goode was shocked by the amount of blood, but the seepage seemed to be slowing. "I'll keep the pressure on for a bit longer, and hopefully it'll start clotting up. If you can keep it higher, gravity will help."

"You threw me with that question about Peter," Vincent admitted.

"Okay, so do you want to explain that to me?"

Visibly trying to shake off the whiskey fog, Vincent answered contemplatively: "The short answer is that Peter thought his wife and I were having an affair, which we weren't, although I was probably still in love with her. He could never get past the fact that Aphy and I dated back in law school. She was quite a woman, but she said I wasn't the one. Next thing I knew she was engaged, married, and pregnant with twins, and in what order, I'm not sure. Thirty years later, Peter still couldn't accept that she'd already picked him over me. When I learned that we'd hired Katrina last week, I invited her over here for a drink. I couldn't get over how much she reminded me of her mother. She's just as beautiful and talented, too, it seems."

So, Vincent was her source.

"This falling-out came after you all went in together on Vitaleron and the Lexicon property?"

"Yes. We were all members of the University Club downtown. Peter saw me talking to Aphy at a couple of speaker lunches and cocktail mixers. Maybe they were having problems at the time. I don't know. But he divested from Vitaleron and the building shortly after that and said he wanted his name wiped from any documents or websites."

"How did he know Simon?"

"We were all in a family drug-and-alcohol treatment group together at the McDonald Center. Our kids were in and out of the group, but we, the parents, still attended the group periodically to share personal stories and challenges, because relapses were common. Simon was looking for investors in Vitaleron, then the property became available, and the rest is history."

Why did you drop the glass when I mentioned his name, then? I've got a hunch you're holding something back, if not lying. Just like your son.

"Where were you the day Victoria and Simon died?"

"I was playing golf at Torrey Pines with some Vitaleron board members," he said. "I've got a receipt from the clubhouse bar if you want to see it."

Well, that's a convenient alibi.

"What time was that?"

"We were there all afternoon and into the early evening," he said.

Well, that doesn't cover the timing of the 911 call. But it could help us flesh out the overall timeline.

"Okay. Yes, I'd like to see the receipt, please."

Vincent seemed to have collected himself. "If I'm going to get it, I'll need my hand back, Detective," he said.

"Looks like it's stopped bleeding," Goode said, opening the towel for another peek.

"My wallet's in the bedroom."

Goode thought about taking the bloody wad of towels on the coffee table as a DNA sample. But he figured he'd better go by the book.

Who knows what these sex-crazed old dudes are up to these days. What if he's the baby's father? We might even find his DNA at the Fontaine house.

After Vincent returned with the receipt, Goode stood up, holding the damp towel wad in his hand. "You want me to take care of this?" he asked nonchalantly.

If he says yes, then it's mine to enter into evidence.

Vincent shrugged. "Sure, thanks. I'm going to leave this broken glass until tomorrow, when it's lighter, so I can see what I'm doing without causing any more damage."

"Where did you go after drinks at the club?" Goode asked, shoving the wad into his pocket like it was no big deal.

I'll put this into a plastic evidence bag as soon as I get back to the car.

"I stopped by the Shores to watch the sunset, then came home and fell asleep watching TV on the couch," he said. "My wife and daughter were packing to leave for Italy the next morning—a trip planned for months, by the way—so they were running around in a tizzy."

"Planned for months?"

"Yes, Warren and I were supposed to play with Simon at our usual annual charity golf tournament this past weekend, but neither of us were up for it after what happened."

Still seems convenient, but at least their stories are consistent . . . though it's not an easy alibi to disprove with mom and daughter in Italy.

"Is it possible Alex went with them?" Goode asked innocently.

"No, they would have told me," he said.

"So, I won't find him if I check the airline manifest?"

"Do what you need to do, Detective, and if you do happen to find him, please let me know so I can call off the investigator," Vincent said.

"What are your wife's and daughter's names, and what airline did they fly?"

"Ruth and Meredith. United to Heathrow and Alitalia to Rome, I believe. I assume we're done here; I need to eat something," he added, turning to walk away. "By the way, was that Katrina Chopin at the door? I was expecting her."

"Yes, it was. She said to tell you she'd come back in a bit. I'd ice that hand if I were you. Keep the swelling down. Then bandage it up."

Back in his vehicle, Goode tucked the bloody towel into a plastic evidence bag so they could run a profile to test for any DNA comparisons that might come up. First thing in the morning, he would call the airlines to check on flights from Halloween night and the next morning.

It was all a little much to be a simple coincidence—the personal history between the Fontaines, the Battrelles, and now Katrina's family too; Vincent Battrelle's fallings-out with both Simon Fontaine and Peter Chopin; and the timing of Katrina's reappearance in town, dovetailing with the Fontaines' deaths.

Stone was looking out for Goode by telling him not to step over the line with Katrina, but now that Goode had found this new information about her father's connection to the Vitaleron clan, he felt he needed to stay even closer to her.

CHAPTER 21
KATRINA

Monday

After moving her Land Rover down the street and out of view, Katrina waited for what seemed like hours for Goode to leave so she could extricate herself from the crafty old man's grip. Tapping her fingers on the steering wheel, she finally saw Goode at the top of the driveway, looking pleased with himself. It was eight o'clock, a good thirty minutes since she'd rung the bell. She watched him get into a black Ford Explorer, then just sit there.

I guess the VW van is his personal car. The Explorer must be his work car. Less noisy and probably more gas efficient, I'm sure.

"What's he doing now?" she whispered. "I hope he's not going to spend hours doing surveillance."

Katrina's phone rang. It was Goode. She let it go to voicemail, hoping he would go home faster. She would call him later.

As soon as Goode started up his car and took off, Katrina swung her heels out of her car and onto the asphalt and marched down the driveway.

Vincent won't be in a great mood after getting grilled by a homicide detective, but this can't wait any longer.

Vincent took even more time to open the door this time, but she could see why: His right index finger was bandaged up, which made it hard for him to open the door while holding a half-eaten chicken drumstick.

"So, that *was* you before," he said, slurring his words. His sweet alcohol breath wafted toward her. "Did the detective tell you to leave? I wish you'd come in. He probably would have left sooner. Look what he made me do."

Waving his bandaged finger, he turned and motioned for her to follow him through a maze of hallways into the kitchen.

"Watch out for the glass," he said, gesturing toward the shards on the floor.

"What happened?" she asked.

"He got me so upset that I dropped one of my favorite crystal glasses and cut a gash into my finger. Wasted a snootful of eighteen-year-old scotch too. Why don't you grab that bottle of Chardonnay in the fridge and pour us both a glass."

"I'm not here to socialize, Vincent. I came on business."

"Do you have news on Alex?" he asked hopefully.

"No, but that's why I'm here."

"Okay," he said, leaning against one of the stools at the counter. "Even if you aren't going to have any wine, can you pour me some? I'm wounded."

"Are you sure you haven't had enough to drink?"

"Excuse me?" he snapped. "You're out of line, missy."

"Well, you did already cut yourself," she said. But since he was still pouting, she handed him half a glass from the nearly empty bottle. "Here."

"That's a measly pour if I ever saw one. I might as well finish it," he said, dumping the rest into his glass.

I can see where Alex got the addictive personality gene.

"I'll have you know that's what's left of the second bottle my wife and daughter drank on Friday night. I've had a rough day and an even rougher night, so give me a break, would you?"

She could see from his mental state that he wasn't going to withstand more bad news very well, but she had no choice.

"I'm sorry you may have lost a grandchild," she said.

That's all it took. A little softness and Vincent crumpled before her eyes.

"It's so sad," he said, his face falling. "My first grandbaby."

Vincent may be a Machiavellian jerk, but he's losing the people he loves, one at a time, and that makes him seem more human.

His eyes welling up, he wobbled off to the nearest bathroom to blow his nose. Even if he was acting like a child, he knew not to cry in front of an employee.

Meanwhile, Katrina was getting a different perspective of the paper's owner than anyone else in the newsroom, possibly even Linda. Still, she couldn't let his mood neutralize her purpose in coming over, and that moment couldn't wait any longer.

After flushing the toilet, Vincent emerged. His eyes were watery, though his face was dry. Except for his sweaty forehead, which he'd forgotten to swab.

"Let's try this again," he said quietly. "What made you come over twice tonight?"

Katrina took a deep breath, shaking her head as she spoke. "I'm sorry for the timing. I know you've had a bad day, but I needed to tell you in person: I can't cover this story for the paper and still help you find Alex, because the two investigations are not just intersecting, they're colliding, so—"

"Hold on a minute," Vincent interrupted. "Are you saying that you can't help me find Alex? I don't understand how any of this is mutually exclusive."

Is he purposely being obtuse, or is he drunk?

"I'm trying to be honest with you. Do you not see that this is a giant ethical conflict?" she asked, looking him straight in the eyes now. "Especially when you asked me not to write anything I learned about

Alex. But it seems to me that the two issues are not only related, they're irretrievably inseparable."

"Well, that's a mouthful," Vincent said, bobbling onto one of the stools and holding back a chortle.

Why is he not taking me seriously?

"Can you explain this in more detail? Because I'm not going to let you quit. I mean, ultimately, I am your boss."

It was no use trying to have a rational discussion with a drunk person. Katrina didn't know what else to say.

I'm reporting a story that has placed you and your family smack in the middle of a murder investigation. Why do I have to be the one to make you face that? Shouldn't that be John Palmer's job?

"This is all very awkward, but I have some promising leads that I don't think I should discuss with you, because it could compromise the story," she finally said. "I mean, come on, a homicide detective was just here interviewing you."

Vincent stared at her noncommittally and took a gulp of wine. "Go on."

"Linda assigned me to this story and told me to focus my full attention on the Fontaines and the dynamics of their personal and business relationships. Well, that directly involves you and your sons, one of whom has mysteriously vanished. I can't keep all this separate or out of the paper."

Even if he was drunk, Vincent had to understand that.

"Listen, I appreciate what you're saying. I do," he said. "But I need your help. I can't trust anyone else. Keep going with this, and we'll talk again in a day or two."

Why is he not getting this? Or is he simply not willing to accept it? Legally, I should be safe because I never signed his damn NDA.

"I don't need another day or two," she said as firmly as she could. "I'm done." Tossing out a Hail Mary, she asked, "Can you give me Michael's cell number? That way I can catch him even if he's not at work."

But Drunk Vincent was not only uncooperative, he was downright ornery. "Why do you need to call him?"

"I need to know more about what was going on between him, Alex, and Victoria. I still need to figure out where Alex went and what happened to the Fontaines, so you'll get your answers one way or another," she said.

"I'd rather you left Michael alone," he said. "You saw how upset he was at the news conference today. He's got a lot on his plate as the new CFO. Why don't you focus on those other names I gave you and go from there. Here's fifty bucks," he said digging into his wallet and pulling out a Ulysses S. Grant. "If you don't want to drink with me, go have one and some food on me at George's. Rick, one of the bartenders there, is Alex's surfing buddy from way back. He does card tricks. Talk to *him* about Alex and Victoria."

"Thanks for the offer, but I can't accept your money," she said. "Although that's not a bad suggestion. I've had quite a day myself."

Walking back to her car, she felt her apprehension building. Any reporter with a brain would suspect that Alex or Michael was either involved in, or knew something about, Victoria's death.

What would happen if she called Michael at Vitaleron? Vincent would be upset because he'd asked her not to, and Linda would be angry because Katrina had defied a direct order.

But what else is new?

Katrina was too tired to go to George's, a pricey, three-tiered hot spot of restaurants and bars in the village of La Jolla. Instead, she picked up a couple of pizza slices in Hillcrest and ate them with a cup of red wine in her apartment, followed by a second cup. She played her guitar for a little while until she felt her mind had cleared a bit.

It was late by the time she lay down, but she couldn't seem to get comfortable on the floor. She had a hard time shutting off her brain, which kept coming up with questions she wanted to ask Michael Battrelle.

CHAPTER 22
GOODE

Tuesday

First item on Goode's to-do list Tuesday morning was to drop Vincent's bloody paper towel at the crime lab. It would give him the perfect opportunity to inquire about the status of the gunshot-residue tests and fingerprint/DNA analysis of the gun. Because he still hadn't heard whether they'd found the missing casing or the fired bullet, he figured they were lagging behind.

Do I need to go look for them myself? The longer they wait, the higher the chance a family member will come in and kick them somewhere else by accident.

While he waited for the lab to open, he called the airlines. Starting with United, he learned that Vincent's wife and daughter did, in fact, fly to Heathrow at 10:00 a.m. on Saturday, and Alex was not with them. A subsequent call to American revealed that Alex had been on a nine o'clock flight for the Cayman Islands the night before.

That was right around the time of the 911 call, although Dr. Thompson said those bodies were down for at least several hours before that. Seems like pretty coincidental timing. But what are the Cayman Islands good for besides financial shenanigans?

"That flight was late taking off, so they didn't hit the runway until nine thirty," the representative said.

Technically, that still gave him time to make the 911 call before boarding or while the plane was still sitting on the tarmac.

Alex was the last known person to see Victoria alive that morning. He also said in his text that he was planning to come back, but didn't, which made him a likely suspect.

"Innocent people don't run," Stone said when Goode called to brief him. "So, does he come back, find her dead, thinks it's an overdose that might incriminate him, and flee? Or do they argue over whose kid she's carrying—his, his brother's, or someone else's—Simon comes to her aid, a struggle ensues, and Alex tries to cover his tracks by injecting them both? Or is Alex on a binge, he and Victoria shoot up together, she dies, he freaks, and takes the drugs and syringes with him? Don't ask me how Simon dies in that scenario. But someone shot him, and why else would Alex take off for the Caymans unless something went bad?"

"Okay, but if any one of those scenarios happened, then why is Michael lying to us?" Goode asked. "Based on his texts, Victoria wouldn't take his call or respond to his texts. So maybe he's the one who comes over, is furious to learn she's been with Alex, and injects her with something to make it look like a suicide, which is why it was so sloppy. As a recovering heroin addict, Alex wouldn't have made such a mess of it, and Michael is the one who's pushing the suicide scenario. Vincent implied that as well, and he didn't seem surprised when I told him Simon had been shot in the head."

"Okay, but then why would either of them inject and/or shoot Simon?"

"Fear? To frame someone else? Or it could be purely financial, to protect Vitaleron or the Battrelle family investments from scandal. Something is definitely off with this clan. The Caymans are a haven for offshore accounts and dubious investment activities. Half the family is lying, and the other half is hopping on the first plane out of here. Vincent's and Dr. Russell's wives and daughters left the country on

Saturday as well. They said they were preplanned trips, but what if they weren't?"

"Alex hasn't been doing anything related to Vitaleron for a couple of years, though," Stone said.

"That we know of."

"What other financial shenanigans could be going on?"

"No idea. We need those tox screens and the security footage."

"Once we have those, we'll be good."

"That's what she said," Goode said.

"Okay, one of us has to hang up now."

CHAPTER 23
KATRINA

Tuesday

Katrina woke up, sweating, with a headache and heartburn at 4:30 a.m. Her heart was pounding and her chest was tight. The two cups of wine before bed hadn't helped, and the weather report predicted that a Santa Ana would blow into town later that day. But she knew that the overall sense of dread she felt stemmed from something more serious—her recurring nightmare, which had started in Northampton, had come back:

After being chased and almost run over by a black Lincoln Town Car, she was tased, blindfolded, and yanked inside. Taken to a recycling plant, she was thrown onto a conveyor belt and sent down a chute to the cruncher, a giant machine that squished enormous piles of sticky soda bottles. She always jerked awake before being sucked inside, but as soon as she drifted off again, snippets of the dream repeated in an infinite loop.

"Not this again," she groaned, digging through her purse for her inhaler. She took a quick puff as the traumatic memories of her mafia series flooded back.

The day her first story ran about Mattie "the Hatter" Sienkiewicz, police found the body of the school superintendent's wife in the brush next to the riverbed. Nearly decapitated, she had a deep furrow around her neck from being strangled with a metal wire. Her eyes were also gouged out and left next to her body, apparently as a cautionary message to Katrina that her source had been murdered for what she'd seen—and done.

What made it even scarier, though, were the calls that came in on Katrina's unpublished home number in Northampton.

"We know where you live," the man whispered with what sounded like a Polish accent. "We follow you to work. We follow you home. You'd better watch your back."

After filing her follow-up story on the murder that night, Katrina lay awake, jumping at every creak inside her old house and every sound outside her window, fearing that someone was coming to strangle her with a wire.

Hearing a car engine, she got out of bed and lifted one of the slats of her blinds. A black Town Car with tinted windows was parked at the curb. As the window rolled partway down, a stream of cigar smoke billowed out and seeped into her room, even with her windows locked. The barrel of a gun slid out of the window, pointed at the house, and stayed there a couple of minutes before the car slowly rolled away.

She immediately called the Northampton police watch commander to report that someone was trying to kill her, or at least threatening to.

"You get a license plate or any other identifying information?" he asked.

"No, it was dark, but I think it was Mattie Sienkiewicz's crew," she replied.

"It could be anybody. Lock your doors and windows."

He was still mad at her, apparently, for her coverage of the sergeants' contract negotiations. Suffice it to say, she got no sleep that night.

The next morning, her editor wasn't happy to hear that she'd gone "outside the family" by alerting the police, but he backed off once he realized how ridiculous that was. If the paper didn't try to protect her, what message would it send to staff if she were disciplined?

Instead, her editor persuaded the police chief to have an officer patrol her house every couple of hours at night, watching out for the Town Car or any other suspicious activity. That was cheaper than putting her up in a hotel or hiring an armed guard to sit and guard her house overnight. The patrols helped, but even when she was able to drop off, it was a shallow, restless doze, broken up by flashes of the nightmare.

She insisted on finishing the series through all of this. Once the crooks were arrested and put behind bars to await trial, the nightmare stopped. Until now.

Katrina knew the situation with Vincent was bad, but she hadn't realized it was *that* bad until the nightmare returned. Her subconscious was clearly telling her to free herself of this psychological conflict.

The question is, how do I stay safe and not lose my mind while balancing all these internal politics? I came back to get my parents' case reopened. I'm not quitting, and I'm not going to let them fire me either.

After failing to get back to sleep, Katrina looked online for a Starbucks that was open at 5:30 a.m. She found one in Bankers Hill, an old neighborhood full of cool old buildings with enclosed gardens and newly built condo complexes, adjacent to Balboa Park.

Katrina was dragging as she climbed the steep set of stairs leading to the carport, looking forward to a double cappuccino to lift the brain fog. Heavy on her feet, she almost twisted her ankle on the last step, where she stumbled and caught herself by grabbing the railing.

The strap of her purse—heavy with detritus she didn't really need—slipped off her shoulder and fell with a thump to the inner crease of her elbow. She was righting herself and pulling the strap up to her shoulder when she saw her car.

Holy shit!

The entire passenger-side window was cracked like a spiderweb, with a hole in the center where the rock had hit. She knew it was a rock because the perpetrator had left his weapon on her hood like a signature, with a note fastened to it by a thick rubber band. A few glass shards lay in the bed of her windshield wipers, but miraculously, none had landed inside her car.

As she unfolded the note, she slowly revealed one of those clichéd untraceable messages crafted out of letters cut out of a glossy magazine:

> Hey, Miss Rock Star Reporter, we see you're back in town, digging where you shouldn't be. Watch your back or it won't be your car window that gets whacked next time. Could even look like another suicide.

What the hell did I do, coming back here?

She couldn't even guess who had drafted the note, because the references seemed so all-inclusive. Was this related to her parents' murders, her brother's suspicious death, or, given the "watch your back" language, possibly to the Mattie Sienkiewicz situation back in Northampton?

I've only written one story so far about the Fontaine case. Is that what triggered this?

Whirling around, she scanned the canyon's edge for anyone hiding or scurrying away. Had they been watching her through the sliding glass doors of her living room from up here? The angle didn't seem right, seeing that the carport was up and around the corner from her apartment. No one could see into her second-floor unit from the driveway below her balcony, either, and the canyon sloped down from there. So, she didn't see any possible vantage point where someone could sit and observe her. They would have to stand with binoculars half a mile away on the UCSD Medical Center's rooftop to do that. Seemed like a lot of trouble to go to, but still doable. The question was, how did they know where she lived?

Did someone follow me home from the paper last night?

She whipped out her cell phone to call Goode, but after thinking it over, decided it was best to keep her work and personal issues separate. She punched in 911 instead.

While she waited for a patrol officer to arrive, Katrina snapped photos of her broken window, the rock sitting on the hood, and a close-up of the note.

Is "watch your back" standard gangster language?

She also left a voicemail for Joanne, asking her to call as soon as possible.

When an officer rolled up to take a report, she told him that she couldn't be sure if it was the work of the Polish mafia in Northampton, someone local who knew her family's history, or if it could be related to the Fontaine case. He took photos of the car and the note as well.

Katrina was still shaking as he drove away, and she hadn't even had any caffeine yet.

CHAPTER 24
GOODE

Tuesday

Due to the potential link to the Fontaine case, Goode got a call from HQ, alerting him to Katrina's 911 call shortly after she made it. But before he had a chance to follow up with her personally, his phone rang with the number he recognized from not-so-pleasant past experiences. It was the FBI.

What the hell do the Feebs want? Did they find out about the threat to Katrina already? I wonder if they have a lead on her parents' murder case.

"Detective Goode?"

"Speaking."

"This is Supervisory Special Agent Martin Watts with the FBI."

"Yes, I recognized the number. What can I help you with?"

"I understand you were calling the airlines, inquiring about Alex Battrelle."

So, it's not about Katrina. They're calling about Alex? Interesting.

"Correct."

"I wanted to let you know that he's under active investigation by the bureau, the SEC, and the IRS. We have him flagged with the airlines, which is how we learned of your inquiries. As you can imagine, this is, well, a delicate situation."

"Why's that?"

"We've been watching him for the past eighteen months and as of this week we have him right where we want him. He's in the Cayman Islands, as you now know, where he's conducting illegal transactions as we speak. We're letting that play out so we can obtain an arrest warrant in the case we've been building."

"I see."

"What's your interest in Alex Battrelle, Detective?"

"He's a person of interest in a special death investigation."

"The Fontaines?"

"Yes. So, I have a delicate situation as well, Special Agent Marty—I'm sorry, what did you say your last name was?"

"It's Martin Watts, and that's supervisory special agent, Detective."

"Right. We need him to come in for questioning right away. He's at least a material witness and at worst a killer, so maybe we can help each other here."

"Well, we don't want to alert him to our investigation at this critical juncture, so I'm not sure how we can help, but I'm happy to look over your evidence and see if it holds water."

Goode felt his blood pressure rising. "Holds water? Listen, I can't just 'send over' my evidence. We're trying to build a case too. How long before you have what you need from him?"

"Maybe a week. It depends on how fast he works."

A week? That's no bueno. Especially now that we have the Katrina potential-victim angle, as unfortunately convenient as that may be.

"I don't know that we have a week. There's another potential victim who might be in imminent danger. That's why we want to talk to Battrelle ASAP. He fled the country hours after the Fontaines were killed, and if he didn't do it, he most likely knows who did. You want that on your head?"

Watts was silent a moment. "I thought you hadn't decided that it was a murder."

"Technically we haven't, but we're definitely leaning that way. What exactly is Alex Battrelle doing in the Caymans, anyway?"

"He's hiding money for some of the wealthiest men in La Jolla, Del Mar, and Rancho Santa Fe. Men going through messy divorces, men having affairs, men being dogs. You're a homicide detective; you know the kind I'm talking about. The men who feel entitled to do whatever they please, screw the tax and securities laws, until they get caught. *If* they get caught. Those men. The problem is they all have very good lawyers who make our jobs difficult, so we need to have them cold, and we don't want Mr. Battrelle dumping accounts because he knows we're on to him."

"Gotcha. So, how about this. There's a two-hour time difference and it's a six-hour flight. Why don't we agree that he has to be at the police station for questioning by Thursday at three p.m., but we won't mention any federal investigation."

"That's not long enough."

"This is not just a professional courtesy. I've got two dead and the life of a third potential victim is at stake. Plus, when my lieutenant breathes down my sergeant's neck, my neck gets pretty hot too. Who is Mr. Battrelle's lawyer?"

"Milton Biggs."

"Of course he is. How 'bout this. I'll tell Biggs that we'd like his client to be at the police station Thursday at three o'clock, but we're asking that he come back voluntarily. Otherwise, we'll have to ask the Cayman authorities to escort him onto a plane. That way, he won't dump any accounts, because he'll think it's about the Fontaine investigation."

Goode could hear Watts breathing as he mulled Goode's proposal. "Okay, Detective. Give it a shot and get back to me, but do me a favor. Don't blow my investigation trying to save a *potential* victim's life."

After they hung up, Goode couldn't help himself.

"Asshole."

CHAPTER 25
KATRINA

Tuesday

Despite the early hour, the café in Bankers Hill was surprisingly busy with patrons dressed in flannel jammies or workout clothes. Katrina ordered her usual double cappuccino, along with egg bites for a protein boost, and a slab of lemon bundt cake to salve that morning's traumas.

Picking up the local news section from one of the tables, she was pleased to see her story displayed across the top. She'd given Norman Klein a tagline at the bottom as a courtesy, but an editor had added his name to hers in a double byline. It wasn't that she minded sharing a byline, but this story didn't warrant it. She already had the quotes he'd sent her, and she'd only included one of them to be gracious.

Is that a message from John Palmer that he wants Norman or Jerry—anyone but me—on this story?

Just then, Joanne called back. Katrina had wanted to discuss the Vincent situation and the deal that Goode had offered her, but now she was going to have to report the death threat as well.

"I need to tell you something upsetting that happened this morning, and I also need some advice, but it has to be on the DL," Katrina said. "Could you possibly come meet me? It's important."

"Sure, I agree, best not to meet at the paper. Let's say eight o'clock at the koi pond next to the arboretum in Balboa Park," Joanne said.

Katrina agreed, pleased that the rendezvous spot was conveniently within walking distance.

With some time to kill before heading over, she whipped out her journal. It had been a while since she'd had the time or the mindset to write in it. She was describing how she'd met Goode at Piatti when he actually sauntered into the café with Sergeant Stone.

The sergeant was stockier and older than Goode, with graying temples and a soft belly, but he had a friendly face and a thick head of hair, so they were both good looking enough to qualify as models in *Middle-Aged Surfing Magazine*. Clutching zip-up leather man-pouches, they looked out of character in jackets and ties.

Huddled up in line, they talked softly into each other's ear. Goode shrugged at one point, as if to say "Hell if I know." They were both laughing when Goode glanced over Stone's shoulder and saw her sitting there. He gave her a discreet nod and whispered to Stone, who turned around indiscreetly and stared at her. She waved at them, Goode waved back, and Stone's face turned red.

After picking up their coffee, they stopped by her table in the corner, brows furrowed with concern.

"Hey, Katrina. I got a call from HQ alerting me to your 911 call this morning. Are you okay?" Goode asked. "Is your car drivable?"

Katrina was taken aback, not expecting him to find out before she had a chance to tell him herself.

"Yeah, I'm okay, the car's fine. A little shaken up is all," she fibbed.

"Did you take photos, I hope?" Goode asked.

"Of course," she said, pulling out her phone to show the detectives.

"Wow," Stone said. "That's not good." Catching himself, he apologized and extended his hand to shake Katrina's. "Hi, sorry. Rusty Stone. Goode has told me all about your investigative talents, which, I guess, some folks are pretty scared of."

"Seems that way. Nice to meet you. I recognize you from both news conferences," she said. Trying to change the subject, she asked, "What's with the ties? Big powwow somewhere I should know about?"

Stone looked at Goode, opening his eyes wide melodramatically, like a cartoon. "Oh, she's good," he said, smiling mischievously, relieved, apparently, that she was taking the rock incident in stride.

"I know, I keep telling you that," Goode said to Stone, then to Katrina he said, "I'll call you in a bit and you can tell me more about it."

"Actually, we do have to run to a powwow, as a matter of fact. Nice meeting you," Stone said. "I'm sure we'll be talking."

As they headed out, Stone tried to whisper, but Katrina heard every word.

"You never said she was *that* attractive. You're right. You'd have to be comatose not to want to hit that. But don't."

Well, then.

Sucking down the foamy dregs of her cappuccino, Katrina picked up her purse and followed the surfing duo from a safe distance down Fifth Avenue, where they headed into an office building.

When she caught up a few minutes later, she scanned the directory of occupants. Only one popped out: Milton Biggs & Associates.

That's where Darren McMurphy works. Maybe they're questioning him?

By then it was seven thirty, so she turned around to head back. She was wearing heeled sandals, but it was such a nice sunny morning that she took them off to go barefoot for the twenty-minute walk to the arboretum.

Turning right on Laurel, one of the cross streets near Balboa Park, which were all named after a different type of tree, she veered onto the wet grass to clean the soles of her feet on the morning dew.

The sidewalk felt warm and comforting as she made her way across the bridge into the Prado, where a light Santa Ana wind blew her hair into her face. Stopping to watch the cars whiz by on the freeway underneath, she recalled taking the same stroll on chilly December nights in years past, when the bridge was strung with festive holiday lights.

A walk through the park always filled Katrina with civic pride. Its history was relatively recent compared to the East Coast, with its intricately carved facades of the Spanish Colonial Revival–style buildings dating back to 1915, when the Panama–California Exposition for the World's Fair came to town. The Old Globe Theatre was even newer, because arsonists had burned it down—twice.

After traveling through the covered walkways that connected museums exhibiting trains, planes, art, and anthropology, she soon reached her destination: an arboretum shaped like a giant birdcage, full of native plants, and the long rectangular pond, where foot-long orange and white koi darted around the lily pads.

I would say it's good to be home, but now I'm not so sure.

CHAPTER 26
GOODE

Tuesday

Goode and Stone headed down Fifth Avenue, their ties and hair blowing askew, for a meeting with attorney Milton Biggs, which Stone arranged right after Goode's call from the FBI. The dynamic duo was adept at double-teaming witnesses to make them and their lawyers squirm.

The hot, dry, and dusty Santa Ana conditions, which often hit in October, exacerbated Goode's allergies, making his eyes burn and his throat dry. The winds also made him feel a little out of sorts as they blew dirt and dust into the air. The only way to push through the discomfort was his standard answer to most any problem: more caffeine.

As Biggs walked them into a narrow room typically used for depositions, Goode sensed that the intent was to cause intimidation, just like in a police interrogation, but he simply leaned into it.

"Yes, we do represent Alex Battrelle, along with *all* the Battrelle family enterprises, including the newspaper and Vitaleron," Biggs said smugly.

"Why am I not surprised," Goode said, eliciting a knee-slam from Stone under the table.

Poor Katrina. What a quagmire. For us too.

"We've already questioned Michael and Vincent Battrelle about the deaths of Victoria and Simon Fontaine, and now we need to talk to Alex," Goode said.

"Why's that?" Biggs asked.

"Because we know that he stayed Thursday night at the Fontaine house and left hours before they were found dead under very suspicious circumstances," Stone chimed in. "He is the last known witness to see them alive."

"What makes their deaths so suspicious, if I may ask?" Biggs asked, looking to Goode for an answer. "And what proof do you have that he was at the house? I spoke with Vincent Battrelle before you arrived, and he claims that his son has been MIA for six months."

"We can't discuss details of the scene, but we have calls and text messages between him and Victoria confirming that timeline," Goode replied. "We also have a statement from Simon's girlfriend that he saw Alex at the house Thursday night and that she and Simon argued about it."

"Okay, so a hearsay statement from another potential suspect?"

"No one said she was a potential suspect, and we have no information that she was at the house like Alex was."

"But you did say she and Simon were arguing right before he was found dead."

"As you may have heard, Victoria was three months pregnant, and it's clear from the call and text logs on her phone that she was having relations with both Michael and Alex."

Biggs raised his eyebrows, his lips curling with annoyance, as if his job had just gotten harder. "I see."

"The Fontaines' deaths are obviously related, but we don't know whether they were the result of a personal or business matter, or both, given how heavily connected the two families are. We do know, however, that a conflict between Vincent Battrelle and Simon Fontaine pushed Alex Battrelle off the Vitaleron board."

"So, you're saying you have evidence of foul play?"

"We can't discuss specifics, but we're leaning that way. We know Alex is in the Caymans, and the timing of his flight is suspicious in relation to the text messages, and also to the 911 call about shots fired near the house at nine o'clock, especially since both victims had already been dead for several hours. So, we'll give your client a couple days—until Thursday at three o'clock—to get to the station for questioning. If he won't come voluntarily, we'll ask the Cayman authorities to escort him onto a plane."

"I'll let him know, but I can't force him to return. He's not going to be arrested, correct?"

"Depends on what he has to say."

"So, what is his standing in this case?"

"He's a person of interest, a material witness, and a possible suspect," Goode said.

"All right, I'll let you know if I can reach him, but he may be totally off the grid. Sounds like you ought to pick up Simon's girlfriend for questioning too."

CHAPTER 27
KATRINA

Tuesday

As Katrina waited for Joanne in front of the arboretum, she tried to figure out when she would have time to get her car window fixed.

I guess I can put some duct tape across the cracks until I can take it to the dealer. Whenever that will be. Getting vandalized is so inconvenient during a breaking investigative story.

She wondered if it was a good idea to confide in Joanne about this. The woman was twenty minutes late and counting. Long enough for Katrina's butt to go numb on the stone bench.

I wonder if news was committed, and she forgot about me. I'll give her five more minutes.

She felt like a CIA operative, developing relationships with all the opposing factions, hiding information from some, sharing it with others, and keeping most of it to herself.

In sticky situations like this, it's better to say too little than too much.

Working as an investigative reporter was never about the money for Katrina, who felt it was her calling to do such important work. She thrived on it. That was the only way to describe it. She wasn't religious, but she'd learned from attending Al-Anon meetings after Franny died that she had to find a "higher power" for the twelve-step program to work. That was difficult, but the meetings helped her to recover from losing him.

When she felt herself succumbing to her own demons, she came back to the same place: Her higher power was the source of wisdom to know the difference between right and wrong, truth, deception, and falsehood. If she started down the wrong road, she could usually feel in her gut which way to turn. But these days, forks in the road kept popping up, and the choices weren't simple black or white. There were more shades of gray than ever before.

Scanning the cement pathways, the only woman she could see approaching was wearing Jackie O sunglasses and a floppy, flowered-print hat, reminiscent of *Laugh-In* or *The Pink Panther*. All she needed were sandals with a white flower between the big and second toes.

As she came closer, Katrina had to laugh. It was Joanne. "Groovy outfit," Katrina said as the editor plopped down beside her and took a few moments to catch her breath.

"Sorry I'm late, I couldn't find my hat. But I'm so glad you called," Joanne said. "Don't worry. This is all between us. I think we're lucky to have you. You might be my last chance to win a Pulitzer!"

"I'm glad you said that," Katrina said. "It's hard to know who to trust. Linda assigns me to your team, then tells me to report to her on the Fontaine story. There's so much second-guessing, and ethical conflicts keep coming up."

Joanne nodded, a neutral encouragement to proceed, listening intently as Katrina explained the morning's events.

"Wow," Joanne said sympathetically. "We need to report this to HR and Linda right away. Are you sure you want to stay on this story?"

"No, I'm sure. I can handle this, and I'd prefer if we don't report it to anyone for now. I don't trust Linda," Katrina said, citing the other reasons she wanted to meet. "She's been telling me to ignore what my gut says to do, which is to interview the whole Battrelle family. Meanwhile—and this is hush-hush—Vincent tried to hire me on the side to investigate the disappearance of his son Alex, but then said I can't write about it. So, I quit, and told him again last night, but he's not accepting—"

"Hold on. You quit what? You know Linda is friends with the Battrelle family, right? She went to college with Meredith, Vincent's daughter."

What an incestuous place. So, does that mean Linda knows about my arrangement with Vincent? But then, why would she put me on a story about the Fontaines, knowing they were so involved with the Battrelles, then prohibit me from talking to them?

"I quit the side gig, and no, I didn't know that," Katrina said, feeling sick to her stomach. Something funky was going on. "Would Linda talk to Vincent about story assignments?"

"I have no idea. I know she often has cocktails at his house when his daughter is over, then stays the night, probably after drinking too much."

"That fits. He lured me over for a drink, too, filled my glass so full I almost spilled it. That's when he said he wanted to hire me as his personal investigator."

"What did you tell him?"

"I said I'd think about it, but then last night I told him I couldn't do it, because it posed an ethical conflict with the Fontaine story, but he wouldn't listen. He shoved a fifty at me and told me to go to George's to talk to some bartender about Alex."

"Did you take the fifty?"

"No, and I also didn't go to George's," Katrina said. "I was too tired. I can always talk to the bartender, but I get the feeling that Vincent is grasping at straws since he hasn't seen or heard from his son in six months."

"Right. Good call."

"Oh, and when I knocked on his door last night, Ken Goode answered, so I left and came back."

"Who's Ken Goode?"

"The lead homicide detective on the Fontaine case."

"Well, that's interesting. Talk about burying the lede."

"By the way, Goode offered me a deal. He said he would give me exclusive access to case information if I promised not to write a story until the end, but I told him that wouldn't fly."

"That's for sure."

"He's already been giving me some good leads, but he's also asking me to trade information. I know that's not kosher, so I haven't done that either."

"Excellent. So far, the only thing I don't like is that Vincent won't accept that you can't be his PI while you're working this story. And what happened this morning, of course."

"Yeah, well, it was awkward last night. He was drunk and bleeding and he kept trying to make me drink wine with him. I just wanted to get out of there."

Joanne shook her head, wiping the sweat from her forehead with the back of her hand. "What do you mean he was bleeding?"

"His index finger was bandaged. He said Goode made him drop a glass of scotch, and it broke and cut him."

"Okay. What else?"

"I think I need to interview Michael Battrelle and ask him about the Fontaines' deaths, because he was romantically involved with Victoria and now he's been appointed to replace her as CFO. But Linda and John Palmer have forbidden me to do that, and so did Vincent. But if Goode is questioning Vincent, he's probably talking to Michael, too, so it's obvious that the Battrelles are part of the investigation."

"Right. I agree. That would seem like a legitimate next step, especially given Michael's personal and professional involvement."

"It feels like they're just trying to protect the Battrelles, which Linda and John Palmer have pretty much admitted to me, and that makes me suspect that the Battrelles are involved in these deaths somehow. Or at least know something about them."

"Which is why you have to be careful, even more so now that you've received this threat," Joanne said, putting her arm around Katrina and squeezing. "I've got some ideas, but I want to noodle them a bit. Can you advance your reporting without calling Michael? I'm going to lobby for you to interview him, but I need to lay the groundwork first. We need leverage."

"I can try calling Simon's brother, William, again."

"Yes, do that. Anything else?"

Katrina mentioned Goode's tip about the politics behind the Vitaleron board members speaking at the news conference.

"Yeah, I wondered about that," Joanne said. "It's not a good look to announce a private corporate management shift at a police department presser when the Fontaines' bodies are hardly cold. Do you have any ideas where Alex Battrelle might be?"

"No, but I went to his house over the weekend and saw a box of cereal and half a yellow banana sitting out on the kitchen counter."

"So, someone's lying—or he's hiding. I'm going to suggest that you take over complete coverage of this case. We don't want the police or City Hall reporters to protect sources or hold on to leads they want to pursue on their own," Joanne said. "I will respect your wishes for confidentiality for now, but if anything else happens, we need to tell Linda and HR. Deal?"

"Deal. One other thing, I'm also wondering why Norman Klein got a byline on my story when he didn't contribute anything I didn't have already. Also, Jerry keeps nosing around, standing over my shoulder when I'm at my desk. Creeps me out."

"Jerry is a brownnoser. He's probably spying for John Palmer, who is trying to keep Vincent Battrelle happy by trying to minimize or sabotage you so they can pull you off the story. But I think Linda sees you as a ticket to the corner office. If she produces good stories and kisses Palmer's ass enough, she can placate him while she orchestrates his downfall, then replace him. I'll talk to Linda about you *before* we go into the afternoon news meeting. That way she can say it was her idea. Talk soon."

With that, Joanne flounced away, holding her hat in place as it flapped in the breeze.

On the walk back to her car, Katrina called William Fontaine at his office.

"I just read your story and was about to call you," he said. "Let's meet. I already spoke with Detective Goode, but he wouldn't say much, so I didn't say much."

William suggested lunch at Mister A's, an old-school San Diego restaurant a block from where she was parked. All she had to do was put more money in the meter.

"I'll be the strikingly handsome man with the prematurely white hair and piercing green eyes," he said.

"Sounds like an online dating profile," she said.

"How did you know?" he said, chuckling.

CHAPTER 28
GOODE

Tuesday

After the Biggs meeting, Stone drove back to the station while Goode returned to Starbucks for another latte, ignoring the inner voice that told him he was about to enter the jitter zone.

Claiming a table outside, Goode tried to reach London at the RCFL, Artie at the ME's office, and the crime lab supervisor, but none of them answered. Byron had gotten another warrant to return to the house to search the grounds again for the bullet and casing and to spray BlueStar to look for hidden blood in any areas they identified as a result.

Goode was mulling next steps when he saw Katrina walking barefoot down the street, carrying her red sandals. She looked so peaceful and innocent. Not a scary, manipulative reporter, but a thoughtful, intelligent woman he wanted to whisk away for that bottle of wine. He wanted to talk more about being orphans and losing a loved one to suicide.

Katrina slipped her shoes back on, got into her car to make a call, put money in the meter, then started walking up the block. As he watched her enter the tall building that housed Mister A's, he downed the rest of his latte and went after her. He knew he was potentially crossing a line, but if she was meeting a source for lunch, he wanted to know who it was—before it hit the paper this time.

Riding the elevator to the twelfth floor, he stepped out and nodded at the ponytailed hostess, who smiled widely, eager to seat him.

"One for lunch, sir?" she said.

"I'm checking to see if a friend is here," he said.

"Very good."

He peered discreetly around the doorway into the restaurant, looking for Katrina's bright-blue dress and red shoes. Thankfully, she was sitting with her back to him, talking to an older man with white hair who resembled Simon.

That's William Fontaine. I recognize him from the photos in Simon's office. Since he and I have already talked, there should be no surprises.

Turning around, he grinned at the hostess, who offered him a menu. "They're not here today after all," he fibbed.

What's a little white lie in the name of justice?

CHAPTER 29
KATRINA

Tuesday

William Fontaine was handsome, despite his melancholy expression, but he wasn't "prematurely" white at his age. Katrina waved as she approached his table—a two-top next to the picture windows that lined the room, overlooking the harbor and airport.

One of the few rooftop restaurants in town, Mister A's offered an even more magnificent view at night, when the skyscrapers were lit up with neon red and green, and guests could watch the airplanes descending diagonally at eye level toward the landing strips below. Katrina always wondered how the pilots could come so close to the tops of buildings and yet never shear them off.

This restaurant was another Chopin family favorite, although Katrina hadn't been there in years—since the waitresses wore cheesy toga outfits and the service was painfully slow. It had since been sold and remodeled by a new owner, who had also modernized the menu.

William pulled out her chair, then ordered the signature chicken Caesar salad for both of them. Normally Katrina would have found this presumptuous, but she didn't mind. She loved their Caesar, the anchovy-rich dressing in particular.

“I’ll have a Diet Coke with lime and lots of ice, please,” she told the waiter.

William got right down to business. “What do they mean, suspicious deaths? This was a double homicide, clear as day. My brother had no reason to shoot himself in the head. He wasn’t depressed. And Victoria had been clean for years, and yet they’re suggesting she OD’d?”

“Wait,” Katrina broke in. “Shoot himself in the head? Where did you hear that, and that Victoria might have OD’d? The police said—”

“When I identified the bodies at the morgue on Saturday, one of the workers showed me where Simon was shot in the temple and the injection bruises on Victoria’s arm. He said they also found pill vials next to her bed and a gun next to Simon’s body. But I know he didn’t own a gun. Would never even have one in the house.”

“Wow. That’s all news to me,” Katrina said. “Maybe you can give me the name of your source at the morgue.”

Someone with loose lips, my favorite kind.

When William didn’t acknowledge her suggestion, she moved on. He was probably still determining whether he could trust her. “Was Simon having any financial problems?” she asked.

“God, no,” he said. “He had surgeries booked out for months and investors clamoring for a piece of Vitaleron. He also wasn’t lonely for female company. Widows and their daughters were champing at the bit as soon as he and Nancy separated. He stayed in shape playing golf, and he was seeing a woman named Lucinda, who gave him the space he needed.”

“Space?”

“He could be distant, always focused on work. That’s why he and I were never close. His bedside manner wasn’t great, but he was a scalpel artist.”

“Speaking of virility, was he the type to test his sex drug on himself?”

“I’ve wondered that myself. Normally I wouldn’t disclose this, but it doesn’t matter now,” William said, lowering his voice as he leaned toward her. "He took Viagra for an occasional boost. Told me, wink, wink, that it was for market testing."

"Tell me about your relationship with Victoria. What was she like?"

William explained that he and his wife had stepped in to help Victoria after she had OD'd because Simon lacked a nurturing gene, and she still called to chat or ask his advice now and then.

"I often brought her here at night for a soda, because she loved watching the planes fly in," he said. "She didn't have many girlfriends, and she was closer to me than either of her parents. Her mother was as self-absorbed as Simon, so neither was a good role model."

After the waiter brought their salads, Katrina let William keep talking so she could eat while taking notes.

"What about Victoria's brother, Cal? What's he like?"

"Ten years younger and more of an accident, really. Nancy hoped that having a baby would save their faltering marriage, but it didn't. When Simon wasn't in surgery, he was in the lab. So, she drank even more after Cal was born, Simon had an affair, and she filed for divorce."

Cal was neglected, too, William said. As a teenager, he filled his world with surfing, skateboarding, drinking, and drugs—though he never took it to the point of abuse like Victoria.

"It took years for Simon to have a decent relationship with Victoria, and that was after Cal gave up and took off for Europe and parts unknown. About a year ago, he called me from Costa Rica. I've tried but haven't been able to reach him with the bad news."

"What's the story with Victoria and Alex Battrelle?"

"Victoria could never stay committed to any man, which suited Alex fine. The two of them always fell back on each other, though never for long. It was an unhealthy, codependent situation."

"Sounds like they both had major intimacy problems," Katrina said, considering herself an expert on the subject.

"Yes," William said. "That's why we were all surprised when she started up with Michael the monogamist, because she normally didn't want exclusivity. I think she hoped Alex would come back even though she pushed him away—hard—a year ago."

"What happened?" she asked.

"She had an abortion. She didn't tell me until after the fact—or him, either, for that matter—that it was his baby. He got bent out of shape, which made no sense, since neither one of them had ever wanted a commitment, and he suddenly wanted to marry her. But she said if he didn't get clean, she couldn't be his friend, let alone his wife or mother of his children. She refused to see or talk to him until he'd been sober for six months."

"Wow," Katrina said, holding her fork in midair.

That could explain why he's been MIA for that long.

"Do you think he was the baby's father this time too?"

"I don't know. He could've caught her at a weak moment, then gone back into isolation, or even relapsed again. Relapse is part of recovery."

"Yes, I'm aware. My brother was an alcoholic. Did Alex have anger issues?"

"He threw a glass prism against the wall after Simon forced him off the board. I could see him getting angry if she threatened to have another abortion, or said, even though it might be his baby, she planned to raise it with Michael because he was more stable. But I've always thought Michael would be the one to explode after all the years of his father dumping on him. Maybe it was the contrary: She told Michael she was going to raise the baby with Alex, and he snapped. If I can't have you, then no one can."

"He told me he didn't even know she was pregnant until the news conference," she said.

"I guess that's possible," William said. "For all we know, the father was the guy from the Vitaleron retreat in Hawaii three months ago."

"What guy?"

"All she told me was that someone sent her compromising photos of her in a sexual situation that she couldn't remember, because someone put a roofie in her pineapple juice. Speaking of codependent relationships, Alex and Michael had one too, just with different origins."

"Sounds like a complicated love triangle," she said.

"Victoria said Michael was jealous of Alex because he was their father's favorite, but he still protected Alex if he got into trouble. Vincent wasn't any better at being a father than Simon was, and I wouldn't call either of them an easy man. That's why they always argued. But they made good business partners, because money was always their first priority."

That's also why Simon didn't approve of Vincent coddling Alex, he said. Simon was concerned that his laxity would hurt the company.

"Vincent could be a tyrant at times. He was often too harsh with Michael, who was trying to please him, and he was equally blind to Alex's bad behavior."

Katrina nodded. "One favor," she said, smiling to soften her next question. "Do you think you could get me copies of the autopsy reports from the ME's office?" She didn't mention that the police chief had threatened to seal them.

"Sure, I'll ask to see the reports as soon as they're available, if not sooner," he said conspiratorially. "I want to see justice done here. My family was murdered, and I don't know why the police are being so damned namby-pamby about it."

Katrina couldn't help but chuckle.

What a great quote.

"Do you think the secrecy stems from the fact that Vitaleron's investors are some of this town's biggest political power brokers?" she asked.

"Yes, and that's why you need to blow the lid off this thing."

"I'm going to try. You've been a big help," she said. "I can see now that the police haven't told me much of anything."

Bastards.

"There's one more angle for you to explore. I didn't think to mention this to the detective because I didn't see it as a factor in my brother's death, but now I'm not so sure. Simon and I discussed using political campaign donations to get this drug on a fast track for FDA approval. I can only imagine how much he and his investors gave to the House legislative committee members with oversight in this area. For full disclosure, I'm an investor myself."

"Go on."

"So, I'd suggest you track the campaign contributions."

"It would help if I had a list of investors' names."

"I'm sure there's one on the computers the police seized from Vitaleron," William said.

"Which neither of us has access to, unfortunately," she said.

"True, but you can check the local delegation's campaign statements online and work backwards. My brother always described his drug as a 'family values' product that would keep marriages together, a tagline he figured the Republican Party, and specifically Christian conservatives, could get behind. In fact, Brandon Winchester, the Republican congressman from Rancho Santa Fe, said he was very interested in helping out. I'd start with him."

"Marketing a sexual enhancement drug to Christian conservatives?"

"Yes, that was the board's strategy."

"It's smart, actually," Katrina said.

"Something else has been bothering me."

"What's that?"

"My brother was shot in the right temple, but he was left-handed. Not impossible for it to be self-inflicted, I suppose, but highly improbable. More importantly, the guy at the morgue said the head wound didn't really bleed, so they think he was shot after he was already dead."

"Whaat?"

"It makes me sick that someone would do that," he said.

Although William had seemed to find relief in sharing his thoughts, he seemed sullen now that he'd finished. He'd hardly touched his salad, which the waiter had already transferred to a to-go box.

"I should get back to the office," William said, sighing as he stood up. "It was lovely to meet you."

After shaking Katrina's hand, he started to drop a credit card on the table, but she stopped him.

"It's on Vincent," she said. When he looked confused, she added, "I have an expense account."

William managed a slight smile. "Thank you," he said. "I'll let you know when I get those reports."

Five minutes later, Katrina was back in her hot car. She couldn't wait to tell Linda—and Joanne—that she finally had some meat on which to hang a story. She couldn't get it all into one take—and the potential campaign donation bonanza would take a while to compile—but William's comments would certainly make for provocative copy.

CHAPTER 30
GOODE

Tuesday

After leaving Mister A's, Goode drove back to HQ to make calls from his desk. The Homicide unit was divided into two rows of cubicles with an aisle down the center. His team sat together, with Stone next to Foster and catty corner to Goode, who sat next to Byron.

Goode's cubicle walls were lined with photos of his favorite surf spots, so he could gaze at them when he needed to grab a few Zen moments but couldn't get down to Windansea. He also had a couple of photos of him and Maureen, one relatively recently with their surfboards, and one of them clowning around at Belmont Park as teenagers.

He tried London again first. Still no answer.

Do I need to go over there and knock some heads together?

But he had more luck with the crime lab this time. "I know they went back to the scene this morning and they haven't returned, so I assume they're still there," the receptionist told him. She gave him the number for the supervisory tech, Dwight Pepper, who was indeed at the mansion when Goode called.

"Where are you now?" Goode asked, picturing the scene.

"On the back patio. We've scoured this whole area, even searched under the bushes, but there's no bullet or casing, Detective."

"Did you try the balcony above to see if you can find any blood or a different trajectory for the bullet from there?"

"Um, no."

I thought that was the whole point of going back.

"Do that for me, would you?"

"Really?"

"Yes, really."

Goode heard the swishing sound of Dwight's pant legs rubbing together as he walked through the house, breathing heavily as he climbed the stairs to the second story. Goode recalled that the man had quite a belly on him.

Less beer and more exercise, Spanky.

"It seems unlikely that we would have missed a casing or blood on the first go-round," Dwight said.

That's a whole lotta attitude there, Spanks. Stand down.

"It was pretty dark when we got there," Goode said, trying to be patient. "Since his gunshot wound was hardly bleeding and the bullet hasn't turned up on the patio, he was probably shot elsewhere, then moved."

"Okay," Dwight said, pausing and grunting. "Wait a minute."

"What?"

"I just found a casing," he said.

"Where?"

"Lodged in the corner of the balcony, between the wall and the railing, like you said."

"It's nice being right every once in a while."

Dwight paused again. "Yeah, sorry," he said, sounding a little embarrassed now.

"We're all human," Goode said, closing his eyes to visualize what he wanted. "So, if he was shot on the balcony, that means he should have bled up there. Do you see any blood? It was hard to see in the dark."

"No, I don't."

"Well, now's the time to spray the BlueStar and see if you can light up any drops or spatters. The killer might have cleaned it up well enough that they aren't visible to the naked eye."

"Right."

"Then try looking for the bullet in a broader radius downstairs, using that side of the balcony to calculate the trajectory. Picture someone leaning the doctor's limp dead body against the railing, then shooting him at close range in the right temple. Maybe he thought about dumping the body over the top but decided against it and carried him downstairs."

Bodies are heavy. Probably would take two people.

"That's pretty creative," Dwight said.

"Yep. So, if you're standing on the patio, facing away from the house, the bullet would probably be to your left. It could also have ricocheted off the side of the house and rolled away. The bullet went through his brain and ended up somewhere."

"Okay," Dwight said. "Man, there's a lot of brush over there."

"You guys have a metal detector?"

"Uh, not with us."

"You don't keep one on the truck? If you can't find the bullet, you should go get one."

Silence.

"You still there?"

"Yeah, I'm here."

"All right, call me back and let me know how it's going."

"Okay."

"Also, now that we know someone was up there with a gun, make sure to collect prints and DNA swabs from the doorknobs on both sides of the French doors, inside and out, and swab any blood spatter you find. It'll probably be degraded from cleaners and the BlueStar, but you never know."

"Will do."

I knew the crime lab had issues, but why did I need to give these instructions three times? Better late than not at all.

Goode rolled his chair over to Stone's desk to fill him in. Stone was also a photo collector, his cubicle lined with shots of his wife Kelly and their three kids, who were making faces or sitting in his lap while watching TV, and the time they drew a mustache on his face with a black marker while he was asleep.

"How'd they miss that?" Stone asked.

"That's what I said. I'm trying not to be annoyed about it."

"Thankfully, you were on top of it. Good work, Goode."

"I'll let you have that one."

"Thought you might," Stone said, grinning. "So, we know the killer shot a dead man on the balcony. Now we have to figure out what actually killed him. What if it's all part of a big cover-up?"

"You mean someone staged a messed-up crime scene to frame someone else or to protect themselves?" Goode asked.

"Yeah, to create chaos and confusion, which is working, for the moment. What if Simon and Victoria were both experimenting with the drug by injection?"

"That would be really twisted, wouldn't it?"

"I meant independently, with other partners."

"Right. Let's see if Alex Battrelle will admit to experimenting with the drug with Victoria. Although we probably won't find any needle marks on him by Thursday."

"We can ask him, although there's nothing illegal about using an experimental drug. Unless he stole it—but how would he get in? He's not on the board anymore. Also, say he used it with Victoria and something was wrong with the batch, then he should be dead too."

"Right, but he's in the Caymans," Goode said. "He's allegedly in recovery, though, so he could've said no but went along for the ride, if you know what I mean. Got scared when shit went sideways, and he ran."

"A bad ride, indeed. Where are those damn tox screens?"

"That's my next call," Goode said.

Stone knew all about recovery. He'd dated Kelly since the eleventh grade, and they got married soon after they both graduated from SDSU. When Stone continued his college routine of weekend drinking binges, Kelly stayed sweet and loyal—nothing like Goode's ex, Miranda—but she firmly told him to hit the wagon or she'd be in the wind. Stone got sober, and he and Kelly went on to have three little ones, who truly loved their Uncle Goode.

Artie answered on the first ring. "I was about to call you. But you're not going to like the tox-screen results."

"Why's that?"

"Victoria had Xanax in her system, but not enough to be fatal. The oxys in her throat didn't get absorbed enough to show up. So, we've got a whole lot of nothin'. It looks like someone sedated her, then shot her up with something that isn't showing up on the standard screen."

"We also still have the missing-syringe problem, which means someone removed it, or them, from the house. What kind of substance wouldn't show up?"

"Could be some obscure drug that the person didn't want us to identify."

"Or to find his or her fingerprints on the syringe. What about Simon?" Goode asked.

"He had Viagra metabolites in his blood, but normal levels for usage the night before. No other drugs for him either."

"Shit," Goode said, smacking the side of his car with his hand. "Owww."

"You okay?"

"Yeah. You're right, that's not what I wanted to hear." Goode paused before asking his next question. "So how do we identify other substances you don't typically test for?"

"We have other options we can try, but it would help if we had some clue what we're looking for. Any ideas?"

"Yeah, Stone and I were thinking it could be Vitaleron's experimental sex drug."

"Can you get me some? We'll have to send it out to a private lab. We don't test for everything, but it wouldn't show up on a screen anyway, because it hasn't received FDA approval."

Goode sighed as he rubbed his bruised hand. "Let me work on that," he said.

CHAPTER 31
KATRINA

Tuesday

Joanne's face lit up as Katrina recounted the highlights of her interview with William Fontaine.

"Get going on the campaign research and don't tell Linda anything until I talk to her," Joanne said. "If I can't get her alone, we'll go in together right before the meeting, because the time crunch will give us some leverage. In the meantime, see if you can get Goode to confirm William's description of the crime scene."

Katrina agreed, but she didn't want to call Goode yet, knowing she would have more questions closer to deadline. So, she started scrolling through campaign records on the Federal Election Commission (FEC) and OpenSecrets websites, where federal campaign donations were grouped for easy analysis.

As William had anticipated, US Rep. Winchester had received a boatload of donations from the Fontaines, Battrelles, and Vitaleron board members and their wives—$750,000 in the past year alone, most of which had been "bundled" at two fundraisers hosted by the Lexicon Group LLC. They were both held at the upscale University Club, a club for businesspeople on the top floor of Symphony Towers.

Where have I seen the Lexicon Group before?

Going back through her research, she confirmed that it owned the Vitaleron building, which was listed among Vincent's many properties around the county.

Great. Another link to Vincent. Just what Linda and John Palmer want to hear.

Anticipating that Linda would ask her to compare the $750,000 to donation totals for the rest of the county's congressional delegation, she put that task aside for the moment to wade through the FDA's bureaucratese about the drug testing and approval process.

After successfully completing animal tests, experimental drugs entered three phases of human trials. Phase one, conducted on twenty to eighty healthy subjects, studied how the drug was metabolized and pinpointed the highest dose that caused no serious side effects. If no "unacceptable toxicity" occurred, phase two began, monitoring the drug's effectiveness on thirty-six to three hundred volunteers. Phase three expanded the test group to as many as three thousand people, watching for safety, effectiveness, and interactions with other drugs. If still deemed safe, the new formula would be allowed to enter the marketplace, with continued monitoring for rare and longer-term side effects. All of this could take years and cost many millions of dollars.

Katrina jotted down the relevant names in the federal drug-review hierarchy, including the head of the Department of Health and Human Services, the FDA commissioner, and directors of the Center for Drug Evaluation and Research and the Office of New Drugs. Drug approvals were under the purview of the House Energy and Commerce Committee, of which Winchester was a member. He was also the minority leader of a powerful appropriations subcommittee that oversaw the FDA.

He's definitely the go-to local guy for expedited FDA approval. This is like shooting fish in a barrel.

Reading further, she saw that Winchester had headed the *Sun-Dispatch*'s circulation department years ago, which meant she might experience some pushback there as well.

Gawd, what an incestuous town.

From there, she checked the federal gift registry, where senators and US representatives were supposed to list items such as golf trips, professional sports tickets, and travel to junkets. Among the numerous gifts that lobbyists and other La Jolla folks, including the Battrelles, Fontaines, and Vitaleron board members, had given Winchester was a most notable trip to Hawaii for the recent Vitaleron retreat.

That can't be a coincidence. But why would he go to a Vitaleron retreat? Wouldn't that be for employees?

Next, she cross-checked Google for images of the names she'd jotted down and up came a photo of Winchester in the *Washington Post*'s Style section. Winchester was looking chummy at a black-tie event with a woman named Marcia Copeland, director of the FDA's Office of New Drugs, who was sandwiched between the congressman and Darren McMurphy, Vitaleron's new board chairman.

Oh my God! They're not even trying to hide their backroom dealings.

Her phone pinged with a text from Joanne: Talked to Linda. The story is all yours. Go tell her what you've got, champ.

Linda smiled proudly as Katrina gave her the details of her fruitful interview with William Fontaine, though she seemed less excited about the campaign donations, gifts, and property records that dragged the Battrelles back into the story.

"Let's hold off on the campaign donations until you've examined the entire delegation. That $750,000 could be an anomaly. We can do that for the weekend, along with a summary of where Vitaleron is in the FDA approval process, with all that nice context you found," she said. "For today, write up your lunch interview and make sure to include that 'namby-pamby' quote."

Katrina nodded knowingly and smiled. "Thanks."

I'll be patient. I'm not going to give up. Don't you worry.

"Oh, and by the way," Linda said. "I'm going to announce at the afternoon news meeting that this story is all yours moving forward.

The cops and government editors will have to warn their overambitious reporters not to covet their sources. Now, go make me look good!"

In the next ninety minutes, Linda stopped by Katrina's desk several times to check on her progress, making it difficult to concentrate.

"What's your lede?" she kept asking.

Micromanage much?

"I don't know yet," Katrina snapped at Linda on her third visit. "I still have more calls to make."

I'm sure she's trying to head off any conflict before John Palmer gets involved, but give me a break and back off, lady.

Katrina made a quick round of calls to Goode, Stone, and the ME's office to allow them to confirm or deny William's claims, but no one answered, so she left voicemails.

After Katrina bristled at Linda's personal check-ins, the editor started sending over editing suggestions on Katrina's half-written story, which Linda was reading from her office on the network server. Annoyed, Katrina went into Joanne's office to complain.

"Does she always read over your shoulder like that?" she asked. "It's unnerving. I'm still trying to report the dang thing. It's not even a story yet!"

"She calls it 'shepherding,'" Joanne said, shrugging empathetically. "But I feel your pain. It will get better. She hasn't edited your raw copy before, so she's anxious. Her ass is on the line because she recruited you, and you keep digging up stuff about the Battrelles."

"Well, if this is typical for an A-1 story, I'm not feeling inspired to write another one."

Due to these constant interruptions, Katrina didn't get a chance to call Goode or the ME's office again until 6:00 p.m. Still no response.

Once Katrina turned in her story, Linda changed the lede, gouged a few holes here and there, then had Joanne do a light clean-up edit before sending it on to John Palmer. By the end of this painful, tedious process, the top of the story was virtually unrecognizable, but Katrina was pleased that the "namby-pamby" reference made it into the headline, even though she knew it could cause some conflict for her relationship with Goode and Stone.

It's such a great quote. I had to put it in the story. If they don't already know reporters don't write our own headlines, I'll just have to edumacate them.

Her story was posted online minutes after she left the newsroom at nine thirty.

By the time Katrina got into her car, she felt wrung out, like a wet rag, but too wound up to relax, let alone sleep.

I hate to say this, but I don't ***want*** *a drink, I* ***need*** *a drink.*

Zipping up the hill, she was in her neighborhood supermarket seven minutes later, buying herself a pricier-than-usual bottle of Cabernet Sauvignon.

You definitely earned it.

Two steps into her apartment, she kicked off her heels and dropped her purse in one fluid moment, heading into the kitchen to pop the cork. She couldn't wait for her boxes to arrive so she could drink her wine from an actual wineglass.

The Cab warmed her throat going down. Despite the presentation in a plastic cup, the extra bucks she spent on the wine were well worth it. Sliding open the glass door, she walked out onto her balcony and gazed appreciatively down the canyon to the freeway below. But the moment was lost as soon as she remembered her broken car window. She quickly came inside to close the blinds and lock all her doors, fearing that someone was watching her with binoculars from some hidden perch.

Katrina topped off her glass. She wanted to shut off her phone, but she had to leave it on in case the copy desk—or Goode—called. She'd been told that there weren't many copyeditors left after the last rounds of layoffs, but they still called with questions after a story had been posted online but before it was sent to the presses. That's why they called it web-first.

Setting the phone on the master-bathroom counter, she felt tired but restless from hours of adrenaline coursing through her system. She knew that a long shower, and probably more wine, was the only way to relax.

Don't drink too much or you'll wake up, brain spinning again, at 3:00 a.m., imagining the contents of the next threatening note.

When the water was hot but not too hot, she let the pulsating jets massage her back, neck, shoulders, and forearms, which were tight and achy after hours of hunching over the keyboard.

Goode's going to be mad about the story, but I did leave him two messages. I wonder why he didn't call me back? He didn't even call to check on me. Maybe he's not as into me as I thought.

After toweling off, she returned to the living room with her wine. Sitting on the floor, she leaned back against the wall and tucked her legs into her sleeping bag. She had a few more sips until her eyelids felt heavy, too tired to get up and pour the rest of her glass back into the bottle. She put her phone into airplane mode, lay down, and drifted off.

CHAPTER 32
GOODE

Tuesday

After the bullet caper, Goode spent several hours trying to chase down a sample of the sex drug for Artie. He started with an informal call to Dallas Fairchild, the Vitaleron biochemist, but that turned into a legal miasma.

"I'll have to run that up the chain and get back to you on that," Fairchild said. "By the way, I'm having those cameras installed after hours tonight, so we should have them working by ten o'clock. As you suggested, I haven't told a soul since Victoria already authorized it. Let's see what happens."

"Great," Goode said. "Thanks for doing that so fast."

Fairchild called Michael Battrelle about getting Goode a sample. Michael called Vincent, who called Darren McMurphy, after which the detective found himself on the phone with Milton Biggs again.

"Did you miss me?" Goode asked facetiously to a wall of silence. "I thought McMurphy handled Vitaleron."

The guy's got no sense of humor.

"Considering the circumstances, we thought it best if I stepped in to avoid any appearance of conflict," Biggs said. "What can I do for you this time, Detective?"

"I think you already know this, but I need a sample of the sex drug so we can get it analyzed," Goode said.

"Right, and we aren't going to hand that over voluntarily. You'll have to go through the courts, and I'll tell you right now, we will fight you."

"What's the problem?" Goode asked. "Don't you want to know if Simon and Victoria Fontaine were murdered, or conversely, if Vitaleron's experimental drug could be fatal?"

"Why would we share the proprietary formula of an unapproved drug, whose development has cost many millions of dollars, with another lab? If your goal is to taint the public's perception of our product, we will fight you even harder."

"We have no such intention," Goode said. "I'm just doing my job, Mr. Biggs."

Once Goode reported back to Stone, the sergeant contacted the department's legal counsel. The preliminary answer was to follow the usual process: Write up a search warrant affidavit and see if a judge would approve it. But an hour later, the attorney told him to back off—at the chief's request via the mayor's office.

"The mayor thinks there's no pressing need for this, so the chief says we should stand down," Stone told Goode.

"You have got to be kidding. Why is the chief even discussing this with him?"

"I have no idea."

"What is in this stuff?"

"I don't know, but let's take a beat. Vitaleron could file for an injunction and demand a hearing, but that would only delay the inevitable. Between us, I've never seen the mayor step into a case since I joined the force. The chief suggested finding another way to get the same information on the QT."

"I'd say this is not only highly unusual but highly improper, wouldn't you?"

"Yes, and I told the chief as much. He just shrugged."

"Is he an investor too?"

"You got me."

Goode took a walk, trying to come up with another option.

You'd think there would be some of this stuff at the Fontaine house if one or both of them were experimenting with it. I should've looked more carefully through Victoria's purse.

It occurred to him that they should check the drug audits and inventories that they seized from Simon's office and the Vitaleron lab for other substances for which to test.

I need to check in with London at the RCFL to see if he's done that yet. But what if Simon—or his surgery partner, or both—were selling this stuff to their patients on the sly? They probably wouldn't keep track of that in writing.

When London didn't answer his phone, Goode decided to go down there in person.

Judging by his expression, London was pretty spooked when he met Goode in the lobby. Goode's crappy day must have been written all over his face.

"Sorry, I haven't gotten to your stuff yet," London said. "We're really backed up, and I'm doing the work of three examiners."

"Well, I need an answer on this, and I'm not leaving until I get it," Goode said.

"What's that?"

"I need to see the computer files with the drug inventory from Dr. Simon Fontaine's office."

London shook his head helplessly.

"What now?" Goode said.

"My wife started having slow contractions a while ago, and she's going to call or text me any minute to take her to the hospital."

Are you kidding me?

"But I guess I can copy the hard drives to see if we have the file you need."

"Okay, thanks," Goode said, relieved. "That would be great."

"Come on back with me," London said, checking his phone as he led Goode through several hallways to a room of metal shelves stacked with computers and tagged with case numbers.

London pulled down Victoria's laptop, Simon's desktop, and the surgery computers and put them on a table. After extracting the data from the hard drives and converting it to searchable files, London uploaded them all to the CAIR system.

"There, that's almost everything," London said. "It's going to take some more time to do the email and browser-history searches you requested."

"I assume you haven't gotten to the security footage yet either?"

"Oh, right, no, sorry, I haven't. Look, my wife just texted me, I've got to run."

"That's a priority, okay?" Goode called after London as he jogged toward the door. "We need to know who went in and out of there that day."

"On it. I've got another examiner helping me, and we'll get to that as soon as we can. Promise."

As he drove away, Goode realized he was grinding his teeth. His dentist had warned him about drinking too much caffeine, but that advice had gone into the ether.

It was getting close to sunset, so Goode headed north to blow off some bad juju at Windansea.

Wait, there were green capsules mixed in with the Viagra in Simon's medical bag. I could also give Victoria's Hermès bag another once-over while I'm there. SDPD property room, stat!

He got off at the next exit to reverse course, feeling a rush of optimism as he headed south toward downtown, where the evidence locker awaited.

I have a good feeling about this.

Within the hour, Goode was going through evidence boxes and envelopes. Bending the rules for his convenience, he transferred the vial of green capsules and blue pills from Simon's medical bag into the Hermès bag.

"I meant to hand this off to the ME's investigator, but I guess we got our signals crossed," he told the clerk. When she looked confused, he added, "We need to look through it for potentially toxic substances or anything else that could have caused their deaths."

The clerk nodded and let him take the purse, which he knew wasn't entirely kosher. Once these items were checked separately into evidence, they both should have been logged out as such when they left the building to maintain the chain of custody.

"Sign it out on the log here," she said, handing him a clipboard.

Well, it's mostly true, and these are unusual circumstances. I'll put the bag back once I look through it again and get these pills to Artie. At least this time I know what I'm looking for.

Heading for Artie's office, he hoped that Vitaleron had made the men's pill green for branding purposes, because "the little blue pill" was already associated with Viagra, their primary competitor.

Once he reached the morgue, Goode turned on the Explorer's overhead light to reexamine the purse's contents for drugs. But other than Simon's vial, which he'd placed there himself, he didn't find any.

"Where'd you get this?" Artie asked when Goode handed over the drug vial.

"Evidence locker," he said. "I meant to submit these to you before. Let's make sure the blue ones are really Viagra, and let's hope these greenies are the Vitaleron sex drug. If that stuff turns up in Simon's blood, it might change the whole face of this case."

"You got it," Artie said. "Who knows? Maybe he was going for super-stud and mixed the two, felt faint, or had a heart attack, causing him to fall down the stairs."

"I never thought of that," Goode said.

"So much to learn, grasshopper," Artie said, chuckling as he put the requisition slip into a padded envelope with the vial and handed it to his assistant. "I'm going out for a cold one. Want to join me?"

"Absolutely," Goode said. "Enough frustration for one day."

They drove separately to a brewery in the Fashion Valley mall, where one beer turned into three, followed by a round of premium tequila shots, which went down nicely with a basket of hot, crispy chips and a bowl of guacamole with fresh chunks of avocado. The music was booming and the acoustics were terrible, so they had to sit close and speak loudly to hear each other.

By the time they split the bill around ten o'clock, Goode had cheered up considerably.

Artie's a good guy. He's going to help us solve this case.

But that warmth faded as soon as he saw that he'd missed two calls from Katrina, along with an angry email from Stone with a link to the story Katrina had posted around 9:15 p.m. Stone had called several times since then, pissed that Goode wasn't picking up.

"Oh, effing hell," Goode said as he read the story in his car. His ear was buzzing as he felt his brain constricting with tension.

He didn't get Katrina's first call because he'd been in the underground evidence locker, where there was no reception. He must have missed her second call while he was at the morgue.

Thick walls or something?

He didn't even wait to listen to Stone's messages before dialing Katrina's number. The call went to voicemail, so he left a message, tainted by alcohol and his own failure to anticipate this situation.

"Namby-pamby? Really, Katrina? I mean, are you trying to get me fired?"

He immediately regretted his tone as soon as he hung up, as the images of Katrina's cracked window and threatening note came back to him. He sat in silence for a minute, then headed north to La Jolla in a dour mood.

You just made everything worse, you dolt.

Goode eased the Explorer into the lot at Windansea, where a stiff breeze was roiling the deep-green water into choppy peaks, and shut off the ignition. Closing his eyes, he focused on the sound of the waves breaking and tried to pull out of the downward spiral.

Stone's messages didn't help. "I thought you had your girl under control," Stone barked. "The chief is on a rampage. Where the hell are you? Call me!"

"How was I supposed to know William was going to tell her that?" Goode told his own image in the rearview mirror. "I don't even know how he got the information."

You should have followed up with her like you promised. Be proactive. Stone thinks this is your fault, and the chief obviously blames you too. Because it is your fault.

"Yes, well, I would argue that it's because of all the shit that went down with Milton Biggs, the mayor, and the chief today," he replied to the voice in his head. "So, I say it's their fault. Plus, London's wife was having a baby, then I had to find those pills and get them to Artie, and I still haven't even had a chance to look at the stuff on the CAIR drive. It was only a few beers."

Looking into his own glassy eyes, he saw disappointment reflected back.

Don't forget the tequila. Maybe next time you'll know better. Katrina is not Norman Klein; she's a force to contend with. You couldn't have stopped her, but you could have tried to mitigate the situation.

With that, he called Katrina again and left her a voicemail, apologizing.

"Sorry about that last voicemail, and I'm sorry I didn't get a chance to check on you today. It was a crazy day. I didn't get your messages in time, obviously, and the shit is already rolling downhill. Next time, maybe you could give me a heads-up that you're going to need to talk to me after hours, so I can watch for your call? I'm going home to bed now before I do any more damage. Goodnight."

CHAPTER 33
KATRINA

Wednesday

When Katrina woke up on Wednesday, she realized that two voicemails from Goode had come in after she'd put her phone into airplane mode. The first one left her annoyed and a little angry, but the second one calmed her down. He sounded so beaten up that she felt bad for him.

He acknowledged that I didn't do anything wrong, which is good, but now he wants me to call to warn him that I'll need to talk to him later?

Checking her voicemails at work, she had a whopping fifteen, which beat her personal record from the day her mafia series started running. The new messages were weighted almost equally in support of and opposition to William's assessment of the police investigation.

One female caller said she thought Victoria and Simon Fontaine got what they deserved.

"That drug will only help sinners fornicate," she said. "The act of procreation between husband and wife is sacred. It's not a recreational sport. God bless you, and I hope you explore this in your next story."

William Fontaine called, too, but with praise. "Great headline. I'm surprised you quoted me so accurately," he said, a sentiment she'd heard before and always found amusing.

Who are these reporters who keep their jobs after misquoting sources?

He also gave her an encouraging tidbit about the autopsy reports.

"My source at the ME's office says the police chief has asked for expedited toxicology reports, so they might be ready by Friday."

Katrina was pleased that her weekend story was getting dressed and ready to go.

In the meantime, I'd better get on that campaign research before Linda tries to send me in a different direction.

Thirty minutes later, she was greeted by a most unpleasant paper plate smeared with chocolate frosting and cake crumbs, a wadded-up napkin, and half a paper cup of cold coffee on her desk.

Why was someone sitting at my desk?

Worse still, she was shocked to see her personal email account was open on her screen, where anyone could have read them, and probably did.

What the hell? I didn't leave my emails open like this. Was this Jerry, snooping? I don't have time for this shit.

She put the napkin on the plate and walked it over to Jerry's desk, where she dumped it into his bin and poured the coffee on top.

That will send a message. If it wasn't him, he probably won't even know the difference. Nosy slobs.

Before she dug back into the campaign donations, she made a quick call to Goode to make sure they were okay.

"Oh, it's you, the investigative reporting star," he said in an unexpectedly passive-aggressive tone, his words hitting too close to the threatening note for her liking.

"I'm confused. Last I heard, you were apologizing," she said.

"I know, I'm sorry. I was trying to make a joke. Too soon? I'm trying to take my mind off the hook my chief poked through my ass this morning."

"Sounds painful."

"No kidding," he said, half-heartedly. "I'm sorry, again, for not checking on you yesterday. I know you're doing your job, but Chief Baxter took my head off in front of my whole team this morning. He's one of those Christian conservatives you mentioned, and he took offense to your story, even though you mention that the Vitaleron marketing strategy was to keep marriages together."

"Yeah," she said. "Weird."

"But the bottom line is that the brass doesn't trust you now, because you've printed details about the investigation that we would never release. As you probably know, we don't do that because we need to assess whether people are lying or know more than they're admitting."

Katrina felt no remorse. She was under attack as well. Had he forgotten that? But she still needed him as a source.

"Not sure what I can do about that. On your other point, I can try to give you a heads-up earlier in the day, but I don't always know. Maybe you should check your phone more often?"

"Easier said than done. Yesterday was a shitshow for reasons I can't disclose, but if things don't turn around in the next day or so, I'll tell you about it."

That sounds promising.

"I'm all ears. But if I'd reached you sooner, what would you have said? Was William wrong about anything?"

"We're off the record, right?"

"I'd rather not, but why stop now," she said sarcastically.

"Okay, well, the answer is yes and no. It's not a simple death scene. We still don't know what exactly went down or how. It's possible that what we saw wasn't caused by one person or even done at the same time."

"Huh?"

"We think someone messed with the scene."

"What do you mean?"

"As in, purposely staged it to throw us off."

"So, William was right. Simon was shot in the right temple even though he was left-handed, so he couldn't have shot himself."

"I didn't know he was left-handed, so thanks for that tidbit. But it's gotten even more complicated. I was off the grid last night because I spent the day running around in ten different directions, slamming into political and legal roadblocks from the top down."

"When can you tell me about that?"

"That's the shitshow I was talking about," he said. "Give me until tomorrow."

"Unless I can find something on paper before that."

"I doubt it, but more power to you. This will all become clearer once I get more toxicology tests back."

"By Friday, right?"

"Friday? I doubt it. We had to use an outside lab."

"So the reports won't be done by Friday?"

"No, because they can't finish the autopsy report before the tox screens come back. Is this William talking again? Please don't do this to me a second time."

"I can't reveal my sources."

"Let's put it this way, if you quote a draft report or the investigator's notes with preliminary results, and you know the cause and manner of death are still undecided, that will be misleading, if not plain wrong. This usually takes weeks, Katrina."

But I bet there's some good stuff in there about what the death scene looked like. So, I'm not agreeing to anything.

"Good to know."

"If you do get ahold of something—unofficially—please call me so we can discuss it, okay?"

"Yes, of course. Just like I did last night."

"Point taken. There's one other thing I've been wanting to tell you, but you didn't get it from me—in fact, you can find it yourself in the property records."

"What's that?"

"Look up the original corporate formation of Vitaleron with the secretary of state and the history of the building and its owner, Lexicon

Group LLC. You need to be careful, Katrina. There's a whole hornet's nest in there."

"Thank you, I think," Katrina said hesitantly. "I already know Lexicon is the owner, although it's listed as one of Vincent's holdings. I didn't go any deeper."

"Well, dig in and call me back. I'm here if you want to talk some more about it."

As soon as they hung up, Katrina took Goode's advice and almost fell off her chair.

What the hell? Daddy and Franny were both involved in this Vitaleron deal three years before Franny died?

Katrina wondered why no one had mentioned this to her when her parents' murder investigation was still fresh. But thinking back, the only reason she knew about the hotel deal on Mission Bay was the *Advocate* article.

Holy effing shit. Did they go into business together because they were all in that family drug-treatment group? Could Vincent Battrelle have been involved in the deaths of my family and now the Fontaines' too?

She called Goode back right away. "Do I need to call security? I thought being threatened by the Polish mafia was bad, and then I come home to this? Do you think that's what the rock and the note were about, trying to scare me off this story?"

"I wasn't sure if I should tell you, because I don't see any direct relationship to this case or any immediate danger. Your father and brother got out of this deal long before either of them died, but their involvement does raise questions. So, all I can say is, be careful. I'll help in any way I can."

"I didn't need this today," she said, shaking her head.

"Try not to worry. If I find any deeper connection, I'll let you know, and you do the same, okay?"

Katrina felt a tightness in her chest. She took a deep breath and let it out slowly. "Okay," she said. "Thanks."

She signed out of her computer to keep the spies away, then made her way to the stairs that led to the rooftop.

I can't breathe. I need some air.

The muscles in her neck and shoulders felt like sheets of metal, and her heart was pounding so hard she could hear her blood pulsing.

I can't tell anyone about this, because Joanne already suggested I give up this story after the death threat. But it seems even more likely now that that was Vincent's plan all along.

Up on the roof, the sky was gray toward the coast, but the marine layer was starting to burn off. Vitaleron board members speaking at a police department news conference, legal and political roadblocks at the SDPD, and now this.

What paper records might connect the mayor, the police chief, Vincent, Simon, and anyone else at Vitaleron? A man's penis can be a powerful, and sometimes irrational, motivator.

Neither the mayor nor the chief showed up on the list of donors who gave directly to Winchester's political campaign. The question she needed to investigate was whether a separate donation stream masked their identity or added a layer of protection. Some, if not all, of the donors could also be Vitaleron investors.

Once she settled on a plan of action, Katrina ran down the stairs as fast as she could. Whirling her swivel chair around, she signed into her computer and typed the chief's name, Tom Baxter, into the OpenSecrets search bar.

The chief getting upset at the Christian-conservative reference could be misplaced anger or fear of being exposed for something more than that.

But nothing came up. She did the same for the mayor, Jack Norton. Still nothing. Thankfully, she was able to reach William.

"Quick question: I'm trying to track the campaign donations as you suggested, but I hit a wall. Did Simon ever mention a particular campaign committee that was set up to funnel money but to also give cover to local officials like the police chief, or anyone else who wanted to donate, so they wouldn't be easily identified?"

William laughed. "You are one smart cookie. I was wondering the same thing after the chief called me this morning."

"Really, what did he say? Was he mad?"

"Not overtly. He expressed his condolences, then said, 'I'm sure you'd agree that your brother's work is very important to the community. I would ask that you not speak any further to the media. This kind of coverage interferes with our death investigation.'"

"What did you say?"

"I told him I appreciated his position, but as a private citizen, and more importantly as a lawyer, I would say and do whatever I saw fit."

"Good for you. I heard that he chewed out the lead detective this morning too."

"He was probably even more pissed after talking to me. But his odd request prompted me to go back into my emails with Simon. I found one that mentioned Christians For Everlasting Marriage, a group that has its own political action committee. Try searching for it. It's a 527, which is under IRS purview."

"That's a great tip, thanks. I did some checking too. The guy you mentioned, Congressman Brandon Winchester, is on the committee that oversees the FDA, so he's the most likely recipient. I found some direct donations to him yesterday, but nothing from any public official. Maybe this will turn up some more."

"One thing I should point out. This is all legal, you know, unless there's a promise of action or quid pro quo in exchange for receiving the donations, in which case they would be considered a bribe. I don't think that's something my brother or Victoria would have authorized, but that doesn't mean it wasn't done without their knowledge or with plausible deniability."

"Okay. One other question. Did you know my father, Peter Chopin? Or did Simon ever mention him or my brother, Franny?"

"No, I'm sorry, although your father's name does sound familiar. Should I know him?"

"He and my mother were judges, and they were murdered six months after my brother allegedly died by suicide. I just found out that they went in on Vitaleron and also the building where it's headquartered, with Vincent Battrelle. Vincent is Vitaleron's largest investor now that Simon is gone. How's that for motive?"

"Oh, God, of course. Yes, I remember now. I'm so sorry for your loss, Katrina. Simon went to their funeral. He said he knew them through Victoria's rehab program, but now I remember he said that Vincent Battrelle was in love with your mother during law school. Simon seemed very conflicted about their deaths, and I never knew why. But I see where you're going with this. It sounds messy, but I think you're on to something, so keep going. I'll let you know if I remember anything else."

"Thanks."

Who gets Simon's and Victoria's shares of the company now, Simon's estranged wife and their son, Cal? Maybe that's why the divorce was still not finalized. Could the wife be a suspect?

The IRS website wasn't particularly user-friendly, which forced her to wade through tedious searches to find the information she wanted. But her persistence paid off.

In the most recent election, the Christian group's 527 committee—which had no legal donation limits—received a whopping $5 million from 350 people. Katrina stifled a squeal of excitement as she scrolled down the donor list, which included the police chief, the mayor, every Vitaleron board member and employee she'd met, the entire Battrelle family, and many socialites she recognized from the newspaper archives.

Ding, ding, ding.

She also recognized names from her previous day's search for donations to Winchester, including Milton Biggs. When she also saw John Palmer's name, her heart sank.

Are you effing kidding me? What kind of horror show did I come to work for?

If the group was prohibited from contributing to or coordinating with a specific federal candidate, how did the money get to Winchester? After checking the rules, she learned that the groups were allowed to funnel money to federal candidates as long as they established political committees to transfer the cash.

After reviewing all the group's expenditures, she concluded that the committee had contributed the entire $5 million sum to the Committee to Reelect Brandon Winchester, which was allegedly run "independently."

This is gold. It may be legal, but it sure doesn't look good for the mayor and police chief to openly mix their own personal interests with city business, let alone a special death investigation. Same for the newspaper's executive editor, even if the donations predate this death case. Ack.

When Katrina relayed her findings to Joanne, the editor almost spit out her coffee. "This is so awful, but it's also tremendous work, Katrina. I'm very proud of you."

"What do we do now?"

"I'm sure you'll be told to bury these names in the story, if we include them at all, but I will fight for you. If we don't do it, some other media outlet will scoop and embarrass us," Joanne said. "Plus, it's the only ethical thing to do."

"I couldn't agree more," Katrina said. "I don't want to get tainted by this. We could all be written up by the Poynter Institute. I'd say it's high time to get Michael and Vincent Battrelle on the record about the Fontaines' deaths and those donations, too, don't you?"

"I wish we could wait until we had more of this nailed down, but my gut says yes. This is a huge development, Katrina. By the way, I wanted to ask, how are you doing? And how did your detective take today's story?"

"I'm fine, but Goode is not so good. The chief's on the rampage, which is what prompted all this new research."

"If you let your detective know what's coming this time, maybe we'll get a quote from the chief."

"Definitely."

"But I need to warn you about one other minefield, Katrina. Milton Biggs's firm not only represents Vitaleron, Biggs is the Battrelle family's lawyer, and he also does work for the paper. He often vets our investigative stories, so that's going to be a tall pile of dung to crawl through today. He'll have to choose his priorities and assign other lawyers to the rest."

"Yeah, I already checked his client list. But it didn't mention the whole family, only Vincent Battrelle Enterprises. Does this town have only one major law firm?"

"No, but it sure seems that way sometimes. To avoid an appearance of conflict, I'm going to suggest we bring in our First Amendment attorney, a fireball named Natalia Gonzales."

"Sounds good to me."

"You'd better make sure Vincent understands that you have officially quit his side job. And don't forget to call Winchester to give him a chance to argue that this is all legal, like William Fontaine said."

"If I go to Vitaleron right now and interview Michael Battrelle, maybe I can find out who coordinated all of these campaign donations before Linda and John Palmer try to pull me off the story."

"Good idea. I wouldn't be surprised if Palmer is having a breakfast meeting with the mayor and the chief as we speak."

"You're probably right."

"Once you get back, he and Linda will be mad that you disobeyed their orders, but it will be a done deal, and I'm sure you'll have more ammunition than just these donations by then. Don't worry, I'll back you up. We're going to the mattresses today. No matter what the cost."

Katrina was pleased that she'd chosen to confide in Joanne. Other than meeting Goode at Piatti, this was the first personal and professional connection that had felt right since she'd arrived. She grabbed a notebook from the supply closet and pushed past Jerry as he tried to stop her for a chat in front of the elevator.

CHAPTER 34
GOODE

Wednesday

Goode heard Stone yelling into the phone all morning, dealing with the media fallout of Katrina's story.

"I wasn't lying to you, she found this out on her own," Stone screamed at Ready Rhona, one of the few reporters he actually liked.

Goode put in his earbuds to block out Stone's voice so he could deal with more pressing matters. He didn't want to scare Katrina, but he meant it when he told her to be careful, and he wasn't exaggerating when he'd mentioned her as a "potential victim" to Agent Wattshispants.

Now that he knew more, he really did believe that Katrina could be in danger. There were too many dead people connected to her and her family for his comfort level.

He'd mostly ruled out the accidental or purposeful overdose scenario for Victoria and decided it would be an unlikely coincidence that both she and Simon would have a bad reaction to the sex drug after experimenting with it independently. He kept coming back to the fact that someone shot Simon after he was already dead, and it was most likely the same person who shoved pills down Victoria's throat.

Although maybe those two acts aren't mutually exclusive. Someone could have come in later and done one or both of those acts, with a different motive but the same intended outcome.

It wasn't a novel idea to stage a death scene to confuse investigators. At Sharon Tate's house in Benedict Canyon, for example, detectives found patches of her blood in places other than where her body was ultimately positioned. Her body was also smeared with dried blood, indicating that she'd been dragged inside from the front porch. Later, Charles Manson privately admitted that he'd come to the house later that night to rearrange the crime scene, because he thought his "children" had caused too much of a mess when they brutally stabbed, shot, and mutilated Tate and the four other victims in a ritualistic fashion.

Goode searched through the files London had uploaded to the CAIR system, hoping to find the drug log from Simon's surgery office. He found some scanned invoices of various medications, but nothing to show how much had been used, discarded, or was still in inventory. He would have to track down Simon Fontaine's nurse, who logged controlled substances in and out.

Calling the surgery office, he asked Regina Russell if the nurse had come in since they'd served the warrant Monday.

"No, Esperanza's still out sick. She was close to Dr. Fontaine and his daughter, so I know she's devastated," Regina said. "We had to cancel all the surgeries this week. We don't have a backup nurse, and Simon and my dad never trusted temps."

"Did you ask her about the drug log?"

"Yes, I did. She said she usually keeps a handwritten log in her desk, but she took it home Friday to put it into a digital format."

That's an oddly convenient coincidence.

"When did she decide to do that?"

"She said she was out running an errand Friday morning, when Dr. Fontaine texted her that the surgery got cancelled and she didn't need to come back. When her afternoon freed up, she stopped in to take the log home with her."

Plausible, but still a little too neat.

"I see. Well, we need it for our investigation, so if you can give me her home address, I'll go pick it up."

"Okay, let me call her and—"

"No, please don't, and that's not a request. I've already tried calling her, and she's not responding. The log is important evidence that's been removed from your office at a critical juncture. I don't want to give her any reason to destroy it."

"Oh, she would never do that. She's a kind, wonderful person."

"We have two dead victims, Ms. Russell. Why don't you give me the address, and let me do my job. We let you keep your computer so you didn't have to close your office. I'm asking you to do this now for me."

Regina was quiet for a moment. "Yes, of course. You're right. But I still don't believe Esperanza had anything to do with this."

"Did you see her in the office Friday morning?"

"No, I wasn't here. I have Fridays off."

"If she came by later for the log, no one would know that either, correct? I didn't see any security cameras."

"Yes, that's true. No one was here. My dad and Simon alternated days off so Simon could be at Vitaleron when he wasn't in surgery. They were able to get in some golf during the week that way, just not with each other."

After he hung up, Goode went searching for the paperwork he needed.

"Hey, Byron," he said to his teammate. "You type up the report yet on the drug inventory from Dr. Fontaine's narcotics locker and cold storage?"

"Put it in your inbox last night, as requested," Byron replied. "Emailed it to you as well."

Goode saw the manila file folder, labeled and waiting for him in his metal inbox. "Yes, you did. Thanks. I'm glad someone is doing their job. Foster, how about your inventory list from the Vitaleron lab?" Goode called over the partition to the other detective.

"Still working on it," Foster said.

"Hurry up, I need it yesterday."

Opening Byron's paper file, Goode scanned the list of drugs but wasn't familiar with any of them. His undercover narcotics gig dovetailed with his surfer lifestyle, which allowed him to wear his hair long and to drive his much-loved VW van for work. But his knowledge of street drugs didn't spill into controlled substances used in surgical procedures, other than fentanyl, which had been gaining ground and taking lives via deadly street trades.

He'd also learned quite a bit from the Kristin Rossum case. In 2001, fentanyl wasn't found much outside hospitals or pharmacies, so the ME's office didn't include it in their routine tox screens. That's why the drug, which is one hundred times stronger than morphine, went undetected in the blood of Rossum's husband, Greg de Villers, who was found dead in their apartment near UCSD, covered with red rose petals.

Rossum, a toxicologist in Artie's office, claimed de Villers had killed himself by mixing sedatives and cough medicine because he was depressed she was leaving him for her married boss, Michael Robertson, with whom she'd been having an affair. The ME's office only learned that de Villers had died of acute fentanyl intoxication after his blood was sent to a private lab due to ethical and procedural lapses within the agency.

Rossum had access to recreational and prescription drugs collected at death scenes by investigators like Artie, as well as a 10 mg vial of fentanyl citrate—enough to kill a roomful of people—that her boss had obtained to start testing for fentanyl. A subsequent police audit found that the vial was empty, and fifteen fentanyl patches, typically used by cancer patients, were missing. This audit helped convict Rossum of poisoning her husband with fentanyl. They couldn't prove exactly how he was involved, but they charged Robertson with conspiracy, an allegation he denied.

That's the kind of smoking gun I need: an empty vial, a discrepancy on the log-in sheet, some kind of proof that a drug was missing from Fontaine's surgery office or the Vitaleron lab.

CHAPTER 35
KATRINA

Wednesday

Parked in the Vitaleron lot, Katrina took a deep breath as she punched Vincent's number into her phone.

"Do you have news for me?" he asked hopefully.

Sometimes I really hate caller ID.

"No, I don't. I'm calling—again—to reconfirm that I can't help you find Alex, or do any other work that falls outside of my job as—"

"Listen, missy," Vincent interrupted. "I don't know why you think you have a choice in this. You still work for me. Are you trying to get yourself sent to the El Centro bureau?"

Knowing this was a metaphor for Siberia, Katrina felt a wave of indignation sweep through her. "If you want to fire me, then you can go through the proper channels. I was hired to be an investigative reporter for the *Sun-Dispatch*, not your personal investigator," she said firmly. "Do you want me to call the Poynter Institute and the *Advocate* and tell them you're trying to force me into an unethical conflict of interest?"

"Don't you threaten me—"

"I've got to go before I say something I regret. I hope you find Alex before the police do, Vincent."

She heard silence, followed by a deep sigh on the other end of the line. Was Vincent finally accepting he was powerless to stop her?

He paused. "You'll still tell me what's going on, though, won't you?" he asked with a hint of sadness and desperation.

I'm not going to say anything more until I know what's going on. I'll be damned if I'm duped by this man. Even if I did see him crying after I left the other night.

Katrina's voice softened. "I may call you later for a comment for the story I'm writing today," she said. "But I've got to go now."

She wished she could prove that he'd tried to hire her to limit or keep tabs on the information she was gathering, or that he was genuinely interested in finding his son.

Landing an interview with Michael Battrelle was much easier than Katrina had expected. Darla Johansen, the blond at the reception desk, immediately called back to the new CFO to announce Katrina's presence in the lobby.

"Katrina Chopin is here to see you," she said, pausing. "Okay, I'll send her in."

It's almost as if they were expecting me.

As Katrina stood in Michael's doorway, she caught him straightening his purple tie and smoothing his dark hair before coming over to shake her hand. He didn't look as trim or handsome as his brother and certainly not as flashy or confident.

"My father just called and told me you fired him," he said, chuckling. "We had a feeling you might show up, and here you are. He said he was getting you pulled off the story, but I guess not."

"Not yet, anyway," she said, smiling nervously.

Is he toying with me?

"I admire you for standing up to him," he said. "I've never been very good at that. Maybe you can give me some tips."

Katrina started to laugh but squelched the urge.

"My father also forbade me from talking to you, but I'm going to take your cue and start asserting myself. So, what can I do for you, Ms. Chopin?"

"You can call me Katrina. Was this Victoria's office? I figured you would take over her desk when you got her job."

"Yes."

"Is that weird for you?"

Michael shook his head and frowned, confused.

"I mean, is it painful, or awkward?"

Nodding, as if he understood now, he said, "Yes, to be honest, it is. But it also makes me feel closer to her somehow. The police were here first thing Monday, then I had to go to that news conference, so I've barely gotten anything done this week. Because I'm the 'boyfriend,' the police seem to think I'm a prime suspect."

"Really?" she asked, genuinely surprised. "What makes you say that?"

"Well, as you know, they served search warrants here, and when I talked to Detective Goode, he seemed awfully suspicious. Then, as he was leaving, he turned and asked me, kind of accusatorily, if I owned a gun, which I thought was strange, because I don't. But then I read your story the next day and saw that a gun was found next to Simon's body. Anyway, that's why I'm going to tell you some things I didn't tell the police."

"I'm all ears," Katrina said, pulling out her notebook.

"First, I want people to know I would never hurt Victoria," he said, maintaining eye contact with her, a sign that he was either telling the truth or was a very good liar.

It's hard to know which one, with Vincent, the master manipulator, as his teacher.

"Or Simon either, for that matter. He was like a mentor to me. I haven't even told my father any of this yet, because it was supposed to be a surprise, but things have gone too far to stay silent any longer. I don't care what he says; I'm CFO of Vitaleron now and we can't afford to have me viewed as a murder suspect."

After letting out a long sigh, Michael continued. "My brother, Alex, is an addict and has been half-assed trying to get clean for years," he said. "A year ago, he learned he'd gotten Victoria pregnant, then spontaneously asked her to marry him, but she turned him down flat. She called him 'pathetic,' said that she couldn't marry him as long as he was still using, and that she'd already aborted their baby."

Katrina nodded, noting the added layers to William's account.

"Over the next few months, I'd never seen my brother crash so hard," he said. "He said he felt like he'd caused the death of his own child."

Before the pregnancy, he said, Alex had thought Victoria would always be there for him. "But the abortion changed him. He finally got serious about his recovery. When he came to me six months ago and asked me to help him to get clean, for real this time, I couldn't say no."

Katrina nodded knowingly.

They decided not to tell Vincent in case Alex failed as he had so many times before. "He never said he was doing it for Victoria; he said he wanted a new life for himself."

So, Alex cloistered himself in the family's cabin in Ramona, away from the temptations of his usual party crowd. "I stayed with him the first week to help him through the withdrawal," Michael said.

After detoxing, Alex kept life simple: He did "financial consulting business" on his laptop, worked in the garden, rode his motorcycle around the mountains, and ate apple pie in Julian.

"Not knowing what Alex's long-term plans were, I started seeing Victoria. I didn't mention it to him because she refused to be exclusive. When she took off for a weekend without me, like the Vitaleron retreat in Hawaii, I didn't ask questions."

"Why didn't you go? You're a board member."

"Because she made it clear she needed space," he said.

In the meantime, Michael said, he and Alex talked weekly. "He sounded healthier than I'd heard him in years. But that's when things got complicated. Alex started talking about getting back with Victoria, which apparently had been his plan all along. Of course, he'd never told me that, and I didn't have the courage to tell him that I was in love with her.

"I dreaded the day he might take her from me, especially after watching him mess with her over the years. All those times they would hook up for a week, then he would run off with another woman or go on another binge.

"Maybe I was being naïve, but I thought I could get her to fall in love with me if I had enough time to show her what it was like to be truly cared for. I actually felt like the wall was cracking."

Looking embarrassed, Michael wiped away a tear. "So, I was pretty surprised when she called Friday and said she was breaking up with me, that there was someone else. I wasn't ready to let her go, but if Alex was my competition, I also knew I couldn't change history."

Michael stopped talking, but he looked like he wasn't done yet.

"Go on," Katrina nudged.

"But I was also concerned because she didn't sound well on Friday. At the time, I wondered if Alex had relapsed and persuaded her to do drugs with him, and that's why she was pushing me away, because she knew I'd take her back to rehab. You know that's where they met, right?"

"Yes, years ago. Your father told me the whole story. My brother was in that same program."

"That's right. I always liked Franny. I should have said this earlier, but I'm so sorry for your losses, Katrina."

"Thank you," she said, impatient to hear the rest of the reveal. "Finish your story."

"Well, that's just it. I never connected with her again, and then she was gone."

"How did you hear about it?"

"On the news, like everyone else, that Victoria and Simon were found dead after a neighbor heard gunshots Friday night and called it in. When the police came, they thought it was a double suicide."

It was an anonymous 911 call. Why did he say it was a neighbor? And the police have never said it was a double suicide. Where is this coming from?

Seeing her expression, he quickly added, "At least that's what Darren told me when he called Saturday afternoon. He said we had to protect the public face of the company to ward off any suspicion that we're in financial trouble. The drug trials had to keep moving forward before investors started yanking funding. And my dad agreed with him."

Recalling the photo of Darren McMurphy with Congressman Winchester and the female federal drug official, Katrina wanted to ask about the campaign donations, but not until he'd finished with Friday's events. "What happened after you talked to Victoria?"

"She didn't respond to my calls or texts, so I called Alex later that day, and he sounded excitable. He said, 'I need to get out of town. I can't be here right now. Don't tell anyone where I am.'"

"Do you think he was on drugs again?"

"I'm not sure. He could've been high, or he might have just been upset. I know I was. Darren hit me up about changing the corporate leadership as soon as Victoria's and Simon's deaths hit the news, demanding we call an emergency board meeting."

"Did you?" Katrina asked.

"No. I told him he was being disrespectful and hung up on him. So, he went around me and called all the other board members, full-on campaigning to be voted in as chairman over my father, who would have been the natural successor as vice chairman. This is off the record, but the guy has a heart of stone, if he has one at all. Sometimes I wonder if *he* was the one on drugs."

"Really?" Katrina asked, jotting down a note to ask Darren's ex, Daisy, about that. "Victoria never told you she was pregnant?"

"No. That was a huge shock, and even worse that I had to hear it from the police—in public in front of TV cameras. It raises a whole lot more questions, doesn't it?"

Katrina nodded sympathetically. "How did you end up taking over for Victoria as CFO?"

Michael explained that although he and his father both had law degrees and MBAs, the board said they'd rather have Michael at the helm.

"My dad can be a bully," he said. "I'm sure the board thinks I'll be easier to control. They're probably right, but I'm not a pushover either."

"So, your dad still doesn't know that Alex was in Ramona all that time?" she asked.

"No, and now even I don't know where Alex is. He never said where he was going."

As an objective reporter, Katrina knew she wasn't supposed to feel sympathy for a witness or suspect in a death investigation, but she couldn't help it. Michael seemed much more genuine than his father.

"The ironic thing is that Victoria had an IUD, so we never used a condom," he said. "I have to wonder how well it worked, though, since she got pregnant twice with it. I don't know if Alex snuck down from Ramona and had sex with her while she and I were dating or if she was with someone else, maybe in Hawaii. I'm not sure I want to know."

Seeing an opening to switch topics, Katrina asked, "Were you aware that Congressman Winchester's reelection campaign committee received $750,000 in direct donations and an additional $5 million from a PAC called Christians For Everlasting Marriage? The donations came from scores of people connected to Vitaleron, including your family and board members."

"Uh, no, I wasn't," Michael said.

As Katrina showed him the stack of donations she'd printed out, he added, "I should clarify. I was aware of the contributions, but certainly not the scope. Darren's our most politically connected board member, and he suggested we all give to Winchester because he's on the FDA committee. Said it's standard practice. Darren handled the Christian group donations too. So, as board chairman, he's the best person to address those questions."

"Okay," she said. "Is Simon or Vitaleron in financial trouble?"

"I honestly don't know, but I doubt it. I was only relaying what he said to me over the weekend. I'm only getting into the financials now. All I know is that our drug isn't considered lifesaving like the AIDS cocktail, which means we aren't eligible for the expedited FDA approval that Simon and my dad were hoping for. That means a longer testing process and a bigger long-term investment."

"Didn't Darren go to that Hawaii retreat three months ago?" Katrina asked. "I know he's going through a divorce."

"Yes," Michael said.

"Is it possible the baby could be his?"

Michael's face turned pale. He stood up abruptly, with a pained expression. "I need to get back to work, Katrina."

"Sorry, I hope I didn't offend you," she said, standing up. "Thanks for your time. I'm sorry for your loss too."

Michael nodded. He had tears in his eyes when she left.

CHAPTER 36
GOODE

Wednesday

Esperanza Cepeda lived in the University Town Center area, a few miles from the surgery practice and the Fontaines' mansion.

When Goode rang the doorbell at her condo, he expected her to answer with sniffles and red eyes, not a cocktail in hand. Whiskey on the rocks, by the looks of it. Her eyes were glassy and bloodshot, but it was apparently from being snockered at two o'clock in the afternoon.

"Ms. Cepeda?" he asked. "I'm Detective Goode, San Diego PD. Homicide. I've been trying to reach you."

That seemed to wake her up a bit, though not enough to break through her inebriated haze. He'd expected her to be Mexican because of her name, but he could see now that she was a Filipina.

"Okay," she said.

"Can I come in?"

Opening the door wider, she motioned clumsily toward the living room. "You want a drink?"

"No, thanks, I'm on duty."

She staggered a few steps ahead of him and plopped into an armchair. He sat across from her, waiting for her to register that this was a serious visit. She didn't.

"Regina Russell said you've called in sick all week. Are you really sick, or are you too drunk to go to work?"

"Of course I'm sick. I'm in mourning," she said. "My boss, Dr. F, and my friend Victoria are dead."

"So, you're upset. I can understand that. I'm sorry for your loss."

She stared at him blankly and blinked as she took another sip. The ice cubes clinked as he stayed purposely silent for a minute, hoping she'd volunteer something useful.

"I'm not sure if you know, but we served a search warrant on Monday, which specifically listed a drug log for all narcotics and drug supplies at the surgery office," he said. "Regina said you spontaneously decided to take the log home the day of the incident."

"Okay."

Given her mental state, Goode almost felt it wasn't right to question Esperanza, but he needed that log. If she'd been involved in these deaths somehow, that might explain why she was so drunk she could hardly talk.

Guilt can do that.

"I came over to pick up that log. I also wanted to let you know that we'll need you to give us an official statement when you're sober," he said.

"I am sober," she said. "Sober as a house mouse." She giggled, then covered her mouth with her hand. "Sorry."

"Ms. Cepeda, this is serious. I'm here because of a special death investigation. We think the Fontaines may have been murdered, and I'm wondering if you know anything about that."

Esperanza wrenched herself out of the chair, set her glass on a coaster on the table with a thud, and disappeared into the other room, where he heard her rustling through papers. She came back a minute later and thrust several handwritten sheets at him before dropping herself back into the chair.

"I was going to type the log into the computer, but I never got the chance, so I hope you can read my writing. I'm quitting anyway."

"Why are you quitting?"

"I can't go back there."

"I see. How long have you known the Fontaines?"

"Ten years. Dr. F hired me right out of nursing school," she said. "I'm really upset."

"So you said."

"I'm sorry, but I can't really talk right—" she muttered before nodding off. Within fifteen seconds, she was snoring.

After checking to make sure she was still breathing, Goode wrote a message on his business card, "Please call me in the morning," and left it on the table next to her before letting himself out.

It was a quick hop over to the ME's office, where Goode buzzed past the front desk and headed for the copy machine outside Artie's office.

Without the log, Foster hadn't been able to tell if any drug vials or containers were missing or unaccounted for at the surgery. But now that Goode had it for comparison with his team's audit reports, he made two copies of the paperwork and handed a set to Artie.

"Let's go over this together to look for discrepancies. Two pairs of eyes are better than one," he said.

Although, if Esperanza was in on this, she could have falsified the log. Or she could have taken a syringe full of something with her and no one would be the wiser.

Unfortunately, as she'd warned, the log was a mess. Neither of them could read her scrawls very well.

"By the way, the lab checked out those green capsules of the sex drug you gave me. They said it's nothing like they've seen before, but there was no trace of it in either victim. So, we can rule out accidental death via sex drug. I'll send this inventory and log over to them for ideas about what to test for next."

"I hope they can do that as quickly as possible," Goode said. "This new reporter, Katrina Chopin, is good. She doesn't have this log, but there seems to be a leak in your office, and I need to stay ahead of her."

"A leak? That's disturbing. I'll nose around about that. But don't worry, we want to find an answer as much as you do."

From there, Goode drove to the crime lab. Dwight Pepper had never called him back.

"Is Dwight here?" he asked the receptionist, laughing to himself. He'd almost asked for Spanky.

"He's in the back office to your left," she said.

After a couple of wrong turns, Goode found the tech—sweaty, flushed, and smiling sheepishly.

"Sorry I didn't call, but I wanted to wait until I was all done to give you my full report. After we sprayed BlueStar, we did find some blood spatter on the balcony, like you said, but it was pretty confined, and there wasn't much of it. We took some swabs for DNA, but it's unlikely we'll get a full profile for the reasons you stated earlier."

"Right. So, good news, bad news, but progress nonetheless. I'm sure it's Simon Fontaine's blood anyway. What else?"

"I had my assistant run back for a metal detector, and we went over the place again as you requested. It took us a while to crawl around in the bushes, but we finally found the damn bullet," he said, holding it up and smiling. "Now we have to see if it matches this gun."

"Excellent," Goode said. "I assume it will, but with a staged scene, anything is possible. The shooter could've used a different weapon and taken it with him."

"Let's find out," Dwight said.

He led Goode over to a vertical water tank built into the floor, twelve feet long and two feet in diameter. After firing the gun into it, he fished out the bullet.

"Now we compare this to the one we found in the bushes, which may have hit bone going through the skull, but we should still be able to tell," he said, leading Goode over to a microscope.

Goode hoped they matched. The paperwork that Dallas Fairchild had sent over looked legit, but this ballistics test was the best chance to confirm, scientifically, if it was his gun that fired that bullet.

"Looks like a match to me," Dwight said. "Take a look for yourself?"

"Sure, why not," Goode said, taking his turn at the microscope.

"Oh, and by the way, the gun was wiped clean. No prints or DNA. And no gunshot residue on either victim's hands."

"As I expected," Goode said. "Thanks."

Stone didn't sound all that pleased by the mix of results.

"What's the matter?" Goode asked. "That's multiple boxes we can check off. No death by sex drug and neither victim shot the gun, which points toward murder and away from accidental death or murder-suicide. We *thought* we had a staged scene, but now we can prove it with the blood, the fired bullet, and the casing found on the balcony as evidence that someone shot Simon postmortem and moved his body downstairs to the patio."

"That's all good, but we have another problem. Milton Biggs called. Alex Battrelle won't come back voluntarily. He's busy with 'client affairs' and claims he didn't kill anyone. Yes, he stayed the night with Victoria, but she was alive when he left her Friday morning, as their texts will show."

"What 'client affairs' does he have in the Caymans?"

"Biggs said Alex is committed to several days of financial transactions that require paperwork to be signed in person. He's devastated by Victoria's death. They've known each other for years. She was the mother of his child, even if she aborted it, et cetera, et cetera. Bottom line is we can eff off."

"So now what? I have to ask Super Special Agent Wattshispants to step in? He didn't want to tip off Alex that the feds were watching him."

"How else are we going to get him back here? We know he was one of the last, if not *the* last, people to see her before she died, and we need answers. If Alex has been doing transactions already, that's got to be enough to get him on something."

"I'll give it a shot."

Stuck in traffic coming into La Jolla, Goode could almost taste the refreshing vodka tonic with lime he was going to have. His car was barely moving when Katrina called.

"Good news, I hope," he said.

"You're not going to like this, but I wanted to give you a heads-up. I also need a quote from the chief," she said.

"Oh, great," he said, his heart thudding loudly. "What trouble are you causing now?"

As Katrina described the nearly $6 million in campaign contributions to Congressman Winchester, including those from the mayor and the chief, Goode shook his head.

"Wow," he said, pausing. "I sure didn't see that coming."

"I know, right? Do you want to pass on that message, or should I call Stone for the quote? I'm on a tight deadline."

"I'll run it up the flagpole. All the board members, the Fontaines, and the Battrelles, too, huh? That's crazy."

"Maybe not. Now we know why the mayor and chief let the Vitaleron execs speak at the news conference."

"Yes, and I didn't tell you this, but my lieutenant had initially wanted us to talk about the search warrants, but that got quashed—by the chief, apparently. The only reason those searches came out is because of your reporting."

"Really? Hmmm," she said. "Can I mention that when I talk to the chief?"

"Yes, as long as you don't say where you heard it."

"Thanks for the tip."

"Sure."

Great. This is not what we need right now, but maybe this will make them be more transparent. Politics and crime investigations don't mix well.

"A couple other questions, though."

I'm scared to ask.

"Shoot."

"Michael Battrelle thinks he's a murder suspect. Is that true?"

"You're going to have to ask Stone about that. But off the record, I find that an interesting comment, considering we still don't know how the Fontaines died."

"He also said that a neighbor called 911."

"We don't know that either. It was an anonymous call."

"That's what I thought. But he specifically said a neighbor reported 'shots fired.'"

"That's interesting as well. What else did he say?"

"That Darren McMurphy told him it was a double suicide."

"Did he, now."

"Yeah, that's what I said. Is Michael a suspect?"

"I can't really answer that, even off the record. But let's say his comments don't lessen my suspicions any."

"How well did Darren McMurphy know Victoria?"

"I don't know. Good question."

"Because he was with her in Hawaii at a retreat three months ago, and she's three months pregnant. I have a source who might know more. Thanks."

"Wait, who—"

Katrina hung up before he could finish his question. Still, she'd given him a new avenue for inquiry: Victoria Fontaine and Darren McMurphy.

Goode was feeling pumped when he called Stone from the parking lot at Windansea.

"Damn," the sergeant said. "She's good."

"I tried to tell you."

"Just wait till the case is over, buddy."

"I am. Don't worry. Since she couldn't quote me, I said you would answer her questions, or have the chief call her about the donation in his name."

"I'll call his cell right now. Then it's duck and cover. You'd better call Watts right away."

"Will do. I'll be at home with a cocktail later, reading through Victoria's computer files. Let me know when it's safe to come out of the bunker."

It was 4:45 p.m., and assuming that Agent Wattshispants left his cush office job promptly at 5:00 p.m., Goode tried to catch him.

"Detective Goode, I had a feeling you'd be calling," Watts said. "Let me guess. He won't come back voluntarily."

"Righto."

"I guess you'll have to wait until next week, then."

"Hopefully not. His attorney said he was conducting transactions as we speak, and I've also gathered more information about my potential victim. She's in more danger than I knew."

"It would give your request a lot more weight if you told me the victim's identity and what evidence you have to support that."

"Remember the Double-Judge Murders?"

"Yes, of course. Our office was asked to assist when your detectives' leads ran dry. What does that have to do with this case?"

Goode explained that his potential victim was the judges' daughter, who was now aggressively investigating this story for the *Sun-Dispatch*, and whose life had been threatened. He also summarized the Vitaleron and Lexicon property ownership ties, the personal and professional connections between the three families, and the campaign donation bombshell Katrina was about to break.

"Damn, Goode!" Watts said, his tone changing dramatically. "You know, if you'd have mentioned some of this up front, you would've gotten a lot more cooperation from me."

"I had a strong hunch before, but I was still developing the information at that point."

"I don't have to tell you that the unsolved murder of those judges is of great importance to the bureau, and to the community at large. If bringing Alex Battrelle back will help with that, as well as our money-laundering case, which now looks like it's part of a political corruption scheme, you'll have our full cooperation, Detective. This may be a quadruple win for our departments, combined."

"Great to hear," Goode said. "So how do we handle this?"

Watts said he would send two agents on the first plane to the Caymans, hook up with local law enforcement, and confront Alex at his hotel. If he didn't agree to come back voluntarily for questioning, they would threaten him with arrest for money laundering and conspiracy to defraud the IRS and escort him to the airport.

"If he's smart, he'll come voluntarily," Watts said.

CHAPTER 37
KATRINA

Wednesday

Katrina had barely laid her notebook on her desk when she felt Linda's presence beside her.

"Follow me, please," Linda ordered, heading for her office.

So much for the friendly, encouraging, editor-reporter relationship.

Once Katrina was seated, Linda closed the door and folded her hands on the desk in front of her, her mouth a straight horizontal line.

She looks pissed.

"Chief Baxter was in John Palmer's office this afternoon," she said.

Was that before or after I called Goode to give him the heads-up on tomorrow's story about their Christian PAC donations?

Katrina shifted in her chair uncomfortably as Linda's voice sliced through the air like a sharp knife cutting a rare steak. "Apparently, the chief voiced some concerns about your story today, not the least of which was the 'conservative Christian' reference. John reminded me that we've only just gotten past our problems with the SDPD, and he's concerned that this Vitaleron story has set us back again.

"Vincent Battrelle also called John to 'strongly suggest' that he take you off the Fontaine story. John thinks Norman Klein should take over, because the chief likes him, and that our biotech reporter can handle Vitaleron's financial fallout."

Katrina held her tongue until Linda was finished. "Okay," she said as neutrally as she could, even though her stomach could've tossed a salad.

"Then," Linda went on, "Vincent called back—and he was shouting so loud I could hear every word. You called him, then you interviewed Michael, both of which I expressly told you not to do." Pausing a moment, she asked her next question and drummed her fingers on the desk as she waited for a response: "Is that true?"

Is she expecting me to cry or something? What a bunch of bullies.

"Yes, it is," she replied calmly.

"Why, Katrina? *Why* would you disobey me like that?" Linda sounded as if she could barely contain herself.

Because this newspaper is a big effing ethical train wreck. But I can't say that, so I'll try the less emotional approach.

"Well," she said. "Did John Palmer tell you that he, the police chief, the mayor, the entire Battrelle family, the Fontaines, the Vitaleron board of directors—and their family members—have funneled nearly $6 million in campaign contributions to Congressman Brandon Winchester, both directly and also through a PAC called Christians For Everlasting Marriage? Winchester, by the way, sits on a committee overseeing the FDA."

Linda's shoulders rose as her head jutted forward, her eyes widening.

"Or did Vincent Battrelle tell you that the reason I called him was because he tried to hire me as his personal investigator to find his son Alex, who has been missing for six months? Or that he invited me over to his house for a drink last Saturday and tried to impede my coverage of this story by asking me to sign an NDA prohibiting me from publishing anything I learned while I was searching for his missing son?"

Linda shook her head, her mouth falling open.

"Or did he tell you that the only reason he called John Palmer today is because I told him—for the third time, I might add—that this side job was a huge conflict of interest so I couldn't do it? And then, when he threatened to fire me, I asked if he wanted me to call the Poynter Institute and the *Advocate* to report that he and the paper were trying to prevent me from reporting the story to save his family personal embarrassment and to hide their possible involvement in the Fontaines' deaths."

Linda closed her mouth, her jaws visibly clenched, and shook her head again. "No, he didn't," she said quietly.

"Did he tell you that Vincent forbade Michael from talking to me, but he did anyway, because he believes the police see him as a murder suspect? Or that both he and his brother were seeing Victoria, who called him Friday morning to break up with him, and that she didn't sound well on the phone?"

By now, Linda had stopped shooting visual daggers at her.

"And did he tell you that Michael said a 'neighbor' called 911, not some anonymous person, and that he described the Fontaines' deaths as a 'double suicide,' when the police have said none of that? He told me all of this on the record, by the way."

Barely able to contain a smirk, Katrina paused for a moment. "I should add that I did talk to Joanne about interviewing Michael, and she and I agreed that I should do it, even if it meant our jobs. So, I did have an editor's authorization."

"Great, now the patients are running the asylum," Linda said under her breath.

Well, at least she's got a baseline sense of humor.

"Should I go on?" Katrina asked. "There's more."

"God, no," Linda said. Leaping out of her chair, she headed for the door. "Wait here."

But Katrina was impatient and couldn't sit still. Standing up, she stood outside Linda's office to watch the Metro editor stride into Joanne's and shut the door.

Katrina didn't know what would happen next, but come what may. With a healthy inheritance, she didn't really need the money; this job was more about following her passion than anything else. But she still didn't want her career derailed by getting fired or by staying at a bad paper that had no ethical boundaries. She invested her soul in every important story, and this was already one of the biggest and most controversial yet. It was shaping up to matter as much, if not more than her mafia series, and, based on the recent death threat, it was just as dangerous.

If and when reporting became simply a job to her, the adrenaline and intrigue stopped streaming through her body, or the calling she'd once felt became more of a burden than a joy, she'd promised herself she would quit the business.

She'd come home to rekindle her parents' cold case, and she wasn't going to leave town again without doing that first. She hadn't gotten this far by giving up or giving in.

Surely Linda must know that, or she wouldn't have hired me.

At first, Linda gestured wildly as she stood above Joanne, who was seated in her chair. Then Joanne rose to her feet and animatedly engaged with Linda, who then flung open the door and marched toward John Palmer's office. Joanne gave Katrina a thumbs-up.

I've got to see this for myself.

Katrina searched for a good vantage point among her colleagues, whose heads were all turned toward the executive editor's corner glass fishbowl. They watched as the editor picked up his phone while Linda was speaking to him, grim-faced. When she turned to go, John held up his index finger and handed the phone to her.

Linda listened as John shook his head, stared down at his desk, and blew air out of his lips like a fish. Visibly agitated, Linda barked out a few sentences, slammed the phone down, snapped something at John, then stormed out of his office and headed back toward Katrina.

"I need a minute," she said before closing her door, sitting down, and covering her face with her hands. After remaining motionless for several minutes, she called Joanne to come over.

"This ought to be good," Joanne said as she passed Katrina.

Joanne was grinning when she emerged a few minutes later. "You're not going to believe this," she said, motioning for Katrina to follow her into her office.

"What?" Katrina probed. "So, we're not fired?"

"No, most definitely not. At first, Linda was pissed that I went behind her back and supervised you on this story, which is ridiculous because she put you on my team last week. After I explained why you came to me, Vincent sealed the deal by ordering her to take you off the story. Given everything you'd told her, she refused. She said, 'I'm sorry, Vincent, you know I can't do that.'

"Linda dictated to John what would happen next, before we all end up on the Poynter website as a national disgrace. If he didn't agree, she threatened to resign. So, I'll be your editor on this story from here on out. You'll be the only reporter unless we ask for help, say, if two big stories break on the same day. But she's removing herself, because of her close friendship with the publisher's family, and deemed, rightly so, that John's conflict was even worse, because his campaign donation specifically violates newsroom policy. So, you and I will be reporting directly to Big Ed, the Nightside Metro and Page One editor."

"Wow. Go, Linda!" Katrina said. "She did the right thing. Good for her."

"Yes, she did. Shocked me too. Great work, Katrina," she said, giving her reporter a bear hug.

For the next half hour, they discussed the two stories that Katrina would knock out that night, which would be featured side by side with a banner headline on A-1 in the print edition.

One would tell Michael's side of the love triangle with his brother and Victoria and their respective struggles with addiction. The other would lay out the gifts, junkets, and nearly $6 million in campaign contributions to Congressman Winchester and the Christian PAC, accompanied by the photo of Winchester yucking it up over cocktails with Darren McMurphy and the female FDA official.

"You'd better get writing," Joanne said, "and don't forget to call Goode, Winchester, McMurphy, the chief, and the mayor too. It's probably too late for a comment from the new drug office in DC, but call and leave a message anyway."

Scurrying back to her desk, Katrina saw the red message light blinking on her phone. There were half a dozen messages, including one from Vincent, threatening legal action.

"I thought you were going to help me find Alex," Vincent said. "And now you're going to plaster my family's personal tragedies all over *my* newspaper? You'd better not use anything I told you in confidence or I'll take you to court."

Because she still had no idea how Victoria or Simon Fontaine actually died, Katrina ended the story by posing several pending questions: Who was Victoria's mystery man in Hawaii, and could he be the father of her baby? Was one of these men in her life so angry about a breakup—or the pregnancy—that he killed her and her father for it? Or was there another motive entirely?

Katrina left messages everywhere, and again, gave Goode one last extra call. This time she caught him.

"You want to tell me where Alex is now, or do you want me to find him for you too?" she taunted.

"Soon, very soon," he said.

"You guys getting close to making an arrest or what?"

"Not yet. Has Stone or the chief called you?" he asked.

"Nope, although the chief tried to get me pulled off the story. So did Vincent. But I'm still on it."

"Of course you are. I'll make sure someone gets back to you. Gotta run."

CHAPTER 38
GOODE

Wednesday

Relishing a vodka tonic at his kitchen table, Goode methodically went through the files from Victoria's laptop and her Vitaleron computer.

He'd been at it for over an hour when Stone called. "The chief says he never made a contribution to that PAC," he said.

"Whaat?"

"Said he never even heard of it."

"Seriously? Katrina wouldn't make up something like that."

"I know, I went to the federal website she cited, trying to confirm what the chief said, but she's right. So, I told him that and conveyed a politically correct response to her—for his own protection. Even he knows he can be a loose cannon. I told him to keep his head down and hopefully this will blow over."

"I don't know about that," Goode said.

Double-fisted with a cocktail in one hand and his phone on speaker in the other, the detective paced around his cramped living room. He thought better when he was moving, even if there wasn't much room to maneuver around the coffee table into the short hallway with the built-in bookcase, which held a few cherished, framed family photos:

his parents' faded wedding portrait; his mother with him and Maureen as toddlers; he and Maureen as kids at their father's ranch in Montana, where they spent a few summers before he died; and a variation of the shot he had at work, with him and Maureen play-fighting with their surfboards as Star Wars laser swords.

"Did he explain why else the Vitaleron suits would commandeer our news conference in front of police headquarters?" Goode said.

"He said that was all the mayor, who, by the way, isn't denying his donation. But he's a politician, so who knows," Stone said. "Either way, the donations aren't illegal."

"You sound just like them. Are you running for office now?"

"Very funny. No, that's the party line from media relations. But we all agreed that it's messy. Maybe his wife sent the check and didn't tell him?"

"Who knows. But I don't see this blowing over. More like blowing up. Super Special Agent Wattshispants seemed pretty interested when I told him about Katrina's story. It should be online in a few hours."

"Yeah, it's going to be a late one for me, doing damage control."

"Better you than me."

"So, we're all set to question Alex Battrelle tomorrow afternoon? I'm going to tip off Rhona so she gets the exclusive. That way the pack will spend the next few days chasing her instead of this donation snafu."

"Yep. I'm looking for ammo for the interrogation right now in Victoria's computer files."

"Call me if you find anything. I'll be up for a while."

Goode poured himself another vodka tonic and a finger bowl of hard pretzels and peanuts. Sifting through Victoria's files was tedious but important.

Where is that memo to the board? I'm betting it has the answers we need, and it's got to be somewhere on this laptop.

Half an hour later, he found a file labeled "Dallas emails," containing exchanges between Victoria and Dallas Fairchild, the biochemist from

Vitaleron, which documented his claims about the stolen drug doses, security cameras, and password-protected locks.

"What should we do?" Victoria wrote.

Goode wanted to trust Fairchild, but he had to consider the possibility that the biochemist was lying.

Victoria's knowledge about the stolen doses is a reason for wanting her dead, so why is Fairchild still walking around alive? Was he playing her? And me?

Still hungry, the detective made himself a ham-and-cheese sandwich. The clock on the microwave read nine fifteen.

Time to check the web for Katrina's story.

As Goode read about Michael's love-triangle account, he felt annoyed, yet intrigued.

Damn. How did she get all of this out of him? Sure would have been helpful if he'd told me some of this instead of lying to cover up his personal drama. It's a touching story, but how much of this is true? He's claiming now that Alex called ***him*** *before leaving town? That means Alex could have gone to the house and killed the Fontaines, or he could have gone by after the fact, freaked, and fled. Where is that damned security footage? I need to watch it before the interrogation. No more excuses.*

Moving on to the campaign donation story, Goode was increasingly impressed with Katrina's research skills, which helped him as well. Now that he had a PAC name, he scrolled back through Victoria's files alphabetically.

He'd previously ignored a file cryptically labeled "CFEM," but clicked on it now that he realized it was an acronym for Christians For Everlasting Marriage. Created only a couple of weeks ago, the file contained screenshots from the FEC and the IRS websites, detailing many of the same donations cited in Katrina's story, including the chief's.

What is the deal? Why doesn't he admit it?

Goode accidentally clicked on the column of file dates, which put the most recent files at the top, and kicked himself for not doing that sooner. He immediately identified the file labeled "Draft board memo," which he'd missed during his previous searches, because he'd been looking in the B's for board. It was created three days before Victoria died:

"I regret to inform the board that we've had a security breach at Vitaleron HQ. Dallas Fairchild reports that portions of several batches of our new drug have recently gone missing from the lab. After discovering that the batches were missing, Dallas reviewed the phase-one test results, which will be submitted to the FDA next month, and said the numbers seemed exaggerated, i.e., 'fraudulently padded.' We discussed possible culprits and whether the two issues could be related. It has to be someone with access to our secure computer server, although it's possible that an outsider hacked into it.

"As you know, Darren McMurphy offered to help facilitate our marketing strategy to promote the drug to the conservative Christian community. He also approached Congressman Winchester about a fast-track approval with the FDA and sought guidance on how to overcome challenges with campaign-donation-limit restrictions."

Well, that's interesting. So, was she in on it, or was she trying to stay on the legal side of things?

"In that vein, I recently learned that $5 million in donations has gone to a political action committee called Christians For Everlasting Marriage. That seemed fine at first, until I discovered that the group gave that exact sum to a committee to reelect Congressman Winchester. This could get us into trouble with the FEC, although I'm not sure how much, because I didn't want to raise red flags by inquiring about it. More importantly, public records show that Vitaleron staff, board members, and dozens of our investors, including Mayor Norton and Chief Baxter, are listed online as donors to this group, as well as myself and Dallas Fairchild.

"The problem is, neither Dallas nor I ever made a donation. Someone apparently believed that Vitaleron investors wouldn't object or find out, but that's not the point. It's fraud. When I confronted Darren about this last week, he denied making the donations without investors' permission, but he admitted that he'd entered into an 'arrangement' with Winchester. He said Winchester asked for a lump sum of 'bundled' donations in exchange for a fast-tracked FDA approval, and a 'token of appreciation' for a female friend at the agency's new products division. I didn't mention the missing drugs from the lab so as not to escalate the situation. However, I did ask if he was crazy enough to bribe a congressman and an FDA official, and he replied, 'It's complicated.' I'm writing this letter now because I told him to get out of this 'arrangement' and reverse the unauthorized donations within two weeks or I would notify the board, but he has completely ignored my demands.

"In a related issue, Darren told me at the Hawaii retreat that he and several board members had invested millions with Alex Battrelle in the Caymans to hide money during their divorces, some of which has flowed back into Vitaleron. I told him that money needed to come back to the States to avoid tax complications or negative fallout from angry spouses that might harm our upcoming IPO. But he again dismissed my concerns, saying that would be 'politically inadvisable.'

"I didn't report this at the time, because I thought I could handle it personally, but I feel I have no choice. During the retreat I was drugged and subjected to an intimate situation with Congressman Winchester and his fiancée, who is a Vitaleron employee. I have no memory of this, because someone spiked my pineapple juice with a roofie, but I subsequently received some photos that were obviously taken to compromise me. I believe Darren only told me about the Caymans investments so he could claim he disclosed it, confident that I wouldn't report it to anyone because of the photos. This is all complicated by the fact that he's been dating Esperanza, my father's surgical assistant.

"One final issue: Last year, Vincent Battrelle purchased a majority interest in Keller Chemicals, which supplies several ingredients for our new drug. I thought that was curious at the time, but it didn't affect the company until Keller jacked up its prices. I questioned Vincent about it a couple of weeks ago, but he shut me down. He said Alex handled the purchase for him, and that it was 'good business' to ensure we have a reliable supplier. I disagreed, told him it was a conflict, and that he should divest from the company within two weeks or I would bring it to the board's attention.

"Since Darren and Vincent haven't acted on these matters as I've requested, as CFO I'm forced to formally seek the board's authorization to determine if we should retain outside counsel to evaluate or investigate them before the IPO next year. They may not only get us into legal trouble as individuals, but they could also cause significant financial losses to the company and its investors, which would endanger Vitaleron's future. We don't need the SEC and FEC in our books, the DEA in our lab, or the FBI in our business. We also don't want any of this leaking out before the IPO."

Whoa. Talk about a smoking gun. So, was Victoria really in love with Alex, or was she having sex with him to get information to protect Vitaleron? How deep was Alex into this financial mess? Would he, Vincent, or McMurphy, for that matter, kill her to save themselves?

Clicking back to Katrina's story, Goode took a closer look at the photo and caption: Darren McMurphy, Congressman Winchester, and Marcia Copeland, the FDA's new drugs director, sipping martinis at a political event in Washington, DC.

There she is. Ms. Token of Appreciation. Nice work, Katrina.

It was fortuitous that the SDPD, working under FBI cover, had prodded Alex Battrelle to come back for questioning, because the content of this memo would necessitate hauling in his father and brother—and Darren McMurphy—as well.

But after reading Katrina's stories, Goode was worried that she'd seriously escalated the danger to herself by placing an even bigger target on her head. The perpetrators would have to assume that she would reveal more details in future stories.

I don't want to see her get hurt.

Still, Goode was in a difficult place. Until he had access to Victoria's emails, he had no way of knowing if she'd ever sent this "draft" memo.

He also couldn't share it with Katrina because that would compromise the investigation.

He'd have to walk the line, somehow. He was prepared to camp outside her apartment to make sure no one tried to shoot her up with something, but he didn't want her to feel like he was spying on her. At first, he thought it would be better to obtain her address off the rock-threat incident report, but he decided he should go the honest, straightforward route. Mostly, anyway.

He tried calling Katrina's cell phone at 10:30 p.m., figuring she would be at home and done with work by then. But he got her voicemail, so he left her a message.

"Can you call me, please? It's important."

In the meantime, he emailed Victoria's memo to Stone with "Motives aplenty" in the subject line. But then he immediately called the sergeant, too excited to wait for a response.

"Did you see my email?" Goode asked.

"No. I'm walking the dog. Good news, I hope. Give me the short version."

Fired up with adrenaline, Goode let it all out in one stream of thought. "So now we've got multiple motives to kill Victoria, and probably Simon, too, because the killer probably assumed she'd confided in her father. But the chief may be telling the truth about the donation after all. I'm going to question Esperanza Cepeda first thing tomorrow, before she gets plowed. Maybe she can fill in some blanks."

"Good plan."

"The whole Battrelle clan seems to have their hands in this, along with McMurphy and Winchester. With the sex drug ruled out as the cause of death, Artie sent the logs and audits to the private lab to determine what to test for next."

"Pretty dumb to make an unauthorized donation in the police chief's name. But that's why we have jobs. Criminals are dumb."

"So true. Gotta run; that's my other line," Goode said.

"What's up, Surfer Man?" Katrina asked with a deeper, sexier voice than usual.

She sounds a little buzzed.

"Out for an adult beverage tonight?" he asked.

"I'm not sure that's any of your business," she said coyly.

"No judgment. I can hear it in your voice. You sound, uh, happy. Great job on the stories tonight, by the way."

"Thanks. It was a long day, but it was good. My editor took me out for some wine. What's so important?"

"I don't want to worry you, but with you getting that death threat even before these stories tonight, I thought it would be good if I knew where you lived," he said, trying not to sound too dramatic.

"Um, yeah, okay. I live in a funky apartment complex at the end of Brant Street, behind the Albertsons in Mission Hills. It's on the backside, upstairs, overlooking the canyon. But there's something you're not telling me. What happened today?"

Goode paused. *Here we go. Be careful.*

"Let's say we're pretty confident now that the Fontaines were murdered. You and I have both uncovered some pretty good motives, and I want to make sure you're safe."

"C'mon. What did you find out?"

"You're going to have to trust me. We're still in the thick of it, but the pieces are starting to come together."

"Well, I haven't gotten any more threats, but my worry level has increased ever since. Back in Northampton, I had a recurrent nightmare of getting abducted by the Polish mafia, and it actually started up again the night *before* I found my car window smashed. It was almost like I knew it was happening, even in my sleep," she said. "I'm trying not to be alarmist, because I need to focus on this story, but I can't stop thinking that all of this might be related somehow to my family's murders."

"After finding those property records, I've been wondering that myself."

"It's sweet of you to worry about me. It's more than I ever got from the Northampton PD."

"That I do."

"I probably shouldn't tell you this, but my entire living-room wall to the outside is made of glass."

Great, she's even more vulnerable than I thought.

"Sorry," she said, unable to suppress a yawn.

"Am I boring you?"

"No, not at all. Anyway, now you know where my apartment is. Maybe you'll see it someday, in our future lives. But I'm sleepy, and I've got an early start tomorrow."

"Goodnight, Katrina. And be careful, okay? Do you have drapes or blinds you can pull?"

"Yeah, I do."

"Do me a favor and close them tonight."

"I'm way ahead of you. Goodnight, Surfer Man."

As soon as they hung up, Goode put on some sweatpants, a sweatshirt, and a jacket, and threw a pillow and a blanket into his VW van.

I'm going over there to make sure no one is lurking around or cutting her brake lines. I'll sit up and watch, maybe even crash for a while. She'll be asleep. Won't even know I'm there.

CHAPTER 39
KATRINA

Thursday

As exhausted as she was, Katrina was wide awake after hanging up with Goode. Before the rock incident, she'd enjoyed falling asleep with the moonlight shining in through the glass doors in her living room. But now that she felt someone was watching her, those blinds were closed.

What the hell happened today, and why's he doing the Vague about it?

She lay down and read her phone until midnight, when her eyelids finally grew heavy again. As she was dropping off, she thought she heard the roar of Goode's VW outside, up the hill in the carport. But she didn't want to get dressed to take a look.

He can't be ***that*** *worried. He would've told me, wouldn't he? Unless something is really wrong, in which case it's good that he's out there. I'm not going to think about it. Go to sleep.*

Four hours later, she awoke to the same roaring sound, only this time it was receding into the distance.

That ***was*** *his van. It's touching, really, that we hardly know each other, but he already cares enough to watch over me during his off hours. If he left, I guess I'm not in immediate danger. Go back to sleep. You've got a big day ahead.*

She managed to catch a few more hours of sleep in between flashes of the recurring nightmare, but they were so light and fitful that she decided to get up and take a quick run around the neighborhood to burn off the excess energy.

Should I ask Goode directly if that was him outside? Don't I have a right to know what's going on?

After climbing the stairs to the carport, she saw that a big asterisk made of duct tape was now holding the broken glass of her car window together to prevent it from imploding. She'd been meaning to do that herself but had been too flipping busy.

So, he was here. That was thoughtful of him.

Smiling, she took off on her run, keeping an eye out for strange or suspicious men who looked out of place.

After showering, she headed into the empty newsroom with her muffin and cappuccino to read the paper and listen to her voicemails without interruption. Once other reporters started straggling in, she figured it was late enough to head north to knock on the Fontaines' neighbors' doors.

Because the mansions on La Jolla Farms Road were spaced so far apart, she hoped she could quickly determine who on the block had heard the gunshot and called 911. By now, the yellow police tape was gone from the Fontaine house, signaling that the detectives had finished processing the house.

I wonder if William Fontaine has been inside yet or if the grief is still too fresh to dive into his family's closets, belongings, and accounts like I did after Mom and Daddy died.

Katrina remembered that time well. The emotional toil of sifting through boxes of her parents' belongings, some handed down over several generations. The sadness that gripped her as she went through her brother's things, and the memories that went with them. She couldn't stop crying.

As she peeked through the Fontaines' gate, she heard a buzzing sound and saw that the security camera moved or stopped when she did.

Is someone watching me here, too, or am I being paranoid? The camera seems to be triggered by a motion detector, but if it's videotaping me now, the security footage will be key to knowing who came in and out of the house last Friday. Maybe Goode has already watched it, and that's why he camped outside my place last night.

She waved at the camera to see if someone would open the gate or talk to her via the intercom, but she got no response. In the middle of the bushes was a blue sign that read **This property is being monitored by Fullerton Security**, with a phone number, which she promptly called.

"I'm standing outside the Fontaine house on La Jolla Farms Road and I'm wondering if you guys are running the security camera from your office or if someone's watching me from inside?"

"I'm sorry, who are you with?" the clerk asked.

"The *Sun-Dispatch*."

"Okay, well, I'm not authorized to talk to anyone but the homeowner."

"That'll be tough. He's dead. You guys wouldn't want me to write that the house isn't being watched, would you? Who knows what liability that could create if this empty house were vandalized."

"I never said we weren't monitoring the house, ma'am."

"I didn't say you did. I said you wouldn't want me to say that you weren't."

"Whatever. I've got to go. My other line is ringing."

"Okay, but I still need to know—"

Click.

He hung up on me? No, I don't think so.

"Fullerton Security."

"We seem to have gotten cut off."

"Ma'am, I really can't help you, and I'm the only one here answering the phones."

"Why don't I talk to your supervisor. Maybe he'd like to help me write an accurate story."

"I'll have him call you."

Two minutes later, her phone rang.

"Hi, this is Charlie Fullerton. Are you calling from a Massachusetts number?" he asked.

What does that matter? Nosy man.

"Yes. I just moved here from there. Do you guys have footage of who went in and out the day of the Fontaines' deaths?"

"Yes, a homicide detective picked it up four days ago. You should talk to him."

"Can I get a copy? The paper will be happy to pay for it."

"Sorry, no can do."

"How about letting me watch it there? You have a master copy, right?"

"Yes, but—"

Before he could say no, she said, "Great, I'll be down in a bit."

As Katrina walked west toward the ocean, the hot asphalt heated the thin leather soles of her pumps with each step. The horizon seemed to grow wider, the strip of greenish-gray ocean expanding in front of her.

I'm sure Goode is way ahead of me on this, because he's finally admitting that he thinks it's a murder case.

Reaching the next driveway, she was relieved to see there was no security gate to prevent her from entering the shadowy tunnel of trees leading to the house. She was about three steps in when she was startled by an athletic-looking, dark-haired man who emerged from the leaves on the right. He was about her age, wearing khaki shorts, a red polo shirt, and a worried expression.

"Can I help you?" he asked in a Latin accent with an edge. But once she explained the purpose of her visit, his tone softened.

"Sorry, we're all a little jumpy after the shooting," he said. "The whole neighborhood is in shock."

Katrina scribbled his comment into her notebook. "Can I get your name?"

"It's Pablo, but I don't live here. I'm visiting from Brazil. It's my sister and brother-in-law's house."

"That's okay. Were you here Friday night?"

"Yes."

"Did you hear the shots fired?"

"No, we were watching a movie, and the surround sound was up pretty loud. We wouldn't have known the difference."

"So, you guys didn't call 911?"

"No. You should try Cat, the lady two houses down on the left. My sister calls her the Gossip Queen."

His words were like chocolate. She thanked him and headed back toward the road, figuring she'd try the homes in between as well.

The next house had a gated entrance and an intercom, just like the Fontaines'.

"Hi, I'm with the *Sun-Dispatch* and—"

"We already take the paper," the woman interrupted.

"I'm not selling the paper, I'm a reporter," Katrina said.

Silence. She tried pushing the intercom again but got no response.

Gossip Queen will talk to me. If she's home, that is.

Her house was much closer to the street than the others and, like Pablo's, had no security gate. A woman in her mid-fifties answered the door in red-framed, cat-eye glasses that matched her spiky bright-red hair and perfectly manicured nails.

A trust-fund hipster?

"Yes, dear?" she said. "What can I do for you?"

After hearing Katrina's spiel, the woman invited her in. "Let's talk in the kitchen," she said, breaking into a wide smile. "I'm cooking spaghetti sauce."

Katrina breathed in the aroma appreciatively as the woman introduced herself. "But everyone calls me Cat," she said, explaining that she sold real estate in La Jolla, and specifically the Farms.

"I was home with a cold on Halloween, gardening out front, and I've been wondering ever since why the police never mentioned that an officer went into the Fontaine house around lunchtime. The news stories said police didn't show up until almost ten o'clock at night, an hour after the 911 call."

"Wait, what?" Katrina asked, confused.

"Yeah. I saw an officer walk up to the gate and make a call on his phone. He didn't use the intercom. The gate opened, and he went inside," she said. "But there was no police car parked anywhere. I don't even know where he came from."

Katrina was befuddled. "Are you sure he was a police officer?"

"Well, he was wearing a uniform. He even had on one of those hats, like you see on TV," she said.

"What time did you say this was?"

"Around noon," Cat said. "I didn't think anything of it until I read your story, but when I called the police's nonemergency line yesterday, they told me I must've been seeing things. The dispatcher was so patronizing: 'Ma'am, it was Halloween, and our patrol officers don't wear hats,' he said. I told him I was only telling him what I saw, that this was an adult, not a kid playing dress-up, and there was no costume party going on at the Fontaines' from what I could tell."

Katrina shook her head with disbelief as she scribbled in her notebook. *Can't wait to hear what Goode says about this.*

"What time did he come out?" Katrina asked.

"No idea. I was only outside long enough to pull some toadstools that popped up after the rain. They were irritating me. Like a hangnail."

"Did you know the Fontaines well?"

"No," Cat said. "They kept to themselves, and they were hardly ever home anyway. Workaholics, the both of them."

"Thank you, this is very helpful," Katrina said, handing her a business card. "Please call me if you think of anything else."

"Will do. I hope they catch the bastard who did this," Cat said. "I haven't slept right since it happened. And you can quote me on that."

CHAPTER 40
GOODE

Thursday

At three o'clock on the dot, a black Suburban pulled up to police headquarters, and Milton Biggs and Alex Battrelle stepped out. Rhona Chen and her cameraman were waiting for them in the plaza.

"Did you kill Victoria and Simon Fontaine?" she called out.

"No, I did not," Alex said.

"Do you know who did?"

Biggs grabbed Alex by the forearm, a signal to stop talking. "Those assholes leaked this as a perp walk," the attorney muttered. "Not a good sign."

Inside, Goode sat across the table from Alex and his lawyer in the interrogation room. Two FBI agents and SSA Martin Watts, who had arrived through the back entrance to avoid the media, listened on the other side of the one-way mirror. The feds would have their turn with him next.

As Goode stared into the suspect's eyes, Alex met his gaze without flinching. Time would tell if this was a sincere form of communication or a practiced business measure, honed from years of cons, both personal and professional.

"I know you were with Victoria Thursday night and Friday morning. Did you shoot her up with something?"

"No, absolutely not. We've both been clean for some time; her for years, and me for the past six months. We made love all night. She wasn't feeling well when I left, but she was most definitely alive. She said she'd been throwing up, but she wears an IUD, so she didn't realize it was morning sickness until she took a home pregnancy test on Thursday. She called to tell me it was positive right away, and I was so excited I drove straight down from Ramona. I spent all day Friday shopping for a ring."

"Did you guys ever experiment with Vitaleron's sex drug?"

"No. We don't need any help in that department."

"Okay," Goode said noncommittally.

"Victoria and I were in love," Alex said. "It just took me eighteen years too long to realize it. I'm not a murderer, and I never would have hurt her or our baby."

"How do you know it's yours?" Goode asked. "You know she was seeing your brother, right?"

Alex's eyes widened and he shook his head, confused. "Michael? No, actually, I didn't." He paused before explaining that even though he'd been in Ramona for the past six months getting sober, he'd texted her one night about three months ago and they'd slept together. "But like I told her, I didn't care whose baby it was, I'd raise it as if it were mine, and we could have another one of our own."

"So why run off to the Caymans? I saw in your text that you wanted to come back to see her that night."

"That's right. After I left her house, I stopped at the store for some groceries and went to my house to eat breakfast before I went ring shopping. I finally found the right one at an estate jeweler on Prospect. I was on my way back with it when Michael called," Alex said, recounting their conversation.

"What have you done?" Michael asked, sobbing. "Victoria and Simon are dead. Victoria is lying on her bedroom floor, and Simon is at the bottom of the stairs, like he fell or was pushed. What did you give her? And what did you do to Simon?"

"What the hell are you talking about?" Alex asked. "Simon was alive when I saw him last night, and Victoria was fine when I left her this morning."

"There's oxy and Xanax on the nightstand and needle bruises in the fold of her arm, just like when you were still using," Michael said. "She was cutting herself again too."

"I can't believe this. There were no drugs or needles in her bedroom while I was there, and I didn't see any cutting marks, because the lights were out. You know we're both sober, Michael, and that I would never hurt her."

"I didn't know you'd been here, but as soon as I saw her arm, I thought of you immediately. If you were the last one to see her, you're a natural suspect. You'd better get the hell out of town."

Alex explained to Goode that his brother never mentioned that he'd been seeing Victoria. "But he was right that you would consider me a suspect, or I wouldn't be sitting here right now. When Michael said he would 'take care of it,' I didn't ask for details. I was devastated. My mind was a blur. I drove straight to the airport, and thankfully they had a flight to the Caymans. I didn't even bring a toothbrush."

Take care of it? What does that mean?

"That's interesting," Goode said, "because Michael told me he didn't know she was dead until he heard about it Saturday on the news. How do you reconcile that?"

"I'm sure he was trying to protect our family name, but he should come clean now that my ass is on the line. Here, I'll show you the call," Alex said, pulling his phone from his pocket. Scrolling through his call log, he showed Goode the incoming nine-minute call from Michael on Friday at 7:23 p.m.

Bingo. All we need are the cell-tower records to confirm that Michael was at the Fontaine house when he made that call.

"Why the Caymans?"

"I do business there. There's nothing illegal about that. My lawyer advised me to come back to deal with this face-to-face rather than have you guys put our family through the public humiliation. But I see by the TV camera outside that you're going to do that anyway."

"Running off to the Caribbean makes you look guilty. You know that, right?"

"If you say so."

"If it wasn't you, then who would want Victoria and her father dead?" Goode asked. "What about Michael? Was he jealous or hurt enough after she broke up with him that morning?"

"I'm sure he was hurt, but he's a pussycat. She did say she was dealing with some heavy stuff at Vitaleron, but our minds were elsewhere."

"Well, there were serious legal and financial issues that she was about to disclose to the board, some of which implicated you and your father. Did she mention any of that?"

"No. That's news to me."

"Really? What about your father? I hear he had some problems with Simon Fontaine. A battle over power?"

"Simon forced me off the board before I got sober. My dad was pissed, but not enough to kill anyone. He's more into mind games than hunger games."

Alex stared down at the table. Goode wondered if he was feeling the weight of the wreckage his addiction had caused, or if he was only pretending to feel remorse, as Goode had seen many addicts do.

"The FBI says you've been doing illegal transactions in the Caymans and that Victoria was aware of this. She didn't confront you about that?"

"Asked and answered, Detective," Biggs interjected.

"Like I said, we were in no mood to talk about work," Alex said.

"Did you know she had a threesome in Hawaii a few months ago, involving Congressman Winchester and his fiancée? Curious timing, given her pregnancy, don't you think? Maybe she told you about that and you got angry?"

"Not my style. But no, she never said anything about a threesome. She was free to see whoever she wanted, including my brother, apparently. I was trying to get clean so we could be together. The night we spent together a few months ago was a weak moment on her part. It was right after she got back from Hawaii, so maybe she wanted to get that scene out of her head. If that's the case, I don't blame her. Winchester is my client, but he's also a sleaze."

"When I questioned your father, he told me you'd been missing for six months, and he didn't know where you were. Was he lying?"

"No. I wanted to surprise him when I came back sober."

"What about the business deal that you two did with Keller Chemicals? Did he tell you that Victoria wanted you to divest those shares?"

"No, I just told you I haven't seen or talked to him for six months. But we knew there would be a strong market for the chemicals needed to make the sex drug. There's nothing illegal or unethical about that. It's simply good business."

"Well, she gave your dad a deadline that he failed to meet, and she was about to inform the board."

"Never heard a thing about it."

"I'm sure your family stood to lose some good money on that. Smells like a motive for murder to me."

"That's absurd. Penny-ante stuff."

"What do you do in the Caymans for your clients?"

"That's not relevant to the death investigation, Detective," Biggs interjected. "He invests in various companies and funds."

"You're wrong. It actually is relevant in this case," Goode said. "And as I told you before, we're pretty sure these are two homicides, even more so now."

"Again, asked and answered," Biggs said.

"If Victoria wasn't using drugs, why would she have Xanax and oxycodone on her nightstand? And with her past history, it seems unlikely that her father would knowingly prescribe either one of those, especially when she was pregnant."

"I've been wondering about that myself," Alex replied. "All I can tell you is that the drugs weren't there when I left around eight fifteen. Something bad must have gone down afterward. What do the toxicology tests say?"

"Nothing so far," Goode lied. "We're still looking."

At that point, Goode stood up and left the room, purposely leaving Alex hanging. His story was believable, but it also left room for a possible Battrelle family conspiracy, which he, Stone, and Watts had already discussed. Based on Victoria's memo, Darren McMurphy had several reasons for wanting Victoria out of his way too.

Even if Alex wasn't involved in the actual murders, he could still be liable for felony murder, when a murder occurs while another crime is being committed by a member of a conspiracy. They would have to bring Vincent and Michael Battrelle in again to clear up the discrepancies in their stories.

"I'm done with him for now," Goode told Watts. "He's all yours. Let me know if he says anything more useful about the murders."

"We've already got the arrest warrant for money laundering and conspiracy to defraud the IRS, so we'll get a statement—hopefully an admission of some sort," Watts said. "I can dangle a deal if he agrees to talk more about the murders, but that would be up to you to pursue further. We'll take him over to MCC when we're done, so your potential victim will be safe for a few days—from this suspect anyway—until a judge sets bail. Justice has been served here, Detective. Well done."

CHAPTER 41
KATRINA

Thursday

Katrina was so hungry she was almost ready to chew her hand off. After stopping to grab a tuna sub on Convoy, she continued past the Vietnamese and Thai restaurants until she came to the Fullerton Security office. The clerk buzzed her in.

"Charlie will be right out," he said, motioning her toward the uninviting chrome-and-vinyl chairs. Katrina paced back and forth until a door opened in the middle of the blue wall.

"Ms. Chopin," Charlie said. "Come on back."

As she followed him down a narrow hallway, they passed a series of cubbyholes, each of which contained a remarkably similar dour-faced, dumpy, bald man sitting at a computer.

Right out of a Dr. Seuss book, "with stars upon thars."

Charlie was bald, too, but he wore a friendly smile, probably because he was the boss. With his paunch, he looked like a bowling ball with stubby legs, draped with a green-and-blue diagonally striped tie.

The viewing room had one large central screen, surrounded by smaller screens divided into four views, one for every camera in or around a client's house.

Charlie explained that a client could monitor these same views from a computer inside their house.

"Is someone inside the Fontaine house right now?" she asked, describing the camera at the front gate that had turned toward her that afternoon.

Confirming her assessment about the motion detector, Charlie said, "I doubt anyone was inside. No one but the police—and you—have contacted us, though we've been keeping close tabs on it due to the recent events. The Fontaines' contract is paid up through the end of the year."

He planted himself in a swivel chair in front of the largest screen and offered her the chair next to him. "What time do you want to start the tape?" he asked.

"How early can we go?"

"There was a power outage here that morning, so there's no footage from six to ten o'clock, but the detective said the 911 call didn't come in until 9:00 p.m. anyway."

Katrina stayed mum about her new information from Cat. "Let's start at 10:00 a.m."

"Okay," he said, shrugging. After typing in the time, he hit "play" and slowly advanced the video.

"Wait, I saw something," she said. "Can you rewind?"

Charlie did as he was asked, and advanced more slowly. At eleven thirty, an Asian woman wearing nursing scrubs and her hair in a bun walked up to the gate carrying two white paper bags. The bigger one looked like it held take-out food, the other was a small pharmacy bag.

Now that the nurse's face was directly in view, Katrina could see that she was a Filipina in her late twenties. Pressing a button, she waited for the gate to slide open, then disappeared down the driveway. It appeared that she'd been there before and that the occupants buzzed her in because they were expecting her.

"Can you zoom in on her face?" Katrina asked.

Charlie complied, but Katrina still didn't recognize the nurse, which wasn't surprising because all her interviews had been phoners. Still, something pinged in her short-term memory.

"Can you print me a screen grab of her face?"

"I'm not sure the police would want me to do this."

"They're your cameras, right?"

"Yes, but it's an ongoing investigation."

"Please, Charlie. You're a private company, and the public has a right to know. That's why I'm here."

As the printer whirred behind them, Charlie swiveled around and grabbed a black-and-white, time-stamped side view of the woman.

"Thanks. Let's keep going."

They stopped the footage again at 12:02 p.m., when the uniformed police officer showed up, just like Cat said.

"Can you zoom in on his face too?"

But as much as the officer's head was magnified, he was looking down and away from the camera, his face mostly obscured by the hat. After he called someone on his cell, the gate opened.

"He didn't hit the intercom. Someone let him in from the inside," she noted, asking for another screen grab.

Charlie advanced the tape again until a shiny, silver Mercedes pulled up to the gate. The white-haired male driver, who resembled William Fontaine but was slightly older, punched a code into the keypad, then drove through at 12:32 p.m.

"Wait, can we watch that again for the plate number?"

"Sure," Charlie said, reaching for a clipboard and flipping through the pages. "Yeah, that's what I thought."

"What?" Katrina asked as she wrote down the number, along with a description of the car.

"That's Dr. Fontaine's car. His daughter drives a red Miata convertible."

"Really? Okay. Thanks. So, we know he was still alive at twelve thirty."

As they advanced the video to one o'clock, Katrina saw the nurse approach the other side of the gate, looking nervous and agitated. Scared, even. "There she is again."

The nurse pushed a button, waited for the gate to open, then quickly walked through it.

Are Victoria and Simon already dead by this point, or is the nurse just late for work? It's still eight hours before the 911 call. It would help if we knew the time of death.

Half an hour later, the uniformed officer went through the same motions, the top portion of his face still obscured by the brim of his hat.

It's almost as if he knew how to avoid being ID'd by the security cameras. Could this officer be a friend of the victims, stopping by for a casual visit over the lunch hour? Or was he off the clock, doing something he shouldn't have been?

The officer looked both ways up and down the street with a tight-lipped expression—until his lips sort of curled upward.

Surely, he didn't just smile if those people are dead inside? Wait, is that lipstick? So, is that a female officer?

The officer looked thin, but strong, and the posture looked more like a man than a woman. After reading about crimes committed by police impersonators, she knew that anyone could buy a uniform, but how many officers still wore hats, let alone lipstick?

Not unless they're on a TV show, in a parade, or at a funeral. Maybe the Fontaines are still alive at this point. The nurse didn't leave until after Simon got home. I wonder why he and Victoria were home, not at work, on a Friday.

The next five hours of video showed no movement until 7:15 p.m., when a midnight-blue Jaguar pulled up. A man with brown hair leaned out the window, punched a number into the keypad, then drove through. But there wasn't enough light on his face for Katrina to recognize him.

"Can we go back and zoom in on the driver's face?" she asked.

Katrina gasped this time through. "Is that Alex?" she asked softly.

"Huh?"

"Nothing," she said, cursing herself for thinking out loud.

"You know him?" he asked.

"I'm not sure. Maybe. It's dark so I can't really tell. Can you print me a still of his face and one of his license plate?"

Charlie handed her a dark, grainy photo that could have been Alex, but also could've been Michael. She'd only seen Alex in photos. The driver was wearing a white dress shirt and tie—certainly not a Halloween costume. Nor was it a black outfit with a stocking mask, as if he were about to commit a murder.

He knows the security code, so he's been there before.

Katrina was antsy to get back to the newsroom to run the plate number with the Department of Motor Vehicles and obtain the registered owner's name.

"Let's keep going," she said. "I'm on deadline."

The next sign of movement was a silver Jaguar pulling up at 7:45. The car looked familiar, but she couldn't place it right away. "Again, slowly, Charlie? Thanks."

"Don't mention it. I'm getting good at this drill."

She couldn't help but gasp again, because this time she recognized the driver as he typed in the security code.

"Oh, my God, that's Vincent!" she squeaked.

"Vincent who?"

"Vincent Battrelle, the owner of my newspaper!" she squeaked again, popping her hand over her mouth. But it was too late.

Dang it, I did it again.

Seeing Charlie's expression, she could see that she had a more immediate problem. "Please promise me you won't tell anyone, Charlie. This is serious now. It's not only my story at stake, it's my job. You understand that, right?"

Charlie nodded noncommittally.

"Let's zoom in on the license plate to make sure," she said.

Yep, it's SDPUB.

Charlie's eyes flitted skittishly back and forth, as if having this knowledge had compromised him somehow.

"I don't know, Katrina. I feel like we should tell the police," he said, his voice going high-pitched now, too, a strange sound coming from such a large, round man.

"They've already got this footage, right?"

"I didn't make the copy, so I don't know what timeframe they got, or if they've even looked at it yet. If you know these people's identities and have information that could help them, I think you should tell them. One of these people could be a murderer."

She knew she had to talk some sense into Charlie before he did something to ruin her story.

"That's not really how this works," she said as calmly as she could. "I don't work for the police. Reporters are independent watchdogs. That's how we protect democracy and regular people like you and me."

She didn't really care if the police had already watched the tapes or if they were too busy holding news conferences, acting like they were on top of things. This was her story now.

Who knows, maybe my story will force an arrest.

As her phone vibrated, she looked down and saw Joanne's name in the caller ID. She asked Charlie for directions to the restroom, where she turned on the tap with the hope of having a semiprivate conversation.

"You're not going to believe this," Joanne told her.

"Same here," Katrina said.

"I'll go first," the editor said. "Channel 10 just aired footage of Alex Battrelle walking into the police station for questioning in quote 'federal and local matters' unquote."

"You're kidding," Katrina said, the adrenaline flooding into her veins so abruptly that she felt a jolt to her forehead.

What the hell? Is this why Goode camped outside my apartment last night, to protect me from Alex Battrelle? So, was that him in the car? Did he kill the Fontaines? Or did he and Vincent do it together?

She looked in the mirror. It could have been the fluorescent lighting, but her face seemed ghostly pale and gray, with a greenish hue.

"So, what have *you* got?" Joanne asked. "Please tell me it's something exclusive that TV can't beat us on. We need to get out in front of this story again. Norman Klein can feed you an insert about Alex from the cop shop, or we can run it as a sidebar. I assume your detective didn't tip you to this?"

"No, he did not. I talked to him last night and he sounded like he was holding something back, but all he said was 'off the record, investigation-blah-blah-blah.' Although he did tell me he thinks it's a murder now."

"Well, that's something, but 'off the record' doesn't help us. Tell me what you've got *on* the record that I can put on the budget," she said, referring to the editors' list of stories for that day.

Katrina was hesitant to say, knowing it would give them enough time to line up lawyers to insert their sticky fingers into her story.

What if they won't run it?

Turning up the tap water so Charlie couldn't hear, she quietly laid out the timeline of who and what she'd seen.

"Wow," Joanne said, pausing. "Wow."

"I know, right?"

Then Joanne went quiet.

"Hello?" Katrina asked.

"I'm thinking. Since we don't know the time of death or how they died, we don't know if the Fontaines were already dead for several hours by the time Alex or Michael—whoever it was—and Vincent got to the house. But if they aren't the killers, what the hell were they doing between seven fifteen and the nine o'clock 911 call? Messing with the evidence? Deleting or stealing secret Vitaleron computer files?"

"That's a good guess, but I still haven't watched all the footage. The 911 call hasn't even come in yet."

"Okay. I'll tell Big Ed, but I'll also need to inform John Palmer about this. Even if he doesn't put his hands on the story, he'll still have some PR issues to deal with," Joanne said.

"Yes, I figured," Katrina said, turning off the tap and flushing the toilet.

When she opened the door, Charlie was standing right outside, as she would expect from a security executive.

"Everything all right in there?" he asked suspiciously.

"Let's finish up," she said. "I've got to get back to the newsroom."

"Did you consider what I said about calling the police?" Charlie asked.

Such an overgrown Boy Scout.

"Don't you worry. I have to call them for my story either way," she said.

That seemed to satisfy him. Back in the screening room, they saw no movement until 8:45 p.m., when the two Jags drove up in tandem from the house to the gate.

"Can you zoom in again on the driver of the first Jag?" she asked.

That looks more like Michael now. Spooked and upset.

After the gate opened and both cars drove through, the time clock clicked past nine o'clock and kept going. But there was no action.

Where are the police?

It was 9:45 p.m. by the time the SDPD cruiser drove up to the gate, where a hatless officer pushed the intercom button. Getting no answer, he got out and looked around, then made a call on his cell.

With the phone still to his ear, the officer climbed back into his car and backed out of view. About fifteen minutes later, a white car with a Fullerton Security logo arrived. A young security guard got out and typed into the keypad, which allowed both cars to drive through the gate.

As Charlie advanced the rest of the footage, a second police car arrived, and then a bit later, Goode came up to the gate.

"Great, that's all I need, Charlie. Thank you so much. You're the best."

"I don't want to get in trouble with the police for interfering in the investigation," he said.

"You did the right thing."

"Maybe. But do me a favor and leave me out of it."

Joanne called again as Katrina was driving to the newsroom.

"Where are you?" she asked anxiously. "John Palmer looked like he wanted to shoot himself when I told him about the footage. But he didn't even try to talk me out of the story. He knows the Battrelles are in such deep doo-doo that we couldn't ignore the story even if we wanted to."

"Yikes. I'm in my car. I was able to get a better view of the younger man as he and Vincent were leaving the house, and I think it was Michael. But I'm going to call the DMV to confirm the plate number as soon as I get back. Whoever it was, he was in the house for thirty minutes before Vincent showed up, then they left together at 8:45 p.m., fifteen minutes before the 911 call."

"Got it. It's almost five o'clock and Big Ed is worried about meeting deadline since everyone but the janitor will need to read this baby before it gets posted, and I'm sure the lawyers will want changes. What's your ETA?"

"Five minutes."

CHAPTER 42
GOODE

Thursday

As soon as Katrina left his office, Charlie Fullerton called Goode, who was trying to track down Vincent and Michael Battrelle for a round of recorded questioning at the station.

"Have you viewed our security tape yet?" Charlie asked.

"No. I've been trying, but the forensic examiners are backed up. Why do you ask?"

"I thought you'd want to know that I just watched it with Katrina Chopin from the *Sun-Dispatch*. Has she called you yet?"

"No. What's on the tape that I need to know about?" Goode asked.

As Charlie recounted the events, he triggered a near panic in Goode that was unusual for him. His concerned responses prompted Stone to come over and stand next to him to listen more closely.

"So, a nurse showed up in the late morning and a uniformed police officer around noon?" Goode repeated for Stone's benefit.

Why would a cop be at the house nine hours before the 911 call?

Charlie also described the arrival and departure of the two guys in Jags, noting that Katrina thought they were Vincent Battrelle and one of his sons.

"I figured I'd better let you know, because she asked me not to tell anyone, and then went to the bathroom to talk to her editor," Charlie said. "It sounds like they're going to run a story tonight."

"Thanks. I appreciate the heads-up," Goode said, hanging up. "Shit."

Stone looked stricken. "How did we not have this already?"

When Goode told him about London and his pregnant wife going into labor, Stone shook his head.

"It's going to look like we dropped the ball," the sergeant said. "I'm going to have to do some serious damage control."

"I know. I'll run over to the RCFL right now and demand that someone run the tape for me."

"I don't know why you didn't do that already."

Goode ignored him and pressed on. "Can you take over getting the Battrelles down here for questioning? I'll be back as soon as I can. Sounds like we have a genuine murder conspiracy on our hands. The Battrelles look good for obstruction and evidence tampering at the very least."

"I can't wait to hear whose bright idea it was to shoot a dead man," Stone said.

"I don't care what Alex said, my money's on Vincent. Seems like the impulsive type," Goode said. "And I'll bet Michael just did what he was told. But what I want to know is, was this one of our guys who came in while the nurse was there?"

"You got me," Stone said. "I'll check with Patrol and Community Relations, but you'd think they would have told us by now if it was."

When Goode came back with a cup of microwaved office coffee to grab his phone, he overheard Stone on the phone with Milton Biggs.

"Michael and Vincent Battrelle need to get down here right away," Stone said, "or we'll pick them up and do a real perp walk this time."

Goode drove to the RCFL as fast as he could, feeling the jitters of cheap java.

Now that I've interviewed the major players, hopefully I'll be able to identify some or all the people Charlie described going in and out of the mansion.

The receptionist said London had just left to take his wife back to the hospital due to some postnatal complications, so she called for his supervisor, a sturdy woman with a short, black, military-style buzz cut.

"Alicia Cortez," the woman said, giving Goode a firm handshake. "How can I help you? You missed London by ten minutes."

"Sorry to hear about his wife. Thing is, we're about to have a PR nightmare. A *Sun-Dispatch* reporter viewed the security footage from the Fontaine mansion today—before we did—and they're running a story tonight. So, I need to see the video ASAP."

"Gotcha. Be right back," Cortez said, sitting him in front of a computer. Returning a few minutes later with the drive, she plugged it in and started scrolling. The footage started at 10:00 a.m.—too late to confirm Alex's alibi via the texts.

Cortez nimbly fast-forwarded to the first sign of action, which was the nurse showing up at 11:30 a.m.

"There she is," he said. "Let's go back a bit and zoom so I can see her face."

Cortez rewound, then slowly advanced and zoomed in until he recognized the young Filipina, who pushed the intercom.

"No shit. That's Esperanza Cepeda," he said, taking note of the time.

Why didn't she mention she was at the house that morning?

From the magnification, Goode could also see the red pharmacy logo on the smaller of two bags she was carrying, which was just the right size for vials of oxy and Xanax. The other one looked like takeout, possibly the chicken soup.

Is she the one who shoved the oxys down Victoria's throat? If she also injected Victoria with something, you'd think she'd have done a cleaner job of it.

The man in blue arrived next, around noon.

"What's with the hat?" Goode asked.

He's purposely turning away from the camera so I can't see his face. He's also not wearing a badge or any equipment or gun on his belt. Doesn't look like one of ours.

"Ready to proceed, Detective?"

"Yeah, thanks."

Goode also recognized the silver convertible that pulled up at 12:32 p.m. "That's Simon Fontaine's Mercedes. I saw it parked in the driveway that night."

Simon is home because his surgery was cancelled, Alex is allegedly long gone, Victoria has broken up with Michael, and Esperanza and the "officer" are both inside. What is going on in there?

When Esperanza appeared at the gate again, it was one o'clock, and she looked shell-shocked.

Is she crying? Does that mean they're dead?

The officer walked up the driveway half an hour later. Observing him closely, Goode still couldn't see his face but noted that his body was slender and athletic.

Like a runner . . . or a bicyclist? Could that be Dallas Fairchild? It was his gun, after all.

Only Fairchild didn't have an arrogant swagger like this dude, who seemed familiar somehow. Goode had seen that swagger many times in the guys he played varsity sports with in high school. Entitled, cocky, and spoiled. And unlike Esperanza, this guy didn't seem upset. If anything, he seemed a little manic.

"Is that a smile?" Cortez asked. "And lipstick?"

"Yes, on both counts," Goode replied. "Lipstick or not, my gut says that's a dude and not a real cop. It was Halloween, after all, so the lipstick could be part of a disguise. It's almost like he knew about the security cameras."

"Dr. Fontaine was shot with a nine millimeter, though, right?" Cortez asked. "Standard issue."

"Right," he replied. "But you can see that this 'officer' isn't carrying one unless it's strapped to his ankle. We've already identified the gun's likely owner, who said Victoria carried it in her purse at night. If one of these people didn't bring it in, then it came home with her."

Six hours later, when the dark-haired man in the blue Jaguar showed up at seven fifteen, Goode couldn't tell which Battrelle son it was either.

Katrina's right, that could be Alex or Michael, but I've met them both and I can't tell. They would both know the code.

But he did recognize Vincent's silver Jag from the SDPUB plates, which pulled up half an hour later.

Timing fits with one of them being the shooter.

As the two Jags left in succession at 8:45 p.m., he said, "Now that I have a better view of the younger one, I'd say that's Michael Battrelle. Looks like he's crying. Alex is older, a little gray at the temples."

Fast-forwarding through the rest of the tape, they stopped with Goode pressing the intercom.

"Thank you, Cortez," he said. "I know this isn't your regular protocol, but would you be able to type up and send me a formal report ASAP, with the time of each person's arrival, identifying description, departure, and plate number? We're holding several suspects right now, and if we're going to make any arrests tonight, we'll need our ducks in a row."

"You got it, Detective," Cortez said. "Stay safe out there."

"Thanks," Goode said.

CHAPTER 43
KATRINA

Thursday

First thing back at her desk, Katrina called the DMV.

I felt bad for Michael, but did he kill Victoria? My reads on people aren't usually that far off.

Before Katrina could say a word, the clerk put her on hold. In the meantime, she multitasked, opening her computer file of typed notes and searching for "Filipino."

There it was: Daisy said Darren McMurphy's new girlfriend was Filipino, like his wife before Daisy.

"I knew I had this somewhere," Katrina blurted out loud.

Could she be the nurse on the video? There are probably a lot of Filipino nurses in San Diego County. It's also Halloween. Just because she was wearing scrubs doesn't mean she's really a nurse, just like the guy in uniform may not be a real cop.

As she compiled her call list, Katrina tried to ignore Joanne waving at her from across the room. Daisy the Muffin might be able to resolve the nurse question. Katrina also needed to ask Goode if he'd watched the footage and checked whether an officer had been sent to the house at lunchtime.

I don't have time to be micromanaged right now. They don't know what I can do yet. But they will.

Finally, the DMV's bad hold music subsided. "Both plates come back to Jaguars registered to Vincent Battrelle on Whale Watch Way in San Diego, 92037," the DMV clerk said, reciting the zip code for La Jolla.

Daddy still pays for his grown son's car? No wonder he thinks he can control him.

Because the clerk couldn't confirm the drivers' names, Katrina would have to describe the younger one in her story as "dark-haired," driving a car registered to Vincent. It would be up to the reader to decide.

Tired of waiting, Joanne came over. "We're out of time. You need to stop reporting and start writing," she said firmly. "Big Ed has asked me where your story is three times in the past thirty minutes."

Katrina tried to explain that she was still making calls to firm up details and answer questions. "I still have so many holes to fill."

"I know, and tomorrow is another day," Joanne said.

But Katrina was determined and persuasive. She finally convinced Joanne that she needed to find out if Darren McMurphy's Filipino girlfriend was, in fact, a nurse, and if so, where she worked.

"I have a hunch that's her on the video," she said. "I also have to call the police to ask about the uniformed officer. Then I'll stop, I promise."

Daisy answered her cell phone on the fifth ring, with loud music and the roar of bar talk in the background. From her wobbly voice, it sounded like she'd consumed a few cocktails.

"Yeah, she's a nurse, but I have no idea where Darren met her. Maybe through work somehow," she said.

"You don't know her name by chance?"

"Don't know. Don't care."

So, even though Katrina believed they were one and the same, she had to turn in her story without that detail.

She and Joanne were five minutes into side-by-side editing her story when John Palmer walked in and covered his face with his hands melodramatically.

"You don't have a TV in here, but you'll never guess who was just on a breaking-news tease on Channel 10," he said.

"Who?" the two women chorused.

"Alex Battrelle has been arrested on suspicion of tax fraud and money laundering. He's also been named as a possible suspect in the Fontaine murders and is being held until he can be arraigned in federal court."

"Wow," Joanne said, looking at Katrina. "Where'd all that come from?"

Katrina shook her head and shrugged.

Goode isn't telling me anything. Now I look stupid.

"He's been working some scheme down in the Caymans, setting up bogus companies, and hiding money for rich clients going through divorces. *Allegedly,*" John said. "The feds said they've been working this case for eighteen months."

"Oh, my God," Katrina and Joanne said in unison.

"That's not all. As Alex was being led out of the police station in handcuffs, Michael and Vincent Battrelle were walking in with Milton Biggs and another attorney I didn't recognize," John said. "Why did I even come to work today?"

Joanne shook her head, a signal to Katrina to stay quiet.

"So where are we, ladies? Is the story done?" John asked, smiling weakly.

"Katrina and I are still going through it," Joanne said. "This complicates matters, obviously. We'll post this version ASAP, then update and repost with the new developments."

John nodded. He arched his back and pushed his thumbs into the lower portion, then slowly hobbled back to his office.

"We'll have to ask Norman Klein for a feed on the two other Battrelles showing up at the cop shop," Joanne said. "Luckily, Big Ed asked him to hang out for a while."

"Okay," Katrina said. "I left messages all around, but I couldn't get anyone. They're probably busy with interrogations."

"That detective never tells you anything on the record anyway," Joanne said. "Better to get something we can use, even if it's not as good."

"Yeah, the police are going to look pretty lame if they can't explain why one of their officers was inside the house before or even *during* the murders," Katrina said. "What do we do about getting a comment on behalf of the Battrelles?"

"Leave messages at the Biggs firm, and on Vincent's and Michael's cell phones," Joanne said. "That's all we can do at this point."

CHAPTER 44
GOODE

Thursday

On his way back to the station, Goode got a call from Stone, letting him know that Michael and Vincent had been successfully corralled into separate interrogation rooms at HQ.

"If they keep trying to lie their way out of this, we have solid proof to confront them with," Stone said. "I've already started grilling Vincent. Once you get here, you can hit up Michael. Byron and Foster will monitor both sessions and feed us info as we go."

"See you in a few."

When Goode walked in a few minutes later, Michael Battrelle was sitting next to a fiftyish man in a suit, presumably one of Biggs's senior associates, while Biggs was next door with Vincent.

Goode wasted no time scolding Michael. "You and your father both lied to me. You said you learned about the Fontaines' death Saturday on the news, but we have security footage showing you were there nearly two hours before the 'anonymous' 911 call on Friday night, which I'm sure one of you made. I haven't listened to the tape yet, but I'll bet my grandmother's birthday cake that it's got your voice on it."

Michael's face went white. He turned toward his lawyer, who nodded for him to answer. "Okay," he said, sighing. "Like I said before, Victoria didn't sound well on the phone that morning. When she didn't answer my calls or texts, I went over there to check on her. I never expected to find them both dead."

"You lied either way, even if it was partly by omission. Alex's statement today completely contradicts the rest of what you told me. I knew you had to be lying, because the scene didn't make sense. You want to explain what you and your father were thinking when you messed with a crime scene?"

"First of all, we didn't know it was a crime scene," Michael said.

"Oh, really? How's that?"

"The first thing I saw was Simon lying in a heap on the landing near the bottom of the staircase. I felt his neck, and he was cold with no pulse. I thought maybe he'd had a heart attack. I called out for Victoria, but she didn't answer. I ran upstairs to her room, because she likes to work on her laptop in bed, and she was lying on the floor. She was cold too. I saw the bruising on her arm and the pill vials on the nightstand, dated from that day. I also found the gun in her purse. I've seen the bruising on Alex before, so I thought the worst, called him up, and basically accused him of causing her to OD."

"Okay."

"She'd told me she was dealing with some serious stuff at Vitaleron, but she'd always taken her work in stride. I didn't think it was enough to cause her to relapse, but she does have a history of trying to harm and kill herself. I've been kicking myself for not pressing her about the cutting, because she must have been more depressed than I'd realized."

"So you were thinking suicide. What would trigger her to do that?"

"My first thought was Alex. She'd been clean for many years, but if he'd relapsed and gone on one of his wild binges, he could have persuaded her to join him, then run off after she OD'd. Or he could've broken her heart again somehow, so she took those pills and overdosed that way. Either way, she seemed prepared for multiple avenues, whatever it took: suicide by pills, the needle, or a gun."

"Didn't it occur to you that you should have seen a syringe or some paraphernalia near her body?"

"I wasn't thinking clearly. But now that you mention it, yes."

"What did you do then?"

"I was reeling from the shock, so I called Alex and demanded to know what he'd done to her."

"What was his response?"

"He said, 'What the hell are you talking about?'"

"Uh-huh."

"So, I said, 'Victoria and Simon are dead. She's overdosed on the floor, and he's lying at the bottom of the stairs. What happened? What did you give her? And what did you do to Simon?'"

"And?"

"He started cursing and crying. It took him a minute to calm down enough to answer, but then he said, 'I stayed over last night, but Victoria was alive when I left at eight fifteen this morning. I didn't give her any drugs. You know I've been clean for six months. I've been out shopping for rings all goddamn afternoon, and I was going to come over and surprise her with one tonight. I haven't seen Simon since Thursday night. He was just leaving when I got there.'"

"Did you believe him?" Goode asked.

"I wasn't sure what to think. He's got a long history of lying and relapsing, but I saw for myself what could have happened. Simon came home unexpectedly and either found her dead or using with Alex, and there was some kind of confrontation. Alex knocked him down the stairs, or maybe they argued and Simon fell, so Alex took off. Maybe he thought Simon was only unconscious. I don't know. He's never hurt anyone before. Not physically, anyway."

"Then what happened?"

"I told Alex, 'Look, I don't know if you're lying or not, but this is bad no matter what. If you were the last person to see her, the police are going to blame you, which will be bad for our family and bad for business.' So I told him to get the hell out of town and I'd take care of it."

"Then you called your father?"

"Yes, as you know, he lives right down the hill. I told him what happened, and he came right over. We debated what to do, but we didn't have much time, because the bodies were already cold."

"Whose idea was it to shoot a dead man?"

"My dad's. He said it would look like Simon had shot himself out of despair that Victoria had OD'd. I tried to talk him out of it, but 'stubborn' is his middle name. We carried Simon's body up to the balcony in a sheet, and my dad shot him in the head. There wasn't much blood there, because he was already dead when my dad shot him, but I cleaned it up as fast and as well as I could. My dad wanted to dump his body over the balcony, so it would look like he'd fallen after shooting himself, but that's where I drew the line. I said that was almost physically impossible, because the railing is too high, and dead men don't catapult themselves over balconies. That's why we carried him downstairs to the patio, so it would look like he shot himself there. I removed the rest of the bullets from the gun, put one in Victoria's purse and put the rest in my pocket. Then we wiped off the gun and placed it next to Simon. I put the bloody towels and sheet in a plastic bag and took it with me when we left."

"It never occurred to you that someone else might have killed Victoria?"

"No. Who would do that? And why?"

"If what you're saying is true, at least some of the crime scene makes sense. But there's no heroin or other recreational drugs in her system, and not enough of the oxy or Xanax to kill her. That's all I'm going to say."

"Okay. But I wasn't being paranoid, because you wouldn't have dragged Alex back from the Caymans unless he was a suspect. Or is there really a federal financial investigation?"

"Yes, there really is, and he was also one of the last people, if not *the* last person to see her alive. Innocent men don't run."

"That's what I said, but he's never been violent before. And he loved her. We both did. I never thought he would purposely hurt her; it was more that he was reckless and they were both addicts. Best case, I hoped it was some kind of tragic accident. So, my dad and I are suspects too?"

"We're looking at your whole family, because this was no accident. But even if your new story bears out, you're not off the hook, because you've both admitted to messing with the crime scene. So, we've got you on evidence tampering and obstruction for sure."

When Goode left the room, Michael was staring glumly at the table and shaking his head.

Outside in the hallway, Stone was baffled by Michael's confession. "How can two smart men be so dumb?"

"My guess is they don't watch enough crime shows," Goode said. "I was thinking we should hold them overnight, but now I'm thinking we should let the rats run loose in a few hours to watch them bite each other. My gut says we'll know a lot more within the next twenty-four or forty-eight hours. I'm going back over to the nurse's condo right now. If she's there, I'll bring her in for questioning."

"We'll be waiting. Call if you need backup."

CHAPTER 45
KATRINA

Thursday

By eight o'clock, Katrina had updated her story with the new developments. As she waited for Joanne to do the final read before sending it to Big Ed, she tried calling Goode one last time. But after getting his voicemail again, she called Regina Russell.

This might be a coincidence, but maybe not. La Jolla is a small town of wealthy elites who know each other. If this Filipina nurse is Darren McMurphy's girlfriend, that would put her squarely into Dr. Fontaine's orbit.

Regina sounded distracted, getting her kids ready for bed.

"Sarah, stop biting your brother!" she said. "Sorry. Darren McMurphy? Yeah, he's part of my dad's golf foursome, with Simon and some of the other board members. He's never bothered with me, because I'm married and not his type, but I know he's been seeing Espee for a while."

"Who's Espee?"

"Our nurse, Esperanza. The stories that woman tells us, you wouldn't believe the man's sex drive and stamina. It's like he always wants to do it where they're in danger of getting caught. He's definitely more than I could handle, but Espee seems to like it. That, or she doesn't want to make waves before she gets that nice house in La Jolla she's always wanted."

Now please tell me she's Filipino.

"What's her last name?"

"Cepeda."

"Is she Mexican?" Katrina asked, disappointed.

"No, actually, she's Filipino."

Katrina smiled. "Did you see her last Friday morning?" she asked, trying to keep the excitement out of her voice.

"No, I had the day off. She was supposed to assist Dr. Fontaine with a surgery, but it got cancelled, so he closed up shop. My dad already had the day off to play golf."

"Would you mind texting me her number? I want to see how she's taking all of this."

A minute later, Regina texted her the number with this message: Just wait till you have kids. I need a martini!

Katrina got Esperanza's voicemail, so she left a message, asking for a return call.

With that, Katrina ran to Joanne's office, where she came to a halt in the doorway. John Palmer was sitting in front of Joanne's computer, where Katrina could see him typing changes into her story.

What the hell?

Joanne, who was standing to the side, mouthed to her silently: "Did you keep a copy?"

Katrina nodded. She always did. Ever since an editor at the *Record* accidentally deleted a story she'd spent three weeks writing, forcing her to reconstruct it from memory.

"That's better. You ladies read it over, then I'll send it to the lawyer," he said and walked out.

Joanne gasped audibly as she started to read his changes. "Go get Linda."

Katrina didn't relish the task and approached Linda's open door with caution. "Knock, knock," she said.

Linda glanced up from her computer, her eyes droopy and tired. "Hi. I hear you've got another big story. Congratulations."

"Joanne needs to talk to you right away. John Palmer made a bunch of edits to my story."

"Shit," she muttered. "Are you effing kidding me?"

Wrenching herself out of her chair, she headed for Joanne's office, with Katrina on her heels.

"Give us a few minutes," Linda said curtly, closing the door in her face.

Katrina's cheeks felt hot to the touch, as if she'd been slapped. But she knew Linda must be furious after already giving John Palmer an ultimatum that he'd boldly ignored. Returning to her desk, Katrina saw that her red message light was on.

"I'm a pharmacist, but I can't give you my name," the female caller said. "I was reading your stories this week when I remembered that Dr. Simon Fontaine's office called in prescriptions for Xanax and oxycodone to our pharmacy on Friday morning for his daughter, Victoria. When I read that she was pregnant, the alarm bells went off for me. Pregnant women shouldn't take these meds, and definitely not together. As a doctor, her father should know they could harm the baby or even cause the mother to overdose, even in small doses, but especially in combination. Remember Heath Ledger?"

Katrina wondered if Goode would confirm that Victoria's prescriptions were dated the day she died.

Ten minutes later, Joanne motioned for Katrina as Linda strode mightily toward the corner office.

"She's going to read him the riot act," Joanne said. "I'm glad she's taking that on. I can't take a man seriously who puts blond highlights in his hair."

"I've got some news," Katrina said excitedly, relaying the tip from the pharmacist and the confirmation that Darren McMurphy's girlfriend was not only Filipino, but also was Dr. Fontaine's surgical nurse, and possibly was the woman in the video who had delivered drugs to Victoria.

"That's all interesting, but we can't quote an anonymous pharmacist. Call Goode again to see if he'll confirm those drugs were at the scene, and ask him what he knows about the nurse."

Katrina tried to reach the detective again, but still no answer. Clearly, he had his hands full.

While John Palmer sulked in his office, Katrina and Joanne revised the updated story to its earlier iteration and posted it at ten thirty. They also had to redo the front and jump pages of the print version, cutting it to fit the holes they'd saved.

"Go home and get some sleep," Joanne told her. "We'll be back at it bright and early. You did good today, kiddo."

CHAPTER 46
GOODE

Thursday

Jumping into his SUV, Goode roared off toward University City. But the lights were off at Esperanza's place, no one answered the door, and she didn't answer her cell when he called. Her driveway was also empty, though her car could be inside the garage.

"Dammit," he said.

Calling Stone, he said, "Wherever she is, I'm sure she's passed out by now and unable to give a coherent statement, but I had to try. If I can figure out where McMurphy lives, I can try to catch her there in the morning. Can you guys get his address from one of those clowns? Don't say what it's for."

"Stand by."

While he waited, Goode imagined what might happen when he showed up at McMurphy's. Drunk Esperanza might put a gun to his or McMurphy's head, like Clover Ziegler did to Norman Klein at Black's Beach before she jumped. Or something even crazier.

Stone came back with the address, which was in La Jolla Shores. "What's your plan?"

"I'm going over there to see if her car is parked outside. Maybe I'll hear them arguing. I don't want to see anyone else dead."

"Me neither."

"Like Katrina."

"Katrina? What does she have to do with this?"

Goode had wanted to wait to update Stone on the possible tie-in with her parents' murders, but he'd run out of excuses, so he gave him the lowdown.

"Wow. I see where you're going with that," Stone said. "I've given instructions to hold the Battrelles until about 4:00 a.m. Might boost their motivation to tell us the complete truth. You want Foster to meet you at McMurphy's?"

Foster's still pretty green. He'll just get in my way.

"No, thanks, I'll be fine," he said. "I want to go in stealth. If it's all quiet, I'm going to check on Katrina when I'm done there."

"Okay, Lone Wolf. You're not going to spill everything to a *Sun-Dispatch* reporter, right?"

"You really think I would do that?"

"And you're not going to accidentally sleep with her, right?"

"Not unless I get really drunk."

"Goode!"

"I'm kidding."

Kind of.

"Okay, don't do anything stupid, trying to be a hero. You know how you are."

Running around all night, Goode hadn't had a chance to check his voicemail. It was almost eleven o'clock.

The first message was from Dallas Fairchild: "Hey, Detective, we got a hit with the cameras in the lab, and I have to say, I'm shocked. Darla, the woman you met at reception, came in around eleven thirty last night and poured off solution from two jugs in the fridge, the different potencies that I'm experimenting with. I checked the levels this morning and she took some of both gender formulas. She funneled them into plastic drug vials she brought in, the jumbo, three-month size you get from a mail-order pharmacy. Seems like a lot if it's for personal use, but not enough to sell on a broad scale, unless she's giving it to another lab to try to duplicate our formula. Either way, I thought you'd want to know. By the way, she does IT work for us, too, which I didn't think to mention, so that means she's got access to Victoria's and my emails. Hope this helps."

Wow. That came out of nowhere. I never even considered Darla as a suspect. Now I'm going to have to recalibrate my scenarios. Unless she's selling the drug to a competitor, Darla is probably sharing it with a man, possibly even another couple.

The other messages were from Katrina at different points throughout the evening, asking for comment on all kinds of details he couldn't confirm. She was obviously making good headway with the case without his help.

"Why would you guys have an officer at the scene nine hours before the 911 call?" she asked. "Was he there for some other reason, like a domestic call? Or was this an imposter?"

As he headed north toward McMurphy's house, Goode briefed Stone on the Darla Johansen news and also relayed Katrina's questions.

"I know it's past your deadline, but were you able to determine if that officer was one of ours?" Goode asked.

"Not that anyone is willing to admit, so I'd say no," Stone said. "I didn't get a chance to call her back either. I read her stories, and I've got yet another media dung heap on my plate for tomorrow."

Goode noticed his gas gauge was dangerously low, so he quickly pulled in to the only gas station in the Shores, which was staggeringly overpriced, just a few blocks from McMurphy's place.

Afterward, Goode slowly cruised by the house. It was a pretty nice two-story place, with a view of the ocean, but it was dark inside, and the driveway was empty.

Did they skip town together? I guess I'll come back in the morning and find out. I'm not taking any chances that one of these characters is Katrina's stalker, so I'm going over there. Long day or not.

CHAPTER 47
KATRINA

Thursday

It was almost eleven when Goode called Katrina back. She was walking toward the elevator to leave the newsroom, strung out on adrenaline, and still very much awake.

"We've got to talk," he said.

"Nice of you to call," she quipped. "But you know you missed my deadline, right?"

"Yeah, I know. I've been interrogating suspects all day and night. And thanks to your little visit to Fullerton Security today, I had to chase down the footage, which I hadn't watched yet."

"Really? Charlie said you picked it up on Monday."

"Long story. By the way, off the record, everyone in this case seems to be a potential suspect."

"Sure seems like it. I wish one of you had called back, because we had a hole in my story big enough for an elephant to thunder through. So, why *was* a police officer at the Fontaines' house at noon that day?"

"That's partly why I called."

"Good. I'm planning a weekend story, which means there's still time for you guys to set the record straight."

"Yeah, well, I think we should talk tonight, but I don't want to do it by phone. Can we meet at your apartment in about ten minutes?"

"Geez, sounds serious. Where's the fire?"

"I *am* serious, Katrina."

Katrina felt torn. She was beyond exhausted, but she also knew it would take a while to come down after such a crazy day. If she were back in Northampton, she'd be on her way to meet the crew at the local watering hole. But she could tell from Goode's voice that this was important.

If he's going to camp outside anyway, I might as well let him in. Maybe if I give him some wine, he'll finally tell me something on the record that I can use. I just hope he can behave in my private little canyon cocoon.

"Okay, sure. Why not," she said. "I need to stop and pick up a bottle of wine first, though. See you in a few."

He's a source on a story I'm actively working. What am I doing? Getting close to the fire again. I guess we'll see how close in the next couple of hours.

CHAPTER 48
GOODE

Thursday

Goode was already parked at Katrina's complex when he called her, but he knew better than to assume she'd say yes. If she rebuffed his offer, he'd planned to leave to let her park and go inside, then pull in behind her car to repeat the same surveillance gig as the night before. He didn't want to spook her, he just wanted to make sure she was safe.

I don't want Katrina getting killed on my watch, but I also like having an excuse to hang out with her.

He felt better now that the Battrelles were in custody, even if it was only temporary, but he would continue to worry until he brought Esperanza in for questioning. She was the only person who knew the identity of the "uniformed officer" and who could reveal what happened at the mansion. Given that she likely delivered the pills that were lodged in Victoria's throat, though, things weren't looking too good for her.

Now that the Santa Ana winds had died down, Goode enjoyed the cool, light breeze blowing through his hair as he leaned back against his car.

As Katrina's Land Rover approached, Goode took a few deep breaths to put up a calm front. His intentions were good, but he was a mere mortal, unsure if he could fight his primal urges once they were inside her apartment.

When she opened her door and swung out those long legs, he took another deep breath. She sat there, smiling up at him and watching him watch her for a long minute before she got out and turned around, her backside raised up invitingly as she retrieved her bottle of wine.

Is she trying to tempt me?

It was almost as if she wanted him to turn her around, push her up against her car and press his body against hers. Take her face in his hands and kiss her. Get lost in her mouth. Unbutton her blouse and kiss those perfect breasts.

It took every ounce of discipline to stand still, feet firmly in place, hands shoved in his pockets as a preventative measure.

"Well, hello," he said softly.

"I see that look on your face," she said, shaking her head and laughing. "Stop it."

"What look?" he asked, feeling the corners of his mouth turn into an involuntary smirk.

"Were you already here when you called?"

"Yes, as a matter of fact I was," he said.

Better to be honest if she's going to call you out anyway.

"A little presumptuous, don't you think?" she asked rhetorically, smirking back.

She's into you. Relax and lean into it. Just not too much.

"Maybe a little. But I know you're a professional and there won't be any funny stuff tonight. We've got serious business to discuss."

"Sounds like it. I've done my part," she said, holding up the wine bottle. "I hope you like red. It's a great Cab I discovered."

"If it's wet, I'll drink it," he said. "I've had an incredibly long day."

"That makes two of us. Follow me," she said, leading him down the stairs that led to the pool, which was glowing softly from the light in the deep end. The only other incandescence came from the sconces hanging between each pair of apartment doors.

"Which one is you?" he asked as they walked down the steps to the walkway, scanning his flashlight over the courtyard for intruders lurking behind a bush or in a dark corner.

"I'm on the second floor at the end and to the right," she said.

"Hold on. Let me go ahead of you, then, and make sure it's safe," he said, taking her by the hips and guiding her around him to switch places on the walkway. "Wait here."

"Are you serious?" she asked.

"Yes, unfortunately, I am," he whispered, tapping his finger to his lips to signal her into silence.

Hearing a rustling sound up ahead, he quickly pulled his gun from the rear waistband of his jeans and crept along the beam of his flashlight, his arms extended and ready to shoot. As he approached the corner at the end, he spun to the right, pointing his light and gun up the stairs toward Katrina's apartment.

As he'd feared, a man was standing at the front door, doing who knows what.

"Police! Don't move," he yelled. The man dropped something metal on the ground. "Show me your hands and come down the stairs, slowly. Slowly!"

"Don't shoot," the man replied. "I'm the manager here."

"Keep your hands up where I can see them," Goode said.

The man complied, stepping gingerly down, one step at a time. "I was leaving Katrina a note that we're turning off the water tomorrow for repairs," he said, his voice shaking. "I dropped my keys up there."

By this point, Katrina was standing next to Goode at the bottom of the stairs, peering up at the man. "It's okay, that *is* the manager," she said. "Sorry, Tom."

A few feet away, a door opened a crack and the curly white hair of an elderly neighbor peeked out.

"Go back inside, ma'am," Goode said. "Everything's fine."

"Sorry, man," he said to the manager, who looked so frightened he might have peed his pants. "You can go back up to get your keys and go."

The manager didn't need to be told twice. After grabbing them from the doormat, he practically flew past them and up the staircase to the carport.

"Dude, you are hardcore," Katrina told Goode. "What the hell is going on?"

Goode stepped back so she could pass and unlock her door. Once they were both inside, he closed the door and turned the deadbolt.

"Nice furniture," he said, surprised to see the living room empty other than the sleeping bag on the floor with a cardboard-box bedside table, and not one, but two guitars leaning against the wall. "Two guitars? So, you *are* a rock star!"

"Ha, I was, kinda, yes. One of those was Franny's. We used to play together. I haven't had a chance to get any furniture from storage yet. That was my plan last weekend, but we both know what I was doing instead."

Following her into the kitchen, Goode leaned against the counter as Katrina opened the wine bottle. "I rented out my parents' house—well, I guess it's mine now—while I was back east," she said. "It was easier that way."

"I have to imagine it would be hard either way," he replied.

"True," she said. "I'm only staying here until that lease expires, and I can ask the tenants to vacate. So, no need to move a bunch of furniture back and forth."

"You're a minimalist," he said. "I get that. I'm the same way."

"Where do you live?"

Katrina listened with a sympathetic expression as he told her about his rental cottage near the high school in La Jolla, in the same neighborhood where he and his sister had grown up with their Aunt Katherine.

"It's difficult sometimes. Being an orphan," she said. "Don't you think?"

He nodded. "Not so much now, but it was, yes."

"So, wait, did you go to high school with Darren McMurphy *and* Victoria Fontaine?"

"Yes, but Victoria was two years younger than me, so I didn't know her. I assume you heard about her crash that almost killed a little girl? Well, it didn't happen until after I'd already graduated."

"Yes, I did. You have to wonder why she was such a troubled teen, coming from an uber-wealthy family, with all those advantages."

"That's exactly why it happened. She sounded pretty neglected to me," Goode said. "Acting-out-in-the-vortex syndrome."

"Yeah, you're probably right."

The cork came out with a pop. She grabbed the clean plastic cup from the dish rack, washed out the dirty one, and poured them both some wine.

"Let's talk on the balcony," she said, "since there's nowhere to sit inside."

But before they could go anywhere, her phone rang. "Hold on, it's Vincent," she said, sliding the glass door open. Although she closed the door, Goode could still hear her side of the conversation.

"*I'm* a troublemaker? You were the one on TV tonight, walking into the police station," she said. "How does it feel being on the other side of the news?"

Long silence.

"I left that message because it's my job. I knew you would be upset if I didn't call, and now you're upset that I did. I can't win. What? Yes, of course I saw you in the Fontaines' security footage."

More silence, then she choked back a laugh.

"No, I'm not laughing. So, what about Alex's arrest and those federal charges? That doesn't sound like *nothing* to me. What were you doing at their house anyway? Hiding incriminating evidence, or were you actually involved in their deaths?"

Again, more silence.

"We did call your attorney, Vincent, all your attorneys. No one called back."

Another long pause.

"I'm not going to call Milton Biggs now, it's almost midnight. I'll do it tomorrow. What about Michael, is that his attorney as well?"

Silence.

"If you didn't want the newspaper and its staff to be hurt, maybe you should have thought of that sooner. Look, I've got to go. It's late and I've got a guest here." Pause. "That's none of your business."

Katrina hung up, set the phone on the railing, shook her head, and took a sip of wine. After a few moments, she pulled the door open and motioned for Goode to join her, which he did. They gazed up at the moon together, sipping wine as he waited for her to speak.

She is so sexy, the way her hair falls over her eye like that. I just want to run my hands through it.

"Vincent is a real pain in my ass," she said.

"Yes, I could hear that."

"It was weird. He asked me specifically if you were here. I wonder if *he's* the one spying on me. He might even have Jerry or one of my other coworkers out there somewhere with binoculars, like he tried to hire me to do."

Goode had had the same thought. "This is really good, by the way," he said, raising his cup to lighten the mood. "You have excellent taste."

"So, what did you want to tell me?" she asked, pulling hair away from her face as she turned toward him. "The off-the-record thing is getting kind of old."

"This has to be off the record, but I think within a day or two, I'll be able to tell you more, or Stone will, and then you can go to town. This is mostly for your protection as, well, a person I care about, not necessarily because you're a reporter, okay? Which makes this awkward."

"Does Sergeant Stone know you're here?"

"Yes, he does."

"Does he know we're drinking wine?"

"He doesn't need to know everything, but I did tell him I'd be a good boy as long as I didn't get too drunk."

Katrina laughed. “You didn’t really say that.”

“Yes, I did, actually, in my usual sarcastic manner. So, now he can’t say I didn’t tell him.”

“You’re a clever boy, aren’t you?”

“Does your editor know I’m here?”

Katrina shook her head and smiled.

“Well, all right then, we’re even.”

“What made you haul in all three Battrelles for questioning today? Was it the security footage? Or something else?”

“We weren’t planning to question anyone but Alex today. After you mentioned that he was MIA the other day, I tracked him down.”

“How did you know to look in the Caymans?”

“Airline manifests. Remember the night you showed up at Vincent’s? That was a whole circus act. I asked him a tough question and he dropped a glass. He was bleeding everywhere, which piqued my attention. I knew Michael was lying too. But after you saw the tape, I had to play catch-up. And then we had to confront them about why they were at the house Friday night, because they’d told us that they’d learned about the Fontaines’ deaths on the news on Saturday.”

“Are you going to tell me why you’re really here?”

He paused. “Okay,” he said. “Here’s what I can tell you. We have no record of any sworn officer going into the Fontaine house earlier in the day. As you know, our first guy wasn’t there until 9:45 p.m., so, if it was one of our guys, no one is admitting to it. The guy’s face wasn’t visible from that angle with that damned hat on, which by the way, no patrol officer ever wears, so we believe he was wearing a uniform that you, I, or Joe Sixpack can buy from the same store. I think he was wearing lipstick as a disguise to throw us off.”

“Really? I couldn’t really tell if it was a man or a woman,” Katrina said. “Do you have an idea who it is?”

“I have my suspicions, but nothing concrete.”

“Okay, so what does all this have to do with me?”

"I can't tell you everything, but isn't that enough? We had all three Battrelles in custody, but I guess they let Vincent out earlier than planned, or he wouldn't have been able to call you. Anyway, I don't want anything to happen to you. I'd just as soon stay here tonight, in your apartment or out in my car. I was expecting you to have a couch, but—"

"But what?" she asked, turning toward him so their faces were only a foot apart. Goode felt the pheromones in the air, drawing him toward her.

"—I'm not really sure where I would crash," he finished.

With their noses only inches apart now, he could feel her breath and couldn't listen to rational thought any longer. Dropping his empty cup on the balcony floor, he leaned in and kissed her, wrapping his arms around her.

"I couldn't wait any longer," he whispered.

She pressed her breasts and hips into his, compelling him to run his hands down her back. She always seemed so tough, but he could feel her emotional wall peeling away as they kissed, gently at first, then harder and longer, their breathing growing faster and louder.

"This is not a good idea," she whispered back.

Goode's mind was reeling, high on a flood of dopamine. "I know."

But her eyes weren't saying "stop." In fact, they reflected a burning, enticing hunger that fueled his desire even more. He buried his face in the warm crook of her neck and breathed in the lavender scent of her ultrasoft skin.

I want her.

Taking a handful of her hair, he tilted her head to the side, pulling her collar away to kiss her bare neck and shoulder. She leaned back against the railing, arching her spine and raising her breasts toward him, her hard nipples poking through her silk blouse. He wanted to unbutton it, move her bra aside and take one of those nipples into his mouth. But based on the incident with Katrina's car and Vincent's comment to Katrina on the phone, they both knew that her stalker, or one of Vincent's goons, could be watching.

Goode wasn't typically one to seek out risky exhibitionism. He also was cognizant of the huge risk he was taking after Stone had scolded him about the Alison escapade and specifically warned him about Katrina. He could be suspended, taken off the case, or even fired for crossing that line.

"You're not going to accidentally sleep with her, right?" Stone's voice echoed in his head. "Just fall into her by mistake?"

But at that moment, Goode wasn't really thinking clearly, with her scent and the feel of her body against his clouding his senses.

Just a few more minutes. Then maybe I can stop.

Luckily, Katrina made the decision for both of them.

"Okay," she said softly, pulling away. "You'd better get out of here before this goes too far."

Goode was a little disappointed, but he was also relieved. He dropped his hands from her tight, athletic hips and slowly backed away, fighting the urge to pick her up in his arms and lay her down on the sleeping bag.

"Just so you know, this is one of the hardest things I've had to do in my whole life," he said.

"In your whole life?" she repeated, chuckling.

"Yes."

Inside the glass doors, she kissed him one last time before taking his hand and leading him toward the front door, where she stopped and whispered in his ear. "Goodnight, Surfer Man."

With her left hand on the doorknob, she turned to look up at him, waiting for him to move. But he stood there, frozen, holding her other hand. Transfixed by those eyes. She seemed so intensely present and in control. She had him. And he couldn't let go of her.

His mind was fuzzy, and his body felt like one big, aroused nerve, buzzing with sensation. He slowly pulled her hand behind her and kissed her gently. Then harder. As her other hand fell from the knob, he took it and put it behind her as well.

Easing her back against the wall, he leaned into her, letting go of her hands and pressing his hips into hers. Her hands fell to her sides as she rolled her head back seductively. She wrapped one of her legs around his thigh, tilting her hips tighter against him as they began to rock back and forth.

He grabbed her around the waist with one arm, cupping her ass with his other hand, and lifted her up. She wrapped her other leg around him and her arms around his neck, holding on to him as he stepped back from the wall, balancing her weight on his hips. Kneeling on one leg at a time, he gently laid her down on the sleeping bag, just as he'd imagined.

Taking off his jacket, he threw it on the floor and set his gun on top of it, far enough away from them that it wasn't a hazard, but close enough to grab if he needed it.

She looked beautiful, half of her face cast in soft light, the rest in shadow, as she watched him unbutton and pull off his shirt. He'd seen a similar expression on a few women before, but never one so fierce or so confident in her sexuality. It scared him a little. She was different. Almost like a man. Yet her eyes said she wanted him to take control. To ravage her.

They had gone past the point of stopping now. Stone's voice was gone. All he heard in his head was white noise.

Kissing the warm skin of her breastbone, he made his way down to the warm crevice between the cups of her bra. He rolled her to the side to wrestle it off and reveal the breasts he'd been longing to see. They were perfect, just as he'd expected. Round, lush, and firm.

As he leaned down and flicked his tongue on her nipple, it immediately hardened against his tongue and she moaned. It had been so long since he'd had a nipple in his mouth, he felt himself growing harder too.

Laying against her, her warm, cushiony breasts pressing against his chest, it was like that first buzz off a martini. The heat spread through his entire torso. She moaned again as he buried his face in her neck, where he kissed her again, and back up to her lips.

She unbuckled his pants and rubbed his stomach, slipping her hands under the waistband of his boxer briefs. As her fingers went lower, he grew more aroused. He wanted her, but he wanted all of her. He wanted this to last.

He unzipped and pulled off her jeans, leaving her panties on. Slowly easing his hand down, he caressed her, guided by her breathing. They were both moaning together now, rhythmically and in sync, like a train. It felt so right—until they heard the sound of tires crunching on the driveway below.

They both stopped, mid-gasp, and turned toward the noise, which was loud and distinct, because, as they both realized, they'd left the sliding glass door open.

How stupid was that?

Although he'd felt lightheaded before, the adrenaline shot through him like a bullet. Still on his knees, he bolted upright and cocked his head to listen. Katrina reached for her bra, fastened the hook, and quickly buttoned up her blouse.

Putting his finger to his lips, he stood up and pulled his jeans back on. Grabbing his gun, he slunk over to the slim strip of wall at the edge of the glass doors and leaned back to peer down below, trying to stay out of view.

Guess it's lucky I stayed.

From his vantage point, all he could see was that it was a black SUV of some kind—with its headlights off.

Not a good sign.

The car's engine idled for a few moments and the driver's-side window lowered an inch or two, then the motor shut off. There was no movement until Goode saw the orange end of a lit cigarette. The apartment complex, as old as it was, didn't have any lighting in that area, so he couldn't see the license plate, especially with the headlights off.

Is he waiting to see if anyone comes out to ask him why he's in a private turnaround at one in the morning? Is this the same dude who hit Katrina's car with the rock, or is there more than one party involved here?

The driver's-side door slowly opened, and a cigarette butt came flying out, followed by a man's leg and a black, rubber-soled shoe, which stomped on the butt. A moment later, the rest of the tall, stocky figure stepped out of the car, dressed in a black T-shirt and black jeans, and silently pulled the door to. As the man turned around and looked up at the balcony, Goode retreated further, hoping he'd moved fast enough to avoid being spotted.

Standing with his hands on his hips in the driveway below, the man's body was a silhouette and his face shrouded in darkness, but Goode could see from his linebacker build that he was not the slender, fake officer from the security footage.

By then, Katrina was standing in the hallway, her arms folded against her chest. She looked to him for some kind of silent answer, but he could only shake his head and shrug.

The man walked a few steps toward the breezeway and the diagonal stairwell that led up to her apartment. Goode's heart pounded as he listened for footsteps on the stairs. But he heard nothing.

With rubber-soled shoes on, he can be quiet. I can't tell where he is. I'm pretty sure I locked the front door and turned the deadbolt. Or did I?

Katrina's mouth had fallen open, as they both waited apprehensively for the man to try the door to get inside.

I'll just have to wait to see if this goon tries to come in, so I have the jump on him.

Goode stepped carefully over the sleeping bag to the door and checked to make sure the deadbolt was set. *Check.* Then he put his ear to the wood for any sound or movement in the stairwell. Still nothing.

A few minutes ticked by, but all Goode could hear was his own heart beating and the blood pounding in his head.

What is he doing out there? Is he still sussing the layout? Or is he done and waiting for another goon so they can enter via the front door and the balcony simultaneously? Then there would be two of them and only one of me.

Goode almost jumped out of his skin when, without any warning, he watched the doorknob turn and heard the door bump against the deadbolt. He'd forgotten to turn the lock on the doorknob, but the deadbolt was set.

Goode backed up and crouched into a firing stance, aimed at the door, and braced for the dude to kick it down. He stood there, his heart racing and his face and body dripping with sweat for several minutes. But there was no more movement, just silence.

Although his heartbeat slowed a bit, he was still not sure what to expect next. Turning to check on Katrina, he saw that she had retreated, presumably to the master bedroom.

Has he gone, or is he still waiting for another goon? He could try to scale the building and climb onto the balcony on his own, so I should close and lock that glass door without him seeing me. The last thing I want to do is call for backup and have to explain what I'm doing here.

Slinking around the kitchen to the narrow slice of wall where he could stay out of view, he crouched down again, pulled the sliding door shut, and locked it tight.

A couple of minutes later, he felt a surge of relief when he heard the car door shut quietly below and the engine start up. The tires crunched again as the car made a two-point turn and headed back up the hill to the street. Goode could see now that it was an Infiniti, and he was able to get a partial plate number.

The question is, how many of them will there be if and when they come back? They would be pretty exposed if they tried to climb the balcony in broad daylight, so it would have to be in the next hour or two while everyone is still asleep. Which is why I'm not going anywhere until sunrise.

Goode knew it was too risky for him to wait in the apartment to find out. He'd already let his primal urges take over when he was supposed to be protecting Katrina.

What kind of savior are you when your little head does the thinking? If this thing had gone bad, the brass would have come down hard on me, and Vincent would have had a field day. I can just see the headline now: "Half-naked cop shoots intruder in reporter's apartment."

Heading to the rear of the apartment, Goode found Katrina pacing back and forth in the master bedroom.

"Is he gone?" she whispered.

"Yes," he said softly. "He tried to open the front door, but thankfully I'd already locked the deadbolt."

"Fuck!" she whispered loudly.

"I know," he said. "I don't think we need to whisper anymore."

The purple mood was gone, and stark reality stared back at them in the full-length mirror.

"I'm going to go sit in my car in case he comes back, with or without reinforcements," he said. She nodded in agreement.

"What kind of car was it?" she asked. "Don't tell me it was a black Town Car."

"It was a black Infiniti," he said. "I got a partial plate so I'll see if I can get any information on the driver. Why a Town Car?"

"The Polish mafia sat outside my apartment in a black Town Car, trying to intimidate me while I was writing the series in Northampton. But I don't know who this guy is with or what his intentions are. What do you think?"

"I don't really know, but I read your comments in the rock report about the 'watch your back' language in the note. That's such a common phrase I didn't attribute it to them necessarily. My gut says it's someone local since the note mentioned your family, and this dude is somehow connected to the Fontaines' murder."

"You're probably right."

He gave her a quick hug because she was obviously still shaken, but she seemed just as relieved as he was that the intruder had been unable to get into her apartment. For now.

"Don't worry. If he comes back, I'll call for backup. At least then I won't be caught with my pants down," he said, trying to make light of it.

"Okay," she said. "Text me if you see anything up there. I'm going to take a hot shower to see if I can calm down and get some sleep. I'm glad you're here. Even if you're out there."

"Me too," he said.

CHAPTER 49
GOODE

Friday

Goode had so much adrenaline in his system, it kept him sitting up and alert in the Explorer all night, jerking to attention any time he heard a car approaching or saw a headlight breaking through the night.

Katrina texted to check on him around four o'clock.

R u still alive out there? I'm having trouble sleeping.

Yeah, it's all quiet. So far, he wrote back. Thanks for asking. Try to get some rest.

He kept watch until the sun came up, then texted Katrina that he was heading home.

All clear. I'm out. Be careful today. Watch out for suspicious linebackers and call me if you need me.

When Artie called at seven o'clock, Goode had just sat down at his kitchen table to drink a bucket of coffee, a form of comfort as much as a necessity to get through the rest of the day.

After a night like last night, to hell with the caffeine rationing.

"Got the email from the lab we've been waiting for," Artie said. "They ran tests based on the Vitaleron drug audit, and nothing matched. Then they noticed that one drug on the surgery log was repeatedly used in combination with others, so they tested for that, but again, nothing came up. Luckily, they checked with another couple of labs, and realized they weren't doing the right test. Once they figured it out, they got a positive result late last night."

"So, what is it?" Goode asked. "I'm dying over here."

"Succinylcholine," Artie said.

"What the hell is succinylcholine?"

"It's a short-acting muscle relaxant that makes it easier to insert a breathing tube, but it can be fatal if a patient gets a big enough dose without a respirator or CPR."

"What happens if you don't?"

"A small dose will relax, then eventually paralyze, all your muscles, including your diaphragm. If you're not sedated, you'll be awake and aware of what's going on. It takes longer to work if it goes into muscle tissue than a vein, and even longer if it goes into fatty tissue. A bigger dose can stop you from breathing, and without external respiratory support, your heart will stop beating within a few minutes. But because it metabolizes into the bloodstream even after you're dead, it can't be traced unless you know to look for it."

"How sure are you that this was the cause of death?"

"Dr. Thompson and I agreed on this, because I did some research and found several cases where the killers used this drug and almost skated."

"Gotcha."

"By the way," Artie said, "how are you doing after those *Sun-Dispatch* stories hit last night?"

"Let's just say we had a busy night. After seeing the security footage myself and talking to the Battrelles, it sounded like Dr. Fontaine's nurse was involved, and what you're telling me only confirms that."

Goode texted Stone to call him for the news, which he did, panting with excitement.

"I agree. The nurse is looking even better," Stone said. "But why would she leave so much bruising on Victoria's arm, unless she was angry and didn't care?"

"Or did it on purpose to make it look like a suicide."

"Right. Who else had access to the surgery's drug supply? Dr. Russell? Because right now, I don't see a motive for him or the nurse."

"Yeah, I'd say no on Russell. The uniformed guy looked a good twenty years younger. But there's always the hired-hit-man scenario. Darren McMurphy has a known financial motive and a beef with Victoria. The congressman allegedly had sex with her in Hawaii, and he's also getting bribed. Dallas Fairchild, the biochemist, is still in the mix. He's got a lean, athletic build like the uniform in the video, and he knows all about drugs. But I don't see how he gets access to succinylcholine or, more importantly, why he would kill his golden geese. Darla is stealing the sex drug, but for what purpose? If the Battrelles are telling any part of the truth, they saw no syringes, so Victoria and Simon Fontaine had to have been injected during the window after Alex left and before Michael and Vincent showed up. Unless we're missing something, these dots don't connect without a conspiracy."

Goode could feel that things were coming to a head. After the visit from the linebacker in black the night before, he was confident that Katrina would lead him to whoever was behind the murders and that he could kill two birds with one stone by tailing her at a distance, without her knowledge. He just had a couple of stops to make first.

I've never used a reporter as bait, and I'm not sure she would appreciate it, but this way I'll be there to protect her no matter what happens.

Goode also didn't mention his plan to Stone, because he knew the sergeant wouldn't like the optics. "What could go wrong?" Stone would say facetiously. "You and your savior complex. Running wild again."

No sense getting him up in my grill. What he doesn't know won't piss him off. Besides, he'll be pleased with the results.

Goode picked up a different vehicle at HQ, knowing that Katrina and her stalker would recognize his others by now. After that, he went by Esperanza's condo and McMurphy's house one more time, but they still weren't at either place. So he called McMurphy's office to see if they would reveal where he was.

"He's taking a few days' staycation with his fiancée. I suggested the Del, and he asked me to book a room," his secretary said, referring to the Hotel del Coronado, a ritzy historic landmark on an island across the harbor from downtown San Diego.

So, he's not even hiding where he is. Interesting.

Heading over to the *Sun-Dispatch* parking lot, he found Katrina's car and parked far enough away that she wouldn't see him but close enough to watch her get into it. At some point, she would come out, and he would follow her.

CHAPTER 50
KATRINA

Friday

As soon as Goode left her apartment, Katrina took off her clothes to take that long, hot shower, noting that her cheeks looked flushed in the mirror. Was that a result of the dopamine rush? Or was she pink with fear and worry about what might have been and the danger of what could still happen? What if Goode hadn't been there to protect her? And what if the man in black came back later, after Goode went home and she was alone?

If I keep all my doors locked, hopefully he won't be able to get in. I wish I had that canister of police-grade chili spray that the lieutenant from Northampton gave me, but it's in the boxes that haven't arrived yet. Time to buy another canister.

For the short term, she felt safe knowing that Goode was outside keeping watch, so she could get a little shut-eye. As she lay in her sleeping bag, she tried to push the fear out of her mind and focus on the memory of his hands on her skin and the warm muscles of his chest against her breasts. But it was a tough slog.

She was worried about him, serving as bait for the bad guys, just to make sure she was safe. When she texted him around four o'clock, it was as much out of concern for his safety as to reassure herself about her own.

After she got his calm response, she was finally able to doze off, though her sleep was light and in spurts. She kept waking up in between an infinite loop of stress dreams to check her phone for a text from Goode.

The ping with his "all clear" text woke her up at six fifteen, by which time she was tired of trying to go back to sleep for the zillionth time. So, she pulled herself out of the sleeping bag, her head pounding as she stood up, and tried to orient herself to her new reality. The man in black was gone for now, though he might come back at any time. But Goode apparently wasn't worried enough about her safety to stay any longer.

Probably more likely that he has to go to work, just like I do.

Still, after going back and forth in her mind, she decided she wasn't going to change her routine or hide out in fear. She would try to shake it off and go for a run. If she didn't, she'd feel crappy and anxious for the rest of the day.

It's too early to buy more pepper spray. That will have to wait until lunchtime. I'll just have to be mindful, keep my phone with me, watch for any black Infiniti or other suspicious cars following me, and just hope that guy isn't waiting for me when I get back.

When she returned, she was relieved to find her apartment door was locked, just like she'd left it, and no one inside.

After showering and changing, she was in the newsroom by eight o'clock, trying to figure out what to do next. Unable to write about the man who had tried to break into her apartment or anything Goode had told her off the record, she also couldn't tell Joanne, let alone Linda, without them pulling her off the story for liability reasons. She wasn't going to let them do that. Not when she was this close.

You're going to have to find a way to get something on the record to advance the story. Somehow.

But she felt torn. Safety issues aside, she had ethical implications to consider.

It was just a few kisses.

She was crazy to think they weren't going to step over the line, no matter how high the stakes were. They were both risk-takers, they'd both had long, emotionally draining days, and, of course, wine was involved. She'd made sure of that. Even though she didn't want to admit it, she'd bought that bottle knowing where it would lead. Still, this guy was different from the others. She really liked him, and it was obviously mutual. After a lifetime of practice, she was an expert at compartmentalization.

As soon as this is all over, which could be any day now, I'll tell Joanne I'd rather not cover the cops for a while. That way, I'll be free to do what I need to investigate Mom and Daddy's murder, and Goode and I can do what we want without any conflict of interest. But in the meantime, that man could come back and be waiting for me when I get home. Like Goode said, he might also bring reinforcements. So, if anything, Goode will have to stay with me full time for the next few nights. One day at a time. In the meantime, I've got work to do.

It was Friday, the day William Fontaine had expected to deliver the autopsy reports. But Katrina figured she should at least make an effort to get the information through official channels. That way, her new sources at the PD couldn't complain.

After leaving Sergeant Stone a couple of messages, Katrina finally got a return call around ten thirty.

"So, we meet again, my fair lady," he said, chuckling nervously.

"Indeed."

"What can I do for you?"

"Let's start with the autopsy reports. Where are we with those? Or is the chief going to seal them?"

"The reports won't be ready until the ME gets final toxicology results, and as you just stated, we won't be releasing them anyway."

"Well, maybe I can get some of the information another way," she said.

"Like what?"

"Can you confirm that Victoria was prescribed oxycodone and Xanax the day she was found dead, or that those drugs were found in her body?"

"Yes and yes, but not in lethal amounts. We are also skeptical that her father authorized those prescriptions, even though his name is on the vials. Next?"

Wow, that's new information. Why didn't Goode tell me that?

"Have charges been filed against Michael or Vincent Battrelle since they were questioned last night? If not, what's their status in this case? Are they considered suspects?"

"No, not yet, and no, they aren't considered suspects. Why don't you call them 'persons of interest,'" Stone said.

"Do you have an official comment about the uniformed police officer who went into the Fontaine house at noon last Friday?"

Stone essentially repeated what Goode already told her, so at least now she had that on the record.

"If it's not a sworn officer, do you have an idea who it is?" she asked.

"We can't discuss sensitive details of the investigation at this juncture, but, off the record, we're willing to give you more information if you can be patient."

"Thanks, but I can't promise I won't come into some independent information today, so I guess we'll have to see," she said.

"I don't know what you mean, but we'd really appreciate anything you can do not to blow up our investigation," he said.

Just doing my job. Not my problem.

If the police weren't going to cooperate, it was time for plan B, which was really plan A, given that they were going to seal the reports anyway. William had already emailed her saying that he had some "informative" documents for her.

He also complimented her on her stories. "Very interesting stuff this morning," he said when she called to follow up.

"They were actually posted last night."

"Yes, I know, but I go to bed early, and I also like to physically turn the pages of the newspaper as I eat my oatmeal," he said. "My friend at the medical examiner's office told me the toxicology results, cause, and manner of death are still pending, but he sent me the investigative reports, which provide new details about the crime scene. Just don't say where you got them, okay?"

"Done."

Katrina felt like a bear, devouring the reports like a stolen picnicker's lunch. As Stone said, the preliminary toxicology results showed that Victoria had Xanax and oxy in her body, but not in fatal doses.

So what other toxicology results are they waiting for?

Dated a couple of days earlier, the reports described what and who was found where—the injection sites on Victoria's arm and Simon's neck, the 9mm gun, Simon's gooey gunshot wound, the open pill vials next to Victoria's bed, the oxys stuck in her throat, the positive pregnancy test, and even the fresh cutting scars on her inner thighs.

I can see now why Goode wasn't sure initially whether this was a double suicide, a murder-suicide, or a double homicide. What an effing mess.

There were still significant unanswered questions, the most important being, what actually killed these people?

No wonder they're being so secretive. Sounds like they still don't know.

Walking the reports into Joanne's office, she discussed with her editor whether she should write a story or respect the detectives' request to wait.

"These reports are not only incomplete, but they're also two days old, which means it could be misleading to quote from them," Katrina said. "But they do reveal some new details for our readers."

"What's the bottom line so far?" Joanne asked.

It looked like someone had interfered with the scene, Katrina said, by trying to clean up or remove incriminating evidence. "Goode and William Fontaine think the Fontaines were murdered, because the forensics don't make sense otherwise. I trust their gut."

"Does it give the estimated time of death?"

"Sometime between noon and three p.m., which is new."

"Right. So there was a major time lag between their deaths and the shots fired that prompted the 911 call. We also know who came in and out from the video."

"Well, we still don't know their identities, only that it *looks* like a nurse and a police officer—on Halloween. What if he's a crooked cop who won't admit he was there because he's a hired hit man?"

"You didn't tell me that part."

"Sorry, Stone told me that. Sort of."

"Which part?"

"He said they have no record of an officer being there hours before the 911 call."

"So, the 'officer' and/or the nurse could have done the deed and left. Michael and Vincent showed up later, found the bodies, and decided to report it anonymously. But then who fired the gun?"

"No one I talked to heard anything."

"Why don't you see if your buddy Goode can help us fill in some of these gaps. We don't want to prevent them from catching a murderer if they're close, but it's also not our job to help them."

Katrina nodded, trying to keep any emotion from her face.

Time to get this over with.

Goode picked up on the first ring. "Are you basking in the afterglow?" he joked.

"Yes, and no," she said, pausing. She really didn't want to have this conversation, but she had no choice. "You're not going to like what I have to ask you."

"That was a short honeymoon."

"Yeah, about that."

"Just kidding. Go ahead. I'll behave."

She chuckled and shook her head.

I can't get mad at him. But he might get mad at me.

"I've got the investigative reports from the ME's office," she said.

"Aw, man, how did you get those?"

"I can't say. I asked Stone for the autopsy reports, and he said no dice, so I had to go to another source."

"I see."

"But Stone did give me a quote about the guy in the police uniform."

"Good," he said, pausing. "Katrina, please don't print what's in those draft reports. They're days old. You know we're uncovering more every day. Even from you."

"I figured you'd say that. But these describe the crime scene, such as it was."

"As I tried to make clear last night, I have some ideas of who the uniform guy is, and he could very well be our killer, but we haven't pinned it down yet. So, if you quote from those reports, he'll know that we know the scene was messed with, and he might destroy evidence. Or hurt someone else. Like you."

"Have you picked up anyone else for questioning yet?" she asked.

"I can't tell you this on the record, but I'm trying to bring in the nurse. The problem is she hasn't been at her place, so she's MIA at the moment."

"So, you know who she is."

"Yes."

"It's Esperanza Cepeda, right?"

Goode paused before he answered, which in her mind was a tell. "I really can't say, Katrina. This is a very delicate situation."

Well, that almost sounds like a confirmation. No wonder she hasn't returned my calls. She's hiding out somewhere. She did look pretty upset in the video.

They both sat in silence for a minute. Goode must have realized that being annoyed was fruitless, because his voice turned playful again, possibly an attempt to deflect. "Have you mentioned last night to your editor?"

"No, and I can hear you smiling. Have you told Stone?"

"No."

"So, I can't tell my editor why you don't want us to print these new details other than we'll screw up your investigation? Do you seriously think my life will be in any more danger if I write about these reports today?"

"Yes, I do. Weren't you there with me last night when a man tried to break into your apartment? If you write that up, I'll have to keep coming over, and you know where that's going. I can't keep sleeping in my car, my back is killing me."

"Funny, I slept like a rock," she joked. "No, seriously, I got a few hours and woke up with a headache, but it was nothing a giant Diet Coke couldn't cure. I'll try to persuade my editor to hold off, but I can't promise."

"Can't you do a follow-up story on the campaign donations?"

That's a great idea, actually.

"That could work. Let me run it by her."

"I know you're just doing your job, Katrina. I only wish you weren't so damned good at it."

"Stop saying my name, you're only making this harder."

"Stop saying harder."

"Ha ha. I'm hanging up now."

Joanne was on the fence about the autopsy-report story, so Katrina offered a few alternatives. She could be pretty convincing when she tried.

"I could do a follow-up on the Battrelles, interview Alex in jail, and give Vincent and Michael a chance to explain why they were called in for questioning," she offered. "Vincent called to yell at me last night after I got home."

"Oh, how awkward. Yes, you could, and you probably should."

"Or I could move on to that weekender about the Vitaleron drug trials and the FDA approval process, and take a deeper dive into the campaign donations."

"Another excellent idea. Probably more doable than the first. Make some calls and let's see where we are in a few hours."

While she was in Joanne's office, the security guard in the lobby left her a message that he had a package for her. As soon as the elevator doors to the lobby opened, he handed her a manila envelope with her name printed in block letters.

"A guy wearing a black leather jacket and a motorcycle helmet handed it to me," he said.

"Did you see his face?"

"No, he had one of those shaded eye shields. Wouldn't sign the logbook, either."

Once the doors closed, Katrina ripped open the envelope to find a thin stack of printed emails between Victoria Fontaine and Dallas Fairchild, who was listed on the website as senior biochemist. Sent within days of the Fontaines' deaths, the emails discussed the installation of security cameras and password-protected locks to catch a thief who was stealing doses of the sex drug from the lab.

Could that be what they're looking for in the additional toxicology tests? The sex drug? Wouldn't that be ironic if Linda was right from the get-go?

Just then, her desk phone rang.

"Hi. It's Darla Johansen from Vitaleron. We met at the front desk."

"Oh, yes," Katrina said, surprised. "I was about to call you guys."

"Really? I was wondering if you could meet for happy hour tonight. Around five at the Hotel Del?"

Regardless of whether this was for business or pleasure, both seemed oddly inappropriate. "Is this a social call or is it related to the Fontaine case?"

"A little of both," Darla said.

Katrina felt a little ragged—and paranoid—given recent events, and Darla's voice sounded a bit off.

"Can you give me a hint?" she asked cautiously.

"No, I'd rather talk in person. My fiancé has been reading your stories, and he wants to meet you."

Rolling her eyes, Katrina was tempted to ask if he liked to dress up as a police officer, but she held her tongue. More often than not, meetings like this were a waste of time. But under the circumstances, it was a good opportunity to get some scoop on Dallas Fairchild, the stolen drugs, and who at Vitaleron rode a motorcycle.

As long as we meet in a well-lit, public place.

"What's his name?" she asked.

"Congressman Brandon Winchester," Darla said coyly. "He knew Dr. Fontaine pretty well and he wants to give you some insights into the campaign donations that William Fontaine mentioned."

Whaat?

"That's what we call burying the lede!" Katrina said brightly.

So, Winchester doesn't return my call, and now he wants to meet me for a drink?

"Don't tell him I told you about the fiancé part," Darla said. "It's supposed to be a secret. His divorce isn't finalized yet."

"Sure, no problem."

They agreed to meet in the Viennese, a hotel bar that Katrina found on the Del's website while they were talking.

I'm betting the congressman wants to give me the "it's all legal" spiel.

That said, only the contributions and gifts he reported could be traced by searching public records. The reports wouldn't cover any secretly exchanged jewelry, favors, or shares in Vitaleron. What if Dr. Fontaine had been trying to bribe and/or extort faster action from Winchester or had threatened to expose him, to which the congressman—or a henchman—responded by killing him and Victoria?

Plenty of links existed between these players, through Vitaleron, the Fontaines, and the Battrelle family. No wonder Vincent had been pushing so hard to get her off the story.

They've arrested Alex Battrelle, so Goode surely knows more than I do after interviewing the whole family. Has he seen these emails too?

Joanne was far more excited about Katrina's happy-hour date with Congressman Winchester than any of the other stories they'd discussed.

"I'll put this on the budget as a follow-up to our campaign donation story," Joanne said, immediately typing it in. "Turn in some A-matter before you go, and you can write a new top when you get back."

Katrina called Goode to share the news about her happy-hour meeting, but also to pick his brain.

"Your possible suspects don't include Brandon Winchester, do they? I don't know much about him other than the donations yet, but I just found out he's engaged to Darla, the receptionist at Vitaleron," she said.

"You're kidding. Really?" he said, sounding genuinely surprised. "That's quite an interesting connection. Where are you meeting them?"

"At the Del."

Goode paused and sighed heavily.

"What's wrong?" she asked.

"I'm trying to decide what I can, can't, and shouldn't tell you."

"So this is something?"

"Yes, it's definitely something. More than you or I probably even know yet."

"Are you telling me to be careful again?"

"Always. Where at the Del are you meeting them?"

"Why, are you going to spy on me? I have a job to do, you know."

"Of course, so do I, which is why you should definitely meet them somewhere busy and public, so they won't notice me."

"Right. That's why I picked the Viennese bar."

"I'll be there, as incognito as possible."

CHAPTER 51
GOODE

Friday

After hanging up with Katrina, Goode realized that Darla Johansen must be the third in Victoria's alleged threesome with Winchester, and the fact that Darren McMurphy was at the same hotel with his fiancée, Esperanza, was no coincidence. Was that the second couple to whom she was supplying the drug?

The rats are gathering, and they're luring Katrina into their nest.

If he showed up early with reinforcements, he could try to mitigate any danger by picking up Esperanza, unsuspecting, by the pool, or, more likely, in a bar, and persuading her to confess, hopefully thwarting any move to harm Katrina or anyone else. He also didn't need to lie to Katrina now about using her as bait, because she'd put herself into this position and had no qualms that he was going to observe the meeting. But he also didn't tell her that he was organizing a sting operation around it.

If Esperanza was with McMurphy, Goode would wait until he went to the bathroom to whisk her away, then go back and grab him too. As long as he had backup, he could make sure Katrina wasn't left unguarded during her meeting with Winchester.

Still camped out in the far corner of the *Sun-Dispatch* lot in his unmarked car, Goode called Stone to discuss options.

"Is she going to write about the autopsy reports?" Stone asked.

"I don't know. I tried to discourage her, but I think she's got her hands full now with a five o'clock meeting with Shady Winchester at the Del," he said. "I don't see how she has time to write anything else before that. If I know my girl, she'll have her head buried in campaign reports all afternoon."

"Your girl?"

"You know what I mean."

"Did you follow my instructions last night?"

"No comment."

"Aw, man."

"Dude, relax, I stayed the night, but I was camped out in my car in her carport. She's got no furniture, no bed, not even a couch. Just a single sleeping bag and two guitars. She's almost like—a guy—only much hotter."

"All right, good."

"Not really, my back is killing me."

"Moving on."

"Happy to," Goode said. "Listen, we'll need the whole team at the Del to spread out around the hotel and mic the tables in the bar. Once I see Winchester in person, I'll know whether he's our 'uniformed' officer. But my gut says he's not the type to get his hands dirty. I suppose it could even be Darla."

"Unless he's the father of Victoria's baby."

"That is dark."

"This whole thing is dark. We can't pick up Winchester simply for having a drink with a reporter. The feds would have to follow up on bribery by campaign donation if that's what happened. But if Darla is stealing trade secrets and IP from Vitaleron and sharing them with the congressman, then we could get them on that."

"We're in the right lane for conspiracy to murder as well."

"That works for me, too, but first things first. The Del is a big property. Why don't you get on the horn with Watts and get him to join the party?" Stone said. "They've got more resources and better recording equipment than we do. If this really is a murder conspiracy, we don't know what all they've got planned, and the bigger the team, the better."

"True," Goode said. "I'm still not sure about Michael Battrelle's role in all of this. He lied to us and to Katrina too. But the only people who have direct or indirect access to drugs at both the surgery and Vitaleron are Dr. Russell and Darren McMurphy, through his nurse girlfriend."

Stone jumped back in: "Just because the sex drug didn't turn up in the Fontaines' bodies doesn't mean one or more of these jackals didn't kill them, hepped up on dopamine and whatever the hell else those pills do to your brain—and your pecker."

"That's why I'd go with McMurphy. The guy's been an arrogant tool since junior high school, and Russell wouldn't leave such a messy injection site. Although I do still like the hit man idea."

"Well, let's go find out."

"I had another dark thought. What if it *is* one of our guys, hired to do the dirty deed? If McMurphy is bribing a congressman, he could easily bribe a cop, and it's a good cover to do it on Halloween."

"I sure hope you're wrong. I always come back to Occam's razor. Go for what makes the most logical sense."

"None of this makes sense. I'll call Watts right now and try to arrange a joint op, starting with a rendezvous a few blocks from the Del at two o'clock. I'll text you once I find a place to park. You know how hellish it can be over there in the afternoon."

"Don't tell Katrina she's bait. Vincent Battrelle and his paper will eat our ass for lunch."

"I'm way ahead of you, chief."

CHAPTER 52
GOODE

Friday

Supervisory Special Agent Watts was surprisingly cooperative. Goode could almost hear him salivating as he listened to the new theory that the uniformed officer could be a real cop involved in a scheme of bribery, theft of IP, trade secrets, and an experimental sex drug, plus a murder conspiracy involving a congressman, an FDA official, and the Battrelles, one of the region's most illustrious families.

"I'll mobilize the Public Corruption Unit, get an emergency warrant, and get those mics planted," Watts said. "But we'll need to move fast to beat the Friday afternoon happy-hour crowd. My guys will stick around to make sure the meeting goes as planned and your asset is secure."

"Whoa, slow down. She's not my asset," Goode said. "She has no idea this is going on. I told her I would be nearby to observe her meeting, but she's not working with us by any stretch. In fact, we've been chasing her tail because she's too frickin' good at her job."

"That's not surprising," Watts said. "Both of her parents were very sharp. You ever wonder if this is all somehow related?"

"No, I haven't," Goode fibbed.

This was his investigation, and he didn't want to share Katrina or his suspicions with anyone else.

Goode and Stone drove separately in case things went awry, as they often did during a joint operation like this.

Coronado was surrounded by water—the Pacific Ocean to the west and the San Diego Bay to the east. If you were heading south, you would cross the Coronado Bridge, but if you were heading north, you could take the scenic ocean route to the village along a finger of land that ran parallel to the mainland.

The Del had always been a special, albeit expensive, place to go for a drink after his annual ritual on the bridge, where he stood with one long-stemmed red rose, peeled off one petal at a time, and released it into the wind at the spot where his mother jumped.

But, for the first time ever, he'd skipped the ceremony this past year. Something had changed after the Tania Marcus case, the homicide of a young girl with long, raven-black hair, turquoise eyes, and an uncanny resemblance to his mother. Stunning even in death. It was almost as if the deep pain of his mother's suicide had dissipated after Clover, the young woman they suspected of killing Tania, jumped to her death at Black's. He'd apprehended Tania's actual killer later that afternoon, the skateboarding biochem grad student he'd seen touching her face when Goode almost ran over her body in an alley.

As Goode drove over the Coronado Bridge, he passed the fateful spot and realized with bittersweet relief that the memory of his mother was still as clear as ever, just less painful. He could still picture his six-year-old self with her, parked in the far-right lane with their hazard lights flashing as she applied a coat of red lipstick that matched the roses on her dress. How she got out and gave him her trademark droopy smile through the driver's-side window before she walked behind the car and climbed over the railing. How he sat waiting for her to return until a friendly young police officer pulled up and took him home.

Turning left on Orange Avenue, Goode cruised alongside the wide, grassy median that ran along the commercial strip of boutiques, family-owned stores, and restaurants in the village. As he approached the Del, he felt like he was visiting an old friend, its red, pointy towers reaching toward the sky with an almost royal grandeur.

John D. Spreckels, the heir to the sugar fortune, had bought up all the undeveloped property on Coronado Island in the 1880s and helped build this hotel in 1888. Since then, the Del had remained an exclusive destination for the wealthy and a staycation treat for the locals. The Viennese, where Katrina was headed, was the most casual of the hotel bars, overlooking the patio and a spacious pool.

At the rendezvous point a few blocks from the Del, his crew joined up with the FBI agents and walked over to the hotel in pairs. Wearing khaki shorts, Hawaiian shirts, and baseball caps, they carried athletic bags full of electronic gear.

At the bar, the agents spread out, sipping iced tea while surreptitiously planting a mic in each centerpiece. Meanwhile, Goode's team circulated around the expansive property, searching for Esperanza or McMurphy, who proved to be elusive. The detectives mostly wandered around, watching, waiting, and taking turns in the men's room.

Where is she? Does McMurphy have her locked up somewhere? Or vice versa?

CHAPTER 53
KATRINA

Friday

Katrina had hoped to arrive first. She wanted to sit at a table where she could watch the entire room and outdoor patio with her back to the wall. But the bar was crowded, and Winchester was already sitting in a booth with Darla.

Waving her over, Winchester stood up and flashed the sleazy smile she recognized from his website, his mouth stretched horizontally to almost cartoonish proportions. He was a good foot taller and a dozen years older than Darla, who beamed up at him as if he were a walking pile of cash. Based on his Armani suit and the sizable yellow-diamond ring on Darla's finger, he appeared to be just that. His smug demeanor confirmed Katrina's sense that he not only accepted campaign donations in exchange for quid pro quos, i.e., bribes, he actively solicited them.

But he's too tall and big-boned to be the police officer on the video.

"Nice to meet you, Katrina," he said, giving her a wimpy, loose handshake.

Like a woman. Ewww.

"And please call me Brandon," he said.

"Hi, Katrina," Darla said with a glassy-eyed sweetness as she emptied the last of her martini into a new one the waiter had just delivered.

"How long have you been here?" Katrina asked.

"About twenty minutes," Winchester said, "but we didn't order any food because we thought we'd take this meeting up to our room."

Katrina had her guard up, intending to follow Goode's advice to keep their interaction in public view—while eating a tasty appetizer that she would expense to the paper.

"Actually, I'd prefer to stay in the bar," she said. "I'm meeting a colleague here in a little while."

When she saw Winchester and Darla exchange looks, Katrina couldn't tell if she'd derailed some nefarious scheme or if they were simply surprised she'd declined their offer.

Leaning toward Katrina, Darla whispered, "I think Brandon is worried someone will see him talking to the reporter who is investigating the Fontaine deaths and think he's involved somehow."

"No one knows who I am or what I look like," Katrina whispered back, "and I'm sure he's talked with plenty of reporters before me. He'll be fine."

I'm not going to any hotel room with this creep. If I ignore him, he'll get the message and sit his ass back down.

Signaling to the waiter, she avoided the congressman's eyes and sat down with finality, while Winchester continued to stand, as if this would somehow force her to accept his invitation.

"I guess we're staying here," he said passive-aggressively, lowering himself into the booth and straightening his tie, all in one motion.

Katrina ignored his tone and turned on her own fake smile. She ordered some overpriced Thai chicken sticks with peanut sauce, deciding against the Chardonnay she would normally order at happy hour.

Got to stay sharp.

"So, tell me, how is your committee involved in the FDA's drug-approval process?" she asked, opening her notebook.

Eyebrows raised, Winchester seemed taken aback by her opening gambit, but, as a consummate politician, he spent the next ten minutes offering an extremely sanitized explanation that she suspected had little bearing in reality. Still awaiting the purpose of this meeting, she wondered what he was so worried she would find out. Or already knew.

"Do all those campaign contributions influence your votes or actions when it comes to Vitaleron?" she asked.

"Of course not," he said with the cartoon smile again, an obvious tell that he was lying. "We don't deal with drugs going through experimental trials."

"Where are Mantabulis and Femtastica in the approval process?"

"I wouldn't know," he said snappishly. "I don't keep track of individual drugs."

A bit testy, aren't we?

"I assume you've met many of the local investors, because they're listed on your campaign disclosure forms," she said. "I found them on the SEC reports for Vitaleron. The donations were all collected at two fundraisers for your reelection campaign."

As she waited for him to answer, he stared at her without blinking.

Ohhh, good party trick.

"I was waiting for a question," he said. "I'm sure I've met some of them, but at fundraisers, it's generally 'Hello, nice to meet you,' and then on to the next donor."

What she really wanted to know was whether *he* was an investor, or even a silent partner, so that only a select few would know he wasn't disclosing the conflict of interest while lobbying his buddies on the golf course—and that female FDA official—over drinks. But she stayed silent, hoping he would feel pressured to fill the space. It worked.

"There are quite a few local investors, or so I hear, but not many with large shares in the company," he said.

"You're aware of who they are, though, right? From your campaign statements?"

The congressman's irritation was showing now, as his jawline and phony smile tightened. "I don't study names on the reports if that's what you're asking. My staff keeps track of them, and I assure you it's all done legally," he said.

"Have you thought about investing in Vitaleron? I noticed it's not listed on your financial disclosure reports."

"Sure, who hasn't? It seems like a very promising drug."

"Darla, you know some of the investors, don't you?" Katrina asked, assessing her tipsiness.

"Yes, but I'll never tell," Darla replied. As she drained her martini glass, the stick of olives hit her in the face, then toppled end over end to the floor, splashing her blouse with the cloudy liquid. "Now look what you made me do. I ordered extra olives on purpose."

Giggling, Darla touched Katrina's forearm as she wobbled her way upright, shaky at best on four-inch spike heels. But Katrina could see that her body was firm, athletic, with narrow hips and small breasts. Like a lean runner.

Could she be the one in the police uniform?

"If you'll excuse me, I need to go to the little girls' room to put some cold water on this mess," Darla said. "You two make nice."

Once Darla was out of earshot, Katrina took a more direct tact. "Okay, Congressman, why did you want to meet with me? You never even returned my call."

Caught off guard again, Winchester was one of those old-boy politicians who traditionally got away with talking around the issue. Deflect, deflect, deflect.

"As I've said, these were all legal contributions, and I'm not sure why you've chosen to try to link me with Vitaleron, as if I had something to do with these deaths. Victoria was known to be unstable, and from what I hear, she overdosed," he said. "Dr. Fontaine had a weak heart, in more ways than one."

"No one has said anything like that to me," she said. "My sources say they were both murdered."

Shaking his head, he said, "Well, my sources are saying the opposite. And as a member of Congress, I'm sure I have access to better information than you do."

"Let's be honest, how much have you invested in the company?"

"I didn't say I had any money invested," he said, a sweaty sheen catching the light on his upper lip and forehead. He took a long sip of his gin and tonic and reached into his jacket pocket. "Excuse me, my phone is vibrating. I need to take this call."

As Winchester headed for the patio, Katrina looked around the bar and saw Goode in sunglasses and a baseball cap a few tables away, nursing an iced tea and nibbling at a bowl of cheese-doodle pretzel mix. He raised his eyebrows with a questioning thumbs-up. She replied with a "who knows" shrug.

When Winchester returned a few minutes later, he had his arm around Darla, who kissed his cheek after applying red lipstick. Thinking he knew better, he swiped at the red mark on his cheek, but simply smeared it, patting her on the butt like a dog.

Is she his pet or his amulet of protection? Maybe sweet Darla isn't so sweet.

"Listen, I have some paperwork I want to show you up in the room," he said.

"What type of paperwork?" Katrina asked.

Sounds like a ruse to me.

"It will prove that everything between Dr. Fontaine and me was on the up-and-up. Your story and your questions today implied that there was something improper about our relationship. I want to be as transparent as I can with you," he said, using the telltale buzzword among politicians that usually signaled they were being anything but.

"Can't you run up and bring them down?"

"No, I can't. They're personal documents, and they don't leave my room."

Katrina's curiosity was piqued, but she didn't want to leave the bar. She trusted this couple even less than when she'd first sat down.

However, she knew Joanne wouldn't be happy if Katrina didn't allow him to explain the donations.

Maybe I'm being paranoid. What if these donations truly are legal?

Despite her fear of mortality, a jolt of adrenaline hit her once again, fortifying her natural tendency to take risks. If she followed them upstairs, surely Goode would watch where she was going and follow if necessary. A congressman couldn't go around murdering people at the Hotel Del, especially reporters. It wouldn't play well in the polls.

That's not going to happen. This isn't a crime novel.

"Okay, but only for a few minutes. I really do need to be back here to meet my colleague."

"Very good," Winchester said.

After exchanging looks with Darla, as if to say "All is well with the world again," he gestured for Katrina to walk ahead of him as they headed for the elevator. She shuddered inwardly as he put his hand on her lower back to guide her up the steps, just as Vincent had.

The touching was not only inappropriate, he'd prevented her from following behind him and signaling to Goode. She jumped at the sound of a hand smacking clothed flesh a few feet behind her, followed by giggling, though she couldn't be sure who was slapping whom.

The three of them stepped into the elevator, where Darla clung to Winchester like a mudpack at a spa in Palm Springs. Laying her head on his shoulder, she winked at Katrina, while Winchester gave her a heavy-lidded look and licked his lips.

Gross. Are they coming on to me? Does he really want to discuss business, or is he trying to compromise me by playing Hide the Olive Jar in their room? What if Darla was the one stealing the medication to share with this creepy dude?

"Fifth floor, please," Winchester said to the operator, whose face was so wrinkled he looked like he'd been around since the hotel was built.

"Yes, sir," the operator replied.

The antique elevator ground its way up the floors, making Katrina feel like they were in slow motion as each floor passed by through the brass grating.

She didn't know if she was more worried that they were going to tie her to a chair and inject her with something or that they were going to force her to have sex with them. She could still feel the spot on her lower back where Winchester had touched her.

It was too late now, but she realized that Goode wouldn't know where to find her because the antique elevator didn't show lit floor numbers on the ground floor like a modern elevator did.

Oh, shit.

"Fifth floor," the operator announced, pulling back the grating with a rattle to reveal a beige carpet with red octagons. The antique floor squeaked beneath them with every other step along the narrow hallway, dimly lit by mushroom-shaped sconces on the ceiling. Her nose itched from the musty smell as her mind flashed to the scene from *The Shining*, where the hallway filled with blood.

Redrum, redrum.

They were approaching the end of the hallway when a door opened and out stepped a tall man, built like a linebacker, wearing a navy blazer, a tie, and one of those earplugs with the coiled wire. Seeing a bulge under his jacket, she assumed he was packing a gun.

How did he know we were here? That must have been him calling Winchester. Wrong build for the officer in the video, but based on Goode's description, he's good for the guy in my driveway.

"Evening, Congressman, Darla," he said.

"Good evening, Walter," Winchester said.

The elevator bell dinged down the hall behind them, but when she turned around, hoping to see Goode poke his head out, no one was there.

"Right this way, Miss Katrina," Winchester said, touching her lower back again as he followed her into the room.

I really wish he'd stop doing that.

Winchester closed the door and secured the horseshoe latch, preventing even the housekeepers or hotel security from getting in—*if* they got past Walter.

Katrina felt a tight ball of anxiety and nausea in her stomach. What had she gotten herself into? She was about to text Goode when Winchester grabbed her phone and set it on a table next to a bucket of champagne on ice.

"We don't really need to be texting or making calls at this point, do we?" he asked rhetorically. "This won't take long."

What won't take long?

Katrina didn't know what to do. There was no such lesson in the investigative reporter's handbook. She'd have to wing it.

She thought of Daniel Pearl, the *Wall Street Journal* reporter who'd been abducted while pursuing a hot story about terrorists in Pakistan and ended up beheaded. This, she imagined, was similar to the dilemma he'd been in, thinking that covering terrorism was dangerous but that his story was important enough to take a risk. He probably hadn't felt entirely safe when he'd climbed into that taxi but chose to do it anyway. And that decision proved fatal.

"Let's see that paperwork," she said.

Tapping two long fingers on her shoulder, Winchester pushed her gently into a chair. "What's your hurry?" he said. "Let's have some champagne first. Don't you think, sweetie?"

"Definitely! Let's break out the hors d'oeuvres too," Darla chirped, lifting the silver-domed cover of the buffet cart to expose a bounty of raw oysters, smoked salmon, crème fraiche, crackers, and caviar on ice.

What the hell are they up to?

The cork exploded across the room so loudly that Katrina almost dove under the bed for cover. But she tried to remain calm as he poured the fizzy liquid into three flutes.

"We just got engaged, and we are in quite the celebratory mood," Darla exclaimed.

If they were simply two people in love who had invited her into their little bubble for a chat and paperwork exchange, then she should be free to go.

So why take away my phone and lock the door? This feels a little surreal, but I'll be fine. Right? Unless the man outside is there to ensure I don't leave.

"I'm not allowed to have sources buy me champagne and hors d'oeuvres," she said. "It's not ethical."

Winchester leaned down and put a full flute on the table next to her. "Who's going to know? We certainly won't tell, will we, sweetie?"

"Don't worry, Katrina," Darla said. "Drink up!"

Did she put something in my drink?

"No, really, thank you, but I don't drink on the job," she said. "I've still got a story to write tonight. So, if you give me the paperwork, I'll be on my way."

The congressman smirked and shook his head. "You didn't really think we were just going to let you leave, did you?"

What the hell?

"I'm sure you don't mean that you're going to hold me hostage, do you, Congressman?" she said, laughing nervously. "That would constitute abduction, a criminal offense, which wouldn't look great in the newspaper or in your opponent's campaign brochures, where you know the story would end up."

"Katrina, what are you talking about?" Darla said in a Valley girl voice before stuffing a cracker heaped with caviar into her mouth, leaving a white, creamy trail on her lips and chin.

Darla curled up like a cat in Winchester's lap as they both sipped champagne on the chartreuse silk love seat. He seemed to be enjoying the head games, thinking he could manipulate Katrina now they were on his turf.

"I was only teasing you, Miss Chopin," he said. "You're perfectly free to go. But there will be no paperwork for you unless we can talk about it. It's pretty good stuff, you know. It would make a really great story. Award-winning, I'm sure."

Even after she'd called their bluff, Katrina honestly couldn't tell if they were planning to hurt her or not. But whatever their intentions, she was leaving while she had the chance.

"Your choice. As I said, I've got to meet my colleague. Why don't you email me that paperwork," she said, grabbing her cell phone and heading for the door.

"I guess I could, but you're being awfully rude," Winchester said. "Sweetie," he said to Darla, who was back at the buffet, "will you make me a plate too?"

"Sure," she said.

"I'll see you later, then," Katrina said.

Opening the door, she couldn't have been more relieved to see a familiar face.

"No, you can't go in there, the congressman is in a meeting," Walter was saying.

"There you are, Sergeant Stone," she said, taking his arm and walking toward the elevator.

"Have a nice evening, Ms. Chopin," Walter called after them.

Katrina hit the elevator call button repeatedly for good measure.

"It's okay," Stone whispered. "I've got you."

"You have no idea," she said.

"Let's get you out of here and you can tell us about it downstairs," he said.

The elevator rose up slowly from below, startling her as Darren McMurphy emerged into view through the grating. He looked equally startled to see her, which seemed strange because they'd never actually met.

After an awkward dance of stepping around each other, he turned and walked toward Winchester's room, where Walter had already opened the door for him.

What's he doing here? Was he supposed to be part of the "meeting" I was just in? Did I escape with my life?

Back in the lobby, Stone led Katrina downstairs, through boutique row, and back to the bar, where Goode was waiting for them.

"Now that we know where McMurphy is, I'm going to grab him for questioning," Stone said, jogging off again. "Meet you up there."

"That was one of the weirdest meetings ever," she told Goode, giving him the brief highlights. "I wasn't sure they were going to let me go."

"Everything is okay now," he said calmly, rubbing the back of her hand.

"If you say so," she said. She still felt goose bumps across her arms and neck. "What's going on?"

"Off the record, we're looking at McMurphy *and* Winchester, especially in light of the article you wrote, which was very helpful, by the way. We have other information linking both of them to the Fontaines, which I'll tell you once this is over. It's looking like a conspiracy case."

"But, of course, I can't use any of that in today's story."

"No, absolutely not, or you will blow everything for us. In fact, for the next day or two, you'll need to be very, very careful. Don't get yourself into a situation like that with any of these people again, because they, or one of their lackeys, might act recklessly. I would encourage you to go to your apartment, lock all the doors, and let us handle this."

"I think that guy from last night at my apartment could be Winchester's bodyguard," she said. "Walter Hall. He's upstairs. But I can't go home and hide. I'm on deadline and my editor is expecting a story. You've got to tell me what's going on."

"Sorry, but I can't say anything more. Go to the paper or go home, Katrina. It's not safe for you here. I'll call you later, I promise, but I've got to go."

"Dammit!" she muttered.

CHAPTER 54
KATRINA

Friday

"Go to the paper or go home, Katrina. It's not safe for you here."

Goode's warning rang in her ears, but she couldn't bring herself to follow his advice, even after everything that had happened over the past week. An intrepid reporter would hang around to watch the cops walk McMurphy and Winchester out in handcuffs.

Maybe I should call Joanne to send a photographer over. How unsafe could I be in a public place, with so many people swarming around?

She could also play it safe and go back to the newsroom as Goode suggested. See if she and Joanne could figure out a way to write it all up, with the hope that Goode's prediction would come true and they'd top the story with a fresh arrest later that night.

In the meantime, however, what would the story say, exactly? Winchester and his fiancée, the Vitaleron receptionist, invited me up to their room for a seafood buffet, played head games, and offered me paperwork I didn't want to wait around for in case they drugged or sexually assaulted me?

She could only hope that she could cobble together a story, possibly with Goode's help. The conspiracy angle sounded intriguing, but it was off the record.

Katrina was scanning the area for a private place to call Joanne when she felt a tap on her shoulder. It was a pretty young Filipino woman who resembled the nurse in the video, one of the last people to see Victoria Fontaine alive. She was petite, in her late twenties, wearing a black sleeveless top, black shorts, and a frantic expression.

"I'm Esperanza Cepeda. You called me, and we need to talk," she said, clutching Katrina's arm. "In private."

Esperanza pulled her into the corner of the restroom, as far from the entrance as possible.

"You have to help me," she whispered, watching the door. "My life is in danger."

"From whom?"

"My fiancé, Darren McMurphy. I think he's going to kill me."

"Why do you think that?"

"You know I was Simon Fontaine's nurse. Well, he and Victoria are dead because of Darren."

Oh, my God. Goode was right.

"Have you called the police?"

"No, it would take too long for them to build a case. I'd be dead by then. I want you to tell my story and get it online tonight. Then they can't hurt me."

"Okay, so why don't you come with me to the newsroom?" Katrina asked. "You'll be safe there."

"No, that won't work. Darren told me to stay in the room. If he comes back and I'm gone, he'll send his people to find me."

"You have a room here too?" Katrina asked.

That doesn't sound like a coincidence.

"Yes, Darren brought me here for the weekend to hide out. He left the room a little while ago, saying he had some business for a few hours. If I take you there and tell you my story, you can post it tonight, right?"

"Theoretically, yes. How did you find me?"

"I called the paper looking for you, and your editor said you were here, interviewing Congressman Winchester, so I went looking for you."

"Yes, Darren was heading for Winchester's room right after I left. Why don't you give me the short version right now," Katrina said, pulling her notebook from her purse. "I saw you on the security video going into the house on Halloween morning right before a police officer came inside."

"Not here, it's not safe," Esperanza said. "Someone could be listening. Let's go up to my room. We can lock the door until we're done and then you can leave."

That sounds risky, but Goode didn't specifically warn me about Esperanza. She sounds sincere, but how do I know this isn't a trap?

"Let me tell my editor where I'm going first, okay?" she said, though she was really planning to call Goode. Joanne couldn't do anything but worry anyway.

But Esperanza shook her head vigorously. "No, we need to go before someone sees us together."

"I'm sorry, I need to do this. What's your room number?"

"Okay, but hurry. We don't have much time. I'm in room 324. I'll wait in here until you're done," Esperanza said, closing herself inside a locked stall.

As Katrina stepped into the crowded hallway, she scanned the bar to the left and peered through the glass doors at the outdoor pool area. Goode was nowhere in sight. Neither was Stone.

He'll understand. He's got to know that I didn't get this far by running from a good story, and I'm about to break this one wide open.

But she knew well enough to call and leave him a message: "I was about to call my editor when Esperanza Cepeda grabbed my arm and dragged me into the bathroom near the Viennese. She says Darren McMurphy is responsible for the Fontaines' deaths, and she thinks he's going to kill her too. She wants to tell me the whole story, but she won't come to the newsroom. She's insisting that we go to her room, number 324, and lock the door. It's six thirty-five, and we're going there now. I know you were looking to question her, too, so can you come as soon you get this? I'm hoping that you already have McMurphy and

Winchester in custody, and we'll be safe in her room until you meet us there."

Hanging up, Katrina headed back into the bathroom and knocked on Esperanza's stall. They walked to the elevator in the lobby, where Esperanza tapped her foot and stared at Katrina impatiently as the operator held the grating open while she looked around one last time for Goode.

"C'mon," Esperanza said insistently. "Let's go!" Once Katrina was inside and the operator closed the grating, Esperanza said, "Third floor, please."

Katrina sighed with relief that they were going to a different floor than Winchester's.

I'll call Joanne as soon as I'm done with this interview. We'll have to swap this out for the campaign donation story, which I can write up as part of the weekender, which is going to be a whopper.

Outside her room, Esperanza stuck her key card into the door and waited for the green light. Still feeling skittish, Katrina was happy to see that no one else was in the room as the door swung closed behind them.

Esperanza selected a few bottles of vodka and a can of tonic water from the minibar. "Want me to make you one too?" she asked.

"No vodka, thanks," Katrina said, reminded that she had refused three drinks so far that night. "But I'll take a tonic."

"I'll go to get some ice," Esperanza said.

Before Katrina could object, her interviewee had left the room with the ice bucket. Katrina was about to call Joanne to leave a heads-up message about where she was when someone knocked on the door. Katrina's heart started thumping.

Esperanza wouldn't knock. She's got a key.

"Who is it?" she asked through the door. Peering out the peephole, she saw Esperanza's face.

"It's Espee, Esperanza," the nurse said in a somewhat muffled voice. "I left my key on the bed."

What if she's got company? I can only see her head.

Whirling around, she confirmed the key was indeed on the bed and opened the door to find Esperanza alone, holding a bucket of ice. She peeked around and didn't see anyone in the hallway.

While Esperanza carried the ice to the table near the minibar, Katrina closed the door, pulling the U-shaped lock across. Esperanza took two glass tumblers off the counter and poured them both drinks.

"Too bad we don't have any lime. Here's yours," she said, handing one to Katrina.

Settled into a chair with her notebook in her lap, Katrina was eager to hear the story.

"Start from the beginning," she told Esperanza, who sat on the couch facing her.

Esperanza took a couple of sips as she cradled the tumbler in both hands and started to tear up.

"This is hard," she said, before the words and the tears came tumbling out.

CHAPTER 55
ESPERANZA

Halloween Friday

When Victoria Fontaine called her father's surgery office that Friday morning, Regina had the day off as usual, so Esperanza was handling the phones. Dr. F, as she called him, was busy and couldn't take the call, so she chatted with his daughter for a few minutes.

"I'm not feeling well," Victoria said. "I've been throwing up."

"Do you want me to come by and bring you some chicken soup from the deli?" Esperanza offered, assuming that Victoria had a stomach bug. "We don't have surgery until one o'clock."

"That would be great, thanks, but I'm not that hungry. Just a cup, okay? And can you also bring me a roll with a bunch of saltine crackers?"

"Sure," Esperanza said, "let me check with your dad and make sure it's okay."

"It's fine, but don't get too close in case she's sick," Simon said. "Be back and ready to prep for Mrs. Stevenson by twelve fifteen."

Then Darren called. When she mentioned where she was going, she was surprised by his response: "I need to go over there, too, as a matter of fact, so can you do me a favor? It will make life easier for me."

"What's that?" she asked.

"I need some paperwork. Simon said he has it at his home office, but I don't want them to know I'm looking for it. It would be great if you could give her something to sleep, so I can run in and grab it."

"Why can't you ask him for it?" she asked. "What's going on?"

"I have, and he's been dragging his feet. It's complicated. It's something the board has been arguing about," he said. "I think the two of them are hiding a problem that could cause a huge blowback down the road.'"

She loved Darren, and she was thrilled that he'd asked her to marry him, but she didn't feel comfortable doing this.

"I don't like the idea of sedating Victoria," she said.

"Why are you questioning my judgment on this?" he said in the same scolding tone he'd been taking lately. "If this is how you're going to be, then we can call off the engagement right now."

Not one to make waves, Esperanza backed off. "How am I supposed to sedate her?"

"She probably has drugs in the house, because that's part of what's going on. She's been acting really paranoid and accusatory toward me lately and I think she's using again, but I need to prove it to the board so I can get them to send her to rehab while I clear up her mess."

"I haven't noticed anything. Are you sure?"

"Yes, I am. I've seen this before. But obviously I don't know where she keeps her stash, so here's what I want you to do: Call in a prescription for her from Dr. Fontaine—a month's supply of Xanax and oxycodone—then go pick it up with her soup. Call me when you get to the house, and I'll be there in twenty minutes. That'll give you enough time to grind up a couple of Xanax and dissolve them in her soup. After she's asleep, open the vials, put them on her bedside table, and take a photo with your phone. This is for our future, baby, I promise."

Esperanza had no reason to disbelieve Darren; he'd known Victoria a lot longer than she had. Darren had told her stories about his family socializing with the Fontaines even before he was born, because their moms had known each other since high school.

It's only a couple of pills, and she isn't feeling well anyway, so she'll just sleep it off. Hopefully she won't even know. But Darren can take whatever photo he wants. I'm not doing that.

She picked up the prescriptions from the pharmacy and soup from the deli nearby, then headed over to the Fontaines', where Victoria buzzed her in at the gate.

"The front door is open," she said.

Inside, Esperanza stood at the foot of the stairs and called up to Victoria in her bedroom. "I'm going to put your soup in a bowl and bring it up on a tray."

Heading into the kitchen, she did as Darren asked, sprinkling some salt and pepper to mask any bitter taste. After calling him as they'd agreed, she carried the soup, roll, and crackers upstairs.

Victoria was propped up on some pillows in bed. She looked pale and tired, but she was beaming.

"Alex and I are going to get married," she gushed.

"Really? So are Darren and I," Esperanza gushed back. "Maybe we should have a double wedding!"

After hugging and congratulating each other, Esperanza sat beside Victoria as she ate the soup, along with half the roll and six packages of saltines.

"What's up with the crackers?" Esperanza asked. "I've never seen you eat so many carbs."

"I'm pregnant," Victoria said. "It's all I can keep down."

Oh, no, she's not sick, and she's probably not using either. She's got morning sickness. I just gave a pregnant woman a double dose of Xanax.

"Oh, my God, congratulations, that's so exciting!" Esperanza said nervously as the guilt sunk in.

They mutually agreed to watch one of the "housewife" reality shows while they chatted, but Victoria was asleep by the second commercial.

A few minutes later, Darren called Esperanza's cell to buzz him through the front gate. When he walked in, he surprised her for the second time that morning.

"Why are you wearing a costume?" she asked, confused. "You never do that. And is that lipstick?"

"I'm going to my son's school for a Halloween party after this," he said. "Where's your sense of humor?"

She'd been making a lot of excuses for his behavior lately—he was stressed at work and not sleeping well—because she didn't like conflict or confrontation. But he stepped over the line with his next statement, which was more of a demand, really.

Pulling a vial of clear liquid out of his pocket, he said, "I want you to give Victoria a shot of this in case she wakes up before I'm done."

"What is it?" she asked, seeing that he'd pulled the label off.

"It's better you don't know."

"No, tell me."

Knowing now that she'd already unwittingly dosed a pregnant woman with Xanax, Esperanza didn't want to make the situation any worse.

"Let's just say it'll keep her knocked out until we're through here," he said.

"I'm not going to do that. She just told me she's pregnant. I wouldn't have given her the Xanax if I'd known."

"Don't you trust me?"

"Yes, but this is not right."

"I'm doing this for us," he said. Then his tone turned dark. "Anyway, look, you're involved in this now. You want me to shoot you up with it too?"

Darren's eyes looked threatening, yet he was smirking with amusement. Esperanza was confused and scared, because she couldn't read his expression.

Is he serious?

"You wouldn't really do that, would you?" Esperanza asked hesitantly, unsure of how he might respond.

"Baby, I don't want to hurt you, but you're not listening to what I'm telling you. Victoria is obstructing what we're trying to do at Vitaleron. This has to be done."

CHAPTER 56
KATRINA

Friday

Katrina's mouth fell open. She couldn't believe what she was hearing.

Esperanza paused, rose from the couch, and headed to the bar to refill her glass.

Katrina was almost scared to ask: "So, what did you do?"

"Well," Esperanza said, her back to Katrina now, "I finally realized that he wasn't bluffing, but I refused to inject her. So, he did it himself. I had no idea what he was giving her."

With her glass full again, Esperanza started pacing. "He made a mess of it too. He jabbed her, three or four times. I'm not sure, but I think he was trying to make it look like she'd shot herself up multiple times. Anyway, I started crying and asked him what was really going on."

"Okay, I might as well tell you," he said. "My dad heads up this secret circle of wealthy men who run this town. They've all invested in Vitaleron, and my father put most of our family's money into it, including my inheritance. He basically ordered me to take care of this for him. For our family. Or we, and a lot of other important people, will be out a lot of cash. I couldn't trust anyone else to do this, so I had to do it myself."

"But why Victoria? What does she have to do with any of this?"

"Because she found out that I've been boosting the results of the drug trials. She also demanded that I force the other board members who are invested with Alex in the Caymans to divest."

"In the Caymans?" Katrina interrupted. "Is that why Alex went down there? To invest or to divest?"

Esperanza stopped pacing and took a sip of her drink. "I have no idea. All I know is that Darren, Congressman Winchester, and several board members are going through ugly divorces. They've been hiding money in the Caymans and then reinvesting it in Vitaleron. Darren told me that Victoria found out, said it would adversely affect the company, and gave him two weeks to clean it up. The deadline was supposed to be today. Darren said he tried to work with Victoria, but she was being unreasonable."

"Does that mean Alex is involved in this whole thing too?"

"Those guys are Alex's clients, but they didn't have anything to do with falsifying the drug-trial reports, funneling funny money to Vitaleron, or giving drugs to Victoria. Alex would never hurt the woman he loved, especially if she was carrying his baby. Victoria said they were going to get married."

"Sorry to interrupt, go back to your story," Katrina said.

By that point, Esperanza said, Darren was babbling. "It was like he was on something. Like speed. He was talking really fast and running his sentences together. After injecting Victoria with whatever it was, he shoved some oxy down her throat before I could stop him."

"Does he ever do coke or meth?"

"He's used coke before, but not with me. I'm not into that."

"Has he seemed hypersexual lately?"

Esperanza frowned quizzically. "How did you know that? We both have, actually. I thought it was because we were excited about our engagement. After he gave Victoria the oxy, he said Winchester was demanding campaign donations, free golf trips to talk up the drug with his buddies at the FDA and some House committee, and that he wanted some of the drug too. Darren said he had Darla go into the lab and literally pour some out of the jugs."

"It's only a hunch, but I think he was secretly taking it and dosing you as well," Katrina said.

"No wonder!" Esperanza exclaimed. "He's always had a preoccupation with his penis size, but lately, he's been so much bigger and harder that he wants to have sex all the time. Sorry if that's TMI."

"No worries," Katrina said. "What happened next?"

"I remember I was shaking and my head was pounding. I knew there was nothing I could do, or he would inject me too. That's when I heard Victoria gasping for breath. They call it a death rattle. But then she just . . . stopped. I went over and touched her neck, and she had no heartbeat. No breath sounds either. So, I turned to Darren and said, 'She's not breathing. What the hell did you give her?' 'Succinylcholine,' he said."

"What is succinylcholine?" Katrina asked.

Esperanza explained that it was supposed to be used in a surgical situation, and what could happen when it wasn't. "I thought he'd only sedated her, or I would've tried harder to stop him."

"How did Darren know about that drug? I've never even heard of it."

"He went to med school for a couple of years before he switched to law. He told me he didn't have the patience. Or the compassion. Plus, his father wanted him to be a lawyer."

"But how would he get his hands on it? Wouldn't that be a controlled substance?"

"It is. We keep it in the storage closet at work. He must have stolen some. He takes me out to lunch sometimes, and he also picks up Dr. Russell for golf. But wait, there's more."

"Sorry. Go ahead."

CHAPTER 57
ESPERANZA

Halloween Friday

Darren checked Victoria's wrist for a pulse, then dropped it as if she were a mannequin.

"She's dead," he said, matter-of-factly.

"You're a monster," Esperanza whispered, shaking her head.

"What did you say?" he asked in a low voice that scared her.

"Nothing."

A few moments later, they heard the front door open and slam shut downstairs. Running to the window, Darren saw Dr. Fontaine's Mercedes in the driveway.

"It's Simon," he whispered. "What's he doing here? You told me he had surgery at one o'clock."

Esperanza grabbed her phone, but Darren grabbed her from behind and pulled her into the bathroom, holding her tight against him, and slapped his hand over her mouth to prevent her from warning the doctor. Esperanza wriggled free enough to show him Simon's text on her phone: Surgery cancelled. No need to come back to the office.

"Victoria?" Simon called from downstairs.

Hearing Simon trudging up the stairs, Darren pulled the bathroom door almost closed, leaving it open just enough to watch for Simon.

"Are you feeling any better?" he asked Victoria as he walked into the room.

When she didn't respond, Simon bent over her body to check her breathing and pulse.

"Victoria?" he said, lightly slapping her cheek. "Victoria! Wake up!"

Simon drew back the covers, picked up her limp body, and laid her on the floor to start CPR.

Freeing Esperanza from his grasp, Darren glared at her menacingly and put his finger to his lips. Then he pulled the syringe from his pocket. From the level of liquid, she could see that it still contained a powerful dose of succinylcholine.

She shook her head violently, the tears running down her face. Darren glared at her again before slowly opening the door. As he snuck up behind Simon, Esperanza watched helplessly until she couldn't stand it anymore.

"Look out!" she yelled.

Still on his knees next to Victoria, the doctor turned to see Darren coming toward him. They struggled to get control of the syringe, but Simon was unable to stop Darren from plunging it into the side of his neck.

"What the hell was that?" Simon asked, touching the injection site.

Esperanza felt an indescribable heaviness as she saw the confusion and betrayal in Dr. Fontaine's eyes. It was chilling how calm and cruel Darren was acting.

"Succinylcholine," Darren said in that same matter-of-fact monotone.

As the drug started to take effect, Simon got up and staggered out of the room. He made it down a few steps before they heard him fall, then the *bump, bump, bump* of him rolling down the stairs to rest on the landing.

Esperanza came out of the bathroom, shaking, to see Darren with the strangest smile. She ran past him and looked down at the jumbled heap of Dr. Fontaine lying near the bottom of the staircase. Her knees gave out and she crumpled to the floor, wailing. She was mortified that Darren had killed these two people, both of whom had always been good to her.

"You need to leave right now," Darren said so unemotionally that she didn't even know him. "Go back to the office and get whatever drug log or inventory paperwork you need to change to prevent anyone from knowing that this vial is missing."

"How could you do this to people you've known your whole life?" Esperanza asked between sobs.

"Simon wasn't supposed to be here. But now he's collateral damage. My dad told me to do whatever it takes, and that's what I did," he said.

"But you killed her . . . and her baby too."

"If anyone asks, tell them she was upset about the pregnancy. She sleeps around so much I'd bet she didn't even know who the father was. Probably tricked Alex into thinking it was his. They're both addicts and always will be. She was under a lot of pressure lately at work too. Then her father came home and found her. With her history of addiction and suicide attempts, he was so distraught that she'd overdosed that he had a heart attack right there on the stairs. He fell, hit his head, and died. This stuff doesn't turn up in tox screens. You know that, right?"

Darren grabbed Esperanza by the neck and put his face two inches from hers. "If you tell anyone about this, you'll be dead too," he said.

CHAPTER 58
KATRINA

Friday

"I still don't understand why you didn't go to the police with this," Katrina said. "They can protect you even while they're building a case."

"This is too big, and they've got someone on the inside. I didn't know what else to do but get drunk. I gave Detective Goode the log, which I never changed, hoping that he'd figure it out. But after you left me that message, I was scared that Darren was going to hurt you too. I've read all your stories. You seem like an honest person."

As nice as that was to hear, Katrina now realized that both of them were in serious danger. She could only hope that Goode wasn't too busy to get them out of the hotel safely.

He can't hide anything from me or keep it off the record anymore, because this time I've got Esperanza's story in my notebook.

"Hold tight," she said. "I've got to make another call."

Getting his voicemail again, she left a rather anxious-sounding message, tripping over her words.

"It's Katrina, and now it's urgent. I'm still in room 324 with Esperanza. You need to get over here ASAP. You're right. We're both in imminent danger."

She was about to call Stone, and then hotel security, when there was a knock on the door.

Katrina and Esperanza looked at each other, neither sure what to do. She didn't expect Goode this fast, and she didn't want to open it for anyone else.

"Who is it?" she asked from across the room.

"Espee, open up," a woman said. "It's Darla."

Esperanza looked at Katrina again, questioningly. Katrina didn't like it, but she apparently took too long to respond, because Esperanza was already opening the door. As soon as she turned the door handle, Darren stormed past her. Darla remained outside, apparently as a lookout, after the door swung shut on its own.

Darren headed straight toward Katrina, carrying a syringe, cocked and ready.

Did Esperanza set me up?

"The police are on their way," Katrina said, backing away from him.

"I'll be gone by the time they get here," he said.

There was no time to think. He grabbed her around the middle and swung her around so her back was to him. Jamming his knee into the back of hers, her legs buckled as he pushed her, face first, to the floor.

Quickly reaching out to try to break her fall, she landed knees first and palms second and tried to scramble away. But he got ahold of her sweater and held it tight.

There was nowhere for her to go. The cramped space between the two beds ahead of her ended with a nightstand.

He straddled her lower back, then sat down, putting all his weight on top of her. She couldn't see behind her, but she heard Esperanza crying and punching Darren's back.

"Stop it, Espee," he said, as if he were scolding a child.

Katrina felt him moving off her a little, only to come down even harder, as Esperanza tugged at him.

"Get him off me!" Katrina yelled. "Help!"

She tried to buck him off, but he was too strong and too heavy. Katrina felt a sharp, piercing pain in the lower part of her right butt cheek.

"Ow!" she shrieked. "What was that?"

Did he just shoot me up with succinylcholine?

"No," Esperanza screamed, "not again."

Darren didn't respond. While Katrina was in shock at being jabbed, he quickly grabbed her arms, one at a time, crossed them at the wrists behind her back, and pushed her face into the carpet to squelch her screams.

Based on Esperanza's earlier explanation, she knew she had only a couple of minutes before her lungs quit working and another minute or two before her heart stopped beating. All she could hope was that he'd hit some of the fattier muscle tissue, which might buy her a little more time.

The paralysis slowly rolled across her hips and up her torso in a wave, surging out to her arms and legs. As she lost control of her limbs, he continued to sit on her until she stopped squirming.

When she was no longer able to resist, he got off her and stood up.

Just like in her childhood nightmares, Katrina couldn't move. She tried to yell for help, but no sound came out. All she could do was lie there.

Is this real or is this another nightmare? Will I wake up, sweating, in my own bed?

"Let's go," Darren said to Esperanza, who was sobbing.

"But she's going to die!" she wailed.

Lying with her head to the side and her ear pressed into the carpet, Katrina couldn't see anything but their legs as Darren dragged Esperanza out the door.

Did she play me? Or was she working both sides against the middle, hoping that someone would rescue them before Darren arrived? And Darla? She turned out to be quite the vixen after all.

Katrina didn't know what to think as she struggled to breathe, feeling panicked and trapped in her own body.

"Go home, Katrina." Why didn't you listen?

She felt woozy.

God, is this what Huntington's feels like? I still haven't accomplished what I wanted in life. I'm not ready to go yet. Where is Goode?

She'd never been so scared in her life. Then, everything faded to black.

CHAPTER 59
GOODE

Friday

Goode thought he'd given Katrina a stern-enough warning—especially after camping outside her apartment for two nights—that she'd go home and lock the door or, alternatively, return to the newsroom.

So, he went upstairs to join Stone in questioning McMurphy. Outside Winchester's room, a man built just like Katrina had described was standing guard. Goode was pretty confident that he was the dude in black from the night before.

"And you are?"

"Walter Hall. And you are?" the bodyguard said, his eyes darting away.

What's with the no eye contact? Did he see me in the doorway last night and know I might recognize him?

"I'm Detective Ken Goode, San Diego PD Homicide."

"You can go on in, Detective," he said, looking directly ahead.

"Damn straight, I can."

As Goode walked into the room, he was only half surprised that McMurphy was long gone.

"Where's McMurphy?" he asked.

"He was here for only a few minutes to deliver some campaign donations, then he left to join his fiancée," Winchester replied. "We're both celebrating our engagements this weekend."

"How do you two know each other, exactly?" Stone asked.

"Through Republican politics. He's helped raise a lot of money for my reelection campaign over the past couple of years. I'm in a hotly contested race, heavily funded by the DNC. He and his dad have also given me some great legal advice."

When Goode got Katrina's first call, he didn't pick up because he and Stone were in the middle of confronting Winchester about his hollow claims and trying to determine if he had a role in this fiasco. After quizzing him about his relationship with McMurphy and the Fontaines and all the campaign donations, they asked him for his whereabouts the day of the murders.

"Congressman, do you like to dress up in uniform?" Goode asked.

But Winchester wasn't very forthcoming. "Are you suggesting that I had something to do with the Fontaines' deaths, Detective? A United States congressman?" he asked, his voice dripping with disdain. "Why would I get involved in something like that? All I want is to do public service."

Goode almost laughed out loud. Winchester was still talking nonsense when Katrina's second call came in. He was going to let it go to voicemail, but decided he'd better go into the bathroom and listen to her messages.

It's not like her to call back twice in a row, and so soon after I told her to go home. She knows this is all coming to a head this afternoon.

As soon as he heard the second voicemail, he burst out of the bathroom and yelled to Stone. "Call the paramedics! Tell them to bring oxygen and be ready to bag Katrina in room 324!"

Flinging open the door, he tore down the hallway, opting for the fire-escape stairwell rather than wait for the elevator.

If I don't get to her in time, she's going to die. On my watch. Damn her. Why didn't she listen to me? Because she's Katrina.

Even in his running shoes, he tripped over his own feet going down the stairs, almost tumbling head over foot. He managed to stay upright by gripping the metal railing tightly and swinging his body back to center. Once he reached the third-floor exit, he heaved open the door and sprinted down the hall. Thankfully, a maid was in the hallway with her cart.

"Police! Emergency! Give me your key card!" he yelled. She scrambled to do as he asked, pulling the cord attached to the card from around her neck.

Quickly shoving it into the reader, he cursed as he got the red light. Trying again, it turned green, allowing him to push the door open.

Katrina was unconscious on the floor. Barely breathing.

Dropping to his knees, he pinched her nose and breathed into her mouth. Continuing until the paramedics came through the door several minutes later, he stopped and let them take over.

Thank God Artie told me what to do. Breathe, Katrina, breathe.

CHAPTER 60
KATRINA

Friday

When Katrina came to, she felt someone or something breathing air into her mouth. Dizzy, she coughed and gasped as she tried to breathe on her own. Then came the oxygen mask.

She opened her eyes but couldn't focus for a moment, though she recognized the voice.

"Thank God," Goode said softly. "Welcome back."

He came into view now, standing over her, with two paramedics on their knees and an oxygen tank beside her. She moved the mask away to ask a question, but all that came out was a hoarse croak. Her neck was stiff and sore, and she felt bruised, battered, and achy all over.

But at least I'm alive.

One of the paramedics handed her a paper cup of water, which she sipped, then coughed again.

"You scared me. I thought I'd lost you," Goode said. "You were injected with succinylcholine, but we got to you in time."

"Was it you?" she choked out in a weak raspy voice. "Did you save my life?"

"Yes, I gave you CPR, but it was a team effort."

Katrina's thinking was cloudy, but she knew she had a story to write. The biggest one of her life.

"I need to get to the newsroom," she said.

"I don't think you're going anywhere tonight," Goode said.

He was right. She could barely move or think straight.

So, who is going to write my story?

Flashes from the hotel rooms started coming back to her. Darla and Winchester trying to give her drinks. Esperanza too. Were they trying to sedate her before McMurphy came with the shot?

"Where's Esperanza?"

"We don't know. She was gone by the time I got here."

"McMurphy injected me," she said. "But Darla is the one who knocked on the door before he burst in. She and Esperanza both kept trying to give me drinks."

"Yeah, no one but Winchester was in his room by the time we arrived," Goode said. "He just sat there, eating prawns and sipping champagne like it was a big joke. But we've got this place swarming with cops. We called in reinforcements from Coronado PD, our department, and the FBI too. Don't worry. We'll find them."

"Can you call Joanne? Let her know I'm okay?"

"Sure. Is your phone in your purse?"

Katrina nodded, smiling weakly back. It was a little personal letting him go through her purse, but after last night in her apartment, she was ready to go there with him. Goode stood over her while he talked to Joanne, but she could no longer keep her eyes open. The paramedic put the oxygen mask back over her mouth and nose for the ride to the hospital.

"She's fine. They're going to take her to Sharp Coronado Hospital for observation," she heard him tell Joanne.

"You're safe now," the paramedic told her before she drifted off. "Everything's going to be okay. You can relax and sleep on the trip over if you want."

CHAPTER 61
GOODE

Friday

Katrina looked so peaceful lying there, asleep on the gurney, as they waited for the elevator. An ambulance was waiting in the parking lot to take her to Sharp Coronado Hospital, the nearest emergency room, to monitor her and rule out any complications. When she woke up, Goode knew she would be frustrated once again that she couldn't leap up and run to the newsroom, but that time would come soon enough.

Goode's phone pinged with a text from Stone: Lobby. Stat. McMurphy down. More paramedics on way.

"There's a suspect down in the lobby," he told the paramedics. "No time to wait for the elevator."

What's going on now?

Running toward the emergency fire exit, he flung himself down the stairwell for the second time in an hour. Bursting into the lobby, he had to push his way through a crowd of lookie-loos.

At the center, Foster was administering CPR to an unconscious McMurphy as Stone stood nearby, craning his neck, presumably for the paramedics. But Goode presumed wrong. Stone was looking for Esperanza.

"There you are," he said. "Esperanza is in the wind. She jabbed him with a syringe, then took off somewhere. Byron and the others split up to look for her, but she could be anywhere. Out on the boardwalk or running down the beach for her life."

"Did we get this wrong? Was she the doer this whole time?"

"At this point, I have no idea," Stone said. "Go see if you can find her. You're the only one who knows what she looks like."

"Is McMurphy still alive?"

"Yeah, we were standing right there when it happened. Slausson and Fletcher are interviewing witnesses in the bar."

Goode paused to let it all sink in, wondering where Esperanza might be.

She pulled Katrina into the ladies' room by the Viennese bar. Maybe that's where she's hiding.

"I have an idea," Goode said, taking off through the lookie-loos. "Excuse me, police, coming through, thanks."

When he reached the bottom floor, he burst into the ladies' room, startling several women standing at the sinks, who scrambled for the door. The six stall doors were constructed with horizontal wooden slats, like shades closed in the down position, so he couldn't tell which ones were occupied.

"Excuse me, ladies, police business," he said, pulling out his gun. "If you're in one of the stalls, please finish up and come out slowly when I knock on your door. And keep your hands where I can see them."

After he knocked on the first door, a frightened woman in her eighties emerged, clasping her purse with both hands over her head, her arms shaking with the effort. "Go on outside, ma'am, thank you."

His next knock got no answer, so he opened up the second door. Empty.

Moving down the line, the next three stalls were vacant. He heard a woman in the last one, crying.

"It's all right, ma'am, I'm a police detective, it's safe to come out. Slowly, now. Hands in the air."

He heard the lock turn, and as he slowly opened the door, he saw Esperanza sitting on the toilet, fully clothed and trembling, her hands above her head, with streams of mascara running down her face.

"You don't have any more syringes on you, do you?" he asked.

She shook her head, looking up at him like a frightened child.

"Okay, stand up and come out slowly. That's it."

Glancing her over, he didn't see any lumpy pockets. He carefully patted her down as they stood in front of the mirror, watching for any protrusions or needles poking out, then cuffed her.

"Let's go. We're going downtown to take the statement I've been trying to get for the past few days," he said, hoping she would say something incriminating or useful as they headed back to the lobby. He didn't have to wait long.

"It was Darren's," she said. "I saw him put the syringe in his pocket after he used it on Katrina. I waited till we got to the lobby, where it was crowded, then grabbed it and stuck him in the neck with it. It still had enough for one person, and I'm pretty sure that was supposed to be me. I don't know if he ever loved me. I'm just a loose end now."

When they got back to the lobby, the paramedics had McMurphy on a gurney, bagged with an oxygen mask until they were sure he could breathe on his own. He was conscious, but Stone and Foster weren't taking any chances. Cuffing his wrists to the metal bars, the detectives escorted McMurphy and the paramedics to the ambulance.

"I'm going with. Make sure he doesn't try something," Foster said.

"Good man," Goode said.

Esperanza stopped in her tracks as soon as she saw McMurphy, forcing Goode to take her arm and pull her along. "I don't want him to see me with you," she said.

"It's okay, we've got you now. We can put you into protective custody if we need to."

"He and his father have people," she said cryptically. "And someone on the inside at the police department."

"Do you know who it is?"

"No," she said. "Sorry."

Great. Just what we need. Can't wait to hear more about that.

Out on the street, police cars were lined up next to the two ambulances. TV reporters were milling around, filming Katrina and McMurphy being loaded into separate ambulances while Goode placed Esperanza into the back of a cruiser.

But that night, leading the news on every channel was Congressman Winchester, cuffed and scowling as FBI agents pushed him into an unmarked black vehicle that would take him to the federal lockup downtown to await his arraignment on some preliminary holding charges.

"Let's let him stew for a night or two before I ask him about the Fontaines' murder again," Goode told Watts, his new best friend at the FBI. "He's got to know by now that he's going down. Have fun."

"Oh, I intend to," Watts said. "I'm kind of excited about it."

Goode completely understood. He felt the same way.

CHAPTER 62
GOODE

Saturday

It was an extremely long night. Goode couldn't be everywhere at once, but, overall, the interrogations went well, because he already had most of the pieces in place.

He and Stone arranged for Esperanza to be held at the station while they followed Darren McMurphy's ambulance to the UCSD Medical Center in Hillcrest. Sedated and chained to the bed, McMurphy had no way to run or lie his way out this time, especially with a two-man detail posted outside his room.

Nonetheless, Goode made sure a couple of officers were also stationed at Katrina's room at the Coronado hospital, in case Winchester's bodyguard or some other mercenary tried to snuff her into silence.

I really wish I knew who the mole was. Because now I'm looking at every badge and uniform and wondering if I can trust them.

It felt good to see McMurphy lying there, helpless. But even as Goode read him his rights, he still managed to act like an asshat.

Victoria's memo made it sound like the "threesome" photos were taken while she was unconscious, so Goode doubted it had even occurred. Still, McMurphy insisted that it had. He admitted to arranging the whole thing, but he tried to play it off as good-natured fun among consenting adults. He was also surprisingly dismissive about the pregnancy.

"She seemed more interested in Darla than Brandon, so I doubt it's his," McMurphy said.

"You saw Victoria as a threat and killed her to get her out of your way, is that correct?" Goode asked.

"I wouldn't waste my effing time killing her. Talk to Espee. She's the nurse with access to narcotics."

What a sociopath. Lying without an ounce of remorse.

From there, Goode headed downtown to take Esperanza's statement at HQ, which confirmed his initial suspicions that she was a victim, not an active player. He was also pleased to hear that McMurphy had told her that his father was the linchpin of the conspiracy, a juicy admission he could use to confront both father and son.

Stone arranged for a prosecutor from the DA's office to come in to offer her an immunity deal in exchange for testifying against Darren and Patrick McMurphy, the latter of whom was immediately brought in for questioning.

"Darren deserves everything he gets. Just show me where to sign," Esperanza said, shaking her head in disbelief. "He thought his plan was so clever that you'd never figure it out. But he never anticipated that the Battrelles would move Dr. F's body and mess with the crime scene, like you said. I wonder if he even knows they did that."

"We'll find out," Stone said. "If they hadn't, we might have actually believed it was a suicide—an overdose and a distraught father, just like he conjured up."

"Except for the nasty bruising and the gunshot wound on the wrong side of his head," Goode said.

"And the security cameras," Stone said.

"And that he injected Katrina."

“Why do criminals always think they’re smarter than we are?”

“By the way,” Goode said, “do you know if the McMurphys knew the Chopin family or had anything to do with the Double-Judge Murders?”

“I have no idea,” Esperanza said. “I’m not even sure if my relationship with Darren was real or if he was only using me to get to the succinylcholine. He’s not the man I thought he was. I didn’t know him at all.”

Based on Esperanza’s statement, Goode was confident they could build a strong conspiracy case to take the McMurphys down, along with Winchester and Darla. Given the Battrelles’ messy cover-up at the house, he doubted that they were in on the murder conspiracy scheme, though obstruction charges were certainly in the mix for them.

In addition to conspiracy to steal trade secrets, Winchester was also looking good for federal corruption charges, soliciting, and accepting a bribe via campaign donations and other illegal gifts. The threat of an additional felony murder charge, and possibly conspiracy to murder, was on the table as well.

While Goode was waiting for Darren McMurphy to be deemed stable enough for jail transport, he got a call from Darla, who had managed to escape amid the chaos. After running to a friend’s house, she immediately called FBI headquarters to try to weasel an immunity deal for herself. Goode was her second call, during which she backed Darren’s claims about his father.

“The FBI is on their way to pick me up, but I’ll tell you everything you want to know,” she said. “I know who planned this, who carried it out, and why. You won’t even believe the full extent of it. There’s a whole cabal of rich men who run this city and make secret deals, and Patrick McMurphy is at the nexus of it. They forced me to participate in all of this.”

“They forced you to steal the drugs from the lab?” he asked. “Did they force you to take them before sex too?”

"That was Darren's idea. He is one kinky dude, and he got Brandon hooked along with him. My career, my reputation, my relationship, and my future were all on the line."

Watts called Goode right afterward, confirming that they would consider an immunity deal for Darla, as well, but not until they got her into a room to hear her story in detail.

"I'm interrogating Winchester, trying to get him to cooperate, right now," Watts said. "We've got him good, but this will seal the deal. Two of my guys are picking her up now. Sounds like she'll be a key witness."

"Be careful, though. She's a wily one. For all I know, this whole scheme was her idea."

Goode planned to inflict a much more stringent grilling on Darren McMurphy once he was behind bars. His pretty-boy face, expensive haircut, and entitled attitude would surely get him a good beatdown from other inmates of lesser means, which often helped facilitate an interrogation. But in the meantime, Goode had a few questions for him before he was loaded into the transport van around 5:00 a.m.

"Why did you wear a police uniform into the house?"

Darren didn't even flinch, his icy, pale-blue eyes devoid of emotion. "I wasn't there," he retorted. "If it wasn't Darla, it was probably a dirty female cop. I told you Victoria liked to play both sides of the bed."

Well, that clinches that. He definitely put on the lipstick as a ruse.

"Sorry, no dice," Goode replied. "We have security footage of you going in and out of there. Lipstick and all. We also have a witness who put you there, and I'm sure your cell phone records will confirm that."

Let's see if Daddy confesses or denies all knowledge of this and lets his son take the fall.

CHAPTER 63
GOODE

Saturday

While Goode's teammates, Foster and Byron, were picking up Patrick McMurphy for questioning, Goode headed back to Coronado to check on Katrina. He was not at all surprised to see her dressed and waiting impatiently in her room for the doctor to sign her discharge papers.

"You're up early. It's five thirty," he said. "Did you get any sleep?"

"A little. It's hard when those machines are beeping constantly. The nurse kept coming in to make sure I was alive," she said, coughing, her voice still a little rough. "She kept saying, 'Your blood pressure is so low.' Must be all that running. Nothing a double cappuccino won't cure. What about you?"

"Yeah, I'm running on fumes myself. I was up all night and was camped outside some chiquita's apartment for a couple nights before that. I wish I could catch a nap, but I've got interrogations lined up like planes on a runway."

"Who would that be? On the record, please. I've earned it, and I'm going straight to the newsroom as soon as I get out of here," she said, pulling a notebook out of her purse.

Goode gave her a quick overview that would suffice for her first blockbuster story, promising to fill in more details as they interviewed and arrested everyone else. As long as she called Stone for the official quotes.

"We're picking up McMurphy's father as we speak. Darla's singing to the FBI right now."

"I'm still not sure about her," Katrina said.

"Yeah, me neither."

"By the way, getting shot up with succinylcholine was a huge pain in my ass," she said, laughing. "What took you so long to come to Esperanza's room? I thought I was going to die."

"I got there as soon as I could," he said, recounting his near face-plant in the fire-escape stairwell.

"Is she okay?"

"Yes. Long story," he said, describing her vigilante neck injection in the lobby before Goode retrieved her from the restroom stall. "She was pretty shaken. She said Winchester had planned to hold you until Darren could come and give you the jab, but you escaped, thanks to Stone."

"I knew they were up to something, but yeah, it was a close call," she said. "Speaking of which, where is that jackass, McMurphy?"

"On his way to jail."

Katrina's face lit up as Goode listed all the state and federal charges that McMurphy and Winchester were up against.

"Basically, they're toast," he said.

"So, they were in it together?"

"Looks that way. Simon Fontaine was most likely unintentional collateral damage, but Darla said Darren McMurphy's father runs a 'cabal'—her word, not mine—that could have ordered the hit. We're not sure of her credibility at this point since she was stealing the drug, which is essentially a trade secret, from Vitaleron for her and Darren's personal use. She's trying to blame him, but we'll see what shakes out."

"Do we know whose baby Victoria was carrying?"

"Not until the DNA tests come back. Alex and Michael agreed to give samples, so we'll all know eventually, but the family wants to give the fetus a proper burial no matter what. I didn't have the heart to tell them that it could be Winchester's, but that depends on whether those photos were staged or taken during an alleged threesome while Victoria was passed out."

"Threesome?"

"Yeah, it's in a memo Victoria wrote, detailing all the shenanigans that give us a menu of motives. I'll send you a copy."

"Awesome. But what I really need to know is whether Vincent Battrelle is involved in this whole cabal conspiracy?"

"That's unclear right now. He definitely plays in the same arena, but that's an open question. At the minimum, we've got him and Michael on evidence tampering and obstruction, so we'll press them for information to force the McMurphys to talk. They could make a deal, I suppose, and get a slap on the wrist. Depends on what else comes out."

"What happens to Esperanza?"

"Since we gave her immunity, she'll be our star prosecution witness. You, too, if you're willing."

Katrina shook her head. "You can leave me out of it, thank you. But now that I have firsthand experience with the same drug that killed the Fontaines, it should make for a great first-person story. When did you learn about the succinylcholine? It wasn't in the toxicology report."

"Not until yesterday morning," he said, outlining his and Artie's detective work. "But we still didn't know who did the injecting or why until last night."

"I can't believe you let me go meet with these guys," she said, shaking her head again.

"What are you talking about? You completely ignored my warning."

"I was kidding. Kind of. But you're right," she said, smiling. "By the way, did I say thank you?"

"Not necessary," Goode said, pausing dramatically before taking a step toward her. "You can just go to dinner with me."

She laughed and playfully raised her hand in a "stop" gesture. "Permission for dinner granted, but not until I'm done with this story and all the follow-ups. So no more inappropriate contact until then. I mean it. I don't want either of us to lose our jobs. After that, you can help me figure out if any of these characters were involved with my parents' murder, because that's what I'm working on next. Unofficially, of course."

Goode nodded respectfully and smiled. "It would be my pleasure."

CHAPTER 64
GOODE

Saturday

As Goode was leaving the hospital, Watts called to say he was finished with Darla and that Goode could stop by FBI headquarters for a briefing and to ask her a few questions before he confronted Patrick McMurphy back at the station downtown.

"So, Patrick was the one driving this train, and he got Darren and Winchester to do the dirty work?" Goode asked Darla.

"As far as I know, yes. I won't testify against my fiancé, but I will say this: Darren told Winchester that his dad instructed him to 'take care of this mess.' I don't know if the rest of the cabal was involved or not."

"I overheard Darren talking to his dad on the phone earlier, and Patrick did not sound pleased, so Darren may have acted on his own," she went on. "Simon was a close associate of Patrick's and he wasn't even supposed to be home when this happened, so I find it hard to believe that murdering him and Victoria was a group directive."

"Maybe things got out of hand. But my guess is that greed and sociopathy run in the McMurphy genes," Goode said.

He also knew that bringing charges was one thing and getting convictions was another.

As Goode sat across from Patrick McMurphy at the interrogation table, he saw the same icy-blue eyes as Darren's staring back at him. Goode stayed silent for a couple of minutes, waiting to see if Patrick would volunteer anything. But Patrick was stoic, his mouth tight, the breath whistling through his nose.

"You all right there, Mr. McMurphy?" Goode asked. "You sound like you're having trouble breathing."

"Not at all. I don't know why you're wasting my time bringing me down here," Patrick snapped. "I had nothing to do with any of this."

"That's not what your son says," Goode lied. "Or my other witnesses."

"My son is not my responsibility; he's a grown man. He makes his own choices," Patrick said.

"From what I hear, you instructed him to 'take care of this mess.' Are you denying that?"

"I'm an investor in Vitaleron and I wanted him to right the ship, which he did by taking over as chairman. That's all I was referring to."

"So, you didn't instruct him to dress up like a police officer and kill Victoria and Simon Fontaine?"

"Absolutely not. That's a preposterous accusation. If that's what he did, it was by his own volition."

"I understand you run a group of businessmen who advise the mayor and other local elected officials, including Congressman Winchester, in exchange for getting your pet projects done. Is that true?"

"I offer free advice, pro bono, as a public service to various elected officials, but that's all. There is no such advisory group. I've been very fortunate, and I like to give back. Sounds like you've got crap intelligence."

"You didn't tell Darren to drug Victoria and make it look like an overdose? The succinylcholine was all his idea?"

"I've never even heard of that drug, Detective."

"And you also don't try to force decisions at Vitaleron, backed by a group of major investors?"

"You keep referring to this group. It doesn't exist."

"That's not what our witnesses say. They claim you instructed your son to take action, and they're willing to testify to that. So that makes you culpable. I'm simply giving you a chance to tell your side of the story."

"I repeat: Whatever my son did, he did on his own. That's my statement. I had nothing to do with the Fontaines' murder. Simon was a good friend of mine. I believe he even has a photo of us in his home office. Why would I kill a close friend and business associate, Detective? It makes no sense."

"Money and control are always strong motivations, Mr. McMurphy. You know that as well as I do."

"That's all my client has to say, Detective," Patrick's attorney said. "Are we done here?"

"For now, yes," Goode said. "But I'm sure the team of investigators searching your house and office as we speak will find evidence to support charges in this matter, so you'd better get your affairs in order. If you change your mind and decide to give a voluntary confession, that *might* make a difference to the DA. Good day, gentlemen."

Let the rats begin to play.

Patrick's face turned pale, and his hands shook as he pushed back his chair to stand up. He didn't meet Goode's eyes as he left the room with his attorney and headed straight for the bathroom.

I'm betting his bowels are telling the truth right now. I'd also bet that Darren changes his tune when he finds out that Daddy is letting him take the fall.

By day's end, Darren had done just that. Unwilling to go down alone, he spilled some good dirt on the mayor to use as leverage: A mansion purchased by an LLC shell corporation owned by Patrick's primary development corporation was given to the mayor as a bribe to spearhead the creation of a new district, allowing Patrick to build a beautiful hotel resort on Mission Bay. The district encompassed the same parcel slated for Katrina's brother's last project. Coincidence?

He wouldn't confirm or deny Esperanza's claim about the inside man in the PD, but his statement was enough for murder, conspiracy, and a host of corruption charges.

Goode was happy. He planned to tip Katrina to the bribery scheme and the possible link to her brother's death in the coming days. Any more charges than that would be gravy, but it looked like they would be swimming in it.

Darren's confession, and results of what proved to be a fruitful search at Patrick's home and office, killed any chance of political fallout. There would be no pushback from the PD's top brass, because the FBI's Public Corruption Unit had taken over that headache by picking up the mayor for questioning that night as well. Goode made sure to pass on Esperanza's tip about the mole so he didn't have to investigate his colleagues on his own, because that was never good.

Knowing he'd done all he could for the day, Goode headed home, where he had two sips of a vodka tonic before falling into bed. He didn't even have the energy to make himself a sandwich.

CHAPTER 65
GOODE

Sunday

Goode woke up fresh and bright at five o'clock the next morning, raring to go. With the primary suspects in jail and the rest anxiously awaiting arrest, Goode was ecstatic to get back in the water for a couple of hours without any blowback from the brass.

It's Sunday for God's sake.

Daybreak was his favorite time to go surfing, and he hadn't been in the water since Maui. He didn't mind if other surfers had the same idea. He'd not only been a Windansea local his whole life, he was also somewhat of a legend as news spread about his recent trip to Jaws—especially at his age.

Stopping at a café on La Jolla Boulevard that opened early, he wolfed down a chocolate almond croissant with a latte, then headed down to the beach.

Paddling out, the quiet was broken only by the seagulls calling. Goode felt a deep sense of peace and being one with the universe. The waves weren't more than a couple of feet high, which meant he mostly sat on his board with his feet dangling on either side, bobbing and meditating.

He planned to ask Stone if he could take a peek at the Double-Judge Murder case files, looking for connections to this one. After wading through this multilayered albatross, Stone agreed that anything was possible.

While Goode was enjoying the serenity of the dawn, he saw a dark form approach, then sprint around and under him. He immediately jerked his legs out of the water, anxious that it might be a shark. But it turned out to be only a dolphin.

The creature swam up alongside the surfboard and raised his snout in greeting. Then, coming a bit closer, he nuzzled Goode's upper thigh.

Goode felt a flicker of his mother's melancholy smile, as if she were coming to say hello, just like the birds who visited him during his last tribute to her on the bridge. By now he knew better than to question those moments. He welcomed them whenever they came.

I guess I don't need to be on the Coronado Bridge to connect with you, Mom.

Lifting his snout again, the dolphin snorted a few times and took another lap around Goode.

"So, you think I can fall in love in a week?" he asked.

The dolphin jumped up and rested his snout on Goode's leg.

"I know, it's been a while. I think it's about time too."

AUTHOR'S NOTE AND ACKNOWLEDGMENTS

I thought my dream had come true when I got my first novel, *Naked Addiction*, published nearly twenty years ago. But sadly, the early versions of this book, which I started writing in 2008, were rejected. Multiple times.

The advice to "write what you know" doesn't come out of nowhere. I knew how to write and tell a story, but at that point I didn't know what I didn't know.

I will always be grateful for the generous critique that uber-bestselling crime writer Michael Connelly gave me on an early version of *Naked*, which features Detective Ken Goode as an undercover narcotics detective who is working his way toward becoming a full-time homicide detective. Michael told me I didn't know enough about police procedures, and it showed. But I did know how to write and build compelling characters, a skill that couldn't be learned. So, he gave me a wonderful blurb that I will always cherish, but more importantly, he offered guidance on how to fix the plot and improve the book overall. I took his words to heart and kept rewriting.

Ultimately, it took me seventeen years to get *Naked* published. It came out two years after the release of my first book, a true crime titled *Poisoned Love*, in which toxicologist Kristin Rossum steals drugs from her lab at the county medical examiner's office, poisons her husband, then stages a suicide scene by sprinkling red rose petals over his body.

At that early stage in my career as an author, I'd been an investigative newspaper reporter for nearly twenty years, but my beat was government and politics, not crime. So, I didn't really know how a detective thinks or talks, which was necessary to write a successful series of crime books, especially one in which the protagonist is a man. Sure, I'd read a lot of detective novels, thrillers, and mysteries, I'd quizzed men on how they think, and I'd even had a couple of homicide detectives do beta reads on my novel.

But the writing didn't come naturally to me. It was a struggle, because until I covered the Rossum case, I'd never seen a homicide case all the way through, not even close. Sure, I'd worked hard to learn my creative writing craft, taken workshops, attended conferences, and joined critique groups, but something was just, well, missing.

After *Poisoned Love* was published, a whole new world opened up to me. I'd always dreamed of being a full-time author, but I still wasn't ready to quit my job as a newspaper reporter yet. Once I got my next narrative nonfiction book deal, I had another in the hopper, and my first novel was under submission, so I was ready to take that risky jump. After two more nonfiction titles came out, *Naked Addiction* was my fourth book to be published. I was on a roll, or so I thought.

But even after writing three nonfiction books about real homicide cases, the sequel to *Naked Addiction*, originally titled *Dopamine Flood*, just wasn't coming together. My first try was rejected by publishers, and later, a rewritten version was rejected by my next agent.

"Open a clean file and start over," he said.

Ouch.

Part of the problem, I told myself, was that I was writing true-crime books, and although I wrote them like suspense novels, using fiction storytelling techniques, they still weren't novels because I had to follow the facts, no embellishment allowed. Promoting them and teaching writing courses kept me too busy to really spend the time figuring out what I was doing wrong.

But I'm stubborn and determined. I did start over with a clean file, and I did a complete overhaul. I showed subsequent versions to readers, other authors, friends. Some liked the book, but it was still not good enough. One said it started in the wrong place; another said it had too many subplots, and worse, one said it felt like dead words on the page.

I did more revisions until I thought it was ready to send out again. I had a new agent by then, one who I thought had more faith in me and was more supportive. He thought the book had something, enough to keep working on it, but he, too, said it still wasn't there yet. He gave me some helpful suggestions, so back to the drawing board I went.

Most people would have given up, started on a new novel, or focused on something that came easier to them. But not me. After another major revision, I sent the latest version to a new set of beta readers, and this time I got a positive, enthusiastic response from all of them. It was alive!

This is that version, and just like my first novel, it took me seventeen years to get published. I always believed in this story, and I loved the characters. I just couldn't let go of it. It's not in my DNA.

For any aspiring authors reading this, the lessons here are twofold. The first is to remember that being a published author, and remaining one, requires great resilience to rebound from rejection. The second is that you not only need to learn your craft, you really do need to know your subject matter. The earlier versions of my characters had parts of me in them, or people I knew, and some were informed by characters in books I'd read or had seen in movies. But it took more than twenty years before they were based on the knowledge and experience needed for them to have verisimilitude.

After writing fifteen books, most of them about homicide cases, I'd now read, listened to, and watched a zillion detective interviews with suspects. I'd also read a zillion investigative reports in which the detectives explained what evidence they'd found and why they thought it was important. I'd interviewed these guys myself and listened to them testify in court. I finally *knew* how these guys talked and how they thought. I knew how they conducted their investigations, what they did, and in what order.

So, Detective Ken Goode grew out of all of that, but he also has grown personally since he appeared in *Naked*, which is the prequel to this series. Because, although this book takes place only a year later, we both grew up a bit over the past seventeen years it took to get this book right. The other main character, investigative reporter Katrina Chopin, and her relationship with Goode have evolved too.

I've been asked if Katrina is really me, and the answer is no. I was told a long time ago that I had to make her different than me, because she needs to do things that I can't and wouldn't or she wouldn't be a compelling character. So, she is her own person, even though we've lived or worked in a couple of the same places and we're both strong-willed, determined investigative reporters who are willing to take risks to get what we need.

Before this book was accepted for publication by Thomas & Mercer, I'd already finished the sequel. Unlike its predecessors, the first draft poured out of my fingers and onto the page in less than two and a half months, so fast that I literally injured my wrists and had to slow down the revisions I completed five months later. Book number three in the series is finished as well, and I'm deep into book number four.

So, I hope you'll stick along for the ride, because I think I finally know what I'm doing.

I can't possibly remember all the people who have read the different versions of this book over the years, but I'd like to thank the ones whose feedback, support, and encouragement stands out in my mind:

My mother, Carole Scott, who told me the book felt dead, and then, after reading some of the rewritten pages, declared, "It's alive!" My stepfather, Chris Scott, one of the few people who really encouraged me to keep writing fiction. My partner, Géza Keller, who lets me read him excerpts every now and then, even though he often falls asleep almost immediately. My friend Onstance Lawford, who read an early version and said the book really started picking up on page 165, which made me realize that I still had a ton of work to do. My former agent, Chip MacGregor, who gave me some very helpful suggestions after reading an earlier draft. My other beta readers, David Byington, Bob Petrachek, Dwain Fuller, Scott Dreher, Amy Wallen, Mary Wotanis, and Michael Foulks. My agenting team at Gersh: Joe Veltre, Hayley Nusbaum, and Joslyn Jenkins. And my editing team at Thomas & Mercer: Alexandra Torrealba, Ali Castleman, and Clete Smith.

ABOUT THE AUTHOR

Photo © 2023 Géza Keller

New York Times bestselling author Caitlin Rother, an award-winning investigative reporter for nineteen years, has published sixteen books, from crime novels to crime narrative nonfiction and memoir. Rother's journalistic work has been published by *Cosmopolitan*, the *Los Angeles Times*, *The Washington Post*, *The Boston Globe*, *The San Diego Union-Tribune*, and *The Daily Beast*. Her more than 250 media appearances include *20/20*, *People Magazine Investigates*, *Crime Watch Daily*, Australia's *World News*, and numerous shows on Netflix, Investigation Discovery, Lifetime, HLN, and REELZ. A popular speaker, the author also works as a writing-research coach and consultant. For fun, she binges on limited series, sings and plays keyboards in a jazzy bluesy trio with her partner, and swims in the ocean. Rother holds a BS in psychology from the University of California, Berkeley, and an MS in journalism from Northwestern University. To learn more, please visit https://caitlinrother.com.